phantom eyes

SCOTT TRACEY

phantom eyes

flux
®
Woodbury, Minnesota

FIRST EDITION
First Printing, 2013

Book design by Steffani Sawyer
Cover design by Kevin R. Brown
Cover images: iStockphoto.com/12157632/Dmitrijs Dmitrijevs
          Shutterstock.com/117253831/2bears
          Shutterstock.com/109736588/Fer Gregory

Flux, an imprint of Llewellyn Worldwide Ltd.

Library of Congress Cataloging-in-Publication Data
is on file with the Library of Congress
Tracey, Scott, 1979-
  Phantom eyes / Scott Tracey. — First edition.
     pages cm.
  Sequel to: Demon eyes.
  Summary: As Braden tries to end Bell Dam's feud once and for all, he must outsmart his father, evade Catherine's dark magic, regain what was stolen from him, trick a phantom that refuses to die, and foil a demon's master plan, knowing that the price of victory could be his life.
  ISBN 978-0-7387-3659-4
  [1. Witches—Fiction. 2. Demonology—Fiction. 3. Magic—Fiction. 4. Gays—Fiction.] I. Title.
  PZ7.T6815Ph 2013
  [Fic]—dc23
                          2013018746

Flux
Llewellyn Worldwide Ltd.
2143 Wooddale Drive
Woodbury, MN 55125-2989
www.fluxnow.com

Printed in the United States of America

ONE

Remember that time a crazy phantom bitch threw me out of a lighthouse and stole my power? Yeah, that sucked the worst. At least until the night she came back.

"Sometimes dead is better, don't you agree?" A month ago, my nightmares had involved demons and torture. Now? Talking. Just talking. It was a simple question, thoughtful and almost kind—if I believed for a second that the speaker even knew what a kind word was.

The woman who stood before me had ripped a curse out of me and thrown me from the parapet of a lighthouse just three days ago. All because five minutes of conversation with me had worked her nerves. If this was my follow-up appointment... well, I was disappointed. She didn't seem to care, though, smiling underneath her veil. "This world is merciless. One shouldn't linger past their time."

Was this supposed to be my time? Ever since the night my uncle had died, I'd been waiting for the other shoe to drop. It wouldn't be enough to cripple me. I'd made enough enemies that someone would want to see me dead. But I was still surprised that it was Grace.

I'd come to Belle Dam to find out who was threatening my uncle and to uncover the secrets of my past. I'd been born with a terrible power—the witch eyes, a curse that let me see the world as it really was. A bubbling cauldron of chaos, memories, and darkness. I thought I'd been alone in my suffering, only to find out that Grace—the woman who'd founded the town a hundred years ago—had held the same power. And she'd built up her sandbox, nurtured two armies, and then vanished into the night.

Until now. Her first act upon her return had been to rip the witch eyes right out of my head. Now I was broken, defenseless, and stuck in the middle of a feud that was about to go nuclear.

Uncle John's funeral was in the morning. For three nights I'd tossed and turned, both desperate for sleep and terrified of it. Every night there came a point where I couldn't keep my eyes open anymore, and then it was … not dreaming. Floating, maybe. Flying. There was wind and the murmur of voices, weightlessness and silver light. That was all I could remember in the morning. That, and the feeling of butterflies in the chasm where my magic had been. A thousand, magic-free butterflies desperate for escape.

Sometimes, when I woke, just for a moment there was a thread. *Sulfur-shaped cries, vagabond hearts.* The lightest brush of visions against the corner of my mind. *Screaming echoes fervor and fire.* But never any dreams. Not in three days. Not until tonight.

It was hard to say how old Grace was. Her face was covered in a sheer veil, her eyes a glowing crimson. It was hard to pick out any distinguishing features, but her voice was unmistakable—equal parts old-world British nanny, Catholic school nun, and long-reigning queen of her own nation.

"You fit right in with a merciless world," I pointed out. I crossed my arms in front of my chest. *Why was she here? Why now?* She'd already taken everything from me. "I've done this before, you know. Lucien already tried using my dreams against me."

"Is that so?" Grace Lansing asked, a careful smile penciled across her face. "There are no dreams here, little boy. Now is the time for nightmares."

The room we were in was small, with tan brick walls and open windows that stretched the length of the room— literal gaps in the wall where it opened into sky. There were lights in the distance—at first, I thought they were stars, remembering the surreal views from the lighthouse, but I quickly recognized streets and houses. The harbor in the distance. We were still in Belle Dam, wherever we were. Some kind of tower, maybe. It wasn't the lighthouse—we were much too close to town.

I shifted around, never completely turning my back to Grace. There had to be a reason she'd hijacked my dreams. But a nervous knot clenched in my stomach. I hadn't been worried when Lucien had haunted me—I'd been *too* calm.

Like some part of me knew it was a dream and nothing bad would happen. I didn't have that now. There was no security blanket to keep me at ease. *I'm in danger* struck only a second before *I can't protect myself.*

There was a book tucked against a cobwebbed, dirty bench in the corner. *Not a bench,* I realized. A pew. "Our Lady of the Sorrows" was written across the front of the dusty hymnal. I looked up, and sure enough there was a bell hanging above our heads. The open holes in the walls made sense now—we were in a bell tower. A church bell tower.

Why here? What was it with the city's supernatural crowd and their fascination with profaning holy ground? First, Lucien turned the Lansing family chapel into his recovery suite, and now Grace brought me to a church that was probably named after her? *Our Lady of the Sorrows? Seriously?* That was Grace to a T. Was there something in the town charter that said that creepers and villains had to conduct their business in a religious venue?

"Go now," Grace said suddenly, and I turned on instinct. Getting thrown out of a building might not have taught me to bite my tongue better, but it made me a little more careful about doing what I was told. But Grace hadn't been talking to me, I realized a moment later. Her eyes were trained on a corner of the room.

A shadow peeled away from the wall, somehow in a corner of a round room that didn't *have* any corners. The moment I saw it, my eyes blurred like I'd suddenly been blasted by a wave of jungle heat. It was like a visual hiccup: one moment everything was clear and normal and the next my eyes had gone glassy and vacant and I couldn't find anything to focus on. My equilibrium shifted, and I threw out my hands, desperate to remain upright. The room was a darkened blob with the occasional splash of color. Grace was just a red haze. A *close* red haze.

As soon as the footsteps faded, everything was as it had been before. I blinked and my vision was clear and easy. Obviously Grace was responsible, but I couldn't understand why. Why bring me here and then hide something right in front of me. What was the point?

Grace was keeping secrets. Things she didn't want me to know. But that didn't make any sense, because she'd already ruined me. She had torn out my magic and left me a shell. She could have killed me. But she hadn't.

"The burdens laid upon me are many, not the least of which is this need for hands in this world," Grace murmured. I couldn't be sure if she was talking to me or herself. "Forced to draw forth phantasms to work my will, they are a necessity, but volatile and mercurial at best."

Phantasms. Another name for ghosts. Which meant that Grace was more tapped into things in Belle Dam than I'd realized before. "You summoned that little girl. The one that tried to kill me?" It wasn't really a question. When I'd first come to town, a little girl in a princess costume had tried to kill me. Later, she'd played the role of muscle, intimidating someone into fleeing town altogether before she'd been banished.

Grace extended her index finger and jabbed it towards

me. "Every pawn had its purpose, some more wily than others. But sometimes, you need to pull your own piece off the board before it does more harm than good. You should be thanking me. Your 'friend' might have been harmed, and I couldn't have that. There must always be an Armstrong in Belle Dam. Otherwise, what's the point in winning?"

I didn't care if it was a dream or not. I couldn't take it anymore. "You keep talking about this like it's a game," I snapped, just as the feeling of butterflies swept through my chest again.

I was wrong. It wasn't like butterflies. It was like being in the middle of the ocean and caught in the middle of a panicked school of fish fleeing a predator. There was an ocean around me, pressing up against me, warm and cool at the same time. *Things* brushed against me on all sides, sometimes even going through my skin entirely. Everything surrounding me was in motion, but I was still. Like a statue in the middle of a hurricane.

"What are you doing to me?" I managed to gasp, feeling a disconnect between my mind and my mouth. The words came out like an echo, broken and stitched back together. "What is this?"

And then ... fragments. *Thorns and thresholds, broken moonlight haze in the distance. Frustration hot and slick like scythes reaping rages. I don't know why it's not working. I don't know why you were wrong.*

A flooding pressure drained from my head, my mind cleared, and I remembered where I was. My mind had gone somewhere else, but it had still cataloged the silence that had followed my questions. Grace always had something to say. She *loved* the sound of her own voice. I could feel her eyes on me—literally feel them, pressing humid and hot against my skin. But she wasn't answering. She was *waiting*.

But what for? What was that?

The feeling passed, and with it, Grace's attention. My head felt fuzzy, like it was floating, but when I closed my eyes I could almost make something out of the shape of lights flaring against my eyelids. Someplace other than this church tower. Somewhere else in Belle Dam. I was there, but I was also here. And also somewhere else. In three places at once, no matter how impossible that seemed.

Now that I was awake for it, I realized that this was what I'd been feeling when I closed my eyes at night. This had happened before—in fact, it had happened ever since the night Grace had attacked me. This... separation. Whatever it was, it had happened before.

"Don't strain yourself," Grace said, as close to warm as she got. Which was to say it was bitten off and sharp, a continent-sized glacier only a few degrees warmer than everything else she said. She began circling the bell that was hanging from the center of the room. Her steps were slow, precise, and even. Like a bridal procession, every step was chosen with care.

She touched a finger to the side of the cast-iron bell, and the moonlit-glowing bell caught silver flame. Phosphorescent fire arced down the side and then around the lip, painting lines and words that were almost human but invariably not. The letters, full of swooping lines and hard angles, constantly moved, each symbol shifting into new shapes from one moment to the next. They were not letters in the way I'd ever thought of letters before, each letter was a word, a sentence, and an intent. And still that only scratched the surface.

"What is it?" I whispered, watching the ever-changing patterns circling the bottom of the bells. I didn't want to be fascinated, but I was. This was magic on a whole other level. This was the kind of power Grace had mastered from the witch eyes. The kind of power I could have had ... if things had gone a different way.

"Something that has slept for many ages," the Widow whispered back like we shared a secret. "Something long missed from this world." Grace held up her palm, thumb extended to the side, and as the bell jerked to the left— nearly knocking me to the ground—the sound pealed all around us, but it sounded like something coming from the outside in. "Something that burns with fires long forgotten."

An ache in my chest flared up every time I reached forward, just a bit, for the magic that wasn't there. It still didn't feel real that I no longer had the power that had defined me all my life. That, to Grace, I was just an empty human, ordinary and worthless.

I wondered what she saw when she looked at the magic she was making. The silver fire burned at my eyes like magnesium flares. The bell continued to clang, but in our own little bubble of the world, the sound was suppressed. However, in the background we could still hear the responding peals of other bells, other churches, ringing in response. Though it was well into the night in Belle Dam, the city was momentarily alive through the sound of a Sunday mass. Could everyone in town hear them? Or just us?

"Did you know that bells can disperse dark energy?" Grace asked, taking on the role of teacher. There was a satisfied, smug little smile on her face. I got the feeling that this was something she'd been planning on for a long time. "They used to say it was the purity of the sound: a bell's peal is like no other sound in this or any world. But it was always just a little more than that. Bells are only instruments." Her eyes skimmed over the language glowing across the surface of the bell. "You have to know the right notes to make them truly sing."

A hush fell over the bell tower then, the aftermath of a significant moment. These bells were a sign of something beginning. Or maybe they were ending.

"The cruelest part of this," she added in a reverent whisper, "is that they will drive him mad. In the whole of demon-tainted history, there were only two who learned the secret languages. Both men. Only men were ever thought to be worthy. And he buried both of them long before either one of us was even a possibility." She was talking about Lucien, the foremost demon of Belle Dam, one of the Riders at the Gate. He was somehow more than most demons.

I saw now what Grace was after. "He's not stupid," I

said. "If he taught them to you, you'll be the first one he thinks of. Maybe that you told someone or hid the secrets here." There were other witches in Belle Dam. And this would make them targets.

"Like your father?" Grace tutted, and inclined her head to study the city laid out beneath her. I hadn't said that last bit out loud, but she pulled it from my head anyway. "Silly pawn. I already told you. Only *men* were worthy. And though you come close, you fall short in many of the most obvious ways. He won't go looking for mortals. Very few beings could hold their own against the full strength of the Riders. Their language was very ... *distinct.*"

"So you want him to think that these things are coming for him?"

She sighed as though I'd disappointed her. Twice in one night. "I want him to remember *fear*. Real fear. There is a difference between fearing you will one day pass from this world. And it is quite another fear to feel the predator's breath against your skin."

"You're just going to torment him," I said. The words fell into the air like pebbles onto a pond. She wasn't the only one suffering from disappointment. After everything Lucien had done. All the people he'd manipulated. Everyone he'd hurt ...

I took a seat in the pew, shifting the hymnal to the side with my knee. No, there was something more to this. The way Grace had shown up tonight, the casual conversation ... she wanted something.

"Why am I still alive?"

She had no problem leaving me defenseless. Every day, I hid in Jason's house wondering if it would be the day that Lucien came after me. I'd killed him once, and I'd tried to stop the ritual he'd performed to restore himself. I would have killed him again if I'd had the chance, but Grace had intervened. She'd destroyed me, but she was just going to *harass* Lucien a little?

"Would you like for me to remedy that problem?" Grace asked in a chilling tone.

"Only if it's not going to disrupt your plans to pull Lucien's pigtails," I snarked back.

"Your contempt means so *very* little to me. Speak to me when you no longer dance on someone else's strings," Grace said with a smirk.

She might be some sort of immortal witch from another dimension, but Grace was also a grade-A bitch. "I'm no one's puppet!" I could feel my hands starting to shake, and worse, tears building in the corners of my eyes.

She laughed. It was a tinkling, perfectly respectable sound, but it still froze me in place. "Fortune may favor the brave," she added with a hidden smile, "but irony certainly crushes the foolish."

"Am I supposed to know what that means?"

"Not yet," she quipped. "But soon. I must admit, I'm surprised the demon hasn't come for you yet. To him, you are nothing more than a broken blade. And he's always been too tidy by far."

Grace was toying with me. That's all this was. She was trying to keep me off my guard. Trying to play me the same way everyone else did. I may not have wanted to be a puppet, but the accusation was on the nose. I reacted far too much, let others set the stage. Even now. Especially now.

"He should know that I'm still sharp. If not, he has no one to blame but himself." I hadn't entirely worked out my plan yet, but it seemed like Grace and I were coming to an agreement. "That goes for you, too."

"Oh, but I am not the threat you should be worried about," Grace said with a small smile. "I am merely the distraction."

"Wha—" But my body was suddenly so heavy, and I felt like I was going to sink straight through the stone floor and plummet down into the earth.

Grace's parting shot was dragged out and slowed down until it was deep and demonic. "Give your new master my regards."

two

I didn't wake up in my bed. Or even in my house. I woke up in the next best thing to a haunted forest.

Jason's house was tucked away from the city, and on one side it bordered the massive forest that took up most of the Belle Dam peninsula. The woods behind the house had been my refuge since moving here. I could disappear into them as easily as a whisper and pretend for a while that my life was okay.

Until now. Because I wasn't in the middle of the woods. I was already in motion. Running like something was coming for me. *"I'm no one's puppet,"* I'd screamed at Grace.

Now I understood that creepy smirk of hers. My body moved on its own, and I had no control over my movements. Someone else was in charge, with a remote control that charted my course. I couldn't even move my arms the way I wanted. I was a passenger in my own head. No wonder Grace had laughed at me. Not only was I a puppet, but I didn't even know who pulled my strings.

My feet never strayed from the path, the route I was taking was one I'd walked a few dozen times before, but all those times it had been my choice. It was the same path I'd used to run with Drew all the time, which led all the way to the coastline. There was a clearing about a quarter mile from here, an outcropping of rocks that overlooked the bay.

Something surged through the branches above my head, shaking loose dead leaves that had managed to cling to their branches. An owl's hoot a moment later emphasized just how quiet the woods were around me. There were no other sounds of wildlife—typically, the forest was a beautiful chaos of noise, but the only sounds were waves in the distance and my own steady heartbeat.

I was barely breathing hard by the time I reached the clearing, even though it was more than half a mile. I could barely keep pace with Drew when we went running.

My hearing returned, or at least it became noticeable again. The sound of water crashing against the rocks down below. Seagulls in the distance. But behind me, the forest was still silent. So my senses hadn't been completely dull. But that didn't explain where all the animals had gone or why they'd all gone so deathly silent. Forests don't normally clear out like that unless there was a predator. *Of course.*

"Long time no see, boy wonder," a voice called out from the woods to my left. I turned, expecting any one of the adults who had my death penciled in on their to-do lists. But it wasn't an adult. It was someone my age.

I hadn't seen Ben since that night at the hospital when

he'd disappeared with a tissue full of my blood. He'd always been a little weird, bloodplay notwithstanding, but in hindsight I realized that this was a far cry from a *little* weird.

He was still dressed like he was on his way to a future business leaders of America meeting, although maybe future sociopaths was more accurate. His dark hair was still carefully disheveled, his suit just rumpled enough to have been on purpose. But his face was leaner, his hair a little longer than the last time I'd seen him. And I couldn't say for sure, but I was pretty sure his shoulders had never been that wide the last time I'd seen him.

Jesus, three days ago. It looked like he'd aged a year or two since then.

He looked towards me like he was waiting on a response, but I decided to wait him out. It was second nature for me to fire back at him with some remark about clandestine hookups under the stars, but I didn't trust my tongue. And I didn't want to even joke about the idea of hooking up with some sort of creepy stalker.

With everyone else in Belle Dam, their allegiances were clear. Or at least it was clear that their allegiances could change at a moment's notice. But Ben was different. He was an unknown. But he'd made it clear that his appearance in my life wasn't an accident.

"Nothing to say?" His smirk widened, even as his disappointment started to show. "I guess I shouldn't be so anxious, huh?" He held up a hand, almost as though he was struck by a sudden wave of self-consciousness. "Sweaty palms."

This was . . . really not what I was expecting. "Is this the part where I beg for my life?" I asked, because I was honestly curious. Dragging me out into the middle of the woods didn't seem like it was going to end with a tea party.

"No," he replied slowly, "this is the part with the screams." Ben made a motion with his hand, the one not clutching my blood, a simple little crook of the finger.

The ring finger on my right hand snapped, the bone breaking in a fluid, invisible, motion. The sound of it was drowned out by my scream, but the *feel of it* raced through my body, heat and shivers as each bone sympathized. My hand was on fire, and this wasn't like with the visions where the pain was all in my head. This was real. I recoiled, stumbling to keep my balance, my hand cradled against my chest. With each wave of pain the fire dulled, but I'd managed to stay upright. That was the important part.

Ben was a witch. That was the only thing that could make sense. My head throbbed and a cold sweat had broken out all over my body. "What do you want?" I asked, finally holding in my screams.

"Isn't it obvious, Mr. Bond?" he quoted with one of the most truly awful British accents I'd ever heard. "I want you to die."

I lunged at him then. I might not have size or strength on my side, but I was still wiry and quick. Maybe if I could knock him off his feet, he'd let go of the things that were letting him control me. Ben stood still, waiting in amusement only to vanish the moment I should have connected with his chest. I stumbled across the clearing, falling once, and then rolling back up onto my feet in a move that was more accident than intention.

"Don't you get it?" he demanded, reappearing a few feet away. "You can't touch me unless I want you to. You can't hurt me. And you certainly can't stop me. I can take my time killing you, and there's nothing you can do."

"Nastier things than you have tried and failed," I said. "Not that it matters. You think Jason won't tear this town apart coming after you? Do you really want that hanging over your head?"

Ben threw back his head and laughed. With an absent wave, my feet tumbled out from underneath me and I went down hard. My teeth bit into my lower lip, and I got a mouthful of dirt for my trouble. Ben's laugh rang in my head the entire time.

Whatever he's doing, he's got total control over me. I should be afraid. The only smart reaction right now would be to be afraid. But my mind was clear. Adrenaline kept me focused and sharp. I eyed the distance to the cliff. Maybe if I could distract him, I could leap off the side. I didn't know if I could survive a fall like that into the water. Probably. Maybe. I didn't even know how deep the water was or if there were rocks. But between a rock and a crazy place ... I'd take the jump every time.

"Oh, that was good," he said, wiping at the corners of his eyes with the end of his sleeve. "Really? What's *Jason* going to do? Kill me?" Ben sneered. "That didn't work out so well the first time."

"What?"

He shook his head to the side, trying to shift the fringe out of his eyes. "Stay down," he said.

"Screw that." I braced myself with my good hand and tried to stand.

As casually as if he was checking the time on his watch, Ben jerked his wrist to the side—and this time I *did* crumple to my knees as I howled. My entire left hand seized up, and my wrist felt like it'd been mangled by some kind of wild animal. The way the pain lanced through me it was like my entire arm had been shattered. There was nothing but fire and red haze and the sound of my screaming. As the initial shock started to fade, I realized that the pain was only in my wrist, shooting up through my arm. I couldn't even feel my hand anymore.

This was how it was going to happen. This was how I would die.

Ben swept down in front of me, dark hair falling into his face. "Why shouldn't I take his son away from him? Kill Jason, and his suffering ends. But kill you, *torture* you, and that's the thing he curls up against at night and wakes up with each morning."

"You don't have to do this," I gasped.

"Oh, of course I do." Ben's voice dripped with contempt. "Gods know how long I had to wait. But then she appeared like an avenging angel. All I had to do was watch the town and interfere when she told me to. Pruning the feud like it was some kind of bonsai." He snorted. "Like I care about any of that. Hannah didn't care. That little psychopath loved it. She just wanted to fuck people up."

Hannah. The ghost girl who had pushed me in front of a bus. Ben was a ghost? But that wasn't possible. I'd touched him. He'd touched me. Hadn't he?

"Oh, yeah, little boy blue's trying to put all the pieces together?" Ben crossed the path to where I lay on the ground. "It's not like the stories. I'm not bound to haunt the scene of my greatest remorse, dressed all in white." He sat down on the dirt next to me, resting his arms on his knees like we were just a couple of friends hanging out in the woods. "Lucky for you."

"Let me guess. You haunt the girl's locker room like the weirdo perv you are?" I said. "Classy."

Half of Ben's mouth quirked upwards, and he reached over as casual as anything and tapped one finger against my abdomen. I screamed again, spasming away from him. I don't know if he'd followed up on his threat and broken my ribs, or if it was just *pain,* but the entire left half of my torso was an electrified minefield of radiating pain. Every time I shifted, every time I even breathed, it was like tripping the sensations all over again.

"It doesn't have to be bones, I can break anything. Make it fester, burn, decay. As far as I can take my imagination." He leaned in, and despite being a ghost, I could smell a sharp tang of sweat. "And I've had a lot of years to decide exactly what I'd do."

"Oh dear, this isn't the yellow brick road," a new voice called out.

three

Matthias emerged from the wooded path in his perfectly groomed three-piece suit, all black as usual. There wasn't even a hint of dirt on his shoes. Another benefit of being one of the few real demons roaming around Belle Dam. "There's a thought," he gasped, as though struck by sudden inspiration. "You should ask the wizard to pull that stick out of your—"

"Stay out of it," Ben snapped, holding up the bloody napkins. "And stay where you are. I'm finishing this tonight. You can't stop me. You wouldn't dare."

"I'm afraid you're going to be as disappointed as your date was on prom night."

I squinted at Matthias through the reddish haze, trying to figure out if he was just another hallucination. The demon sauntered forward, one measured step after another. Like he had all the time in the world and I wasn't a broken mess on the ground.

"Are you kidding me?" Ben looked down at me. "You

just got rid of one demonic godmother and now you've got another one lining up to take his place? Haven't you learned *anything?*"

"I'd say the boy's learned a touch more than you," Matthias responded easily. "Then again, you were never the brightest star in the sky, were you? The rebel with the secret insecurities. Such a forgettable cliché."

"That reminds me," Ben continued, his attention returning to the demon. "I'm pretty sure I told you not to move." He flexed his fingers and made a sharp twisting motion.

My ankle snapped, but this time I bit down on my wrist. If he wanted my screams—if hearing me suffer was part of what was getting him off—I wouldn't let him have it. Breathing became more difficult, something in my chest stealing the air out of my lungs. But I bit my teeth into my uninjured wrist, adding a thimble full of pain to the flood that was already coursing through my body.

It took minutes for the pain to recede enough to pull my mouth away from my hand. Minutes that Ben was more than happy to wait. I muttered under my breath.

"What's that?" he asked brightly, leaning closer.

"I said no wonder Jason killed you," I repeated, my voice hoarse. "But it must run in the family."

Matthias kept walking forward, slow and even. "What's that, now?"

"Killing people that don't stay dead," I said.

Well, it made the demon laugh, at least. I noticed

something from my position on the ground. Matthias approached ... and Ben backed away from me. Not noticeably at first, but the closer Matthias got to his space, the further back Ben shifted. Until he wasn't close to me at all.

"You know him?" I finally asked, when Matthias came to stand over me instead of the crazy guy.

"*Knew* him," he corrected gently. "Though I should point out that when I knew him before he wasn't such a ... how can I put this delicately?"

"Troll-faced psychopath?" I suggested weakly, then gasped as the pressure inside my stomach intensified.

"I think deviated little shit-stain covers it better," Matthias offered.

I inhaled, and inhaled again, but couldn't get enough breath into my lungs. The squeezing sensation increased, and it felt like hours before even the slightest bit of air seemed to reach my lungs. My body was screaming for oxygen, and despite my best efforts, I couldn't seem to get any in.

"Oh, stop that," Matthias said over me. "The boy's no part of this. Your quarrel is with Jason."

"My *quarrel* is with Jason's son," Ben snarled. "And since he was sweet enough to provide his blood on a silver platter, I couldn't help myself. It's almost like he was begging for it. The powers were a problem, of course, but he was kind enough to get rid of those for me, wasn't he? And then all that blood on his face. Blood is always potent, but that night it was especially so. But you didn't tell him, did you? Didn't warn him or anything. So why are you here now, Matthias? This is between Braden and I."

"*Braden and me*," the demon corrected. "But actually, this is between you and Jason. Though even *that* isn't quite right. You know who was ultimately responsible, weren't you? The man behind the curtain. He pulled Catherine's strings just as easily as she pulled Jason's. And she got you out of the way without even lifting a hand to help."

"And I'm not stupid enough to go after either of them," Ben said, vaulting to his feet. "But I can take out the town pariah no problem. Maybe I'll even follow it up with the Lansing golden boy. Put a nice dent in this feud of yours."

"Oh, it's not my feud," Matthias demurred, ducking his head down as if he was too embarrassed to take the compliment. Though how the feud was a compliment, I would never understand. "But as I've said, I'm afraid you're going to walk away disappointed today. You're operating under the assumption that the boy is no longer on the board. But I'm afraid he's still very much in play." He turned back to the path expectantly, like reinforcements would be arriving any moment.

There was a hushed moment where our eyes followed the demon's, waiting to see who next would be joining this insane menagerie.

But the joke was on us, because the woods were silent. Help, or whatever it was that Matthias had been expecting, wasn't coming. "Where is that thrice-damned girl when you need her?" Matthias snarled, looking upwards. "Always right where she's not wanted, but then the moment she's supposed to be somewhere, she's distracted."

"Girl?" Ben asked, almost like he couldn't help himself.

"Unimportant," the demon responded crossly, waving it off. "I'll have to take care of this myself."

Matthias extended a hand, and shadows swirled against his fingertips. At his feet, a pool of black began to ink up, seeping up from the ground as though there was always a well of demonic oil lurking under the surface of the world. He whispered a word, although his mouth didn't move, and another voice—an inhuman growl of a voice—repeated the same word, which sounded somehow much more proper in a guttural tongue.

The creature that dug itself out of the darkness was as much like a hellhound as a Doberman is to a German shepherd. For one thing, where the hellhounds had fur that was more like spines, this creature looked hairless, cast in shades of ashes and soot. It was almost skeletal, bones protruding visibly at the top of the spine and near the tail. Its eyes were a solid, murky cataract gray. As soon as its feet were underneath it, the helldog's muzzle turned sharply towards Ben.

"Another hellhound?" he scoffed. "You should know better than that, demon. You can't hurt me. No one can."

Matthias held up a finger, his face schooled into impassiveness. "Barghest."

Ben shook his head. "Bar guest? The hell is that?"

"*Barghest,*" Matthias repeated. "Not my particularly favorite breed, but surprisingly useful under the right circumstances."

He held up a second finger. "Would you like to know what those circumstances are?"

All it took was a single click of Matthias's tongue and the barghest sprang forward, snarling. Ben didn't flinch—and why should he? He was only as corporeal as he wanted to be, which meant he couldn't be hurt.

At least that's what I thought until the barghest slammed into Ben's chest, jaws snapping for his neck as the pair tumbled to the ground. From where I was, I had a perfect view of the look of shock in Ben's eyes, the white-eyed panic as he tried to scramble out from underneath the devil dog.

"They're an accident, of course. Hellhounds are remarkably resilient creatures—I'm rather proud of them—but even they can be put down. But if the hound is pregnant, the litter refuses to die. They'll continue feeding off the mother, growing stronger through her death until the body finally is sucked dry of anything nourishing. The pups all die, one by one. And then, curiously enough, they come back, clawing their way out to the surface. Dead, but not dead. Alive, but not alive. Sound familiar?"

Matthias crouched down to where the barghest had Ben pinned and casually tucked a strand of his hair out of his face. "You're going to forget this little vengeance quest of yours. The boy is off-limits. Besides, we both know that you've got another weakness."

The rage on Ben's face only magnified. "You wouldn't touch him."

Matthias raised a shoulder in a half shrug. "Wouldn't I?

I care very little either way. So unpredictable, you boys with your mercurial minds. Wouldn't the city be safer without such a threat?"

"I'll back off," Ben said quickly. "Just leave him out of this."

"Crawl back in your grave," Matthias said, his voice growing harsh. "Or go beg a witch to return you to your repose. Catherine's always willing to do you a favor, isn't she?" Ben's rage surged again and he tried to push himself back up, but the barghest was like a lead weight on his chest. As Matthias stood and turned, the boy's eyes shot to me again. It was clear that no matter what Ben said, this wasn't over. He'd come back. It was only a matter of time.

I started shivering, crawling in on myself as much as I could. It caused Matthias to look up, his expression annoyed. "You're going into shock," he announced, coming back to where I lay on the ground. "I suppose you want me to burp you, too? Tell you a bedtime story, perhaps?"

"I wouldn't mind if you went and fucked right off," I said, as my teeth started chattering. I hadn't noticed the temperature before, but suddenly November in Belle Dam was seeping into my bones like a toxin.

"I'm still in play," I said, repeating his words back to him. "If I die, you get nothing."

"Spare me the histrionics," Matthias replied, striding towards us. "When you have to choose, simply choose to live. Simple."

"It doesn't *work like that*."

"It doesn't?" Matthias looked positively dumbstruck. "I suppose that explains a bit. I never understood why people would choose to die, especially not when they look so ravaged and sagging." The demon glanced down at me, and he took a deep breath. He looked uncertain. Maybe even a little nervous. "Some lesser minds might choose to blame me for what happened to your family. I bore you no malice." It was hard to say if Matthias looked uncomfortable or if his grimace was about having to talk about it. Feelings, eww. "I would not be punished for the actions of another. Let the blame hang solely around his neck so that he might choke on it."

He wanted forgiveness? Matthias was the reason Lucien had found those girls to hurt in the first place. He'd practically braided Lucien's hair while he set about trying to pull himself back together. But no, that wasn't right. Even as cloudy as my mind was, and despite all the pain I was in, Belle Dam had sharpened my mind too much to ignore what had happened here tonight. Grace had pulled me away for a pleasant conversation. Matthias thought I was still a game piece to be played. The city wasn't done with me yet. But without my power, I wasn't capable of doing anything. Unless that meant . . .

The hole in my chest where my magic had been was suddenly an aviary, a thousand flapping wings brushing up against the sides of the void. It was like a rush of excitement, but muted. *Something's happening.* I didn't know where, and

I didn't know what, but something on the other side of the city was in flux, and it had to do with me.

A crown of sorrows milky white weddings ravish and spinning the beginning of the world sisters till the end her empty eyes shocked brown like ground underneath the strikes of lightning. And then Grace's face. Grace's voice. Grace's magic. "Find a way to make it work. Or I'll feed you to the Rider next."

As the feeling faded and I dropped back into awareness of my ravaged body, I shook my head as best I could. The pain wasn't so bad now. For a moment. "No," I moaned, "No chance." Matthias was indirectly responsible for John's death. He'd helped Lucien, and Lucien had killed my uncle. None of that would have happened if Matthias had stayed out of it. But there was more to it than that. I wouldn't let him dictate the terms.

"You're *dying,*" the demon said, leaning into my field of vision. "Now is not the time for misplaced pride. This isn't like the times before, where the same power that was killing you was also keeping you alive. You're an empty vessel now. Fate has washed its hands of you." And then he smiled, and it was terrifying. "What better time for a resurrection?"

"Immunity," I agreed. "But you'll ... owe me a favor," I managed to say between heaving breaths that didn't do any good.

Matthias looked down at me, and I got the distinct impression that he was passing judgment on me even now. Weighing my life against his potential gains. He pressed his lips together and shook his head. "I'm not that foolish.

Owing you a favor would make my life … complicated. I prefer simplicity. *You* will owe *me* a favor."

"Fine." I wiped away the blood that was trailing down my forehead, only managing to smear it into my hair. "We'll shake on it."

"You're a devious little biped, aren't you?" Matthias said slowly, a smile curling around the corners of his mouth. I knew I had him then, and collapsed back onto the ground. He crouched down over top of me, hand poised over my chest. "I can't promise this won't hurt."

One moment I was dying, and the next moment I was *dying*. Black lightning poured into my veins and tore each one of them to shreds. I collapsed into a hundred thousand pieces, and each piece was an unbearable agony. My body getting charred and splintered apart, and the liquid fire I was drowning in, was nowhere near as painful as the bubbling green acid flowing through my veins.

I screamed. And screamed. And somewhere in the midst of the pain, somewhere far beyond my mind and sanity, there was a moment. A single, crystallized moment buried underneath layers of loathing, rage, and desperation.

I was going to live. And if I was going to live, I damn well was going to take back everything that was mine and take them all down. I was done being the victim. I was done letting everyone else pull my strings.

They wanted a weapon?

I'd give them a war.

four

I woke up sometime just after dawn on a lounge chair behind the house. A giant blue tarp lay discarded at my feet, emphasizing the line of flattened grass and groove lines in the dirt that suggested something—most likely me—had been dragged out of the woods.

Nice to see that I still rated so highly in Matthias's affections.

I stretched out, feeling muscles popping in relief and not in agony. All at once, I remembered what had happened last night and what Ben had done to me. I looked down at my wrist, but there was no trace of the damage from last night. The more I concentrated, the more I noticed how *good* I felt. Certainly not like I'd taken a beating the night before. Certainly not like that beating had been bad enough to get me admitted to the hospital.

But then I remembered everything else that had happened. Grace, and then Ben. Matthias. Grace had opened up the lines of communication for a reason, and it had something to do with the weird feeling in my chest. And Matthias had maintained that I was still useful.

And lastly, I remembered finding my center just before I must have blacked out. I was done being a pawn. I was done being a victim. And I sure as hell was done with being everyone's punching bag.

I needed to figure out a plan. But first, I needed to take a shower and dig out a suit. Because we were still burying my uncle this morning.

¤   ¤   ¤

In Belle Dam, when a Thorpe died, there were two services. A service for the public, giving people who'd spent their lives hating and fearing my uncle a chance to relax and put those old feelings to rest. Where people who'd never known or spoken to John while he was alive could grieve his death as publicly and obnoxiously as they could. It would be standing room only, with an eager town pressed in tight like cattle, falling over themselves for one last look.

Death makes us targets, Jason had told me several days ago. *When we're dead, we can't collect on old debts or make new threats. There's no reason to fear us. And so they try to forget us.*

But those feelings also make some people cocky, and the last thing either side of the feud needed was for someone to explode at the wrong moment. So Jason and I had a private service with a priest who'd apparently known the family since my great-grandfather's days. I'd never been to a funeral before, but it wasn't nearly what I expected. There were prayers, but they were strangely formal and formulaic. No mentions of God, no talk about souls. It was a lot about "committing him to the earth" and talk about duty.

"I thought he'd never stop talking," I said, shoving my hands into the black leather gloves Jason handed me.

"Father Patrick knew Jonathan as well as anyone, Braden," Jason said wearily. Everything he did lately was with an air of fatigue. If I were a nicer person, I would say that his brother's death was weighing heavily on him. But I wasn't a nicer person, I knew that had very little to do with it. Jason hated to lose, and right now he was coming up, forgive the pun, dead last.

"If you knew him at all, you'd know he hated being called Jonathan," I muttered. I was just happy to get away from the chapel, with its stale stench of pretentious decay, and the priest, who looked like he'd be more at home with a knife and a butcher's block.

We went out of the chapel and through the Thorpe cemetery, and Jason left his attempt at parenting at the chapel doors. That there was a family plot surprised me only a little. My mother was buried in the city, as was the empty grave that should have held me. But John was a true Thorpe, with Thorpe blood in his veins. He wasn't a token offering for the town. As much as the Thorpes and Lansings pretended they were a part of the city, they always held something back, keeping their blood to themselves.

A cemetery full of Thorpes. I'll be buried here someday.

Jason was pragmatic enough to have already picked out my final resting place, I was sure. I could ask him to show me it while we were here. *Especially since I might be coming back sooner than anyone expects.*

There was a code to the headstone engravings, Jason had pointed out on our way in. *Augustus Thorpe, Taken By the Water* was right next to his brother *James, Lost Before His Time.* Every Thorpe, back to the very first to settle in Washington, was either Taken or Lost. Taken through the never-ending feud with the Lansing family, or Lost to anything that didn't fall to an act of war. It was sobering to see how few were Lost.

"You don't need those," Jason commented, looking at the sunglasses covering my eyes. It was as close as he ever came to asking me what had happened. One of his mysterious business trips had taken him out of town when everything had happened with John's death and the lighthouse. When he came home, it was to find his seventeen-year-old son, his *weapon,* staring back at him with ordinary, human eyes and not even a drop of magical power left to his name.

"I have a headache," I said, my words terse. Jason wouldn't tell me where he'd been or what had been so important that he'd left when I could have used his help. So a stalemate developed—I kept my secrets, and Jason kept his.

That was only part of the truth, though. What had happened in the lighthouse—hell, everything that had happened that *night*—was a wound that wouldn't close. I didn't want to talk about it with anyone, least of all Jason.

"We'll be expected at the repast," Jason explained, for the thousandth time. After the funeral, there was a gathering. Normal people had a wake, but not Jason. It was always a repast, and it had the sound of a particular Belle Dam kind of tradition.

"I'm aware."

He looked down at his watch. "It's nearly ten. The funeral will be letting out soon." His pace quickened, legs longer than mine. He was taller than me. I'd never really noticed that before. Taller than John had been.

John had been taller than me, too.

Had been.

I struggled to keep up, made all the more difficult by the sudden shifting of gravity around me. The dizzy spells came without warning, as blood suddenly ran to my head and things looked out of focus. It was one of the many changes I'd had to get used to. Everything inside of me was jumbled and *wrong*.

"Was Braden even supposed to be my name?" I asked suddenly. The footpath through the woods was a short walk to where Jason had left the car. I'd always thought that the access roads on the back half of the Thorpe property were for something official, like power lines or telephone lines or something. But it seemed like they served a more obvious function—ease of circumventing the house to one of the several buildings tucked away in the woods.

Jason looked up, startled out of his own thoughts. "What?"

"My name," I reiterated. "Did Uncle John pick?" I shrugged, reaching into my pocket for a cell phone that wasn't even there. "I'm just wondering what they'll put on my headstone." Then again, I already had a headstone in town. Maybe they'd just toss me in the empty box.

Actual *emotions* crossed Jason's face, whipping by so fast they forced him into a halt. Of the few things I knew about the man who was supposed to be my father, one of the most important was that he *never showed emotion.* But just for a moment, a brief flash of seconds, I caught shifts in his face and truly, honestly saw the family resemblance. I could always read Uncle John's face like it was an open book: I knew every single scowl, frown line, smirk, and twitch. And just for a second, I could do the same for Jason.

Rage, and frustration, and an anger that was made up more of despair than hatred. All replaced by the weary look I'd come to recognize. A look that had my name all over it. "Your mother picked your name," he said, each word sharp like axes. "Braden Michael Thorpe."

Braden Michael Thorpe. I'd been raised as Braden Michaels. It made sense. Not the most ingenious of secret identities, though. Then again, it didn't seem like I'd been in hiding so much as just being kept away from Belle Dam. We'd only moved once during my childhood, from the desert up to Montana.

Those eight words looked like they'd cost Jason something precious. *Does he really need to be reminded of this right now?* Jason and I might not get along, but I didn't need to torture the guy.

"I was just curious," I said quietly, trying to absolve at least some of the guilt I was feeling. My skin flushed, and at first I thought it was embarrassment, but quickly realized it was something more.

Ever since the night of Grace's attack, I'd felt *off.* Like parts of me were missing or weren't doing their job any longer. Phantom pains stretched along my skin, nipping at me with increasing frequency. Moments of vertigo so strong that I had to lie down until they pass. Hot spells. Cold spells. Nausea.

"We're going to be late," Jason said, and just like that, our conversation was forgotten. We had a city full of condolences to accept.

I didn't care for the grief. Grieving people wanted to touch, wanted to *hug,* and if anything it made me want to be touched even less. Every time anyone came close, even if they just wanted to pat me on the shoulders as Jason had tried to do earlier, I had to move away, as quickly as possible. I couldn't let them touch me.

After all, it was my fault. The feud, John's death, the slump in Jason's posture. I'd set all this in motion by coming here, and it was almost too late to leave.

five

"The Harbor Club?" I said when the car finally stopped.

"It's a large enough space to hold everyone," Jason said stiffly.

"And remind them that Jonathan Thorpe was so much more important than they could ever hope to be," I muttered. "Lucky them."

It was the Belle Dam version of a country club—perfect for the port town with a need for pretense and class warfare. Close to the harbor, its giant wall of windows looked out onto the bay that surrounded the city.

"The church had a meeting hall they offered to us," Jason said, sounding suddenly uncomfortable. "I thought you would prefer something a little less..."

"A little less what?"

He slid his phone back into the breast pocket of his suit. "I didn't know... I was never sure if... Jonathan was never very..."

The answer dawned on me. "You didn't know if we

went to church. If I'd be comfortable with an actual church service." That's why the service had been so formal, so carefully devoid of words like "God" and "heaven."

Jason's jaw tightened, but he didn't respond.

I really, really don't understand you. I watched him from behind pointless sunglasses. He hadn't cried at all, but that didn't surprise me. Jason didn't strike me as the type to let anyone see any of his weakness. But I hadn't cried, either. I'd been numb for days, and that was the only thing keeping my feelings at bay.

It was like John's death had happened to someone else. I knew it couldn't last. I knew it would be awful when it set in. But I felt like a freak. Who buries the man that raised them and doesn't shed a tear? Who doesn't even get the sniffles?

Did Jason cry at his own father's funeral? *There is the most fascinating tradition of patricide among the Thorpes,* Lucien had whispered to me once. But Jason had resisted, he said, and Lucien had had to take matters into his own hands. Did Jason know how his father had actually died? Should I even tell him?

I didn't actually know what Jason thought of me. When I first came to town, it was like I was an item on his agenda. A new toy he'd purchased. But later, after I was hurt, I'd become an inconvenience. And no matter how many doctors he threw at me, none could tell him how to fix what was broken.

Now I was broken, but maybe in the best way possible. The only problem was that the list of people who wanted me dead seemed to double every day. Unless I was under lock and key for the rest of my life, at some point, they would come for me and the curtain would fall.

"Where were you?" I asked, the words stumbling out of my mouth before I could catch them. "Why weren't you here?"

I expected him to disappear or to walk away without answering. But Jason stopped short, and it wasn't until then that I realized I'd yelled at him, accused him, blamed him, but never once in the last three days had I ever just *asked* him.

"I ... should have been here," Jason admitted, just as quietly.

"I tried to save him." It was cold enough outside that I could see my breath. I focused on that, instead of him. "I deserve what happens to me. I deserve all of it."

Jason lifted a hand and reached out, but I flinched. Backed away. Some part of my brain expected to be hit. To be attacked again. Hurt. But Jason looked like I'd been the one to attack *him*. I realized my mistake too late, but before I could apologize, or—I didn't even know—Jason's phone rang.

"I have to take this," he bit out. He didn't wait for me to respond, just spun around on his heel and kept his back to me.

I couldn't even play nice with Jason for an hour. What was wrong with me? I ducked my head low and went inside, figuring that the sooner I got inside, the sooner I could find someplace to hide.

The Harbor Club was a paragon of elegance. Gleaming

marble tile floors, rich, creamy white walls. Spaced around the lower floor were blown-up images of a much younger Uncle John—school photographs, birthday parties, family portraits, and pictures with Jason and a salt-and-pepper-haired man I took to be my grandfather.

I sifted through the crowd like a piece that didn't fit, sinking to the bottom while they all rose. A bar was set up at the far end of the room, and I made my way there. A pair of women dressed all in black reclined against the bar, talking to each other but both were more focused on the crowd. More interested in who spoke to whom, and where everyone was positioned.

I reached out, snagged a glass of white wine just as the bartender dropped it off for one of the women. Meeting her eyes, I took a sip, challenging her to argue. The wine burned going down, but I refused to let it show. She knew who I was—it would surprise me if there was anyone here who *didn't*.

She didn't say anything, and my lips quirked up in a faint half smile. I could have poured the drink over her head, and she wouldn't have raised her voice. She might later, in private where there was no one important to listen in, but not now. Not when she was face to face with me. Not when her friends and neighbors were only a few footsteps away, ready to turn on her in a moment's notice.

"So sorry to hear," the woman murmured, so quiet I could barely hear her. But I ignored the wasted sympathy. I didn't deserve it. John's death was my fault. All of this was my fault.

So I drank. When the first glass was drained, I replaced it with a second. The bartender eyed me, but didn't hesitate to pour.

It was easy to tell when Jason arrived. Crowds parted when Jason Thorpe walked into a room. His mask and armor were on full display, cold and aloof and utterly untouchable. He could have been getting his taxes done, not burying his brother.

Almost immediately, *he* was besieged with thinly veiled condolence calls. There were tears, handkerchiefs, and trembling, but very little truth. He accepted each bit of sympathy like he was a stone. Everyone knew the brothers weren't close, that John had fled years ago, but that didn't stop their attempts at seeking favor. All in all, it was quite a performance. Jason was impassive because nothing could ruffle his feathers.

Well, other than me. I was insanely good at driving him insane.

I watched him for a couple of minutes, the burning in my gut bringing a surprising amount of relief. I should feel *something*, so if it had to be pain I'd caused myself, then that would have to do. Jason mingled his way through the crowd, taking time to talk to everyone who approached. I saw a dozen different variations on "We appreciate your concern" and "Thank you for coming."

As Jason continued to mingle, I dropped my glass on a

table and slipped through the crowd. At the far end of the room was a staircase leading to the second floor. A week ago, it was where I'd had one of my first real confrontations with Catherine Lansing—where she toyed with me while pretending not to know why girls were disappearing in her city.

From my second-floor vantage point, I scanned the crowd for her. There was no way she wouldn't show up. It wouldn't be a victory if she couldn't lord it over the competition. I hadn't seen her since the night John did.

The night she killed him.

I should have been looking for Lucien, the demon in the three-piece suit, because there was no way he'd miss it, either. For much different reasons, I was sure. Lucien had been manipulating events in Belle Dam for a long time, and I'd become a thorn in his side. It was one of the few things I was proud of since I'd come to Belle Dam.

But today wasn't about me, and it definitely wasn't about demons. It was about John, and the bitch who had taken him from me. I'd promised to kill her. It was only fair. When John tried to kill Catherine's husband, she retaliated by killing my mother. At least that's what the stories say. The papers suggested a different story. That my mother was "sick." That there was an "accident." Coded words that implied a suicide that might not have been self-inflicted at all.

I felt the shadow closing in on me before he appeared at my side. I could see both stairways from where I stood, which meant he hadn't come from there. He must have been on the balcony outside, the one that faced that city instead of the bay. Waiting for me. I don't know how he knew, but he did.

I spoke over my shoulder, not trusting myself to turn around. "You can't be here."

"You need me," he said quietly. I closed my eyes. If I looked to my right, I knew what I would find. A boy, only a few years older and a few inches taller. Strong and solid. And nothing like his mother.

"Go away, Trey."

"No."

"Please." It was a whisper.

His response was just as soft. "No." A hand reached out, hesitant, and grabbed the back of my coat. My eyes flew open at the same moment that Trey started pulling me backwards, away from the prying eyes downstairs. He dragged me into one of the corners, half hidden by a potted ficus. I focused on it, the way the leaves curled down, like they were shamed.

He took one of my hands and set it against his waist. Then the other. And then he carefully wrapped his arms against me, pulling me tight against him.

"It'll be okay," he said, his cheek pressed up against my ear.

But it wouldn't. He knew that. I knew it too.

I counted to ten. It's all the time I allowed myself to have. Long enough to memorize the way his arms slid over me, familiar and new all at the same time. His head pressed against mine, his breath on my skin.

I pulled myself and pushed at him until there was an icy hollow between us. *All my fault. If I'd done what Lucien wanted in the first place, none of this would have happened.*

But Trey would probably be dead. Would I have traded their places if I could? Sacrificed Trey for John?

I couldn't do this. It would be too easy to fall under Trey's spell. To forget that I was supposed to suffer. I had to remind myself, and him. I had to make it hurt. "Do you know what I see when I look at you?" I asked, licking my lips as the blood rushed to my head again and tore at my balance.

"Braden, don't."

But I didn't listen. That was the price of getting what you wanted. You had to serve penance. The words had to be said out loud. "I see *her.* I see the look on her face when she killed him. I see the way he hit the ground, and I can hear that last little gasp of air, the one that said he was dead already."

Trey was marble, sharp and perfect, his face expressionless.

"He's dead because of me. Because I was weak."

"That's not true," he whispered.

"Your mom's going to come for me, and there's nothing I can do to stop her," I said. "I'm all used up inside. She won't even have to break a sweat."

"She won't."

"You don't know that." I shrugged. "I'd do it if I had the chance."

"No you wouldn't," he pressed. "You're better than they are."

"I'm really not." I walked back over to the landing, looking down at the party. Because that's what it really was. Everyone may have been dressed in shades of black, and there might have been a hint of melancholy in the air, but this was a party with eager eyes and electric anticipation in the air.

"Don't you get it? If I had my power, I wouldn't care. From here," my voice was so calm, "I could stop her heart. I wouldn't fight fair—Thorpes never do."

"You're not a Thorpe."

I pretended I couldn't hear him. Kept talking. Musing on all the ways I would commit murder if ever given the chance. "I could take a page out of her book and poison the food, but that would take time. I'd need to see *her* eyes catch in surprise, that last imprint before she's gone." *John's eyes, widening just a fraction as he fell. I used to read his face like a magic eight ball, deciphering his mood from the lines on his face.*

"Stop," Trey implored.

Anytime Jason and Catherine shared the same air it was jarring, like a sharp, piercing sound that shattered a moment of Zen. It was an energy that the town thrived on, moments of utter possibility. Anything could happen. So many opportunities to get ahead, to push someone else down, adults all jockeying for position like a high school election. Belle Dam denizens scurried beneath me, climbing over one another for favors. No one cared that he was gone. Except me.

"I remember what she did," I said casually, over my shoulder. "I saw it. What it looked like, how it felt. So effortless." I snapped my fingers. "And then it's over."

"Braden ... " But he didn't have anything else to say. I knew it wasn't fair to him, knew that this had to be hard on him, too. He'd watched his mother kill John the same as I had. Penance, though. It had to be done.

"Where would you be right now, if that night had gone differently? If John was still alive and their plan had failed?"

I could feel him staring at me, knew his expression would be perplexed. His fingers were probably tapping against his pants, a restless rhythm betraying his nerves.

"If things had gone differently, we'd still be dressed in our funeral finest," I said it casually, like were discussing nothing more than the weather for all the emotion in my voice. "This might have been her wake."

"I don't know what you want me to say."

I closed my eyes. "No. You're a good son. You'd be with her." I opened them again, took off the sunglasses, and faced him. I had to squint—unfiltered light was still hard to handle during the day. "But you don't have to worry about that. She's not the one that's going to die."

He lunged forward, put his arms on my shoulders. Trey went to speak, but I cut him off.

"You need to pay more attention." I looked to my left, down below us. "She's here," I said quietly.

Down below, on the first floor, Catherine Lansing had made her entrance. I knew they'd come together, but even still, seeing Lucien's thin-lipped smile as the pair of them stared up at us made my stomach churn.

All of the Lansings were blond, but Catherine made it somehow ... more. Maybe it was her presence, the innate sense of entitlement that she shared with Jason. That's what happened to warlocks in a town full of plebeians. Belle Dam had been taught to adore what it feared, and it had never adored anything as much as Catherine Lansing in the spotlight.

She wore a black pantsuit, the jacket's sleeves coming up short and exposing the cuffs of her white business shirt. Her collar had been pulled over the top of the suit coat, a flare of white against her skin.

Lucien, unsurprisingly, had gone black on black. His pinstripe suit gave just a touch of whimsy, a humor that no one else seemed to share. If possible, his dress shirt was even darker than the suit that surrounded it.

Grace said that Lucien was still in hiding, licking his wounds. But he wouldn't miss this. Neither of them would miss this. They'd gone to so much trouble to make today possible. I looked down at my watch and almost started to smile. Had Grace known? Had she planned this out from start to finish?

Trey reached for me again, like he needed to prove to me that he was no longer his mother's pawn. But I'd used Catherine's arrival for the distraction it was and darted out of his reach.

I was halfway down the steps before anyone realized what was coming.

s|x

Even a week ago, dramatically descending the stairs without my sunglasses would have made an impact. The witch eyes had been physically devastating, but it was how they *looked.* They were ever-changing—eyes that could be cobalt blue, amber, and then a vibrant viridian all in a matter of seconds. Never the same shade from one minute to the next, the same way I never saw the same sights twice.

That was then. Ever since the power had been ripped out of me, my eyes had settled on just one color: an unnatural, pale green like limestone battered by the sea. People still stared, my eyes still called attention to themselves, but now they were just a cry for attention.

I flew down the stairs, moving faster than I thought I could. The rest of the world had slowed, and I'd been quickened to move faster than ever before. Trey called my name from the stairs, but he'd hesitated too long. By the time he realized I was gone, I was already at the bottom.

On the way down the stairs, I'd slid my watch over the

bones of my wrist and onto the lowest part of my palm, where my fingers could dig into the leather band with ease. There was a countdown in play, all I had to do was to keep them busy long enough for the payoff.

I strode up to the two of them, defiant and unafraid. For the first time, I met Catherine's stare eye to eye. I expected to see something in hers, something vicious or cruel or mocking. She'd drawn her line in the sand. But her eyes were blank—walled off and empty. Just like Jason's. Revealing nothing. Up close, I saw the differences in her from the last time. Her skin was more pale than I remembered, and the makeup around her eyes was thick, but it didn't disguise how sunken her face had become.

"They'll let anyone into these things," Lucien murmured in a low drawl at my approach.

I didn't break my gaze. "Pipe down—the humans are talking."

Catherine raised an eyebrow at me. "Are we now?"

I spread my arms, inviting. The international symbol for "come at me, you psycho warlock bitch."

"Braden, come on." Trey was suddenly between us, his hand pressing against my chest. Pushing me backwards. "Don't."

"You'd better kill me," I said, not caring how my voice carried. Actually, I wanted it to carry. I wanted the crowd to hear me. I wanted them to *know*. When the time came and someone found my body, I wanted them to know without a shadow of a doubt who was responsible. "Come on, Catherine. What are you scared of?"

Like a volume switch had been pressed, the conversational din surrounding us had almost completely diminished. My words rang throughout the club.

"This is everything you've been waiting for," I shouted, not caring that I was throwing myself right into the path of predators. My skin was hot, my insides burned, and *I just had to do this.* "Kill me, Catherine."

Several seconds passed. No one in the room even dared to breathe. Everyone waited on Catherine's reaction. I could feel them all around me, people who'd been raised in this town and had never before seen a confrontation between a Thorpe and a Lansing quite like this, where there were no agendas to hide behind, no minions mouthing words written by someone else.

The city held its breath.

Catherine, of course, was not one to disappoint. "Deal with this," she said, framing her voice just loud enough to carry to the ring of observers around us. They would eagerly spread her response for her, and Catherine wouldn't have to resort to shouting to match my fury. When she turned back to me, it was with the cold, empty mask I'd seen her wear before when she was dealing with people of no consequence. Like I didn't matter.

"I came to pay my respects," she said clearly. "A pity if that offends you."

Trey stayed by my side, one hand still braced in front of me. "You are *unbelievable,*" he breathed.

Catherine couldn't have missed the utter contempt in his voice, but she pretended not to notice anyway. She took a step forward, her eyes measuring mine. "You are a very stupid boy," she said softly, her lips barely moving, and her whisper just loud enough for me to hear. There was no chance anyone else would.

Upstairs, I'd told Trey that if I had the power, I would have turned it on Catherine. Killed her with as little mercy and care as she had killed John. But being in front of her like this, seeing her breathe, and blink, and the faintest hint of anger blossoming in her cheeks ... it was too much. Catherine was alive, and John was dead, and there was nothing I could do about it.

Oh no. Tears that I had spent three days expecting suddenly sprang up, and my vision shimmered for once because of weakness and not because of magic. My face grew hot and my skin felt too tight for everything that was trying to force its way out. This couldn't be happening. Not now. Now in front of *them.*

"A pleasure as always, Gentry," Lucien said, rubbing his thumb up and down the surface of his glass. He acted like he hadn't just witnessed my verbal assault on his pet human. Or that he cared. "You and I should get together. We have something to discuss."

"You're insane," Trey said with a sneer.

The crowd parted around Jason as he strode towards us,

a smooth pace that suggested his timing was more coinciden-
tal than planned. His arrival halted things before they could
degenerate even more. Relatively speaking. "Lucien," Jason
said, greeting the man as if he was just any ordinary business
associate. Pleasant, but flat. "I'd heard you were dead."

As quickly as Jason appeared, Catherine vanished into
the crowd with only a tip of her champagne flute to my
father before she departed.

"Rumors of my demise and all that." Lucien didn't seem
bothered by the fact that Catherine had abandoned him.

"Pity," Jason replied dispassionately. "I liked you better
that way."

I could feel the conversation drawing to a close, and I
started to panic. The parry and riposte between Jason and
Lucien was formulaic at best. Another few moments and it
would be over. Nerves and wine chewed at my gut.

"Do we really need to play this game, Jason?" Lucien
asked.

"You're threatening my son," Jason said, without any
trace of hospitality. "You should praise whatever bottom
feeders you cling to that you still have all your teeth."

"And who do you thank that the boy still draws
breath?" Lucien asked with an arched eyebrow.

Catherine had walked away. Another of my enemies had
walked away without even so much as a scuffle. A few nights
ago, she'd used everything in her repertoire to try and take
my life. And now we were trading remarks in public and no
one was the wiser.

I get people wanting to kill me. I understand it. But I really didn't understand why they *weren't*. Only Ben had seemed like he was really committed to killing me. Everyone else, including Lucien, had backed away slowly. And then it hit me. I knew what to do.

"Why am I?"

My question was an instant quiet to a building storm. Jason and Lucien both turned their attention to me. Trey dropped his arm. "Why am I still alive, Lucien? You can't use me anymore, right?"

My breath caught as Lucien paused, and I could feel the sweat starting to seep through my shirt. Seconds were ticking down, but as much as I wanted to check my watch again, I knew that the wrong motion would tip him off.

"I get why you switched sides. The Lansings are probably your best bet next time around." It had taken Lucien a hundred years of careful matchmaking to create another Grace. If he wanted another one, it might take that long or longer. "But why am I still here? Or Trey, for that matter."

"Do you have such a death wish?" Lucien breathed, a sudden spiral of black smoke filtering through his eyes. The crowds around us had diminished with Catherine gone; no one seemed to care as much when only one side of the feud was in attendance.

It was hard to say what happened first. One moment, Jason was to my left and Lucien in front of me. The next, Lucien was on the ground and Jason was standing above him, his face a dark scarlet. And in between each moment, breaking them apart like snapshots, came a sonorous ringing of bells from all sides.

Goosebumps formed all over my body as I shivered underneath the sound. Jason and Trey both froze, their heads cocked to a side as though they were hearing something they couldn't quite understand. But Lucien ... Lucien suffered.

I'd seen Lucien broken and hobbled once before. This was worse.

The demon lawyer's body *rippled,* as though there were a thousand independent parts shifting and writhing underneath the surface. The darkness was chased from his eyes until they were *too* white, pupils rolled up into his head in hiding. I'd seen his body split apart once before, saw reptilian skin and demonic eyes hidden under the skin in places that eyes weren't meant to be. But now it was like his human mask was pulled too tight, and as each of those interior eyes shifted, so did the flesh that hid them.

Lucien writhed on the ground as his body started to shudder apart. I looked up in sudden fear, but the rest of the wake had their eyes turned away. In fact, no one was paying us any attention at all.

That's when I saw the look on Jason's face, equal parts appalled and unsure about what he was looking at. Even still, there was a sense of concentration in his eyes, like he knew exactly what was going on everywhere else in the building, and he was making sure no one else noticed *here.*

The bells rang twelve times in total, and they coincided with twelve different seizures on Lucien's part.

So that was what Grace meant. The bells had done more than just make him a little uncomfortable, which is what I would have expected.

I crouched down in front of Lucien once the last bell had started to fade, and straightened the front of his suit coat, easing the lapels back into place before patting him on the shoulders. "You really should have seen that coming, asshole," I said, smiling for the first time in days.

SEVEN

Jason pulled me out of the wake immediately. I expected rage, or at least some yelling. Something to express just how pissed off he was at me. At how stupid I'd been to provoke Lucien the way I had. But Jason didn't say anything at all as he led us back out to the town car that had driven us across town.

Trey followed us outside. I pulled my coat closer against my chest as a harsh wind swept up off the harbor. Both of them kept *looking* at me, snatching glances every time they thought my eyes were somewhere else. What had happened to Lucien was unexpected, but they both thought I had something to do with it. I didn't have the heart to tell them that my power hadn't secretly returned. I wasn't playing possum. I'd let Grace do all the heavy lifting for me.

"Take him home. Watch him," Jason said gruffly once we reached the car.

I turned around, confused, before realizing that Trey was ushering me into the car and then taking Jason's place next to me. "What—" I started to ask before my father slammed the door in on the two of us. I shifted in my seat towards Trey. "What's going on?"

Trey's forehead was lines of tension, college ruled. "How'd you do that?" he questioned. "Did it come back? You should have said something."

"I didn't do that," I said, and then I followed it up with a lie, turning away from Trey. "I don't know what happened. I'm still empty."

"*Something* happened to him, Braden. You're the only one I've ever seen hurt him before."

"That's because I'm the only one stupid enough to try." I looked out the window. We were heading along the harbor, and I stared at all the ships that had been pulled from the water for the winter. Lucien would never forget what had happened. I'd already earned his enmity, but now I'd not only humbled him, I'd tweaked his nose while doing it. If he hadn't wanted me dead before, he'd want me dead now.

Was that why I did it? I could have left well enough alone, let him be hobbled by the bells and gone on with my life. But I'd had to engage, had to be there to witness it. And now he was going to come after me in revenge.

Of course, he'd have to stand in line.

"I think Jason's starting to warm up to me," Trey said from next to me, sounding entirely too pleased with himself.

"He let you get in the car; he didn't buy you a friendship bracelet," I said dryly. "Plus, I think he's expecting you to play babysitter. Make sure I don't go on a demon-taunt-ing rampage throughout the city."

Trey eyed me, a hint of a smile threatening the corners of his mouth. "I wouldn't mind keeping an eye on you."

He just didn't get it. I sighed, and Trey frowned like he expected another round of protests. But I didn't say any-thing this time. I could only push him away so much, and I'd had enough for right now. I needed to catch my breath before the next time. Getting through the funeral service, and now the wake, was enough for me. I just wanted to crawl up into my bed and forget that there was a world out-side of Jason's house. At least for today.

We pulled up into the drive before I said quietly, "Don't you think it's weird? That I'm still here?"

Trey was quiet for a long moment before he finally said, "Lucky. Not weird."

"Lucien has more reason than anyone to want me dead. Grace just wants to talk, now. Ben's the only one who seems like he still wants a pound of flesh, and I still don't get why."

"Wait," Trey commanded, suddenly serious. "Go back. Start again. What happened?" Now he sounded pissed.

"Oh, right." I probably should have told him what had happened first. I started going through what had happened the night before, first Grace in the church and then Ben out behind the house. Trey's good mood popped like a balloon, a sudden jolt that changed the pressure inside the car. As soon as it pulled to a stop in front of the house, I bolted out, like that would somehow make things better.

"When were you going to tell me?" he demanded, like he had any right to do that.

"I wasn't." Trey wasn't even supposed to be here today. "This isn't your problem, Trey. It's mine. And I have to figure out what to do about it." Because bending over and taking it wasn't an option. And neither was relying on Trey to be there to help me. This wasn't his fight. It was mine, and the truth was that I couldn't protect him.

"Figure out what to do about *what*?" Jade asked, appearing in the doorway before I had even reached the door.

"Both of you?" I groaned. I'd thought that I'd just missed her at the wake—of course she'd have to show up at some point; she was a Lansing.

"Figured you might need some reinforcements," she said with a soft smile, and then added in a rush, "Jason said it was fine."

Drew appeared behind her, an amber bottle tucked into his catcher's mitt–sized hand. "Did Jason say we could raid the bar, because I need tequila if I have to share a roof with your pretty boy Rom—oh, hey Gentry." Drew offered him a bright, full smile.

"It's fine," I said, unsure about which one of them I was actually talking to. I made a split decision to keep my sanity, though. Drew and Trey couldn't share a roof without someone getting punched in the face, and I wasn't in the mood to play referee. "Trey's not staying."

"Yes, I—" But when Trey tried to get in the house, I blocked him at the door.

"I keep telling you I can't do this," I shook my head, "but you just don't listen. You keep thinking it's going to be fine, like I'm going to forget what happened and we can be together and life will be grand."

"How do you know it won't?" he asked, crossing his arms in front of him. His eyes kept shifting to the place behind me where I knew Drew was standing. Drew was no doubt smirking and doing everything in his power to silently antagonize Trey from inside the house.

"Let's be realistic," I snapped. "There's a pretty good chance I'll be dead before the year's out. I've got enough people out for my blood. Maybe they're just toying with me now, but eventually they'll get tired of it. Someone will make the first move. And that'll be it."

"Why won't you let me help you?" he pleaded.

Why won't you let me help myself? I thought to myself. But maybe that was just how Trey was wired. He wanted to save me. Even if he didn't know how, he wanted me to be okay. I couldn't say that I wouldn't do the same for him. I'd done it before.

But I couldn't do this Trey's way. He would want a solution that would keep me out of danger. He wouldn't want me to try to aggravate the hornets' nest any more than I already had. But Drew was a schemer. I knew he would help me figure out what to do.

It shouldn't have felt like a choice between the two of them, but that's what it came down to. "I'm sorry," I said, and my stomach lurched because I couldn't decide what I wanted more: to push him away or to pull him close. Trey didn't react as the door slowly closed in his face.

Jade looked uncertain where she stood, casually shifting her weight from one leg to the other. "Do you want me to … " she gestured towards the door.

I shook my head. I barely had what it took to keep my distance from Trey, I didn't think I could stand to push the other two away. The tie around my neck was suddenly a noose, and I ripped it off with a snarl, tearing myself out my suit with a rage I hadn't felt a moment before. Damn Trey, and damn Lucien. Damn all of them. The cuff links that Jason had given me earlier that morning went tink-tink-tinkling away, swallowed up by the dark cherry wood floors underneath us. I think one of the buttons in my shirt followed suit.

Jade and Drew watched me cautiously through it all, not saying a word between them.

I was heaving by the time I was done, but my shirt was unbuttoned, my jacket a pool of fabric on the floor. "I need a shower," I muttered, leaving the two of them as I headed upstairs to my bedroom.

Drew's gleeful voice floated up from the floor below, just before I closed my door. "So if Gentry rode back with him, does that mean the little prince has to walk home?" His bellowing laughter echoed throughout the house.

¤　　¤　　¤

A half hour later, I couldn't get my leg to stay still. After a shower that had done little but clear the remaining alcoholic fog from my head, I'd gone downstairs and promptly devoured everything in sight. I hadn't even realized I was hungry until after I nearly licked the first plate clean.

The food tasted weird, bland, but my body was on autopilot and didn't seem to care much. Drew and Jade joined me—Drew ate, while Jade just watched, alternately amused and horrified at everything we ate. There had been a spread in the kitchen that would have fed everyone at John's memorial, but there was just us in the house. I hadn't caught a glimpse of any of Jason's staff, not even the grumpy, iron-haired woman who ran the household and did most of the cooking.

Drew leaned back in his chair, the legs teetering in the air. His eyes watched my leg. "Anxious?"

I meant to deny it, meant to hide behind a lie like I always did, but I nodded.

"Come on," he said, springing to his feet.

"Where are we going?" Jade asked, because of course she was coming with us.

"*We* are going to work out. *You* can go do your nails or something," Drew said, dismissively. But he smirked at her while he said it, and I realized I wasn't the only one he liked to poke at. With me, it was come-ons and flirtatious behavior. With Jade he ... became a misogynist?

"Should I take my shoes off and keep to the kitchen,

too?" she asked acidly. "Try that again with someone who doesn't know how often *you* get a manicure."

Really? I glanced down at Drew's hands as he scowled and shoved them into his pockets. He grabbed me by the arm and dragged me towards the rear of the house, chased by the tinkling sounds of Jade's laughter.

Before I was even out the back door, I knew that trusting Drew was a bad idea. After less than five minutes of him bobbing and weaving, slapping me on the back of the head, the anxious energy inside me wasn't getting any better.

We hadn't gone far, just out onto the covered patio that sat tucked between two wings of the house. Even Drew didn't seem like he wanted to risk much more than that.

I'd been told, time and time again, that the safest place for me was inside the house. But, Jason would admit with some hesitation, as long as I stayed close to the house, I could still go outside. Not into the woods, of course—I'd seen for myself how that had worked out. Not that the house had been very safe for me last night. I'd gotten out *somehow.* Whatever Ben was doing with my blood had gotten him around all of Jason's defenses.

It took almost ten minutes before Drew's "exercise" started to turn around. Jade had settled into the same lounge chair that I'd woken up in this morning, and I shivered a little at the memory. Drew cuffed me before I got too bogged down by the memories of last night, but all it did was give me a focus for my anger.

I couldn't beat Lucien. I couldn't beat Ben. But maybe

I could beat on Drew a little. Instead of trying to block his pot shots, which had been the point all along, I started taking shots of my own.

Drew barked out a laugh, just the one, but the air around us changed sharply and so did his mood. It stopped being about a little horsing around between friends, and it started being about competition. Just because Drew was stronger and faster didn't mean he had the right to push me around. No one had that right. I'd meant what I said last night. I wasn't a victim. I wouldn't be any more.

My muscles stretched out in relief, and I found myself moving with the same sort of heightened agility that made Drew a threat in a proper fight. My awareness of my body seemed to pull back until I was like a spectator in my own skin. It was different from the puppet master feeling I'd had last night—I hadn't been in control of anything then. But now, I was still in control, and I was also so much more *aware*.

Drew landed some hits on me, blows softened so that he didn't leave me black and blue, I'm sure, but he never caught me off guard the same way twice. The faster he moved, the more he bobbed, the more I weaved and blocked and countered him. It only seemed odd for a moment, the way I seemed to be picking up skill quicker than I should be. Drew's expression got more and more grim, and I stopped thinking about it at all.

It became a dance. Drew would throw a punch, I'd glide out of the way and retaliate with a jab of my own. His expression became more and more tight the longer we went on, irritation framing his face.

He bounced back a couple of steps, wiping his forehead off with the back of his hand only to go suddenly still. The tension left his face and he smirked, looking somewhere over my shoulder. "Oh, hey Gentry. Got him nice and sweaty for you," he called. I spun around, my focus crackling like a lake during spring thaw.

But there was no sign of Trey. I started to turn back around, to ask Drew what the hell he was thinking when my legs were swept out from underneath me and I fell to the ground.

"That," he panted, "is why you never let them distract you. Now what the hell was *that*?"

I waited for the sky to stop spinning before I even started to consider his words. The way I'd moved, the way my body had responded ... that wasn't me. More mysteries. More things about myself that I didn't understand.

"You're a good teacher?" I offered, because soothing Drew's ego usually seemed to work.

Twin snorts from both Drew and Jade, who looked up from her phone. "He's a terrible teacher. Almost as bad a teacher as he was a student."

"Hey, there was no one better at cutting class than I was," Drew said as he lifted up his shirt to wipe off his face.

I turned my head, because while the view was nice, Drew was one of the last people I'd want to check out. At least not as long as he might catch me. I'd never hear the end of it.

Jade turned her head away, too. The relationship, or not relationship, between Drew and Jade had confused me ever since I'd come to Belle Dam, and I'd given up trying to figure them out. They claimed to hate each other, but they were always *around,* hovering at the edges of the other's orbit. But each of them denied that there was anything between them. Maybe they had even convinced themselves.

Drew offered me a hand up. "Explain it again."

With his help, I climbed to my feet. My body felt calm for the first time in days. *Sated,* like this was how I should be feeling every day. "She showed up last night and we had a chat. For someone that hated me on principle a couple of days ago, she was almost friendly. But I think she kept me around for a reason. I just don't know what it is yet."

"Maybe she's changing her mind about what she did. If she took your power, she could give it back, right?"

"I don't even know if that's what I really want," I said. "Maybe she did me a favor. I could go somewhere far from here and start over. Be normal."

"Yeah, but you can't protect yourself," Drew pointed out. "Is it really worth it?"

"He can be *normal,*" Jade interjected, turning a cold stare onto Drew. "How many times has he almost died? Maybe this is a good thing. He's cured."

Drew's eyes narrowed. "Just because he doesn't have his gifts doesn't make him normal. It doesn't mean everything's going to be okay. The world doesn't work like that."

We weren't talking about me anymore, were we? The

air between the two of them was charged with sharp emotion. "Do you guys need a room? Because," I gestured back towards the house, "I'm pretty sure there's about seven hundred of them inside. You could pick one. Hell, pick a few."

Drew was the first to look away from their impromptu staring match. I took a closer look when his head dipped down. Was he ... *blushing*? Exactly how big were these lies that the two were telling?

"Do you think Lucien would come after you?" Jade asked, studiously ignoring Drew's presence.

"Probably. He's up to something, too. I'm useless to him now, so in theory he could kill me whenever he wanted. But he hasn't. I don't get it."

"So Lucien's got a backup plan," Jade said slowly. "One that involves you, I guess?"

I nodded. That made about as much sense as anything.

"So what do you want to do?" Drew asked impatiently. "Run? Or are you going to stay and fight? Because I'm not going to waste my time teaching you if you're just going to bolt at the first chance."

"I don't even know where to start," I said. Because that was the crux of my problem. Fight or flight. Someone needed to stand up to Lucien and Grace, and all the other monsters in Belle Dam.

"Start with Grace," Drew said immediately.

"Start with Matthias," Jade said, at almost the same time. When we both turned to stare at her, she shrugged.

"You said he helped you last night. At least he's picking a side."

"He didn't really pick much of anything," I said. "I owe him a favor."

"Yeah, and what kind of favor is powerless you going to be good for?" Jade asked. "From everything that Drew's told me about him, he's not going to get involved unless there's some benefit to him."

From all Drew's told her? I turned to him, raising my eyebrows. He pretended not to notice me, instead staring at the house. "Daddy's home. I'll catch you later." And without another word to either one of us, Drew shifted out of his human form and into something four-legged. I expected to see a wolf emerge from the silvery blur of Drew's power, but Drew changed it up on me again.

"A snow leopard?" I said out loud as Drew trotted away from the house and into the woods. I'd done a report on leopards when I was ten or eleven, and they'd been my favorite animal for all of ten days until I realized that falcons were way cooler. "What a drama queen."

Jade started laughing and couldn't stop. After a couple of minutes she wiped at the tears in her eyes, her hand on my shoulder. "You have no idea," she chuckled.

eight

Jade stayed for dinner. Jason didn't say anything at all, which would have surprised me, but then again Jason had turned around and walked out of the room as soon as he'd realized I wasn't alone. Jade and I were left to fend for ourselves for the rest of the night, which was fine between us.

There was a living room down the hall from my room, one of three nearly identical rooms I'd found in the house, but this one had a fireplace and a working television, so we holed up in there. Jade had come prepared and brought movies—comedies about teenagers coming of age in stupid ways, which were some of my favorites.

We were halfway through the second movie and a bowl of microwave popcorn when Jade paused the movie and turned to me with serious eyes. "I know you don't want to talk about—"

"No."

"Braden, come on," she pleaded. "You should know he hasn't gone home since ... well, since that night." She spoke quickly, like she expected me to cut her off. But I didn't say anything at all. Every time I got some distance from Trey, any time I thought I could clear my head from what was going on around me, there were flashes. Images in my head. Catherine's smirk, the detachment in her eyes. Purple motes of darkness. And then John. On the ground. Empty.

I nodded, because that was all I could trust myself to do.

"Trey wants me to leave," she added, and my head snapped up, staring at her. "He even called the school to see how many credits I had. To see if I could graduate a semester early."

Jade might be leaving? I hate that my first thoughts were selfish, but they were what they were. *What am I going to do without her?* We weren't the closest of friends, but she was always *there* for me in a way no one else ever had been. If anything, Jade and I were so close because our friendship was *normal*. What I could do, and who her family was, had very little to do with why we wanted to hang out together.

My heart lurched in my chest, and I had to duck my head down again. *But it would be safer for her if she did. Trey was right, this town wasn't safe for any of us.*

"When I leave, I don't think I'll ever come back," Jade said quietly, going to stand over by the window. "I mean, I'll miss it a little, but I've never wanted any of this. I don't want to have kids just so they can play a starring role in Bigotry part two. I'd rather go off and be fabulous somewhere far from here. My aunt did that, did I ever tell you about that?"

I shook my head.

"She lives in New York. She's this crazy artist, which is weird because she and my mom look so much alike, but they're totally different. Anyway, she ran away after high school. She comes to visit every so often, but whenever she's with mom, it's always strained."

I looked at the movie on the screen, paused just moments before the big reveal, where the heroine's whole world was to be ripped out from underneath her. My stomach soured and I flicked the television off. "Done with that," I said under my breath. And I was.

Jade followed me back into my room, crawling onto the other side of my bed when I flopped down. We stared at the ceiling, not each other. "Maybe—" she hesitated. "Maybe we could go." Her words picked up speed as she warmed up to the idea in her head. "Together. New York's a big city, we could start over. No crazy parents, no demons leering at us from across the room. I'll take my diploma early, and you can always finish school there."

"Come on, be serious."

Jade rolled over and lay flat on her stomach. She turned her head towards me, hair falling in her eyes. "You turn eighteen in a few months, right? My mom might try to drag me back, but she'd have to find us first."

Her hand slid over mine, squeezing once. I sighed, closing my eyes. I knew this was just a momentary whim of Jade's, but I couldn't help but wonder *what if*? I'd come to Belle Dam without knowing anyone and look how that had turned out. What if I had someone there who had my back. Someone who liked me regardless of what I was capable of. "We can't just pick up and leave. Can we?"

She twisted her wrist until her palm was facing up, and mine down, and then she slid her hand under mine. Slowly, though, like she expected me to pull away at any second. "Why not? There's nothing tying you down here anymore."

Wrong. There was Jason. And Drew. Riley, who was still broken and who I'd promised to try and fix. Trey. How would they be if I left? Would they stick together? Or would Lucien and Catherine pick them all off one by one?

She squeezed my hand again. "You remember the first time we met?" I nodded. "I don't remember what I was talking about, but you had one of your attacks. That probably should have been the end of it, but I couldn't get you out of my head that night. I was *worried,* you know? And then the next day at school, you were like this lost puppy. But I could tell you understood. You weren't meant for a small town life any more than I was."

"I've never lived in a big city," I pointed out. Jade wasn't making much sense.

She waved a hand dismissively, her expression a frown. "I never said you were. But you weren't meant for *here* either. We're bigger than this place."

"Maybe," I shrugged.

She scooted up on the bed, and nestled her head against the side of my shoulder. "You know he'd follow us, right? If that's what you're worried about."

I wasn't worried about Trey. "You have to stop," I said, resting my cheek against her hair. Jade smelled like vanilla and spice. "I can't … Trey and I … I just can't."

"I know," she said. "Not right now. Just … he'll be there someday if you change your mind, y'know? And you guys can figure out what you're both like when your life isn't being threatened all the time. Maybe you won't even like him. I'm telling you, he snores. And he's a total slob."

"Jade … "

"I'm just saying," she added defensively. "Just something to kick around in the back of your head."

"For your birthday this year, I'm going to teach you what 'subtlety' means."

"I'm surrounded by idiots, Braden," she said, squeezing me. "Subtlety gives them an excuse not to pay attention to what's really going on under the surface. I like when people confront their feelings up front."

"How's Drew?" I asked.

I was a good friend who didn't point out how long of a pause she had before she responded, "No one likes a know-it-all, Braden."

"What would we even *do* in New York? Do you know the first thing about how to live on your own?"

"Do you? I'm not saying it's going to be easy, but it's a better option than staying here and waiting to see what my mother and her demon are cooking up next." She barely suppressed a shudder.

"I don't know what *I* would do," I amended. "I mean, I

always thought, in the back of my head, that the witch eyes would kill me sooner or later. Especially since I've come here. But now they're gone, and I have to worry about everyone else trying to kill me. I never really thought about what I'd do if things were different. Who am I if I'm not the kid with the freaky eyes? If I'm not the kid with the over-protective uncle and the house in the middle of nowhere? If I'm not the enemy of half the town?"

"You'll figure it out," Jade said, a confidence in her voice that neither one of us seemed to believe. "That's all I want. I deserve to figure out who I want to be, and make the decision for myself. Not because of my last name or because my family has fallen into the same damn cycle over and over again. All I know is that the only thing I can learn by staying here is how to lie, cheat, and kill. I don't want that."

"I'll think about it," I murmured quietly as a content silence wrapped around us. I drifted off to the sounds of Jade's even breathing. At least she didn't snore like her brother.

NINE

Jade left sometime the next morning. I remembered waking up long enough to tell her goodbye before gravity dragged my head back down to my pillow. It was almost the afternoon by the time I woke up, and I felt good. Rested. The twelve hours of sleep I'd gotten was really working for me.

The fridge was full of leftovers when I walked into the kitchen. I portioned a little bit of everything onto a large plate and tossed it in the microwave. My appetite was still out of control, but that was fine. It was better than when I couldn't stomach eating anything.

I devoured everything on my plate and went back for seconds. Last night hadn't gotten me any closer to figuring out my next move. It came down to fight or flight. One way or another, I was going to have to make a choice. Did I want to stay, and try to fix the problems I'd caused? Or could I really just run away, and never look back?

Jade had suggested talking to Matthias, and Drew had suggested going back to Grace, but neither one of those options felt like the right choice yet. I didn't want to deal with Grace again until I knew what I was doing—until I knew I could convince her to restore my powers. And Matthias...he'd saved my life the other night. But he'd done that because my head had been filled with thoughts of vengeance. What would he do if he thought that I was going to run?

"Hiding from Captain Crankypants?" Drew asked from behind me. I stopped my contemplation of the microwave and turned to see him perched on the countertop like he'd been there all along. Or like he'd magically appeared there.

"Only because I can't run away with my tail tucked between my legs," I said, eyeing him. "What do you want?"

"If you're serious about that exercise thing, there's no time like the present," he said. "I figure I can make you cry within an hour or two."

"You want to work out with me again?" Drew stared at me like I was the simplest person he'd ever encounter. "After what happened yesterday?"

"Look, that was weird, but maybe it's a side effect of your new life. Maybe you've secretly been allergic to sunglasses your entire life, and now you're like...a scrawny, midget-sized version of a pro wrestler."

"Or maybe you're still an idiot." I paused. "No, you're definitely still an idiot."

"I'm an idiot that doesn't get pushed around, though," Drew pointed out. "I—" And then he stopped, cocking his head to one side.

"What is it?"

Drew shook his head immediately, holding out his hand like he wanted me to shut up. His eyes were locked somewhere to my left. When the microwave beeped to signal that my food was done, I jumped, and whatever spell Drew was under was broken.

"You didn't tell me Gentry was hanging around," was all he said, taking off deeper into the house.

I trailed him through the halls, realizing halfway there that we were heading for Jason's study, the one he used the most often. It was where he'd had me meet with the eye doctor right after I'd gotten out of the hospital, and where we'd met with the funeral director and the priest for John's services.

Jason's voice carried into the hallway. "Braden won't be your concern for much longer!"

"I can help you," Trey insisted.

"What the hell is he doing here?" I demanded in a whisper.

Drew glared at me and mouthed an exaggerated "Shut up!"

"She might say he's not worth her time, but we both know that's not true. You know as well as I do what happens when she smells blood in the water."

"If Lucien doesn't want him dead, then she won't kill him. And Lucien was never one to part with his toys before he's squeezed out every last bit of usefulness."

Trey's voice got even louder. "Are you kidding? He may have partnered up with my mom, but that doesn't mean she's going to do what he tells her. In case you haven't noticed, she's not exactly known for her listening skills. Your brother was gone for half his life and she still went after him with a vengeance when he came back."

"Leave my brother out of this," Jason snapped, strangely sharp.

"Then what about your son?" Trey pushed. "You know I'm right. She doesn't care that he's not a threat anymore. You tricked her, and she's not going to just let that go."

Okay, that was it. I'd had enough of this. I went to push my way past Drew and force my way into the conversation, but the shifter glided out of my way and merged into my wake. "Stop talking about me like I'm not even here. If you're going to plan stuff, I should be involved."

Jason exhaled in annoyance, the very picture of an exasperated father. "You couldn't keep him occupied, Drew?"

Drew puffed up, Jason's words triggering the undercurrent of hostility that was always running through his veins. "I don't work for you. And I'm not his babysitter."

"Thank God," Trey muttered under his breath.

"Well?" I demanded, looking between the two of them. "I'm right here. If you're going to start planning out my future, why don't we get started."

"Now do you see what I have to deal with?" Jason said in an aside to Trey. The two of them. Conspiring! They *hated* each other! What the hell was going on? They couldn't just go around changing sides now.

Trey's resulting smile was brief and humorless.

"I'm not kidding," I snapped. "I swear to God, if you

don't start filling me in, you can't blame yourself when the plan goes all to shit. Would you rather I just go pester Catherine all over town until she gets annoyed and she death-whammies me? Or maybe I should just save everyone the trouble and go jump off the cliffs out back. Would that make it easier on everyone?"

Trey winced, and even Drew looked uncomfortable. Also notable, neither of them would actually look at me. Jason stared down at the floor, his expression thunderous. Silence hung in the air, but the tension radiating off of Jason made it clear we were all waiting for him to react. No one wanted to precede that.

I took a step back, just in case. I didn't know what I'd said exactly, but whatever it was, I was the only one who didn't see the deeper meaning. I'd never seen Drew look so uncomfortable.

"If you ever threaten to kill yourself again," Jason said, his voice so low it crept down along the marble floors, "I will lock you up where you can't do *anything*. It will be a beautiful cage, but make no mistake that it will be a cage, and I will leave you there for the rest of your life and not lose a minute of sleep over it. Do you understand?"

"Jason—"

"Do you understand?!" he roared, an explosion of emotion that had both Trey and Drew rearing back in alarm. I was the only one who didn't move, but only because my feet were rooted to the ground.

No one spoke. No one even breathed. I think we were

all trying to come to terms with the fact that Jason Thorpe, the cold, clinically detached steel facade of a man, looked dangerously close to losing the last bits of his control.

He took a deep breath, still staring down at the floor. "Goodbye, Gentry."

"Jason, seriously. Let me help. Let me do *something*."

"*Goodbye*, Gentry," Jason repeated firmly.

Trey took one last look at me, eyes full of emotions I didn't want to see. I turned away, mirroring Jason and staring down at my shoes. Scuffed gray tennis shoes that were falling apart at the sides. I had a closet full of shoes upstairs, but I still wore the same ones I'd brought with me to Belle Dam.

Trey walked out of the library. Jason waved his hand sharply, and the library doors slammed shut behind him.

"Keep up with what you've been doing," Jason continued, looking over at Drew. "I haven't seen this much color in his cheeks since before the hospital."

"Excuse me?" The words carried a not-so-subtle undercurrent of *Hey, fuck off and die in a fire.* The change in Drew was instantaneous. The moment Jason addressed him, his body went taut and his expression flattened out into a scowl. He shifted his stance, the same one he'd been in when he first taught me how to throw a punch.

"You're teaching him to defend himself, right? It couldn't hurt, especially now." Jason's eyes flicked to me. "He's been very ... spirited lately. I'm hoping the exercise will channel his energy into more constructive endeavors."

Constructive endeavors? I still hadn't told Jason about the other night, or about anything really. So what exactly did he think I was getting up to that was so destructive? Or did he already know, somehow?

Drew moved forward until the two of them were nose to nose. He had several inches on Jason and glared down daggers at him. "Just so we're clear," Drew said, in a voice every bit as dangerous as Jason's could be, "I don't work for you. I don't *like* you. I'm here because of Braden."

"There's no need—"

"You killed my father," Drew said, seething. He was like a pot about to boil over, his body humming with tension and his eyes glowing the electric, silvery sheen that only appeared when he used his powers. "So save your petty words and your fake charm, and remember that none of it matters at the end of the day. Because you're a murderer. If there's any justice in the world, I'll be there when you have to pay for what you've done."

"Drew!" I moved forward and grabbed his arm. It was like trying to move a statue. "Come on."

Sometime before I was born, Jason had killed Drew's father and basically ran his mother out of town. The Armstrongs had been a long-established family in Belle Dam, second only to the Thorpes and Lansings. I didn't know the whole story about what had happened with Drew's father, but I knew it had been bad.

It was easy to forget that Jason had done things in the past—horrible things. I knew he wasn't the hero of the story.

His hands were just as bloody as Catherine's. That was how life worked in Belle Dam. Evil begot evil, stains begot stains.

Drew was right. Jason killed his father. And I was an idiot for never realizing it before. All the times I'd asked him to meet me here at the house because it was more comfortable for me. Drew always wanted to meet in the woods, or he caught up to me somewhere in the city.

How does he stand to be around me? Maybe it was different when no one knew who Jason was to me, but as the secret got out, his actions never changed. He never acted differently around me. How could he do that? How was it so easy for him, when I couldn't be in the same room with Trey without wanting to scream and explode?

Drew threw off my arm and stalked to the library doors without another word. I flinched when the door slammed behind him and held my breath in the aftermath.

I counted to thirty before I trusted myself to speak. So many different feelings were welling up in my stomach that I wanted to scream and vomit at the same time. "Jason—"

"He's right," Jason said, so quiet I almost didn't hear him. He stood by the door that Drew had stormed out of only a couple of minutes before. "I'm not ... I don't expect you to understand the choices I've made in my life, Braden. What happened with Drew's father was ... a mistake." He shook his head, eyes closed for a moment, like he could shake the memories free like they were nothing more than cobwebs. "I've made many mistakes," he added, voice growing bitter.

"We don't have to do this right now," I said, unsure where *this* was even going. Jason didn't confide in me. That wasn't how our relationship worked.

"You say that like we have all the time in the world," he said, flashing a humorless smile at me. "It's alright. I know what you think of me."

"You're acting like you're going to die or something," I said, my voice shaking.

"No," Jason said, that sad smile reappearing. "I'm acting like I have to send my son away again."

It was true that Jason had been *off* since he'd come back home, but now he was really starting to scare me. What was he going on about? Why was he sending me away?

"You should ... sit," Jason said, gesturing to one of the couches. Warily, I crossed the room and started to lower myself down. He sat next to me, a gulf of space between us, positioning himself awkwardly. His body was shifted towards me, but his face was angled away.

"When you fought with Lucien," Jason said slowly, deliberating every word carefully, "before you woke up in the hospital, you almost died. I thought for sure that you would, and it would be my fault. I'd lose my son again, just a few days after I got him back." He looked down at his hands, perched in his lap like he didn't know what to do with them. I'd never noticed them before, the long, tapered fingers that were so like my own.

"I don't ... I'm not ... " Jason rolled his head, an audible pop as his neck cracked. "You thought I was more interested in replacing Lucien than I was in your recovery," he continued. "I let you think that. I thought it would be easier. But I wasn't looking for another seer, or a prophet, or anything like that."

"No," I found myself arguing. "That's not true. You went searching for a *curandero.* Everyone knew."

"Ahh, *that,*" Jason said, sighing. "That was a fool's errand, but I suspect you knew that already. *Curanderos* are healers first and foremost."

"You were hoping for a cure. For me." My mouth was so dry I could have spit sand. "So where were you the rest of the time? If that was the exception, then what were you doing? What were you searching for?"

"Family," Jason said simply.

"You lost your *family?*"

"Not mine," he replied quietly. "Yours. Jonathan knew where they were, of course. Of course he did." He shook his head, a flash of a smile at some hidden memory. "He kept in touch with them, even after all these years."

"What do you mean, *my* family?" I whispered, harsh and tremulous.

"We've never talked about your mother," Jason said. "What do you know?"

"I know she wasn't from around here. Lucien found her for you." The fact that my parents had been some sort of breeding stock for a demon's designs was another thing I tried not to think too much about.

"Lucien matched us, and I allowed it, but I *did* love her," he clarified. For one moment, and one moment only, he looked at me and there was a fierceness in his expression. "I should tell you that Jonathan did, as well. It was hard not to."

"What was her name?"

"Rose. Rosemarie. She never let anyone outside of the family call her Rose." Jason chuckled at that, looking away again. "Her family was like ours, although they used their gifts so differently. Not for war, like ours. Your mother didn't have much in the way of power, but she had fire in so many other ways. Even on your worst day, she had a way of making you smile." He seemed lost in his thoughts for a moment, fingers reaching absently towards his lips. A muscle in his cheek flexed, and he very nearly smiled before it fell away like the memory that had sparked it. "She had siblings, and they are not ... inconsequential. You have an aunt and an uncle."

"Why are you telling me this?"

"Because they can protect you, Braden." Jason shook his head, and then added, "If you want. You'll never have to spend another day worrying about Catherine, or Lucien, or ... anything else that weighs on you." He didn't say John's name, but he might as well have. Or maybe he was talking about Trey.

"So you're going to send me away," I said. My legs were screaming in pain, and I looked down to see my fingernails clawing into my own skin. "Just throw me away because I'm useless now." I didn't bring up that I'd been thinking of leaving all on my own because this was different. Jason was trying to get rid of me.

"I'm going to save your life," Jason responded gently. "Or at least I would like to. If you'll let me."

I looked up in shock, meeting his eyes. "What do you mean?"

"You're old enough to make your own decision. You're right in that much, at least. But I…would like you to meet them, at least. I mean it when I say that they can protect you. They stay under the radar, in more ways than one. Unless I'm mistaken, they're the ones who taught my brother how to disappear."

"But you knew where to find him," I pointed out. Jason had once showed me a spell that allowed him to spy on John and me back at our home in Montana. *To have to watch someone else raise your kid through what was basically a television. Getting no input at all. No wonder Jason was so cold.*

"I didn't say he tried to disappear from *me*," Jason said. "If he hadn't been my brother, things might have been different. If I had known … " But I could only imagine what Jason was thinking. Maybe if he'd known the bargain struck between Lucien and Uncle John, if he'd known what John was really trying to avoid.

The mysterious phone calls that John had always gotten, I didn't remember them happening when I was younger. Maybe they hadn't. Maybe Lucien had waited until I was old enough and then he started drawing John back in. And John hadn't run, because how far could you run from something that could predict your every move?

"You can always find family, Braden. It's more than just

the blood you share. It's a connection. Deeper than anything else, a well that you share between you."

My mom had a family. A brother and a sister. I'd always wanted a brother or something when I was younger, even though I knew it would never happen. Siblings were for kids that had two parents. I only had John. Besides, I wouldn't want to be the oldest—I wanted older siblings to follow around and learn from. Growing up seemed like it would have been easier if I was the baby. Maybe I wouldn't have ended up here at all because I would have had someone else looking out just for me.

"I—I'll think about it," I said, pulling my hands away from my skin.

Jason nodded, eyes widening a fraction. It was nice to know I could still surprise him. *You didn't expect me to agree, did you?* And if I was willing to admit it, it was nice that I cared enough to notice.

"I'll make some calls. They won't come into the city itself, not with our ... issues. They're aware of Lucien's limits. As long as they don't cross the town line, he can't touch them."

Lucien was bound to the city, trapped through a complex spell that Grace had created that used the lines of the town as a binding to keep him here. "But he can still leave. He had to, he came to Montana and put the vision in my head that brought me here."

Jason nodded. "But had a connection to my brother, acting like a beacon. Even still, he was likely at an incredible disadvantage. In order to even send a projection, he would have had to leave the bulk of what power he had behind. And no one likes to be helpless." His face blanched as the implication of what he'd just said occurred to him. "I'm sorry, I didn't—"

"It's fine." After that, neither one of us had anything to say, and we sat there, the only sound the ticking of the grandfather clock in the corner. I looked up several times, thinking Jason was looking at me, only to see his eyes vacant and relaxed. Whatever he was seeing made him look ... relaxed. And sad.

"What happened the night she died?" I asked, my voice reverently quiet. Ben had brought my mother up the night he'd stolen my blood. I hadn't forgotten, but there'd never seemed like a good time to ask.

As easily as Jason had opened up moments ago, the gates slammed closed and his posture stiffened. His silence stopped being a thing of feelings and regret, and returned to the constipated, prissy quiet that I'd come to know and loathe.

"I'll let you know when your aunt and uncle are ready to meet," Jason said, his voice almost robotic in its monotony. As if only a minute ago we hadn't been discussing my mother, and Jason had smiled.

Nothing's ever going to change. Maybe he's right, and I should just run while I've got the chance.

It was a surprise how much that thought hurt.

ten

Trey wasn't lingering by the door ready to pounce the moment I left Jason's study. Drew wasn't lurking around the back waiting to seethe in my general direction, either. It was a little disconcerting. I expected one or both of them to vent about Jason at me, so the unexpected silence was ... uncomfortable. It threw my day off a little—I'd hoped getting Drew to kick my ass a bit would soothe the itching in my legs and maybe clear my head a little bit.

What did it say about me that my entire sense of normalcy rested on Trey intruding on me and Drew being a dick?

I wanted to go for a run, but without Drew there, I didn't feel comfortable going out back into the woods. But there was nothing to stop me from using the treadmill that Jason had in his exercise room. It was more like a suite, full of top-of-the-line equipment that didn't have a speck of dust on it, but still didn't look like it had ever been used.

I stopped by my room to pick up a pair of shoes and

change into running shorts, and then I headed back, intending on only going for a mile or two. Just enough to take off the edge to this nervous energy. But once I hopped on, and my stride started to lengthen, I found myself falling into a rhythm. It was like the moment I really hit my stride my mind cleared out of all the stress and the tangled thoughts, leaving me with clear canvas.

I had family other than Jason. He'd gone in search of them. *That* was why John had come back to the house that last day. He'd told Jason exactly where to find them. But the knowledge still chafed against the memory of my uncle. John had known all along that they existed, and he'd never even said a word. Never told me there was somewhere else I might be safe, if not for him. Maybe things would have been different.

But I could leave. If not with them, then with Jade. I had options.

Leaving meant that they would all get away with it. Lucien for destroying so many lives. Catherine for what she did to my uncle. Grace, for what she'd done to me. Walking away meant giving up on any of that. Was that cowardly? Or was it a strategic retreat? *I wish you were still here, Uncle John,* I thought. *Because I don't know what to do.* I zoned out for a bit, staring out the window at the forest behind the house.

It had seemed like only a few minutes since I'd jumped on the treadmill, but by the time I looked down at the screen, I was supposedly crossing my seventh mile. I looked around, realizing the light in the room was different.

Brighter, since we were on the western side of the house and it was getting to be midafternoon.

There was definitely something wrong with me. I'd never been weak and housebound, but I'd never had the kind of energy I had lately. Last time things had started to get strange, I'd ignored it and it had turned I had a part of Lucien's ... I don't even know what the winter voice was, but it had been in my head, manipulating me.

But who was I supposed to ask? Jason? He was already half tempted to lock me up where no one would ever find me again. There wasn't anyone else I thought could help that I would even remotely consider going to.

When I got back to my room (after pushing through and finishing the eighth mile), my phone was blinking.

Catherine knows we want to leave. Lucien told her, Jade had texted almost an hour ago.

How???? I sent back.

A new pair of sunglasses says it involved entrails.

It was stupid of me to even be surprised. Lucien had the ability to see the future as a series of threaded timelines that split off from each other at the slightest deviation. I'd tapped into his power before and been almost immediately overwhelmed. At any given moment, there are thousands upon thousands of possibilities in play. Our conversation last night must have triggered something, set a particular future into motion or something.

That was the main problem in wanting to work against Lucien. The only way to really get the best of him was to be truly random. I hadn't planned to shoot him in the head, which was the only reason it must have worked.

She said if I try to leave, she'll just beat me there and bring me back, Jade texted. *What are we going to do?*

Figure out something else, I sent back, then tossed my phone onto the bed where it vanished into the messy pile of blankets. But the idea of trying to do anything at all was almost paralyzing. The moment I started, Lucien would know everything I was up to. He'd know exactly where to strike to cut me off at the knees. He'd see through any feint, any attempt at subterfuge.

If I kept stressing about everything, and didn't actually *do* something, I was going to go insane. What I needed was a change of perspective. A reminder of just what kind of monster I was up against.

¤   ¤   ¤

The hospital was almost my second home by this point. If I wasn't a patient myself, I was visiting one. I'd never liked hospitals—it was more than just an ordinary thing, though, like hating the way all hospitals used the same neutral color scheme. Or the way all hospitals seemed to smell identical—like disinfectant, tension, and emptiness.

Mostly, it was because hospitals were chock-full of emotions. All of those feelings, memories, and especially all that pain would build up over the years. Seeing the hospital without my sunglasses on was always a thousand times worse than whatever had landed me into the hospital in the first place.

Riley's room was almost unrecognizable when I walked in. She was up on one of the top floors, in a private room where she could be monitored better. Her mother couldn't afford it, but Jason could. There was even a guard at the door, just in case anyone got too interested in her. He'd already had it all taken care of before I'd even thought to ask. Even then, he tried to play dumb when I brought it up later to thank him. For whatever reason, Jason didn't want any of the credit for making sure Riley was taken care of.

The room normally had an exceptional view of the city through the forest. But ever since her second night, when Riley had had some sort of epic freak-out, the drapes stayed drawn. Every wall socket had at least one night light—most had two, and the overhead lights in the room were never shut off. Even while she slept. Her bed was covered in quilts that smelled faintly of smoke and sadness, worn along the edges and colors a pale imitation of what they'd once been. Fitting for the girl who was a faded impression of who *she'd* once been.

There were pictures taped to the far wall, a collection of them artfully displayed to highlight all the people that Riley had known on a daily basis. I didn't have any proof, but I had a feeling that was Jade's contribution. She and Riley didn't get along, at least that was how it looked on the surface, but I never got the impression that Jade actually hated her. Riley might have seriously disliked her, but Jade was more resigned on the matter. Like there was nothing she could do about the problem, and no easy way to fix it.

There were even copies of the school newspaper were spread out along the bedside table in case Riley ever woke up and wanted to do some light reading. But Riley wouldn't, because her mind had been shattered. By me. Now she was somewhere between schizophrenic and a vegetable, speaking in riddles that sounded like nonsense.

My vision wavered as I crossed the room's threshold, and the bottom dropped out of my stomach. Suddenly I felt every last one of those miles I'd run, and my legs were like soup. I fumbled towards the wall, holding myself upright through sheer force of will.

What better place to fall apart than the middle of the hospital? But I didn't want to through another round of "let's try and diagnose Braden's freaky problems." Nothing certain ever came of them. Medicine couldn't help me control the witch eyes, and it almost certainly wasn't going to solve whatever was wrong with me now.

"I know you're there," I said, once I realized just how quiet the room was. Too quiet.

Matthias rose from his seat in the corner, where he'd been hidden by one of the big gift baskets that kept accumulating. Likely by someone who thought Jason would be stopping in to check on her personally.

"Hush now, indoor voices," Matthias murmured, giving me a smile. "We wouldn't want the little miss to wake early from her slumber, would we?"

I forced myself to stand up straight, ignoring the shiver in my limbs. I'd already showed him enough weakness lately. "What are you doing here?"

"I'm not the one with interesting agendas. And seeing as how some small part of that life you've got draped around your shoulders belongs to me, I don't think I care to answer. You came to see the girl. Why? What do you think you can do for her?"

"You can't be here," I insisted. "Don't come here again. Riley's suffered enough." I would have to involve Jason, tell him that the demons were starting to circle. That would only make him more interested in Riley, but better him than a closet full of monsters.

"Hasn't she just," Matthias said with a small chuckle. "But I'm afraid I can't abide by your wishes. After all, someone needs to be looking out for the girl's best interests. Ask yourself if you can protect her?" He waited a moment during which I was uncomfortably silent. "I thought not."

My eyes moved, involuntary. Since coming into the room, I'd tried not to look. Tried not to see.

Riley lay in her bed, feet and legs pulled up tight against her body. She wasn't rocking today, so that was an improvement. Wasn't spitting out a stream of crazy conscious thoughts that resembled word salad. Wasn't screaming, or clawing, or scaring the living crap out of hardened women who thought they'd seen everything.

I hadn't been here for it, but I heard one of the nurses had never come back to work after dealing with Riley. Riley had grabbed her by the wrist, and started reciting dates. Times, months, years. They didn't mean anything to the other nurse on duty, but they meant something to the one Riley had grabbed. She'd bolted out of the room shortly after the dates switched from past to future, to things that hadn't happened yet. Tragedies and triumphs that no one had any right to know yet. Least of all a broken girl tucked away in a town full of darkness.

Riley was another casualty of going up against Lucien. He tried using her as his final sacrifice, wanting to kill her to hurt *me*. I'd killed him once before, only to find out that a creature like Lucien can't just be *killed*. But I had broken him, cracked the foundation of whatever existence he currently had. The sacrifices were all part of a restoration ritual, but I'd interfered and kept him from taking Riley. Back when I had power. Back when that power had been just as deadly as Lucien.

"Oh good, you're feeling sorry for yourself," Matthias grimaced, turning away like the look on my face was somehow offensive. "I thought that would have passed by now."

"It's been *three days*," I snapped.

"Worlds and empires have fallen in less."

"Easy to say when you've still got your creepy demon powers," I muttered.

"Forgotten hells, aren't you bored with being the victim by now? Do something new!" Matthias asked, an unusual sharpness cutting at his words. "Be the villain. Be *interesting*. You can't say Belle Dam hasn't earned it."

"I don't know how I feel about taking a civics lesson from a demon," I said stiffly.

"*Someone* needs to remind you of your place. Have you forgotten our friend in the lighthouse?"

"And look where that got me! What do you think I'm going to do, Matthias? *Sarcasm* Lucien to death? He's right. I'm nothing now."

"You're everything you were a week ago," Matthias said. "Maybe more."

"You're insane."

"You've been manipulated since the moment Lucien set his good eye on you," Matthias replied, his eyes narrow. "There hasn't been a single decision that you've made that someone else hasn't prompted you into. You don't act. You react. Try pulling your own strings for once. Better yet, pull someone else's."

"With *what?*" I tore off the sunglasses that were just for show. Stared at him with eyes that had once held a curse, but were now a flat, unnatural green.

Matthias took in a slow breath, clearly taking his time and drawing this all out. "In all of this, you never thought to ask the most important of questions. It never occurred to you to wonder."

I hugged myself, staring down at the floor. "Wonder what?"

"You've pitted yourself against a creature of the primordial. They called him the Fateblinder once. Did you know that?" Matthias sighed. "Nearly a demon's lifetime ago.

Regardless, you dance where he tells you because he holds the cards. If there is a string to pull, his fingers will tangle on it at the worst possible moment. So tell me how your friend the Rider doesn't know who's hiding in the lighthouse?"

Jade and I had talked about leaving, and suddenly Catherine knew. Even when Lucien was hunting for his sacrifices, using Matthias to find them, he'd sent me out looking in all the wrong places. Lucien always *knew.* "She exists in another world," I said, because that was the answer, wasn't it? Grace wasn't under his purview?

"Follow it down to the rabbit's warren. *Think.* Maybe the lighthouse is shielded from him, but how does he not know about what she did to you? Even if she is hidden, wouldn't he know you were stolen from this world, even for a few moments? How was it that your fate was hidden from him so neatly? Without even a wrinkle in the fabric of life."

I didn't want to play games. Didn't want to wonder. "Tell me."

He frowned. I wasn't playing the game, and he loved games. "She hides herself. I suppose it's a simple enough talent, once you have a little demon succor in your veins."

That was how Grace had stayed under the radar all these years. Lucien hadn't seen any of it, hadn't found out the *reason* behind my sudden power outage. The gaping hole in my metaphoric chest that had plagued me ever since. And then there was Riley. Attacking him the way I had, accidentally using Riley's mind as a battleground. Afterward he'd screamed at me. Demanding "What did you do?" like the truth was too alien to comprehend.

"She hides herself," I repeated in a whisper.

"And that made all the difference," Matthias murmured with a satisfied smile.

"And you? You know how to hide yourself from him, too, don't you?"

Matthias laughed. "Who do you think showed the lovely Widow how to disappear in the first place?"

I looked over at Riley. She was awake and watching me. Our eyes met. "There's a Bishop in Black's house," she confided, as though it was a secret only the two of us were privy to. "He's so tiny now, and likes his tea too sweet."

"So I am, little seer," Matthias chuckled, sounding unusually fond. "And so I do."

It was exactly what I'd been looking for. If Grace could hide herself, it was only so that she could maneuver around Lucien like an equal. So that when she came at him, he wouldn't hold the advantage. If I could convince her to teach me to do the same, I could . . .

No. I had to shut that down now. Not until I had time to think it through. But it was the seed from which my plan would form. *If I choose to stay,* I thought with increased guilt as I looked to Riley. If I could get my power back, I was sure I could find a way to fix her.

"He'll come for her soon," Matthias added, stepping away from me. "He knows she didn't die, and he'll wonder at the dynamic you conjured together."

I looked to Riley, who seemed to be listening even if her eyes were caught by the fraying at the edge of her blankets. "What is she? Is she dangerous? Can I save her?"

I don't know why I went to a demon looking for hope.

"Why would you ever want to do that? Maybe she's the ignition you needed all along. The city could use a villain like you."

"I'm not a villain," I snapped. "I won't be."

He cocked an eyebrow. "You weren't a weapon once, either. Times are changing. The girl's been reshaped by two repelling powers. There's a bit of you in there. And a bit of him." Matthias smiled again. "Which do you think is more dangerous?"

"White is winning and there's no king to castle," Riley told me solemnly.

"*If* I chose to do something," I said carefully, trying to keep my words vague. A conversation with Jade had been all it had taken to alert Lucien that something was up. "Could you do what she does?"

Matthias pretended to consider what I was asking, though the smile started forming before I'd even finished my question. "You want me to tie a string to you?" He was pleased. "You know I can yank on it whenever I want. Dangerous thing, for a puppet to go finding new masters."

"I'm asking for … " I fumbled for a second before my own smile started to form. "Attorney/client privilege."

"I'm sorry, I think you dialed the wrong number," Matthias replied. "You don't want the sexy black man in a three thousand dollar suit," he said, picking at a bit of lint on his shoulder, "you want the mewling, petulant shell of a thing wearing eyeballs in between its green scales."

I didn't let the dismissal faze me. Demons struck bargains with humans; it was their nature. There were contracts involved. Just because Lucien was more up front about it didn't mean he was the only one. "You can negotiate a contract the same as him."

"*Can* is not *will*," he pointed out. "Tell me what you're thinking, and I'll consider it. Sheltering you will not bode well for me if our mutual friend decides to grind you up and feed you to my hellhounds."

"I tell you anything, and it sets something in motion," I said. "This is all hypothetical. Give me an hour, free from Lucien's spy games."

"So you *are* up to something." His demon eyes gleamed. "Tell me more."

I shook my head, holding out my hand. "Shake on it. One hour." There were too many variables. Take the wrong action and Lucien might see the ripples and trace them back. But this was just a handshake, not a partnership.

"One hour," he agreed. Matthias's hand was on mine even before I could see it. Dark eyes flashed a cornflower blue as he peered inside of me, seeing all the secrets in my life, old and new. Lucien could read the paths that the future might take, but Matthias could see into the dark parts of man. The kind of secrets that a man might only share with the closest of confidants. The kind of secrets that might spell revolution.

Just as quickly as he'd snatched my hand out of the air, he flung it away. The demon-blue faded from his irises and he stumbled away from me. "You're on your own. I won't help you." His bravado was shattered; he looked *terrified*.

"What's wrong? What did you see?"

Matthias didn't respond, but Riley did. "He sees the endgame. He fears deep down into the marrow."

"You're damn right I'm afraid," Matthias snapped. "You never said that *that* was a possibility."

"He needs to suffer," Riley's voice became a horrible snarl. "He needs to be broken for what he's done."

"Someone needs to tell me what's going on," I interjected. "Riley?"

She glared at me, and it was like seeing something else in control of Riley's body. The slant of her demon blue eyes, the tightness in her arms and legs. Her expression. This wasn't Riley. This was something else entirely. It was like there was an alien behind her eyes now.

"Is this what you've been waiting for?" Matthias asked, half in shock.

The thing that wore my friend's face revealed nothing. "Knights fall, and the end of all things. There is only victory in the breaking. He will become what he was, and what he will be, and then the world will tremble."

I looked to Matthias for translation, but he was looking down at the floor, a puppy who'd been scolded. *Where is this coming from? Was this part of Riley there, waiting underneath the surface? Is this what she's been waiting for?*

"I don't understand." I admitted. "What's happening? What's wrong with her?"

"She's ... something complicated," Matthias said, sullen. "Partly who she was, partly who you will be, and partly what he *is*. And apparently, she's been keeping secrets."

She turned her glare on me. It was enough to make me forget that she was in a hospital gown or that we were even in a hospital. All it took was one look, and I squirmed and dropped my own head. My nerves screamed at me to hide, to wait out her displeasure. "You will take your place as what you were and will ever be, violet-eyed prince. Break the board and lay them all to waste."

Violet-eyed. In the vision that Grace had forced into my mind, my eyes hadn't been the ever-changing kaleidoscope I'd grown up with, or even Grace's sun-flare red. They'd been violet and inhuman, burning with maddened fire.

"No," I whispered, shaking my head violently. "I won't become *that*. I refuse."

She climbed up onto her knees, never looking away from me. It was creepy, the way her head always stayed at the same angle, despite the contortions of her body. It was like her head was the one static point on the entire bed, held in place by some sort of invisible ties. "You *will*. Or you will fail. Run while you can, broken-eyed boy, or you will become what you fear most."

When he spoke again, Matthias's voice was low and tired. "If you want any hope of stopping a monster like Lucien, you must become a monster yourself."

eleven

My shirt was soaked with sweat by the time I made it down to the lobby after stumbling out of Riley's room. The nervous energy that had only started to build up a little was a raging inferno by the time I got to the parking lot. I was going to rip free of my skin and leave it behind, I was sure of it.

It never even occurred to me to arrange a ride back home to the house. My feet started down the gravel path at the side of the parking lot, and before I knew it I was running like my life depended on it. The faster I ran, the faster my heart pumped in my chest, the more the racing fear was drowned out by everything else. Maybe it was just the endorphins that kept me sane, but running managed to put some distance between me and Riley's prophecy.

All the real players in Belle Dam were terrified of what I could become. Lucien had tried to kill Trey specifically to keep the vision of me from becoming a reality. Grace had stripped me of my powers because of it. And Matthias had refused to help because of what he'd seen.

If I tried to fight, that's what I would become. That made the decision for me more than anything. I had to go.

I made it home without any other disturbances, but I'm sure there were half a dozen panicked citizens making phone calls and sending text messages about Jason's tempestuous ward running the streets like a crazy person. My nerves had calmed a little by the time I made it back to my room and grabbed a change of clothes and a towel.

The shower helped, but only after I cranked up the music player on my computer and had the speakers blasting through the walls. I needed to not think. As long as I was distracted, there was a fragile truce in place where I couldn't dwell on what had been said.

There was a text from Trey on my phone once I was done. *Can I come over?*

Why was this my life? Why wouldn't he get the hint? *It's not a good time,* I texted back, though there might not ever be a good time again, if I really took off. I hesitated, staring down at the screen and waiting for his reply.

Please. It's important.

As much as I needed to keep pushing him away, now more than ever, part of me still needed to see him. Especially since it could be the last time. *Ok. See you soon.*

Once it was done, I was filled with a different kind of nerves. I changed outfits five or six times, each time for reasons that got more and more ridiculous. I knew I was being stupid, but I couldn't stop myself. The idea of seeing Trey for the last time—and I couldn't tell him I was going anywhere, because that's all Lucien would need—made me want to throw up. In fact, I tried to do that, only nothing came out.

It wasn't much more than a half hour later before the front doorbell was ringing, and I was contemplating another trip to purge the rest of my breakfast. I actually made it as far as the hallway next to the kitchen before Trey appeared and cut me off from the bathroom. He was wearing a thick gray sweater, which looked like the softest thing ever, and a pair of jeans. I pushed down the urge to go to him immediately, instead leaning against the wall. Pretending to be cool and collected. Like anyone would believe it.

"I would have tried to talk to you earlier," Trey said awkwardly as soon as he appeared, "but I didn't want you to think I was pushing you. That's why I waited."

"You were talking to Jason about me," I said, "so you should have talked to me first anyway."

"Actually, that wasn't about you," Trey said, shoving his hands into his pockets. He looked more nervous than I had ever seen him before. "It was about me. But Jason wouldn't go for it."

"Go for what?"

He looked around slowly, the uncertainty on his face growing. "Can we go out back or something? Just... I don't want him to come out and see us talking and turn me into a ceiling fan or something."

"He wouldn't do that. He might have you neutered, though. I'm pretty sure he'd be one of those overzealous pet owners."

"You joke," Trey said under his breath, clearly not laughing, "but he probably would."

"And you thought he was warming up to you," I said, only a little smug. I led him out onto the back porch and sat down on one of the lounges. "What's up?"

It took Trey awhile to get himself comfortable. He looked around at the furniture, decided on one of the other lounge chairs, and then once he sat and realized how much distance was between us, he got up and moved it closer. Then he sat down again and was quiet for so long I started to get frustrated.

"Trey? You wanted something."

Trey gave me a thin smile and nodded. "You remember in the chapel basement, when Lucien had us trapped?"

How could I forget? Lucien had known I would follow him, and he'd carved a binding circle into the floor before our arrival. Only, he'd only been expecting me. Trey had been a surprise, but what had been *more* surprising was that Trey had been bound inside the circle, too. A circle that should have only trapped someone with magical power. As far as either of us had known, Trey wasn't a witch.

Then again, Belle Dam *was* a town full of secrets. What was one more?

"Is that what you're here about?" I asked. "Because I can't help you."

"Yeah, you can," he said earnestly. "I want you to teach me. Show me how to use it."

It felt like my entire body froze like a computer. It took

a minute for me to reboot, at which point I swallowed. "I'm sorry, you want me to *what?*"

"I want you to show me how to use magic," Trey said. He made it sound so simple. *Show me how to ride a bike. Teach me how to play the piano. Train me in the mystical arts.*

I stared at him in dumbfounded shock. This was some kind of joke. But he wasn't smiling. "You're not serious."

"I am."

I pulled off my glasses, wincing at the light. Even though it wasn't as bright outside as it had been a few minutes ago, it was still more than I was used to. "You're not serious," I repeated, my voice growing harder. "You can be a dick sometimes, but you're not usually an asshole. You know I can't do that anymore."

"I'm not asking you to," he said, looking me dead in the eyes. "I just want you to walk me through it."

"Walk you through it?" I shook my head, already thinking through the thousands of hours John and I had spent trying to get my own gift under control. I didn't have a choice—the witch eyes had made my power wild and unpredictable. It seemed like the more control I'd gotten, the faster it was killing me. "Do you really think it's that easy? You can't get *tutored* in magic, Trey! I've been learning it since I was a kid and I barely know anything at all."

"You've done well enough against everything so far," he pointed out.

"That's because I'm a freak. It came easily to me because of what I was. John barely knew what to do with me half the time. I was the worst student ever. So why would you even think I'd be the person for the job. I mean, hello," I snapped, waving a hand in front of my face like *see the gaping hole where all my crazy eye magic used to be?*

"I wouldn't be asking you if I didn't trust you," Trey said stiffly.

Why was Trey uncomfortable? "Oh," I said, now understanding the conversation he'd had with Jason last week. "You tried Jason first, and he turned you down. And you're still not talking to your mom, so that's out." I paused, letting all that sink in. "So I was your last choice. Great. Awesome."

"Five seconds ago, you were pissed because I asked you after what you've gone through. Now you're pissed I didn't come to you first? Maybe I was trying to respect that this would be hard for you." He swallowed. "Especially since you can't seem to look at me anymore."

I pressed my lips together rather than say something neither one of us wanted to hear. "I can't help you, Trey."

"But that's just it. Maybe I can help you. If you show me how to control it, how to make it work, maybe we can figure out a way to take back what you lost."

God, why was he doing this to me? There wasn't enough on my plate so Trey had to come in and add more? And he was being so *sincere* about it. Like he really did just want to help me. Just like always. Only now he'd be the one with the power. The one who could do the fighting. "Why would I want it back? I'm healthy, maybe for the first time ever. I'm pretty sure I can run a six-minute mile, and I've never been able to do that before. I haven't had so much as a real head-ache in days. I sleep through the night, and I won't look like a raccoon if I spend all summer on the beach!"

"First we have to get you to next summer," Trey said, trying to sound gentle but just coming across as pompous.

"Go to hell," I said. Because I was the only one allowed to worry about that. I turned my back to him, already regretting this conversation. Why did I think he needed a proper goodbye? Trey was a dick.

He moved so quickly. One second, my back was to him and the next he was standing in front of me, standing so close we were nearly nose to nose. I couldn't help but look at him then. "Sorry," he said quietly. "Jade told me about ... the two of you. Are you?" he asked quietly, eyes darting over my shoulder as if confirming that no one was eavesdropping on us. He didn't even use the word. Leaving. Running away. Abandoning ship.

"I don't know," I said, suddenly irritated. I took a step back, and he took a step forward. I looked away, and he reached out and grabbed my chin.

"Hey," he said. "Come on. Please."

"Why are you such an ass all the time?" I demanded. "I tell you to leave me alone and you're worse than ever."

Trey let his fingers slip from my face, and he pressed his forehead against mine. I sucked in a breath at the contact, feeling any resolve I had start to pool down into my legs and out of me entirely. "I'll leave you alone if that's what you want."

But I couldn't answer that. Even the idea of putting my feelings about Trey into words caused my throat to constrict so tight I couldn't get air in. I had to talk about anything else. "Do you know that Lucien spent over a hundred years trying to put everything into place so that I'd be born?" I scuffed my foot against the ground. "I get why he seems to think I'm his … possession or something. If I spent half as long as that trying to make something happen, I'd feel like it belonged to me."

"Okay," Trey said warily. "Where are you going with this?"

I shrugged. "I used to think Jason didn't want anything to do with me because I was broken. But that's how Lucien feels. I get it now. I may be broken, but I'm still *his*." And he wouldn't let me go until he was done with me.

"Your life isn't over just because you can't see through walls," Trey said. "And the Braden I've come to know in the last few months wouldn't just roll over, no matter what happened to him."

"I'm not that kid anymore," I snapped. "Do you know what I'd do if I had my power back? Without even stopping to second-guess myself?"

Trey swallowed, but after a moment he gestured for me to continue. I could see it in the way he wouldn't quite meet my eyes, the little hunch in his posture. *He already knew.*

I'd spent enough time thinking about it in the middle of the night. What I would do? How I would begin? Lucien would take a while. He had to suffer properly. But he wouldn't be first.

"I'd kill her. I don't know how, but I'd make it sudden. Make it *hurt.*" No, that wasn't enough. A moment of relief wouldn't make me feel better. "No," I said slowly, "it wouldn't be enough to kill her. She'd have to lose everything first."

"Do you think that will solve anything?" Trey asked.

"I don't care." I eyed him, waiting for the moment it became too much. When he saw the wrath inside of me, bubbling through my veins, lurking just beneath the surface. "Taking you from her would hurt," I mused, "but it wouldn't be enough. I'd have to take you both."

"Kill us?" Trey sounded nonchalant, like discussing his murder was a normal occurrence around here.

I shook my head, my thoughts stuttering over a hurdle I hadn't anticipated. Trey wasn't supposed to play along. And I wasn't supposed to think about hurting him or his sister. They weren't involved, not really. As much as I know it would destroy Catherine to lose her children, I couldn't do that to either of them.

Trey took a step forward. Then another. Then he was crowding into me. He took my hand in his and brought it up to his neck, laid it against the even pulse of his heart. "How would you do it?" his words the kind of whisper that was more appropriate for a clandestine tryst, not a daylight conversation about murder.

"Stop," I pleaded. This was all wrong. Trey was supposed to look at me in horror, to turn away and never look at me with all that stupid idealism, like we really could find a way to be together. It was stupid, and juvenile, and it had to stop.

"I deserve to know how I'm going to die," he said good-naturedly.

"You wouldn't see it coming," I said, my words choking off into a gasp as Trey's mouth hummed against my ear.

"Keep talking," he said, his lips a tease against my skin. Fractions of a touch, ghost impressions down my jaw. "Details. The details are important."

"I … uh … " The feeling stopped, as fleeting as it had begun.

"Keep talking," he reprimanded, nipping at the bottom of my earlobe and knocking every coherent thought completely out of my head. Trey seemed to realize this, because he kept talking. "Would you do it from far away? You could, couldn't you?" His nose traced a line up along my temple. "No, that wouldn't be like you. You'd have to be there, right?" For just a moment, he let his cheek rest against the side of my head, but only for a moment. Then the game was back in motion, and it was all touches so brief they were just fragments of connections.

"I wouldn't do it," I finally managed to say, trying to swallow and focus on the conversation at the same time.

"You *have* to," he insisted. "You don't have a choice."

"You told me there's always a choice," I said, gasping as his mouth traveled down to my neck and he nipped again at the skin there.

His movements were more forceful now. Proprietary.

Trey struck me as someone who was too classy to leave a hickey on someone else's skin, but his lips kept moving, claiming one inch of skin at a time.

I never should have let him this close to me. That was the problem with Trey. If I wasn't forceful up front—if I let myself think about it for even a few seconds—my mind wavered. Convictions that had been so firm only a few minutes before were now tenuous guidelines I could ignore easily, because it was *Trey*.

My fingers wrapped around his wrist, holding him, claiming him. His eyes sunken and dull, clothes that had once fit so perfectly now hung loose and low on his stooped frame. He wasn't anything that he'd been, but it mattered not, because he was *mine.*

I pulled away from Trey so fast I nearly threw myself onto the ground. The vision that Grace had put into my head was never far from my thoughts. The *thing* that I'd become. The reason she'd started the feud in the first place—to make sure that Lansing and Thorpe would never align. But it had happened anyway, maybe even *because* of the feud that she'd created.

My breath came hard and fast, and I knew my eyes were wild but I had to get away. He reached for me and I skittered backwards, brushing up against one of the lounge chairs. I almost fell backwards, tripping over the frame, but Trey caught me. I scrambled out from his reach and around the chair, keeping it between us.

"What's wrong?" I expected Trey to sound astonished,

or worried. But it wasn't that at all. He sounded like he'd been expecting that.

"Nothing," I lied automatically, not even stopping to feel bad about it anymore. I was a liar. Liars lied. It was what we did.

"Braden ... " He didn't push me. The intense expression on his face melted away, like I'd imagined the last few minutes. "You can teach me. Then we can figure out how to help you."

"Trey ... I can't."

Trey, who loved to push at me, who always seemed to know when my mind was never fully committed, chose to believe me. He slumped down a little, a man who'd had his last, and best, hope taken from him. "Okay," he said, exhaling. "Okay."

"I'm sorry, I just—"

"It's okay, Braden," he said. "It's my problem, not yours." But there was a look of determination in his eyes that I didn't like. Something that made me a little bit nervous.

I walked out into the yard. There was a breeze coming down through the forest. I closed my eyes for a moment, trying to take it all in. Trey. Jason. This city. These people. What if I never had anything like this again? What if this was the closest, and the furthest, I'd ever get to being happy?

"I wouldn't mind throwing Drew around the next time he put his hands on you," Trey muttered. I looked up in surprise, saw the way Trey's head was dropped down, a hint of red creeping up his neck.

I laughed, and the sound caught me so off guard that I had to stop immediately afterwards. It was like ripping off a bandage, only it was one I didn't know I had. I couldn't remember the last time I'd laughed. Really laughed. The last few months had been one issue after another, and especially in the last couple of weeks, things had gotten so grim I'd forgotten how it felt.

Once I started, I had trouble stopping. "You..." I gasped. "Jealous... of Drew!" And then I was howling. Tears sprang up at the corners of my eyes, and I fell backwards onto the grass and stared up at the sky. Of all the people to be jealous of, Trey was jealous of Drew! Anyone in their right mind would have known that Drew was the last person I'd ever be interested in. Plus there was the fact that he was still hung up on Trey's sister. But the same way that the heart wanted what it wanted, the green-eyed monster hated what it hated.

Trey loomed over me, his expression dark, but I couldn't stop. I grabbed at his arm, pulled him down with me. He dropped to his knees, then carefully laid himself down next to me, brushing up against my side.

I laughed until I thought I might start crying. Once the floodgates were opened, there was no telling what would sneak out. But laughter finally started to fade, and I stared up into a relatively blue sky. It was almost December in Belle Dam, and I was alive. Maybe not the person I'd been two months ago, but I was still someone who could laugh.

We lay there, barely touching, until I took the initiative

to reach over, and lay my head down on his chest. I could hear his heartbeat, steady and solid. His chest rose and fell, and for just a few minutes, we were normal.

Of course it couldn't last.

twelve

Trey only stayed another hour, and we didn't move from our spot on the lawn. But just as I started to drowse, to slip under completely, he roused the me and led me back into the house. I was so tired and out of it that I didn't even say goodbye, just wandered up the stairs and into my room while he let himself out the front.

I barely even remembered getting up from the back lawn at all because the moment I hit my bed, I was out. It wasn't normal sleep, as some part of me was aware the whole time. My mind was covered in blankets of shadow, each time I managed to squirm out from underneath one, there was another dozen piled on top.

Garden statues lamenting burn the witches in olive hubris under ivory chains there are no two ways to bleed them dry dark melancholy grown on a bed of dire lies told and lies hidden shadowed gold boundaries of this land where blood runs counterclockwise burn this garden with weakness rip the humanity from her heart like weeds. Everything that was ours shall always be ours.

I was already standing at the side of my bed when I woke up. *Not again,* I nearly whimpered. But it didn't look like I'd been bodyjacked again. Waking up came all at once, the first shocking moments of pond-jumping in spring, the way the water stabs the body into sensation.

It took several minutes before my body started to feel like mine again. Sleep was starting to become a wild card in my life—I never knew how I would wake up. Or where. My stomach started growling while I was still trying to figure out if I was okay or not.

The house was a quiet din as I left my room and headed through the winding halls down to the kitchen. I didn't even know what half the rooms in Jason's house were supposed to be for, other than getting lost in. At any given time, I really only knew my way to my room, the bathroom, the kitchen, and the library.

Someone else was already in the kitchen when I walked in. Expecting the gray-haired maid that prepared most of my meals, I was surprised to find Jason standing at the counter.

"Gentry made it home okay?" he asked. There was an undercurrent of *something* to his question, but I didn't have the first clue about what he was implying. Jason was still a mystery to me, especially now.

"I needed a nap," I said slowly, "so he went home."

"Okay." But it was not an "I take what you're saying at

face value" okay. It was more of an "I'll accept that this is the lie you're going to tell me" okay.

"You don't need to check on me," I said sharply. "I know what I'm doing." Which was the biggest lie of them all.

"Braden," he started, then sighed and shook his head. Jason walked to the end of the counter and scrubbed his hands with a dish towel that had been left there. Then I noticed his outfit: the rolled-up sleeves of his dress shirt, the lack of a jacket and tie, the frustrated scrub that had left his hair unkempt and scattered. Jason looked more relaxed than I'd ever seen him as well as more exhausted.

It was another side to a man who never showed me the same side twice. It was hard to get a read on him because the readings always changed. At first he was cold, then he was calculating, then concerned. Now, what? What was the role he was going for? Weary parent, tired of fighting the bad fight? Emotionally drained and morally bankrupt?

"Sit," Jason said. "I'll make you something."

Did I get swallowed up by a tornado or dropped down a rabbit hole? Jason was offering to *cook*? But he paid people to do that! Wary, like this was some kind of trick, I took a seat at the table, watching him pull out ingredient after ingredient from the fridge.

His movements were quick and precise, barely any motion wasted, and he arranged each of them on the counter evenly spaced from the next. Then he opened one of the lower cabinets, pulled out a saucepan and a skillet, and set them on top of the stove.

Things were washed, chopped, and poured all in a matter of minutes. Something sizzled in the skillet while he started deftly chopping something small and white, either an onion, or garlic.

"I thought Catherine was the one with a restaurant," I said, trying to make a joke. At the sound of my voice, Jason flinched, and then all at once grew still. I flushed, and my voice dropped considerably in both tone and enthusiasm. "Sorry."

"I'm just not used to other people in the kitchen when I cook," Jason said, keeping his back to me. "For a second, I forgot you were here." It was clear he felt just as awkward about the situation as I did. "But don't ever apologize for speaking your mind," he said, turning his neck enough to make it clear he was addressing me, but not enough to actually *look* at me.

"You hate when I speak my mind," I said, still cautious.

He made slow, even slices over something wrinkled and red, sun-dried tomatoes I guessed. He was almost finished before he answered again. "You almost died... *twice.* I watched my brother raise you, sneaking peeks when I could. He kept you alive for seventeen years. I could have lost you within the first month."

There was another one of those moments of stillness, as if Jason only allowed himself a second to succumb to whatever feelings were clawing at him, and then he was in motion again. The tomatoes were poured into the saucepan, then a few other ingredients, and he started to stir.

I kept opening my mouth, intent on saying *something*. Anything to drown out the silence that crept through the room and made the words that hung between us all the more awful. There were times that I thought I hated Jason, when I found him reprehensible and cruel and unfeeling. But I was starting to realize that no one could ever hate him more than he hated himself.

"I thought you would be more like me," he said finally. "I knew you'd be strong-willed, of course, but I thought... Christ, I don't know what I thought," he muttered. "You have to understand, for most of my life, I knew my son would be the one to end the feud. He made me think my son would be the ultimate weapon. He was the one who said you had to be hidden away, for your own safety."

"Lucien," I said.

Jason nodded. "In forty years, he never steered me wrong. Of course I trusted him implicitly. Why wouldn't I?" His laugh was bitter. "And then he almost killed you."

He poured something else into the pan and then switched focus as he carefully laid several chicken breasts into the skillet and turned up the heat. "I saw my brother with you, you know. In the hospital. He was always so calm. Maybe that's why I didn't understand what it was like. Sitting there, hour after hour. *Waiting.* Feeling like you're hanging on the edge of a cliff, and every moment is a chance for rescue or ruin. I do not understand how he did it. Just... so *calm.*"

"He got used to it," I said slowly. "A trip to the ER probably never gets easier, but he had a lot of practice keeping himself together. That's probably a Thorpe thing, how you never let people see you sweat."

Another silence crept up between us, but this time the tension from a few minutes ago had diffused. There was a bridge building between the two of us—a shaky, tenuous bridge that could collapse into chaos at any moment, but it was a start.

"I never should have let him bring you back here," Jason said. "But that's no worse a crime than the rest of my behavior since your return. I should have seen the boy, not the magic. If I'd known that this was where we'd end up, I would have made different choices. Maybe. At least I'd like to think so."

"I don't know if it would have changed anything," I said, thinking it over. "Lucien had all this planned. He would have brought me back, regardless of whether or not he had your blessing. And everything that's happened since ... I'm just as much to blame." I thought about John, and the way he'd come back trying to protect me. Knowing there was something wrong before anyone else. Knowing *me*. Knowing the right thing to say when everything was going to hell.

It wasn't Jason's fault that he couldn't be the replacement either of us needed. "You've done the best you could under the worst of circumstances," Jason said. "John raised you well."

"He did," I nodded. "He was the best."

"When ... when John came home, I put out feelers. I

had people looking for him. But he wasn't trying that hard to hide," Jason said with an exasperated laugh. "My brother, always making things harder than they needed to be." Jason flipped over the chicken over and stirred the sauce in the other pan. "I told him everything would be forgiven, I would do anything he wanted, if only he'd tell me how to help you. I'd give you back to him, I'd leave him everything. *Anything.* But he had to help you."

"He told you he would, didn't he?" Jason didn't have to admit it, I already knew. "And then he sent you after my mom's family." Maybe to get him out of the way, or maybe just so he wasn't around to get underfoot. Because John knew that if he ever came back to Belle Dam, there would be a price on his head. He'd come after me, knowing it would probably be the last thing that he'd ever do.

I couldn't say anything after that. There was a single moment where I thought it was going to be too much, where I was going to crack and break down and nothing would ever be okay again. And then there was John's voice in my head, calm and placid the way he could get some-times on summer nights. *"You're the strongest boy I know. You'll be capable of such great things someday."*

Jason put down the spatula and turned to look at me. His face was gray and tired, and he checked his watch. "The last ferry leaves in about an hour. Your aunt and uncle … they'll meet you on the other side." And it was clear he wanted to say more, but the words caught before he could get them out.

"Do you think they'd be able to protect me?"

"*Yes.*" I could tell it cost Jason to admit that. That someone could do something he could not. "They take family seriously. More seriously than anything else. They'll protect one of their own with everything they have."

Neither one of us said much after that, not until Jason portioned out the meal he'd cooked onto a plate and set it down in front of me. Bow-tie pasta, some sort of brown sauce, and a chicken breast. As soon as the food was put down, Jason went immediately back to cleaning the mess he'd made.

"It looks good," I said, but it smelled even better.

Jason responded to my surprise with a wry, "I *can* cook, Braden. There are a lot of things you don't know about me." He paused. "And I about you, I suppose."

Another silence eased up between us, but this one lacked any of the previous tension. It snuck up on me, I'd started tucking into the food as soon as the plate was in front of me, and it was only after I started eating that I realized how hungry I actually was. I'd scraped the plate clean and gotten up for seconds before I realized that Jason had been watching me for several minutes, all the mess already cleaned up. He'd combined the rest of the chicken and the pasta into the saucepan, and it was the only evidence left of the meal.

"What would you do, if you were me?" I asked, hungry for something other than food now.

Jason spread his hands in front of him. "I ... don't know."

"But what do you *want* me to do?" I pressed.

It took a lot longer for this answer. "I want to know that you're safe. What happens to me, or this town, that's not your fault. It's not your responsibility. I think I understand that, now."

"So you want me to leave with them."

"I ... yes."

Jason wanted me to leave. Lucien wanted me to stay. Grace wanted me for ... I still wasn't sure. No matter which way I turned, there were strings. People manipulating me. Even Jason. He might have been sincere, I *wanted* to believe he was, but he would use that against me in a heartbeat. Everyone wanted to make my choice for me, decide the path I was going to take.

"Just ... be safe, Braden," Jason said, before he got up and walked from the room.

Safe was just a word, though, and words could only get me so far.

thirteen

One of the drivers was waiting out in front of the house when I was done. I'd tried to find Jason before I left—unsure about what I would even say—but I couldn't find him anywhere. I let it go. If Jason wanted to hide, then who was I to judge him for it? He'd already done more than enough for me.

The ferry was on the south side of the marina, almost at the edge of the city. I hadn't spent much time around there other than the visits to the Harbor Club. Matthias's club was a few blocks away, tucked away in the middle of an industrial zone.

There was no time for me to second-guess anything, because as we pulled up in the parking lot, the dock workers were hustling the last few people on board. I bolted out of the car, worried about what would happen if I ended up getting left behind. Would they wait for me? Or would they take it as a sign of bad faith and take off?

I couldn't risk it. I ran for the ferry, even as I was remembering the bus I'd gotten on that had ultimately led me to Belle Dam in the first place. Back then, all I'd cared about was trying to keep Uncle John safe, and maybe figuring out where I'd come from and why I was born with the powers I had.

The strange feeling in my chest returned the moment I set foot onto the ferry. I was one of the last ones on, making it just under the wire. Guys in plastic ponchos hustled me forward, and I ended up speed-walking towards the cabin. The sky was a thick sea of clouds, and the rain started even before we pulled away from the harbor.

The fluttering in my chest, the strange sensations that had been bothering me for days now, intensified and reminded me of the visions. But the visions always came from the outside in—seeing things that had happened in the rest of the world. But this was like something from the inside, coming from the void in my chest where my power had once been. This time, though, it wasn't an aviary. It was a hurricane of feathers, tracing lines up and down the emptiness, marking its vastness.

It had been the worst when I was with Grace. And she'd stared at me while it happened, like she was waiting to see something. Were we connected now? When she stole my power, did something else get created in its place? I'd attacked Lucien once and tapped into his ability to read futures. Maybe this was something like that?

Although I didn't know how the echolike feelings that coursed through me could do any good. They were just reminders of what wasn't there anymore. That Grace could do whatever she wanted with my power, and I was helpless to stop her.

I sank down on one of the benches and watched the sky open up all around us, blanketing the ferry in a curtain of water. "Great," I muttered. I was going to get drenched when I got off later.

"What are you?" I don't know why I thought to question it out loud, but there was predictably no response. When the winter voice had been a part of me, it would answer my questions. Maybe I expected this new feeling to work the same way.

The feeling kept strengthening, more and more invisible birds added to the process, until I thought it couldn't possibly get any more distracting. It felt like actual butterflies in my chest, except that there were thousands more than should have actually been able to fit. I knew I'd put on some weight and all, but I was fairly certain I hadn't swallowed a quarter of a million overgrown bugs.

Like the crescendo in a song, the feeling built to a fever pitch, and was suddenly silenced as quickly as it had started. For a moment, just a fraction in time, the hole in my chest stopped aching. I felt *connected*. Like it wasn't a hole, but a rope, and hanging on the other end was something familiar.

I smelled vanilla perfume and fresh-cut flowers. Earthy smells, but ordered. A garden, not the forest. A hint of rust and iron and the smell of the sky right after a lightning strike.

"I'm sorry, mistress," a girl said. Elle. *I heard her voice as*

clear as if it had come from my own mouth and felt the rumble of my own chest.

"It is the price and the balance," another voice responded, but this one had no sound. It was like hearing without ears, thoughts given a form that was not audible nor visual. "It seems your counsel was wise, and the boy retains a purpose."

The connection snapped closed.

Grace. And Elle. I should have figured that out already. Elle had started moving around town about the time that Grace started to get more active. She'd showed up right around the time that I'd needed saving from the psychotic little girl in a princess dress, and banished her back wherever ghosts came from. She'd been tall and gorgeous, and liked flirting with me too much.

Elle had also been the first one to see that there had been something wrong with me. The infection of Lucien's power that had started to cloud my judgment. That must have been how Grace found out about me—Elle had been telling her everything.

Was she a ghost like the others? I'd seen her use magic, but that didn't mean anything. Ben was a ghost, but he was able to use my blood to control me.

The wave of dizziness caught me off guard, and it was a good thing I was already seated. I leaned over, pressing my fingertips against my forehead. I couldn't tell if it was being on the ferry or from what I'd just seen, but the way dinner was roiling in my stomach, I knew this wasn't going to end well.

What a cliché. First time on a ferry, or a boat of any kind, and I was going to have to drop my dinner over the side.

No. I refuse. I lowered my head down to my knees and spent the next forty minutes breathing slowly and surely, forcing myself to keep everything in my stomach where it belonged. It was a slow battle, and for some reason when the ferry docked on the other side of the bay, I felt like it was the best kind of victory. I was immeasurably proud of myself all for doing nothing more than keeping myself from throwing up.

The pier on the other side looked identical to the one I'd just left, but now I wasn't in a rush, so I could actually notice all the details. The railings were red-painted metal, thicker than my arm. I was the only one who got off. I walked down the dock, noticing the nearly empty parking lot. *That's not creepy or anything.* I had a healthy appreciation for what could be hiding in the dark. This close to midnight, there was no telling what could be waiting for me.

The couple standing under one of the corner lot lights didn't exactly fit the mold as far as supernatural terrors went, though. I wondered if they planned it like that, standing under the light like some sort of message. Or maybe they just wanted me to see them.

They didn't look like witches. Not that witches looked like anything in particular, but Jason seemed to think they could protect me. I didn't see it. The man, my mother's brother, looked world-weary in his black pea coat and days of scruff. He had dirty blond hair, but maybe that was a trick of the light. His hands were tucked inside the coat pockets, the expression on his face pensive. Sad.

The woman, though—my aunt—was completely different. Her hair was long and honey brown, and she looked both nervous and excited. When her brother nudged her in the side at my approach, a full smile blossomed on her face, and it made my stomach churn again.

My footsteps faltered. *They're going to expect too much out of me. I'm just going to disappoint them.* I stopped where I was, but I didn't turn away. It would be easy enough to turn around and run back to the ferry. I doubted they would follow me. The ferry would be docked here for almost half an hour before it made one last trip back to Belle Dam.

The woman put her hand on her brother's arm, and even at this distance I could see her squeezing him. Her face was an open book, and I could see the dismay. But they stayed where they were, and I stayed where I was, and there was a stalemate.

Anxiety flooded through my system, and it was an endless stream of thoughts that started with *They're going to want,* or *I don't think I can,* or *What if they?* Each one was crazier than the one before. I *knew* it was crazy, but I couldn't stop myself. The panic needed a voice, only there were too many voices in my head already.

I pulled my phone out of my pocket, and did the only thing I could think. I called Trey.

He answered immediately. "What's wrong?"

I exhaled as I laughed, but I could hear the quaver in my own voice. "I don't think I can do this."

I heard traffic sounds in the background. Trey's voice was tight. Troubled. "Where are you?"

"I ... took the ferry." I couldn't admit to Trey that I was thinking about leaving. "Jason found ... my mom had family. He thinks they might be able to help me." I closed my eyes, swallowed down my shame.

"The ferry," Trey mused, which was not the part I thought he'd get stuck on. There were sounds of movement and a low voice in the background, but I couldn't make anything out. "Okay, Drew's going to be waiting for you when you get back."

"What? Why? Trey, I'm fine."

"It's just for my piece of mind," Trey said after a long pause. "You shouldn't be walking around without someone there."

"Fine, whatever," I said. Clearly, overprotective Trey wasn't going anywhere. "Did you hear the rest of what I said? Jason found my mom's siblings. They're here."

It was like a switch flipped, and the weird tension was gone. "Are you okay?" Trey asked, his voice dropping down.

"I don't know. It's weird."

"Where are you? Are they there?"

I eyed the distance. "They're like fifty feet away? Maybe more. I suck at depth perception."

Trey made a hmm-ing sound. "Do they look like axe murderers?"

I barked out a laugh, not expecting that. "I don't know. How do I know if they're axe murderers? Is there a dress code?"

Trey's tone was dry. "There's usually an axe."

I snorted, cradling the phone against my shoulder. "Don't make me laugh. This is supposed to be serious. You're ruining it."

"I'm a terrible human being," he agreed, the phone line crackling.

"You're starting to sound a lot like Drew," I said, looking away from the relatives. "I don't know anything about them," I said a moment later, my voice dropping. "What if they're evil? Jason says they're not, but he thought Lucien was a cuddly version of a demon." And then even softer. "What if they hate me?"

"They won't hate you. Unless they're Amish. I'm pretty sure your sarcastic ways would be lost on the Amish."

I smiled, but sober thoughts took over far too soon. I couldn't laugh this conversation off. There was too much attached to it. There was more to this conversation than just a first impression. I'd be leaving everything behind. "What do you think I should do?"

"I think you should walk fifty more feet and then say 'Hi, my name's Braden. I'm only mildly annoying.'"

This time, I didn't laugh. "Stop trying to distract me. This is serious."

"Well, are you still panicking?"

I...wasn't. There were still nerves rushing through my system, but the stifling panic wasn't part of the equation anymore. I could move my feet, and that meant I had to go. There was only so much time until the ferry left for its return trip back to the city. "I have to go."

"Remember, you're only mildly annoying," Trey said encouragingly from the other end.

"I hate you," I laughed.

"You really don't," Trey said, sounding the most serious he had the entire phone call. "And if they don't figure out how lucky they are to get to know you, then screw them. We'll figure something else out."

This time my hesitation didn't have anything to do with my fear. "Trey..."

"Go be brilliant," he said gruffly, ending the call before I could respond.

I started walking forward again, sliding my phone back into my pocket. Their expressions hadn't wavered, not since I made the call, but I could see some of the woman's tension ease when I started approaching again. Maybe I wasn't the only one who was nervous.

There was no joyous reunion or anything like that. I approached, and they waited. Even though I took my time and let my nerves run free, they didn't move. They let *me* approach *them* like I was an abused dog they were trying not to spook.

When I was finally close enough to introduce myself, I opened my mouth but my tongue was frozen. She was younger than I thought she'd be. My mother's sister was maybe in her thirties, and something about her reminded me of Catherine. It wasn't just that they were both blond, it was something I couldn't see. The way they carried themselves, the sharpness in their eyes. Inner steel.

She might not look like it, but she's a predator. I could almost picture her taking on hellhounds with nothing more than a couple of knives. It was all there, in the way that she stood, in the way she looked at me and still watched the rest of the parking lot. Even still, I wasn't scared of her. If anything, it put me at ease.

"Hi," I said, looking down at my shoes. "I'm Braden." I wouldn't repeat the rest, no matter what Trey said.

"Rose's son," the woman said warmly. "Look at you."

"Braden," the man said in greeting, tucking his hands behind his back. Unlike his sister, he was exactly as old as I expected, in his forties like Jason. His skin was weathered and lined and dark from the sun. He didn't look like he smiled much. Jason would have liked him.

"Sorry, I'm off my game," the woman said with a sigh. "I'm Anna. And this is my brother Patrick," she said, gesturing to her brother.

"Hi," I said again.

The smile on her face warmed even more. "Hi," she replied. Tears started to shimmer in her eyes, and when she opened her mouth, the words tangled up. She shook her head, laughed, and looked away. It took her a minute to pull herself together.

"Jonathan never said a word," Patrick said, taking the lead from his sister. "You have to understand, it's a little raw for us. We never knew ... we thought that when your mom died, that you ... "

They believed the story that Jason had spun. That I'd died with her. "He kept in touch with you, though? My uncle?"

"Yeah," Anna said, wiping at the corner of her eye. "Not often, but enough to keep in touch. I hadn't talked to him in almost a year, though."

I hunched my shoulders and turned around, facing the ferry. "He ... he's gone. Just a few days ago." If I didn't look at them, I could pretend we weren't talking about this. That it wasn't real.

"Yeah, your fa— I mean, I heard," Anna said. I heard her take a step forward, but that was all. "I'm sorry. He raised you all by himself, huh?"

I nodded, not trusting myself to speak about that. "So why are you here?" I asked, feeling myself grow colder. "What do you want from me?" I turned to face them, and wished I hadn't.

Patrick looked like he'd expected this. Knowing, and a little condescending. But Anna looked stricken. "You're our nephew," she said, as if it was obvious. "You're in trouble. We want to help."

"But *why*? You won't set foot in Belle Dam, so obviously you *get it*. Jason says you can protect me, but neither one of them could protect me when it really mattered. So why do you think you can do so much better? And why would you want to?"

Anna seemed to realize there were many questions layered in between. Her insight just managed to annoy me. "We can't do better," she said gently. "No one's ever going to be able to do better than John did. But we *can* help you. We can keep you safe. And we want to. Besides," she offered a tiny smile, "Patrick's daughters would love to get to know their cousin."

Patrick hadn't said much in the conversation so far, but he looked up at that, a fierce expression I didn't see coming. His unease now made a little more sense. He was worried about his family.

"How much do you know about what happened to her? Jason won't tell me anything."

Patrick gave a sharp look to Anna, and she raised her hands, deferring to him. He cleared his throat, looking at something just past my shoulder. "A few days before you were born, your mother called us in the middle of the night. She was seeing things, and from the sounds of it, she had been for a while. If we'd known, if she'd said anything, maybe we could have done something. But she kept it from us until just before the end."

Jason had said the same thing. That my mother had seen things, the way that I'd seen things, as though my power were being channeled by her in fits and spurts.

"She told us there was a darkness lurking in the town and that we had to swear that we would never set foot in the city ourselves. She was adamant, telling me to swear on the lives of my daughters." There was a pause, and he looked up at me like he'd just said something significant.

I didn't see where he was going with this. "Okay?"

"Patrick didn't have any daughters," Anna said, when Patrick faltered. "He hadn't even met his wife back then."

Okay, that made sense. Well, it didn't entirely, because even if she'd tapped into my powers, I couldn't see the future. Only the present and the past. "She knew. And you believed her," I said.

Patrick nodded. "I knew my sister. Whatever had happened to her, she was convinced we were in danger. She said that if either of us," he gestured towards his sister, "even so much as crossed the town line, it would be horrible. So she made us promise never to try."

"So you left her there." Everyone had a story about what had happened to my mother, every version had its own villain. And now there was a new pair being added to the mix. "You abandoned her when she probably needed you most."

"The next morning, she laughed the whole thing off," Anna said. "She tried saying it had just been a nightmare. That everything was fine."

"Two days later, she was gone," Patrick said tightly. "But not you."

Anna gave her brother a sharp look. "Is that really necessary?" she demanded in an acid tone.

"Jason got the kid he wanted," Patrick fired back, turning to face his sister. Anger and something like cinders started coming off of him in waves, absences and smudges in the air that hurt every time I looked at them. I winced, rubbing at the sudden blood rush clouding my thoughts. "And now that his plan failed, he's hoping we'll clean up his mess."

I shook my head. "This was a mistake." I started to back away. Anna might have been on board with taking me away, but Patrick definitely was not. As far as he was concerned, I was just a proxy for his Jason hate.

"No, Braden," Anna pleaded, holding out a hand to me. "It's not—this is just hard." She fixed her brother with a dark look. "*On all of us.*"

"Jason Thorpe is a poisonous serpent and he deserves to have his son ripped from his arms," Patrick spat, turning away sharply. *So that was his stake in all of this.*

"Hey!" I grabbed him by the shoulder and shoved him back around to face me. "He's my *father*, and you don't get to talk about him like that!" I'd earned the right to be pissed at Jason for every little thing, but I was also the only one that probably gave a damn about him. That made it okay. Neither of them could understand the way Belle Dam twisted things. Maybe Jason was responsible for their sister's death, but I wouldn't believe he did it intentionally.

"Thorpe *murdered* my sister," he snarled. "Your mother. I get to talk about him however I want. Don't tell me you actually believe he's the hero in all this? How long were you in Belle Dam before someone tried to kill you? How many days after that did you get admitted to the hospital?"

"And where were you when my mom died?" I spat out.

In hindsight, I deserved it. If anyone had said something like that to me about John, I would have decked them, too. I just didn't think it would *hurt* so much.

The next thing I knew, I was on the ground and Anna was standing between us. I could still feel his fist colliding with my face, the press of each knuckle into my skin. It replayed in my head over and over again.

Now my head throbbed for real, and the blind spots swirling around Patrick were even more frenetic. It was like snowflakes viewed through a photo negative, speedy black trails flaring around him.

I picked myself up off the ground and started backing away. Whatever Anna was saying to him had finally started to calm Patrick down, and now that it was over and his temper was fading, I recognized the shame in his expression.

"Braden, I'm sorry," he started, "that was completely uncalled for."

I shook my head. "It's fine," I said, shrugging. "I deserved it."

"No you didn't," he said. "I'm supposed to be helping you. Not assaulting you."

"No, really," I said, "I'm used to it. I can't start my day unless someone's already tried to beat the crap out me." I ignored the looks on both of their faces: hurt and worried and *concerned.* "Thanks for this. Meeting me. I mean, it's nice to know that you'd come all the way here to try and help me out."

"Braden ... " Anna said softly, but the resignation in her voice said she already understood.

I wasn't going with them. I couldn't. "I'd like to get to know you ... " I trailed off. Knowing my mom had family made me feel hope. There was more to me than what Belle Dam had given me. "But I have to do this first. I'm sorry."

"Braden, don't do this," Patrick said. He reached out a hand.

"If I run now, then everyone else has to pay for my mistakes," I said. "But I meant what I said. Maybe if I find my way out of this. But right now, I have responsibilities." Who'd be there for Jason to cook dinners for? Or work to find a cure for Riley? Or referee Drew and Trey?

It was easy to run from the home I'd grown up in to come to Belle Dam. But running from Belle Dam was harder than I ever would have thought possible. It hadn't become my home exactly. More like it was a puzzle, and I was the last piece. And once I was fitted into place, the puzzle was complete.

I couldn't leave that behind, even if I wanted to.

fourteen

The wind picked up again on the way back as the temperature dropped significantly. Another storm was inching its way into the city. The ride back was quiet, leaving me ample time to think about what a moron I was.

I should have left while I had the chance. Anna and Patrick might not have been perfect, but that was the smart choice. The easy choice. But something had held me back. I wasn't the kid who ran away from his problems. There were two types of people in the world. People who ran from trouble, and people who ran towards it. Actually, there were three types of people in the world, because someone had to cause the trouble in the first place.

I definitely wasn't the first, probably was the second, but almost wished I was the third. *"Be the villain,"* Matthias had said, before realizing just what that would entail. *"So what do you want to do?"* Drew had asked, snippy and to the point as usual.

I was already looking for him before the ferry finished

docking. Drew had set up a perch on one of the metal railings that lined the pier, and he didn't seem to care that everything was still soaked through from the rain. In fact, it looked like he'd been caught outside during the worst of it. He looked more scowly than normal, which meant that "bonding with Trey" had gone over more like "advanced trig without a calculator."

"I hope you're not trying to get me home in time for curfew," I called out as I approached, shoving my hands into my pockets. "And since when do you take orders from Trey, anyway?"

Drew rolled his eyes and hopped down off the railing. "You got big plans tonight, manpain? Got some epic sulking to do while you stare longingly out a window? Guess again." He cuffed me on the back of the head, and added, "Also, fuck you. But I got to hang up on Gentry four times before he managed to spit out enough to get me here. I should thank you for that."

I rubbed my head and glared. "Dick."

"Stop flirting, you're giving me butterflies," Drew said absently, awkwardly texting with a phone that looked positively doll-sized in his too-big hands.

"Is that Trey?" I asked, trying to peer over and catch a glimpse of the screen.

Drew raised his hand again, only this time it was a fist he waved at me. "Personal space, moron."

"You forgot to take your Midol, didn't you?" I said sympathetically. "Well, too bad, because we don't have time for stops." I clapped him on the shoulder and then started walking away before he decided to retaliate. "Come on, we haven't got all night."

"Did someone spike your sippy cup? Because you're extra sassy tonight," Drew fired back. Despite the fact that I was walking fast, Drew's long legs meant he didn't have to struggle to keep up.

"I just figured a few things out, that's all," I said. "And now we need to go. I need to sneak onto the Lansing property, and I need *you* to help me not get caught."

"What's the rush, little boy? Afraid Prince Charming won't be waiting patiently for you until tomorrow?"

I spotted Drew's motorcycle parked on the sidewalk and changed directions to head towards it. "Who said anything about going to the house? We're going into the woods."

His curiosity was piqued. "Oh?"

I nodded. "Going to see a woman about an eye exam."

Everything was fine one moment, and the next... not. There was an extra bite to the wind, an extra layer the darkness. Drew felt it too, he grabbed me by the shoulder and pulled me to a stop. We were fifteen, maybe twenty feet from his bike, and alone underneath one of the buzzing parking lot lights.

With the ferry docked, the crew had followed me off and gone home for the night. The parking lot was a forgotten field, the lights only managing to illuminate just how alone we were. But still, I could feel something. Drew could feel it too.

I started to spin around to check all the angles, but Drew wouldn't let me go. "Something's coming," he growled.

The first drop of rain struck down the moment I felt him appear like a mirage forming at the edge of my vision. He was wispy around the edges, smudged into the landscape around him like a spirit conjured out of the earth at a pagan rite. He stood with one of the lot lights behind him, and the halo around him washed out the features of his face. But I knew it was Ben.

"I don't have time for this," I said under my breath.

"Don't worry," he called out, smug and fevered. "I learned my lesson last time. Quick and fast. Especially now that there's no one to interrupt."

"Blind *and* stupid," Drew responded, moving to stand in front of me. "Which idiot are you working for?"

"Drew, don't," I said urgently, grabbing at his arm and trying to move around him. But the Shifter wasn't having any of that. Every time I tried to move, he was already blocking my way and crowding into my space. His eyes locked on Ben, and I *felt* his body tighten, like I had the day when he'd threatened Jason.

I didn't flinch. I was proud of myself for that. "It took you long enough," I called back to the ghost. I wasn't nervous or scared. Because of all the things I've faced down in the last few months, the ghost with a grudge was pretty much near the bottom. If this was where my story ended, I'd gotten off easy. Nothing surprised me anymore.

Ben stepped forward, leaving behind the corona of light that bled out his features. Beside me, I felt Drew shudder.

"*Dad*?" he whispered, confusion and heartbreak making his voice tremble.

Well, fuck.

fifteen

"What do you mean, *Dad*?" I demanded.

But it was like Drew couldn't hear me. Even Ben exercised his right not to open his mouth and make some stupid comment. The only response I got was from the storm, which continued to whip the winds up around us and open up into a deluge.

"*What do you mean, Dad*?" I shouted. Because this . . . I didn't know what to do with this. Jason had killed Drew's father. And now, it seemed like Drew's father wanted to do the poetic thing and kill Jason's son. *That* was what Matthias was talking about the last time. He'd known who Ben was all along, and never said a word.

"I told you Ben was short for something," the ghost said, sharing a smile with me. Not Ben. *Bennett.*

I should have seen it coming. Ben had been too eager to help, too knowledgeable about what was going on in Belle Dam. About the players involved. Now I knew why. He'd worked with Jason and Catherine, and they'd betrayed him in this quest for power. Matthias had used *Drew* to make Ben back down last time, threatening the life of his son.

"I know what you're thinking," Ben added, "but the demon didn't quite understand the rules. There must always be an Armstrong in Belle Dam. The boy is as safe as houses."

"What are you talking about?" Drew asked, once he found his voice.

"Do you really think he won't come after Drew?" I demanded. "He's a demon. They can't be trusted. He'll do it just to spite you, whatever your 'rules' say."

"Trusted? No. But bought ... ?" Ben's smile grew even wider.

Drew turned to me. He looked ... lost. I'd never seen a picture of Drew when he was a little kid, but now I knew I'd recognize him anywhere. He probably looked lost like this, vulnerable and sad. Drew's mouth opened, and it took a second for him to force the words out. "You know him? He's come after you before?"

I nodded. "He's the guy who gave me the information about Grazia." A girl I'd never met before Lucien had attacked her, only a victim of his rage because her name was Italian for Grace. "He pretended he was friends with Riley, then he showed up at the hospital and took some of my blood." The simplest explanation seemed best. "He almost killed me with it."

"Like a poppet, or a voodoo doll," Drew said faintly. "But he'd need a witch to prepare it ... " he shifted his stance, back to facing his father. "Why would you do this? *How* could you do this?"

Being chastised by his son didn't affect Ben. "Do what? Make Jason pay? Better question, why am I doing your job? You know it wasn't an accident. You knew who was responsible. Are you really that much of a coward that you'd suck up to them now?"

It was the wrong approach to take. Drew didn't do well with *anyone* telling him what to do, let alone his deadbeat father. He shifted his feet just slightly, putting himself back into a fighting stance, and offered a feral grin. "Course not, but I've been thinking about asking good old Jason to adopt me anyway. Might even start calling him Pop. What do you think?"

It was almost easy to see the relationship the two would have had, had Bennett lived. Hard, demanding, and a constant push and pushback. But there wasn't twenty years of history to soften the exchange, and for whatever reason, Drew was ignoring the fact that it was his *father* across from us and treated him just like any other opponent. And Drew had never met an enemy he didn't like to bait with every low blow he could summon up.

"You're going to want to stand down, son," Ben tried, even though he looked no more than maybe a year older than Drew. But it was there in his voice, the confidence of someone well beyond their years. "I don't want to hurt you."

"Can't hurt me, if all your crazy talk is true. I'm the only Armstrong in Belle Dam."

"Can't *kill* you," Ben said in almost exact same tone. "Didn't say anything about hurting you."

The two of them tried staring the other down. A long moment passed before Drew finally lowered his head and looked away. "Just give me a second," he said, voice dropping.

"Take a minute if you need it," Ben said magnanimously.

I wanted to feel surprised, but I didn't. Not really. "I get it," I said softly. "It's fine." I didn't blame him. This wasn't his fight, and I was surprised he'd stuck around as long as he had.

Drew peeled himself out of the shirt he was wearing and handed it to me. It was already soaked through, so the timing didn't make a whole lot of sense. Also, it weighed like twenty pounds. "You … want me to have your shirt?" I asked. As parting gifts went, it defied understanding. When a guy gave someone their letter jacket, it had a meaning. But what did a blue henley imply? Was it a promise to go steady at the local Old Navy?

He rolled his eyes. "Just hold onto it." And then he turned back to his father. "Someone bought that shirt for me, I don't want it to get ruined. You're going to beat the shit out of me? You'd better get started." Like it was any other bully on the playground, Drew started stalking towards his father, hands clenched into fists. "But just to warn you, Mom dated a lot of assholes while I was growing up. I know how to take a beating."

Ben's face darkened.

"She said Jason was better in bed than you, too. In the interest of fatherly loyalty and all."

As much as the idea of Jason having a sex life made me want to cringe, the low blow caught me off guard and I barked out a laugh. This definitely wasn't the time for laughing, but that was Drew. Always getting an inappropriate reaction out of me.

I'd seen Drew fight demons before, shifting between animal forms from one second to the next, capitalizing on the strengths of one even as he shifted into another. I'd never actually seen him go for a straight-up fight in his human form, though.

And I definitely had never seen him get his ass kicked so easily.

Drew was fast, but his father was faster. Every lunge, every jab, every attempt at offense was easily and effortlessly dismantled. It wasn't like the last time I'd seen Ben, when he'd gone out of his way to make it as painful as possible. With Drew, Ben showed mercy, but it didn't strike me as any sort of fatherly concern. The smirk on his face only got wider the more Drew tried, and failed, to even get a single hit in.

Drew dropped to the ground, a busted lip smearing red all down his chin. Ben stood over him, dead eyes as disturbing as any demon's, and grabbed his hand. He snapped Drew's index finger like it was a butterfly's wing, his eyes eagerly watching the reaction in his son. Drew tried not to howl, choking off his yell almost as soon as it started, but he didn't have enough in him to pull away.

"Stop it," I demanded, running forward. Ben looked over at me, and without breaking my gaze, proceded to snap another finger, like a child slowly and deliberately disobeying. Or like a cat continuing to scratch at the walls even after being yelled at. Staring, and dragging claws against the wall slowly and insolently. The unspoken "fuck you" was obvious. Ben didn't take orders from me, and if he had to beat his kid bloody to prove it to me, he would. And stare at me with those blank, empty eyes as he did it.

"He'll heal." Ben offered, staring down at his son. "That's part of the fun. You can decimate him all afternoon, let him shift a few times, and he's nearly as good as new. Then you can start all over again."

"He's your son! Doesn't that matter to you?"

Ben looked down at the body lying there in front of him. Still, there wasn't the slightest bit of remorse on his face. There wasn't anything human in it at all. He shrugged, smirking. "Not really, no." Ben raised his hand, again, and I ran for him.

Stupid move. Stupid, *stupid,* move. I went flying back before I even got close to him. I flipped, and rolled, and somewhere along the way, I slammed into the concrete base of one of the parking lot lights, right against my kidneys. I cried out, grabbing at my back once I finally stopped moving. It was like a sharp knife to the organ, but it lessened just a bit every time I took a breath. I just had to wait it out.

"I still have your blood," he said, jiggling a little vial in front of me.

"Just let him get it off his chest," Drew said weakly, from a few feet away. He turned his head and looked at me, though for once he didn't try to immediately get back up. "He hits like a girl anyway." Drew raised his voice, "Right, *Mom*?"

"You have some mouth on you," Ben said, his face screwed up in the kind of hatred and loathing I'd come to expect from demons, but not someone that used to be human. Then again, Hannah the princess Barbie bus-pusher had been a sociopath, too. Maybe that was why Grace had chosen them.

The wind died to a crawl and the storm let up in stages until it was nothing but rogue drops of rain escaping the sky.

"Bennett Amadeus Armstrong!" Trey's voice rang out from behind me. He strode across the parking lot like he was the biggest badass in the state, an undercurrent in his voice causing goosebumps to break out on my arms. *Trey was here?*

The first step in banishing a ghost was to invoke his or her name. The name was important, because knowing something's name gave you power over it. But only a witch could banish a ghost—and Trey might have had it in his blood, but he'd never been trained to use it. So what was he thinking?

I met Drew's eyes from across the lot. "Amadeus?" we mouthed at each other. At Trey's intrusion, Ben had let his attention be dragged away from his son. When he started walking towards Trey, I began inching towards Drew.

Ben went silently still, but it only lasted a moment. A

fleeting glimpse of surprise flickered across his face, like he couldn't believe what had just happened. *Something's wrong. What's Trey trying to prove?*

"That's not my name," Ben said, his smile widening as his body relaxed. "Next time, double-check your sources."

"Only Trey would come to the rescue with the *wrong goddamn name*," Drew snarled into the grass, beating his fist into the dirt.

It was almost funny. But then I remembered that Ben was a sociopath and I was probably going to die. So it became even *funnier.*

Trey looked down at me, annoyed. The hysterical laughter probably wasn't helping. "Of course it's not his middle name, but it got your attention, didn't it?" The other two were silent for a moment, and I only started laughing harder once I realized that *Trey had made a joke.*

Trey came to the rescue with the wrong goddamn name, and he only did it to be a dick. It was like Drew, Trey, and I had somehow started sharing one single sense of humor, and it was obnoxious, irritating, and absolutely fucking hysterical.

"Bennett Andrew Armstrong," Trey said, more formally this time. The reaction in Ben was immediate. His head *whipped* around to stare at Trey, and there was fear in his eyes. My laughter died out like a bike skidding to a stop. A few laughs still escaped, but they were humorless bubbles sneaking out minutes too late. *Something* was wrong.

The goosebumps I had had before were a full-fledged panic attack surging through my body like a lightning storm.

Normal people can't banish ghosts, I thought. *And Trey isn't a witch.* And yet, when Trey held out his hand and a pair of golden flames sprang into existence above his palm, I wasn't surprised. The flames hovered there, reflecting in his eyes so that it looked as though his eyes were glowing much like mine had.

He didn't go through the ritual the way Elle did. He didn't do *anything* like she did. The air pressure compacted into a dome around us, careening in so quickly that my ears popped. A low rumble started to build in Drew's chest, and his lips peeled in a growl.

My teeth rattled, and I was pretty sure the filling I'd gotten when I was fifteen was about to unfill itself right out of my mouth. The wind was a howl, an angry mistress that writhed and struggled against Trey's will, but still did as she was commanded. Overcast skies turned dark with angry intent, a crackle and rumble of thunder preceding a new storm.

The sky ignited into lightning and a blinding sheet of water that instantly washed out the world outside the dome. Beneath us, the ground shook just enough for the loose gravel to shimmy and shake like Mexican jumping beans. My skin was electric, an entire menagerie of goosebumps swarming over my skin until I could feel each individual hair on my body stand at attention.

Trey was using magic, and he was like a pro.

"I banish you." Three words. Three simple words, and the world rushed to obey. I felt a tightening in my chest, a compression and familiarity of something that had once been second nature. I could *feel* it in the air. Maybe for the first time since the lighthouse. Magic. A *lot* of magic.

This wasn't ordinary power. And it wasn't the kind of power a boy like Trey could have harnessed in an afternoon. My mind cataloged all the signs, even though I already knew what it all meant. I saw the pieces laid out in front of me, and no matter how much I didn't want to acknowledge what was happening, more evidence became filed away.

Trey had magic. Trey had a *lot* of magic, maybe more than me. And what was more important, he had the kind of control that Jason and Catherine did—control that came with decades of effort. I couldn't have handled it. Every time I tried before nearly killed me. But Trey was *glowing*. Not literally, but it was like the magic was feeding him and in some way that he'd always been malnourished, but now he was whole. The one glaring imperfection had been smoothed away and now he was complete and *right*.

Ben was trying to speak, his mouth kept opening but either the wind stole his words or he was fading so fast from the world that his voice was the first to go. He started to flicker the same way that Hannah had, but in Ben's case the flickering came fast, like a flashlight rapidly being clicked on and off. On, off, on off, on off.

Faster and faster, flickering. Real. Faded. Transparent. The wind shrieked. The ground vibrated. There were tears in my eyes. I felt like if I reached out, I could touch the magic. Feel it against my fingertips.

Even in that perfect moment, when I could almost pretend that I was whole again, a deep and creeping fear had taken root inside of me, and it worked its way through every part of me until my hands were shaking, I was sweating, I couldn't catch my breath, and my mind was going a hundred miles a minute.

The dust settled and the wind died. I stared at Trey in horror. I knew what he had done. I *knew* where this power had come from.

"No," I said, shaking my head. "You wouldn't... This isn't happening." It had to be wrong. I *wanted* it to be wrong more than I'd wanted anything before. It was just a mistake, an accident that the universe would fix at any moment. Because Trey hadn't... he couldn't...

At John's wake, Lucien had come up to him. "You and I should get together. We have something to discuss."

Trey went to Jason for help. Then came to me. He let the subject drop when I refused to teach him. Didn't push, even though that was completely unlike Trey. Accepted that there was nothing he could do. Even though that was completely unlike Trey, to just let something go like that.

Treyaskedademonforhelp.

"We both knew he was going to come after you again," Trey said, without a hint of remorse. "I did what I had to."

"What did you do?" I screamed. I went to shove at him, but he grabbed my hands before I could and held me by the wrists. I twisted, shoved, tried anything to free myself but Trey wouldn't let go. Rage kept me in motion, kept me pushing. Trey was impassive, resigned with the choices that he'd made. But he didn't look sorry. Not even a little bit.

"You already know."

I struggled and fought, but Trey refused to let go. "What the fuck is wrong with you?" I couldn't see straight, my vision was a constantly jerking haze of red and black. "How could you—"

"How could I?" he asked sharply. "Don't be naive. I knew what I was doing. I know what I've done."

"You struck a bargain with a demon! They're the only ones that could have given you that kind of power! Just... tell me it was Matthias. It was Matthias, it had to be... " I trailed off at Trey's stony silence, the way his eyes dropped down.

The fight drained out of me like poison from a wound. "There's a loophole, there's got to be a loophole." Lucien wouldn't make a contract without several different ways to screw Trey over. But there was always a way out. *But you don't have anything he wants anymore,* the practical part of my mind pointed out. A month ago, Lucien would have done anything to get me to do what he wanted. *But why would Lucien make this bargain? Why now?*

"Power has its price," Trey said, his hands sliding up my arms. "I knew what I was going to have to pay. It's okay."

"It's not! Why would you even say that?" In the last few weeks, I'd felt weak and broken many times. I'd been determined to get my feet back under me and figure out a way to survive. But this... this was something else. There wasn't any coming back from a demon's contract. Trey had signed on the dotted line. He was Lucien's now, and Lucien got to set the terms.

I don't know if I can deal with this. Why would he do that?

Why would he sacrifice himself? For *me.*

I bent over and heaved, needing to suddenly vomit out everything that was churning in my stomach. But I heaved, and I heaved, and nothing came out. My face burned, tears leaked out of the sides of my eyes, and once I started, I couldn't seem to stop. I just kept trying to expel it all.

It took some time, but I finally pulled myself back under control. I sat there, curled up into a ball, my head on my knees and I breathed. Slow, deep breaths, shaky and closer to gasps sometimes, but soon I got close enough to fake it. Trey had his arm over me, and his head pressed against the back of mine, shielding me as best he could.

With my newfound calm, I tried to put things into order. First, Trey had sold his soul to Lucien. Second, Trey was the biggest moron known to man. Third, no really, the *biggest moron known to man.* There would be documentaries and feature films starring guys not nearly as hot as Trey.

Fourth, I had to find out a way to get him out of it. Because I couldn't let him do all of this... because of me. That wasn't the way we worked. Or at least that shouldn't be.

I stood up, but I didn't completely break away from

Trey. He touched my hands, my face, like he wouldn't believe I was okay until he actually felt for himself. It was nice, but unnecessary. I wanted to be mad. I wanted to be so mad. But all I could do was wrap my arms around him and pull myself up into him.

"Hey, you're okay," he said, like *he* needed to be consoling *me* right now!

"No really," a caustic voice interrupted from behind us, "I'm fine. Don't trouble yourselves." Drew's body could have been sculpted by Michelangelo, with all the perfect little curves of muscle and cuts of bone. But in that moment, I barely noticed. I just held on to Trey and tried to think my way out of what he'd done.

Later, I was going to be furious. But right now I was too busy feeling relieved to hold on to much of anything else.

"Oh, his shirt," I mumbled, finally pulling away from Trey. Drew's shirt was still in my hand.

"Hey, that's..." Trey said, looking down at the shirt with a quizzical look.

"Drew's shirt," I supplied, but that didn't ease the confusion on his face. I shrugged and walked it over to Drew, who just like he said was fine now. He was dirty, like he'd rolled around in the grass a few times, but otherwise there wasn't a mark on him. Trey came up behind me, slid his arms around my waist. I know it was a clear sign of staking a claim or something, but Drew didn't rise to the bait.

The Shifter rolled the henley up and squeezed the last

little drips of water out. A side effect of whatever Trey had done—the three of us were almost completely dry. All the water from the storm had evaporated inside the dome. Drew pulled the shirt back on, and managed to do so without a single sexist remark. "Wow," I said, and Trey's arms tightened around me, but Drew's abs of doom weren't what I was wowing.

"So my dad's a total psycho," he offered a few moments later, his tone dismissive. "That just makes me one of the cool kids. Everyone in Belle Dam's got a fucked-up family tree. Psycho dad is probably a step up from plain old dead dad."

"Drew—" But he held up a hand before I could continue.

"Your turn to play chauffeur. I've suddenly come down with a need to go raid that legendary Thorpe liquor cabinet." Drew nodded at me once and then headed for his bike. Trey and I watched him go, and waited until he pulled out of the harbor parking lot before we moved again.

Trey spoke first. "Do you think he's going to be okay?" I shook my head, unsure. I pulled away from him, sliding in to his side and wrapping my arm around his waist.

"You always do that," he chuckled.

"Do what?"

Trey shrugged. "Nothing, I just thought it was funny."

"*What* was funny?"

"You're always," he struggled to find the words, "jockeying for position. You don't like to be touched unless you're the one doing the touching. If I grab your hand," he made a point of pulling away long enough to take my hand, "you'll let go, then take my hand again."

Did I do that? Maybe. It was hard to say. Just to prove a point, I didn't let go of Trey's hand, even though I definitely felt a little uncomfortable. *It was just because Trey called attention to it,* I told myself. *I don't really do that.*

"We should get you home," Trey said, looking towards his car. He'd parked on the street, I was surprised no one had hit him yet. "Before anything else happens."

"Let's go somewhere," I said suddenly. "Just us."

He laughed like he thought I was kidding. When I didn't laugh too, he turned to look at me, his expression heavy. "Like where?"

sixteen

By the time Trey caught up to me, I was already climbing into the passenger seat of his truck. "You're serious," he said flatly. "What's going on, Braden?"

"I don't *know*!" I snapped. "I just... I don't want to go home. Can we just go somewhere? Or are you going to keep making this difficult?"

"We need to talk—"

"No! We're not talking about it. As far as I'm concerned, it didn't happen. Not for the next few hours. I... can't. I just can't." Right now, the idea of Lucien having his hands all over Trey's future made me want to go catatonic, vomit, and scream until I lost my voice. Probably all at the same time.

He didn't say anything else, and a chilly silence crept into the car with us as Trey drove. I leaned my head against the glass, letting the chill seep into my skin. Too much kept happening, and the better I thought I was getting at dealing with new blows, the faster and harder the next set came. I couldn't keep up.

My heart started racing, and I couldn't seem to catch my breath. A couple of times I went to take a breath and it was like I just … couldn't. Like my lungs had forgotten how to inflate. Like there wasn't enough oxygen in the world to make the next breath okay.

Trey gripped his hand against my knee, and I flinched so hard I slammed my head against the window in an effort to get away.

"Pull over." My eyes were blurring and the world had gone askew, but I felt it when he took his foot off the gas. My head throbbed, and the panic subsided by degrees, but each of those things was only a distraction. I might have been the passenger in a car someone else was driving, but I was still running.

And it was time to stop.

"He's not going to kill me," Trey said once he'd pulled the car over to the berm and cut the engine. "I got it in writing."

"He won't." The brief wash of relief through my veins only cleared the way for a fresher, darker hell. Because if Lucien wasn't going to kill him, he was going to do something even worse. Something unforgivable. "He's going to drain you," I said slowly, pulling away, my voice wooden and flat. "He's going to leave you the same way he leaves all of them. With an empty future."

"But alive," Trey said, trying to make it sound lighter than it should. "So I don't become the businessman I figured I'd be some day. So what? I don't save the world. I don't win the lottery." His smile was sad, but selfless. "You'll be able to do those things. I made sure of it. That's the other part of our deal. He can't hurt you, either."

I couldn't handle this. Trey had sold himself to Lucien. I needed air.

"We should talk about this," Trey said.

"I don't really feel like it," I sneered. "Why not go talk to Lucien about it? But then I'm sure he already knows what a completely idiotic ass-bag you are."

"Do you want to hear my side or not?" His fingers traced the lines of the steering wheel, but he didn't make a move to cross the aisle again.

"I—I can't," I said quickly, and threw the door open. It took me a second to remember how to undo my seat belt before I slid out. Coming back out into the cold was bracing but welcome. I couldn't trust myself to speak more than that. I couldn't decide *how* I felt right now. I was frustrated, desperate, fuming, terrified, depressed, fatalistic, and on the verge of tears. But none of that was going to help me right now.

Trey came around the front of the truck, resting his hand on the hood.

"I want to punch you," I admitted. "And if you really understood what you've done, you'd punch yourself, too."

But Trey wasn't so easily swayed. "You were going to die," he said calmly. "Bennett won. Game over. Lucien may hate your guts but he needs you alive. So we made a deal."

"So Lucien showed up with a convenient threat and

suddenly you're on board?" I slapped my hand down on the truck, and *damn* that was a bad idea. I winced, cradling my hand against my chest. But the pain only made the anger that much stronger. "Why the hell would you trust him? He *lies*. It's what he does."

"Do you think that I don't know that?" Trey's jaw tightened. "But this way I can help you. I can keep you safe."

"You're giving Lucien exactly what he wants. Control over you. God, have you always been this stupid and I missed it?"

"Better that I pay that price than you," Trey continued. "You keep trying to sacrifice yourself for everyone around you. You think I don't know that? You wound up in the hospital because of me. If I hadn't followed you through the portal that night, maybe you'd have been able to save your uncle. You lost everything that night." He looked down at his hands. "And I was just happy that you were alive. I know that's selfish, and stupid, but it's true."

"*You sold your soul, you absolute fucking moron!*" I screamed, my voice deafening in the night.

"I knew what I was doing," he snapped.

"Really? Because if it acts fucking stupid like an idiot, walks into danger like an idiot, and tries to be so fucking noble like an idiot, it's probably an idiot. The king of idiots." No, there were not tears in my eyes. I refused to cry over this . . . this . . . .jackass.

"Braden—!"

"I get it, you want to talk! But I can't do this. Especially not right now. And fuck you for doing this to me. Do you know what it's going to be like, knowing that the reason you got turned into a drooling jackass is because of me?"

"I'll still be *me,*" he said in his stubborn voice.

"You'll be *less.* That's the point. You won't be *Trey* anymore. You'll become the smallest, most insignificant version of yourself. That's what happens. That's why you should know better than to strike a deal with the devil."

"And I'd do it again." Trey's body was shaking in anger, and I swear for a moment I could see the air rippling around him. "Do you think that tonight was it? Do you really think you'll be safe for the rest of your life? This wasn't about *tonight,* Braden. It's about tomorrow, and the day after. And the year after that."

I turned around and walked to the end of the truck, just to give my feet something to do. Because right now all they wanted to do was kick Trey in his stupid, fat head.

"You're not going out there by yourself," he said, and it was like the starting shot at a race, because I whipped around and ran full speed at him, not stopping until we were nose to nose.

"No," I said sharply, "you don't get to make any decisions. Not anymore. Because you can't be trusted not to be a *stupid fucking asshole.* So we're done with that, and I'll figure out how to fix this."

"Don't you get it? I don't *want* you to fix this. Lucien can't go after you. I got it in writing."

"I DON'T NEED YOU TO PROTECT ME!" I screamed so loud they probably heard me in Maine. "I've never needed you to protect me. You're not my knight in shining armor. I thought you got that!"

He crossed his arms in front of himself, closing ranks against what I was saying. "I'm not going to apologize for what I did."

"You are the most frustrating, arrogant—"

What I had been about to say was interrupted by Trey crossing the small chasm between us, and simultaneously grabbing the front of my shirt and pulling me towards him. His hand slid under my jaw, tilting my mouth upwards, even as I was berating him, his lips captured mine and claimed my anger as their spoils of war.

Because it was a war. Our hands vied for position, bodies shifting, limbs blocking the way, fingers tangling in hair, in cloth, against skin. Trey kissed me like it was the last time, and I kissed him like it was the first time again and again.

And I wanted to hate him. I really, really did.

But I cared about the ass-bag.

¤   ¤   ¤

One of the public beaches passed us by. Trey had driven us through the rest of town and was heading past the turnoff for his own house. But he didn't slow down and instead kept following the road south, away from the water and from Belle Dam itself.

Just as signs for the highway started cropping up, Trey turned onto a dirt road that was nearly invisible in the twilight. I didn't ask any more questions, since it was clear he knew where was taking us. I took the opportunity to watch the scenery and pretend today had been anything other than what it was.

When we pulled up in front of a cabin, almost completely swallowed up in the trees, I hesitated for a second. It had a certain "this is where the serial killer hides the bodies" quality to it. The sun was setting and the wooden structure was crime-scene dark. There was barely a five-foot gap between the house and the woods. A recently escaped mental patient could appear at any time.

"Relax," Trey said, climbing out of the car. "It's perfectly safe." He walked around the car and opened my door for me. "I come down here when I need to decompress."

"Or when you don't want anyone to hear the screams," I muttered under my breath.

"Dirty," Trey said, flashing me a full-wattage smile. "Come on, the temperature's dropping. It's going to be freezing tonight."

He was right. A cold front had followed the storm in, and it was at least twenty degrees colder now. Neither one of us was dressed for this, and the sun hadn't even fully set yet. Trey slung an arm around my shoulder and led me up to the door. He pulled a key from his key ring, prompting a raised eyebrow from me, and led me inside.

The first thing I realized once he started turning on lights was how messy the place was. I'm not the picture of a perfectly clean anything, but I'm not entirely a slob. Trey, on the other hand, didn't seem to fit that mold. There was a collection of shirts tossed over the back of the barstools lining a breakfast bar, the kitchen table was covered in papers and books, and a small stack of bowls filled the sink.

"How long have you been staying here?" I asked, biting down on my lip. I'd been apprehensive just seeing what the place looked like, for some reason seeing that Trey was actually *staying* here made my stomach start doing somersaults.

"Ever since ... " he trailed off, and then his voice hardened. "Ever since."

Jade had said he hadn't been home since that night. I guess she hadn't been lying. I shuffled a stack of papers so they were more in order. Trey looked from me to the mess and back again. A faint blush started creeping up on his cheeks and he took the papers out of my hands and started to do it himself. "You said you wanted to get away. If I'd known, I would have ... "

He's nervous. It was almost cute. I let him take a few minutes to try and clean up, staying out of the way. I certainly wasn't about to *help*. Besides, seeing Trey struggling with uncertainty made me forget for a time that our lives weren't normal.

I built a fantasy world while he cleaned his real one. A world where John and I had moved back to Belle Dam, and there were no such things as witches, and Trey and I could just be ... Trey and I. No lawyers, no curses, no lighthouses. A world without a feud.

He'd probably take me on a date to the beach, and when it started raining just as we got there, he'd just laugh to him-

self. Then instead of a picnic on the sand, we'd eat in the car, each taking turns to find the most ridiculous songs on his mp3 player and listen to them. Jade would probably text us about a hundred times each, furious that we weren't giving her the play-by-play as it happened. And then at the end of the night, he'd drop me off at home and insist on walking me to the door, and Jason wouldn't even pretend not to be waiting up. And since Jason would ruin the moment at the end of the night, the next time I saw Trey, he'd offer me a handful full of chocolate kisses, because he didn't want to miss out on it again, and then he'd smile and say—

"You're sitting on my shirt."

I slid off the barstool I'd sat down at, and avoided his eyes, a little blush of my own coming on. "Sorry," I said, but my voice was a little rusty.

"There," he said, relieved, once he'd grabbed the shirt and stuffed onto what was a laundry basket crammed full of clothing. "Come on," he said, avoiding my eyes. "This isn't even what I wanted to show you."

"Not your dirty laundry?" I teased. "Because I do declare, Gentry Lansing, that I'm positively shocked. Waving around your unmentionables. I'm an impressionable young boy!"

He shot me a level-eyed look that nearly wiped the smile from my lips. And it reminded me, in an instant, that if Trey was staying here, then his bed was here. Trey's bed. A bed with Trey in it. Suddenly, I was back to nervous again. *Tell him you need to go. Make up an excuse.* But try as

I might, I couldn't think of anything. Nothing plausible. Trey would see through anything I said.

It wasn't the first time I'd thought about sex, or more specifically sex with Trey. But the problem wasn't so much about whether or not I wanted to have sex with Trey. I was more concerned with not wanting to have sex with Trey and have it be *bad*. I mean, he was most likely not a virgin. He'd done this before. And he'd know in an instant that I couldn't say the same.

"Come on, moron," he said affectionately, tugging on my arm. It was hard to say whether he'd seen the look of panic on my face, and decided to distract me, or if he just hadn't noticed. "You haven't even see the fireplace yet."

He pulled me towards the back of the cabin, waffling his fingers with mine. The log cabin vibe of the house reminded me of Montana, and the house that John and I had lived in. That was as perfect a distraction as anything else I could think of. Nerves and anxiety were dwarfed by equal parts of nostalgia and regret.

"I grew up in a house like this," I said softly.

Trey squeezed my hand, showing he was listening. The cabin wasn't huge, but the kitchen and the living room took up a majority of the floor space. I could understand the kitchen—it was set up to entertain. And the same for the living room, and the fireplace that dominated the corner.

The first time I'd set foot in the kitchen at the Lansing home, I'd been caught off guard by the culture shock. I expected a woman like Catherine to have a kitchen that looked like it could double as a torture chamber, and instead I'd gotten Martha Stewart. Which was still a bit of a torture chamber, but I had the feeling that Martha did that a lot more than Catherine did.

But the fireplace in the cabin, that was exactly what I would have expected. It was a fitted structure of dark old stones and slate, and I wouldn't have been surprised to see a few human skulls wedged in there for atmosphere. The rounded interior of the fireplace was an almost solid black, also serving as the stunt double for a portal to Hell. There was even an iron bar running along the top of the interior where Catherine could hang her cauldron while brewing up a batch full of poison.

"I take it back; you would plan a terrible first date," I said, almost laughing.

"What?"

I remembered that none of the first date stuff had been out loud. Trey was watching me, his eyes on mine. It was a lot easier to deflect when I wore sunglasses. Not for the first time, I missed them. He was looking at me like he expected an explanation, but I just shook my head.

"I thought we could hang out here for a while, watch the fire." There was something wistful in his tone. *He might not have many of these,* I realized. Memories. Or nights where anything could happen. Tonight Trey had banished a ghost. Who knew what tomorrow would bring?

"Do you even know how to start a fire?" I asked with a

smirk. I dropped down onto one of the couches, acting as though I couldn't be bothered.

That was just the opening Trey had been waiting for. He sat down next to me, and pulled himself up along my back. "You're easy to please, aren't you?" he asked, as he flicked his wrist towards the fire. Of course he'd want to show off a little. Trey's power was still new to him, like a gift he'd forgotten he'd been given, and he was proud. And I knew I should be mad, but I just couldn't deal with it right now. Sitting on the couch, with his arms around me and his forehead pressed against my neck, was all I could handle. All I wanted to.

Just one night, that's all I need.

I seriously expected Lucien to storm in through the front door at any moment. Nervous tension kept me on edge, but the longer we lay on the couch, quietly talking, the more I started to relax. By unspoken agreement, we didn't talk about anything important—our conversation ranged from places we wanted to see one day, favorite movies, and all the things that we probably should have known about each other by now. Sometimes I turned into him, or he into me, and the kisses that replaced conversation were just as slow and calm. For all my worries, nothing felt pressured.

SEVENTEEN

Hours passed, and the fire started to dwindle down. "I should get you home," Trey said, running his nose along my cheek.

Leaving the house would break the spell and bring it all back. I played with his fingers, splaying his hand out and tracing all the different lines on his hand. "This was perfect," I said quietly. I was afraid that if my voice carried, if the world heard me admitting that I'd had a nice time, something would happen to ruin it.

He put out the fire the same way he started it, with a little magic. It was interesting to see him work, because it wasn't just the knowledge that Lucien had given him, but it was also a bit of practical application as well. It wasn't enough to just put out the fire, which Trey willed away with very little effort. The ashes and embers were still going. I watched his face narrow in concentration as he held out a hand over the metal pan of old ashes next to the fireplace. He transferred the heat out of the embers and into the ashes, and then carefully carried the container outside. As he tossed the ashes into the air, he focused again and a wave of warmth swept out as the air was heated quickly.

It wasn't just how to make magic work that he'd learned, but the principles to apply, like how to transfer energy from one source to another. It was like he'd downloaded a lifetime of knowledge in just a few minutes. Whatever the terms of the bargain, Trey hadn't gotten screwed on the basics. At least not yet.

On the drive back we were both quiet. We both knew that reality waited on the other side of tonight. "Thanks for saving me," I finally said, once Trey pulled into Jason's driveway.

"Don't be stupid," he said, offering me a slow smile. His expression changed as we reached the house, though. There was a car in the driveway, a car I recognized.

"Is that ... Jade's?"

Trey looked at the clock in the truck's console. "It's almost midnight. What's she doing here?"

We were both thinking the worst by the time Trey cut the ignition and we hurried into the house. "She's upstairs," Jason called out from the kitchen as we walked down the hallway. I detoured us towards him, though I didn't fully walk inside.

"You decided to stay," Jason said, an unusual frown on his face. *He thought I would go, and I surprised him by staying.*

"FYI, your brother-in-law is a dick," I said, letting that be the end of it.

Jason recovered quickly, I'll give him that. There was only a moment of frustration and worry on his face before he regained his composure. "If I'd known I was running a home for runaway Lansings, I could have applied for a tax credit," he said, trying so hard to be casual as he sipped his coffee. He eyed the two of us, but thankfully I was spared the awkward moment of having my father and boyfriend try to make small talk.

"Is she okay?" Trey asked.

"I think she just needed a friend," Jason replied, a hint of reproach in his tone. "She said something about no one answering her calls."

Trey looked at me with guilt in his eyes. He'd turned both of our phones off in the truck on the way out of town. I hadn't thought to turn mine back on. Clearly neither had he.

"I take it you asked Gentry to take the ferry with you?" Jason asked. Skirting the issue about why I'd decided to stay, I noticed.

"That happened later," I said quickly, distracted. "Bennett Armstrong." The name caused Jason's head to snap up fast enough that he could have whiplash. "Was he always a total psycho? Because he's one sadistic box of crazy now."

"What happened?" Jason's face went smooth and blank, even though I could see the calculating ferocity behind his eyes. Trying to figure out what had happened, how he could handle it. How the feud was involved.

"Someone brought his ghost back," I explained. "Not sure why. But he decided revenge was a better option. He tried to kill me, and when Drew got in the way, he started torturing him."

"He hurt his *son*?" Jason's tone was venomous and sharp. Interesting. There were lines that even Jason thought were too abhorrent to cross. "Is he okay?"

"I think so," I said, awkwardly shrugging my shoulders. "He didn't want to talk and I wasn't going to push. His dad was like ... seriously disturbed. I don't know if that was a Bennett thing or a ghost thing. But he was enjoying himself way too much."

"You should have told someone!" Jason yelled, looking between the two of us before deciding to turn his rage on Trey. "You just let him wander off with you? Where I— where *no one* knew where he was? Anything could have happened to the two of you. What if Bennett had come back to finish what he started? What then?"

"Bennett's gone," Trey said, in a cold tone. "He's not coming back."

"But there will always be an Armstrong in Belle Dam," Jason said, his expression sour. "I should have known better—"

"Don't blame Drew for what his father did," I interjected quickly, failing to stamp down on my fury. "You of all people don't get to do that." There was too much on my head already for the things that Jason had done.

"You told me he said that before," Trey said, trying to be both the voice of reason, and a distraction. "'Always an Armstrong in Belle Dam.' I've never heard that before."

"Old family legends," Jason said, waving it away. "Most people have forgotten them by now. But the important thing is tracking down where Bennett's gone to lick his wounds. Something summoned with magic can only—"

"—be sent back by magic," I interrupted. "This isn't my first day." I debated how much to tell Jason, but figured he needed to know at least some of it. "Trey sent him back."

Jason scoffed, but I stepped between them before tempers could flare any worse. "Trey protected me. It's fine. Besides, I walked away with just a couple of bruises. Way better than the last time." The words were out of my mouth before the klaxons could go off in my head. All it took was the look on Jason's face as he processed *"the last time."* I hadn't told him about any of it. At the time, it had seemed easier. But now, the look on Jason's face had me second-guessing that.

It was like there was a great, pressing weight on him that was invisible to the eye but crushing him nonetheless. In all the time I'd known Jason, I'd seen him with mask after mask, feigning emotions and saying only what people wanted to hear. And seeing him like this now, looking broken and completely out of his depth, I felt more shame than I'd ever felt before in my life.

"You're never going to trust me, are you?" he whispered, and the knife inside me twisted just a little bit deeper. It wasn't a question. Not really.

"Jason … " I said, but he got up from the table and calmly walked from the room. I remembered the first few weeks living here, the way that Jason would walk out of the room in the middle of our conversation. It hurt to think that we'd slid back to that place. But I couldn't change who I was.

I watched the hallway he'd left through for a long time, wishing that somehow things could be different. Maybe Jason and I had gotten off on the wrong foot, and maybe he wasn't the heartless monster I'd assumed him to be, but...that still didn't mean I could be the kind of kid he deserved. He'd never be John. I'd never be the son he dreamed up in his head. No matter how many times I wished it.

I pasted a smile on my face and tried to pretend everything was alright. What was one more trauma? "Come on," I said to Trey, leading him through the house. When we came to my room, we found Jade curled up on my bed, already fast asleep.

Her short, caramel-brown hair was spread around her like a halo, and if I didn't know any better I would have expected that she'd arranged herself just like that so she'd look perfectly photogenic when we walked in.

"She almost looks sweet and innocent," Trey said, leaning against the door frame.

I bumped into his side. "She'd kick you in the balls if she heard you say that," I said, looking at her closer. "She looks tired. I've never seen the circles under her eyes before."

"So you want to let her sleep?" Trey's voice had gotten suddenly stiff. "In your bed? All night?" But even his weird bit of jealousy couldn't stop his eyes from curiously roaming over everything in my room, taking it all in.

"I'll sleep in one of the guest rooms," I said, trying to hide a smile. I closed my door quietly behind us and headed across the hall to one of the many spare rooms in the house.

Trey tried to stop at the door, again, and I dragged him in behind me. The beds were fully made, but I didn't know how often the sheets were changed, so the first thing I did was pull the comforter off and leave it in a puddle on the floor. I went into the closet, fairly sure there'd be a stack of blankets just like there was in my room. Jackpot. I pulled a couple of them out, and cracked the window.

"Okay, well," Trey started.

"Stay," I said. I looked up to see my own nerves expressed on his face, too. "Just until I fall asleep? Please?"

Trey gave me an inscrutable look, but he kicked off his shoes and closed the door behind us. He cut the lights, and I was thankful for the darkness as I started undressing. Trey sat at the edge and slid across, making room for me. It was surprisingly easy, jockeying for position on the bed. We moved with a comfort that I didn't expect, and when I laid my head down on his chest, Trey adjusted his arm so that it curled around behind me.

It wasn't until I started to unwind, until my body settled against the warmth of Trey's, and I could hear the low and steady beating of his heart through his chest that everything really started to hit me. I wouldn't cry—I refused to break down, but again, Trey reacted like he just *knew,* and tightened his arm around me.

"I'll be here until you fall asleep," he whispered, and it was the balm I needed. Everything started to slip away, and I fell asleep to his heartbeat.

"I own him now. And that means I own you, too." Lucien stood next to me, standing on the pier.

I don't want this, *I tried to say, but I lacked a voice. A mouth. There was a smooth lump in the front of my face where my lips should have been. My fingers were clay digits, thick and unwieldy. With every movement, I saw the flash of golden strings. In my wrists, my feet, my head.*

"I promised not to kill you. I promised not to torture you. But I never promised not to teach you the error of your ways," Lucien said with relish.

My head was pounding, a legion of winged creatures trying to burst through my skull. My shell was cracked, breaking apart. Everything I was had become something less, and now I was being torn apart by the pain, my skin split tore shredded screaming pain—

This wasn't a dream. This wasn't a nightmare.

My skin was filled with fire, sculpted by a thousand suns. There was light in my veins, and if I opened my mouth even a little, it would start to escape and then everything would be blind.

It was coming. I could feel it, breaking my bones in all the best ways. I screamed in triumph. I screamed in torment.

Eyes like molten fire twisting and violated claws scratching at your mind and rending apart your power savage like all

*bad things to boys who sin and sing melodies instead of dirges
because that's where traitors dwell in the spaces between holy
and hell angels spirited against rising tides and demons quake
below your rage this power that was yours, boy, was never really
yours only pillaged and stolen back now all of it mine mine
mineminemineMINEMINEMI—*

The screams woke me. My screams. I'd soaked through
the sheets, my body was dripping sweat like I'd spent the
month in a sauna, and worst of all, I was alone.

It took me precious seconds to catch my breath and
remember how I'd ended up here. Trey. The ghost. The
bargain. Jade. I closed my eyes and counted to a hundred.
Anything to focus on, to not think about what I was going
to do. By the time I left and headed back to *my* room, I'd
managed a good facsimile of control. It was a simple plan.
Figure out how to engineer a conversation with Grace.
Convince her to give me my powers back. Use those powers
to wipe the floor with Lucien. Get Trey out of his deal. Pray
that I survived.

Jade wasn't in my room anymore, and the bed was
made. *Maybe Trey woke her up before he left.* But she was in
the kitchen waiting for me, in a shirt that I recognized from
my own closet. She was alone, seated at the table in the same
seat Jason had been in last night. Lost in thought looking
out at the backyard, she didn't hear me come in until I made
a beeline for the coffee maker.

"Trey left already?" I don't know why I assumed he'd
stayed the night, but I did.

"Gentry was here?"

I nodded. "It was a Lansing slumber party, but I wasn't allowed to cuddle with you." I pretended to pout.

Jade laughed, tucking a stray strand of hair behind her ear. She pulled one of her legs up onto the chair, and hid half of her face behind her knee. "Sorry about falling asleep. I figured I'd just wait for you to get home, and then the next thing I knew it was morning."

"It's fine. Yesterday was ... a lot. We got back pretty late."

"And then Trey stayed the night?" Jade raised an eyebrow, but the look seemed fake somehow. Like she was just going through the motions.

I looked at her a little closer. The bags weren't as bad as they'd looked last night, but there was still something in her eyes. Worry. "Are you ... are you okay?" I asked.

Jade smiled and deflected the concern with ease. A roll of her shoulders, a short laugh, and she looked more like the Jade I'd known than ever before. "I'm untouchable," she said lightly, with a teasing tone. "So Trey stayed the night?"

I shook my head, trying not to blush. "Can you get ahold of Drew for me? I don't know if he'll pick up if I call." He'd been quick to go off and lick his wounds last night, and god only knew how long it was going to take before he calmed down.

The clatter of Jade's coffee cup yanked me out of my own head. Looking at me with terror, she quickly picked up the cup she must have knocked over. "I'm ... we don't talk. Why would I talk to him?"

I explained about Bennett, and everything that had happened last night. About how Drew had met his father for the first time, and it appeared that his dad had been a total sociopath.

"Wow," Jade said, some of the color returning to her face. She was still a little pale, though. "But why me?"

I shrugged. "Because he doesn't want to talk to me? And Riley *can't* talk to him. Maybe you could say something that would help. I don't know. I just don't like the idea of him wandering around the town like everything's fine while he's got this on his plate."

Jade twitched, a movement that turned into a nod. What was going on with her? She wasn't normally this scattered, or this freaked out. "Yeah," she said quickly. "I can do that. I should get going anyway. Sorry to crash your breakfast."

"Jade," I called, before she left the kitchen completely. "It's no big deal. If you want to stay for a couple of days, I'm sure Jason won't care too much."

"Catherine will, though," she said sadly. "And that's a headache no one wants."

I let her get changed in my room and then walked her to the door before she left. She hugged me, an impulsive, tight movement that nearly choked the air from my lungs. Whatever Jade was going through, she'd share when she was ready. I was sure of it.

But I started to put it together almost as soon as she

left. I walked into my bathroom, and it was just sitting there on the floor, right next to the trash container. I bent down, picking up the blue-and-white piece, not recognizing it immediately. The cardboard was a piece of a box that boasted "Know five days sooner than the leading brand." A pregnancy test.

Jade.

eighteen

"I told you I'd let you make your own decision," Jason said a couple of hours later when he walked into my room. I'd turned the cardboard piece over and over in my hands like I was a magician, and I was suddenly going to turn it into *not my problem*. "But you have no idea how hard it is not to knock you out and drive until we're on the wrong side of dawn. John did it once, it couldn't be that hard."

"He never escaped, though," I said. I slid the cardboard into the palm of my hand, and very carefully slid it under the pillow. The fact that Jade might be pregnant left me with a whole host of worries, and I couldn't put my finger on what exactly was the problem. Intuition was a fickle bitch sometimes. I knew it was a bad news, but I couldn't figure out why.

Jason stopped less than five feet from the door, and he looked around him awkwardly. I nearly smiled when I recognized the discomfort in his expression. He squared his shoulders when he was uncertain, and one corner of his mouth quirked up even as his lips pressed together.

"Lucien was always watching," I explained. "So were you," I added, waving a hand. "But it was always more than that. I've tried to figure out why John took the bargain with Lucien, why he agreed to undergo the *geas* and let Lucien into his head like that. Why *Lucien* would want that. Maybe keeping me in the dark was a victory, but he never won a victory when he could win two." I scratched my leg, suddenly aware of Jason's eyes on mine. The heavy look that increased the pressure in the room a thousandfold. I don't think I've ever had his undivided attention before. "Lucien wanted a window into John's head. And the *geas* was the perfect way. No matter how far he'd gone, Lucien could find him."

"That is … very astute," Jason said, and it was so grudging and uncomfortable that it made him sound so much like his brother. A sound I thought I'd never hear again.

Neither one of us knew what to say, it was obvious. I knew we were building up to something, but I wasn't sure what. So I took a moment and looked at him. Really *looked* at my father. The first time we'd met, all I'd seen was the arrogant warlock businessman. Then later in the hospital, things had been awkward and uncertain, and boundaries were just starting to change. Until I came back to this house, and the walls slammed up again. It was easier for Jason to hold me at arm's length. It was easier not to feel anything, and so he tried.

But somewhere along the way, he'd changed again. Or

maybe I'd changed, and he'd been forced to follow suit. And now, no matter how hard he tried, he couldn't get the doors closed fast enough. And I was starved for every scrap of knowledge I could pry out of him.

"You are the most headstrong little shit I've ever met," Jason sighed, lowering himself down into my desk chair. "Nothing like me at all. I was too busy trying to be perfect. You're more like him than you know. Jonathan, I mean. He was impulsive, and reactionary." It *sounded* like a compliment, but it was coming from Jason, so understandably it took me a few minutes to process.

It took him a long time to look me in the eyes again. "Tell me what you're planning. I can help you, Braden. You don't have to do this by yourself."

There was a chess set on a tiny table in the corner of my room near the window. I didn't know if it had always been in the room or if someone had just assumed I'd play and put it in there for me. Either way, I hadn't had much use for it before. But now I dragged it over by the window seat and started setting up the pieces. The set was old, carved out of wood, and polished by countless generations of Thorpe boys no doubt. What better introduction to the feud that would be their livelihood than the civilized game of kings?

"Do you remember right after we first met? When we had lunch at the place across from the high school?" I asked, as I began to methodically set up the pieces on the board. John had taught me to play years ago, but my skills had always been rusty.

It helped me to think, and it reminded me of Riley. She'd talked about a Bishop in Black's house . . . *Matthias*. *What if it really was as simple as a chess game? Make a move, anticipate their reactions.* It sounded easy in theory, but probably not in practice.

"Yes," he said cautiously, like I was leading him into a trap.

Which I was. Sort of. "You told me how you and Catherine had been friends once. How you went searching for Grace Lansing's treasure. Did I ever tell you what it was?"

Jason didn't bother responding. He waited. But I had his complete attention.

"It's the power that she stole from Lucien. She ripped it out of him, trapped him in this town, and then I think she expected to come back for it later. Only that didn't happen. But that's not the important part." I let a silence build between us, pretending to feel the anticipation that was clearly going to annoy Jason so badly until he—

"Braden! Just get to the point."

"I know where they are. There's still two wellsprings left." And now with some distance from the situation, I knew what the butterflies in my chest had always been. Someone had accessed my power, and they were trying to use it to open the wellsprings and claim the power. That they had to keep trying—that Grace had even summoned me so that she could study me while it was in progress—meant that something was very wrong. She couldn't claim the wellsprings' power on her own.

When Grace tore Lucien's power out of him, she hid the power in three places deep below the Belle Dam soil. All the power of a Rider, the oldest of demons, buried and forgotten. Until now. I unlocked the first wellspring on accident, and drained it dry by trying to use it on Lucien. Now there were only two left, and each one had the potential to be devastating.

"What would you do with it?" I asked. "If you had more power than Catherine could even dream of? Unparalleled knowledge of the future and the way to shape events to your choosing." I let Jason ponder the question. I gave him time. And then I quietly asked, "Did you spend even one second trying to think about how to make things better? Using that power for good things? Or would you just punish and break Lucien and the Lansings?"

"I . . ."

"That's why I have to do this by myself," I said gently. "Maybe I'll screw it up. Maybe I won't even make it to the end. But I'm the only one who really knows what he's getting into. That power's not passive. It's a virus, sneaking into the cracks and exploiting all your weaknesses. Making you a hybrid, a demon with a human's ability to be clever and cruel in the same breath."

"How do you . . ."

"That's not important," I said. I didn't want to think about the winter voice. About what I'd started to become while it was inside of me. What I still might have become if Lucien hadn't pushed me and Grace saved me by tearing out my power.

"I need you to tell me about my mother," I continued. "About how she died."

He gave me a long look, and it seemed like he shrank in on himself, like his clothes were suddenly too big for him. "Fair enough," he said under his breath. "We didn't tell anyone that we were expecting. No one. Rose thought it would be bad luck. But Lucien knew. He told me before, my child would be *special*. But that night, he was beside himself. And just a few weeks before Rose reached the first trimester, she . . . .she *saw*."

"Had anyone who knew me seen me that night, I never would have heard the end of it." Jason's eyes were distant, and there was a soft smile playing out on his face. "I'd left work early to be with her. I had her feet in my hands because she was always complaining about how much they hurt." And then the smile jarred, a movie that had suddenly frozen. It was a moment trapped underneath seventeen years of grief. The warmth drained out of his face and voice. "She gasped, and her eyes flashed like diamonds catching light. She took one look at me and said—"

He left it hanging there, and I almost leapt off the window seat and went for his throat. "What did she say?" I demanded.

He shook his head, looking at me like he'd forgotten we were talking. "She said, 'You'll have to tell him that I love him. Do it every day.' It was so . . . *matter of fact*. And then later, I'd ask her about it, and it didn't seem to register. It never worried her, these things she was saying. These visions. She acted like they were a normal part of her pregnancy."

I didn't bother to wipe my face off. "What happened next?"

"These … incidents kept happening. Saying things that made no sense. Anecdotes. Warnings. Wishes. She read books on spirituality, things that talked about the equilibrium between life and death. She even looked through our family books, journals, anything she could get her hands on. She became a voracious reader. She never told me what she was looking for, but I always got the sense she was looking for meaning."

His head turned down, and this time there was no upturn to his mouth when his lips pressed together. *Shame. Self-loathing.* "You knew something was wrong, didn't you?" I said slowly.

"I suspected," Jason admitted immediately, like he'd been waiting for the question. "Lucien tried to tell me that it was just your powers bleeding through her and that there was nothing to worry about. Worrying would only stress out Rosemarie, and with her, you as well."

"She talked about me like she wouldn't be here to watch me grow up," I said. "You didn't think about what that would mean?"

"Of course I knew what that meant," Jason snapped, looking at me with a suddenly stoked fire. It didn't matter that he was my father, or I was his son, self-loathing fueled the burning inside him. "You think I didn't second-guess everything Lucien was telling me? That having a child would take my wife from me? That if only I'd had the courage to schedule an ab—," he looked at me with panic, and dropped his eyes. The rage burned out of him, leaving only quiet and confession. "Every time I turned, Lucien was there trying to dissuade me from what I was worried over. Tried to turn my focus back to Catherine. And then traces of workings started to appear. Magic that wasn't mine, and wasn't your mother's. Little scraps that I could feel but not decipher, enough to dig into my mouth like a toothache."

"Someone was using magic against you?"

"Even now, I couldn't tell you. I don't know if Lucien convinced Catherine to make a move against us, or John had experimented with something new, or maybe even someone new had been brought in to raise suspicions. All I know is that there were scraps of magic twisting around my house like motes of dust, and I couldn't determine where they were coming from. And my wife's behavior got stranger by the day."

"But what did you *think*?" I asked, surprised at how gentle my tone was.

He snorted. "Catherine, of course. I thought she'd found out, somehow. That she worked against your mother and me, hoping that Rose would lose the baby. But then she had you, and you were perfect." He smiled, looking at me quickly before a quick flush of red struck his cheeks and he looked away. "Your eyes were the same color they are now. I never noticed that before."

"Then came the depression, and I still didn't do anything. I was so busy trying to catch Catherine in the act, that I never . . . " Jason scrubbed his hands over his face. His mouth was a bitter frown. Each word chosen with ultimate care. "I went into the office one morning. Lucien was there. Waiting on me. He couldn't have been involved, he was with me the entire time. It was the only time I ever suspected him in twenty years of service."

Jason saw my look of disbelief. If anyone in Belle Dam had the ability to arrange someone's death while giving himself an alibi, it was Lucien. "I've seen his temper only a handful of times. Never as bad as that day. Lucien *always* knew what to expect. Except for that day. That day was a shock to both of us."

"What happened?"

"We got back to the house, and he just," Jason made a motion with his hand, "*relaxed.* 'Your son is fine,' he said, like that was the only thing that mattered. When I asked about Rose," Jason licked his lips and looked away. "When I asked about your *mother*, it was one of the few times I realized that he was just a *thing* pretending to be human. He turned back to me, like my question was almost an afterthought, and said, 'I'll send someone to collect the body.'"

"And yet you continued working with him for the next twenty years," I pointed out with a fair amount of bitterness.

I half-expected him to explode on me. To rage and yell and unleash some of that terrible anger I knew he had bottled up inside. But he sat there like a sad, ruined thing. "I should tell you that all I cared about was my weapon. My vengeance on Catherine," he said wearily. "You could hate me properly again. And it's ... easier when you hate me."

"I'd rather hate you for the things you've earned," I said. It was a surprise he heard me at all, I could barely force the words out as a whisper.

"Bennett said that what really happened to my mother was more interesting than the story," I said slowly. Something about Jason's story still seemed off.

"I don't know what else could possibly make the story worse," Jason said. The mask faltered again, and I saw the grief that Jason had tied himself up in for the greater part of my life.

I believed him. Whatever Jason knew, he'd told me. If he'd wanted to spin me a story, he would have chosen something that left him in a better light. Something that didn't expose the raw, seething parts of him that had never quite managed to heal.

A moment hung between us, and I had to decide what to do. Did I tell Jason what I was planning? No, I couldn't do that much. Every word I said out loud brought me too close to things that Lucien might pick up on. And he might still think of me a bit player in his grand plan, but it was almost definite that Jason was still a major player.

"If I asked you to forget the feud," I said carefully, playing with the hem of my shirt, "forget Catherine and revenge and everything else that has kept you going ... could you do that?"

The problem with asking a question you already know the answer to, is that you already know the answer. "Braden..." It was a pitying tone, a sad but sincere expression.

"Just don't do anything rash. I can't handle anyone else getting caught up in something they can't handle."

"I'm the adult here," Jason said, a measure of his old stiffness evident. "I'm the one who should be protecting you."

"Trey struck a bargain with Lucien. That's how he saved me last night." I don't know why I had the tendency to blurt things out to Jason without the buildup.

"I figured as much," Jason said slowly. "Do you know what the terms are?"

I shook my head. "Not exactly. It's on my agenda." I looked down at my hands. "It's going to get bad, Jason. I can feel it."

"It wasn't going to get any easier. I could try to negotiate with Lucien, but I don't know how much either one of us has to bring to the bargaining table." He eyed me from the desk chair. "He let you live for a reason. That's not negligible. I don't know how much latitude that would allow you, though."

I doubted there was anyone in Belle Dam outside of this room who would believe that Jason Thorpe would ever actually offer to try to negotiate on behalf of one of the Lansings. Jason had never looked older, and as usual, it caused a rip of guilt in my chest. It was like I couldn't walk into a room without tearing down the people inside. I was less dangerous than ever, but I still caused chaos wherever I went.

"Don't," I said. "I'll figure something out." And because I felt like I had to give him *something* I added, "I'll let you know if I need help."

Jason eyed me gravely. "Do you promise?"

I nodded, forcing a smile. "Sure."

It was one of my best lies ever.

Nineteen

There was another chess set in the library, identical to the one from my room. I brought mine with me and set it up so that the boards were less than a foot from each other. Then I set up the pieces, dark cherry red and ivory, and stared at the two boards.

There wasn't just one feud in Belle Dam. There were two. The Lansings versus the Thorpes. And Lucien versus Grace. But then there was also a third feud. Lucien and Catherine versus me versus Grace. But that was a feud that was, for now, contained only in my head. The minute Grace made a move, Lucien was going to be there to strike. And I was going to be there to . . . well, I didn't know what I was going to do yet.

I knew there were journals and other books about the feud tucked away on the shelves, but right now reading about the past didn't seem like it would do much good. I couldn't learn anything about Lucien or Grace that I didn't already know—I knew more about their weaknesses than anyone else in town.

The office desk in the center of the room was swallowed up in paperwork, as Jason worked diligently from his computer tablet. He would flip the stacks from time to time, searching out a particular file. I was surprised that most of his work was done on the computer. He seemed the type to stick to old-fashioned mediums.

I don't know if it was our morning conversation or some other pressing need, but Jason had come in a few minutes after me, and neither one of us said a word to the other. He worked behind the desk, and I studied the chess sets.

Lucien had told me once that all demons were adept at contracts. That it was they who taught humans the concept of a binding document. I let my fingers run along the edge of the board until they brushed up against the red/black bishop. That would be the most important part. Without him, I wouldn't be able to build to anything.

I kept trying to figure out what else I would need— what other pieces were still critical if I was going to do this. Plot a revolution. But something that wasn't discomfort kept surging up through my chest, distracting me. At first I thought maybe I was nauseous, having skipped breakfast, but it wasn't that. It was a melody without music. Inside me, where I felt an aching hole all the time now, it was like … a resonance. *Yes,* the emptiness inside me seemed to say, *I know you. I still remember.*

"Do you feel that? I—" I broke off in the middle of

what I'd been saying. It was like in physics, when we'd learned about sound waves and resonant frequency. How an opera singer could shatter glass if she hit the right pitch.

"Braden? What is it?" Jason stood up immediately.

The feeling was getting stronger. No. The feeling was getting *closer*.

I didn't expect the sharp inhale that followed. I looked over at Jason, whose eyes weren't trained on me. They were trained on the door. His mouth was open, the little crinkle appearing between his eyebrows the same way John's did when he was confused. He was rigid, like someone had forgotten to wind him up.

At first, the girl was a shade of black out of the corner of my eye. But as she sauntered into the library, as carefree as a bird, I had to blink twice. She wore all black like she'd gotten lost on the way to the funeral—black dress, black heels, black clutch, black sunglasses, black gloves, the whole nine yards. Even her thick, black ringlets were pinned up with a pair of raven-colored sticks.

I knew her, but Jason beat me to the punch. "Elle?" he whispered, but he didn't say her name like he saw the girl. Or the witch.

He said her name like he'd seen a ghost.

"Hello, Jason," she said. To me, she just nodded.

I looked between them. "You know her?"

Jason finally broke his gaze, looking from her to me and then back again. "Braden, this is … "

He trailed off, and Elle bit her lower lip. "Adele," she said gently. "I used to work for your father."

Adele. I knew that name. "But that's not possible," I said. Elle was only a few years older than me, but the girl who'd worked for Jason had disappeared almost a decade ago. Unless he hired her when she was still in middle school, there had to be some kind of mistake.

"I took a new position," Elle continued to Jason. "Which is why I'm here." Elle worked for Grace—hell, I already knew that Grace was the reason she and the other witch had come here in the first place.

"Are you dead?" I demanded. "Another ghost like the others? Are you here to try killing me, too?"

"What is he talking about?" Jason demanded. "Adele?" Maybe I wasn't the only one getting better at reading him, because his nose wrinkled up, and he heard something in my tone. Because he realized this was something more than just the feud. "She's not working for Catherine."

"No," I agreed. "She's not." But that didn't mean I had the slightest idea of why she was here.

"I'm not a ghost, hot stuff," she said, but there was no fire in her voice today. Normally, Elle was flirty and fun. This Elle seemed more like someone who'd just come off a week-long bender. "And I work for—"

I cut her off, my voice harsh. "I know who you work for. I'm not an idiot. You're the reason she got involved at all. I'd be *fine* if it wasn't for you."

"Dead is a kind of fine, I suppose," she said evenly.

Outside, the sun must have emerged from the cloudbank because the light coming in from all the windows suddenly intensified. Behind her sunglasses, I noticed Elle's twitch, and the way her head dropped down.

I took a step forward. "What's wrong with your eyes?"

Elle brushed by me to address Jason directly. "I really *am* sorry about Jonathan. I wish there was something I could have done." As an afterthought, she added, "You know I always liked him."

"Really?" I snorted. "I think your boss made sure everything happened just the way she intended."

"Braden," Jason warned. It was hard to say if he wanted me to stop being a dick or if he thought I was picking a fight I couldn't win.

Elle shifted her weight from one foot to the other.

"Take. Off. Your. Sunglasses." I said, because I wanted to *see*. I wanted Jason to see, too.

There's nothing more annoying than a standoff with someone when you can't see their eyes. I understood why people always hated getting into them with me, because thirty seconds of it was almost all that I could take. I came really close to just lunging forward and ripping them off of her when an eyebrow flexed upward and the windows all went dark.

Jason didn't flinch, but I did. I still had a long road to go towards being a badass. Once the light in the room was dimmed—the windows didn't all have curtains so some were simply darkened until the light couldn't get through—Elle slowly, and reluctantly, pulled the sunglasses off her face.

"Oh my god," I whispered.

¤ ¤ ¤

I thought that when Elle took off her sunglasses, we'd see the ever-shifting kaleidoscope of colors that I'd always grown up with. The witch eyes, ripped out of my head and put into hers. She was the one that Grace had walking around the town, trying to unlock the wellsprings. It made sense.

What I didn't expect to find was the damage.

Her eyelids were both red and crusted, like scabs that had never been allowed to heal properly. There wasn't any white left to her eyes: now they were either blood-red or ravaged pink. Her eyelashes were completely gone, and the skin around her eyes was puffy, cracked, and still oozing in places.

And I didn't feel a moment of pity for her.

"She's been trying to use my powers," I said, answering Jason's unasked question. I could feel his shock from behind me, but he saw the girl he'd nurtured, the girl he'd thought dead these last ten years. All I saw was Grace's pawn.

"Are you satisfied?" Elle asked, the challenge returning to her voice.

I managed a smile. "Almost. Tell me about her offer."

"My lady doesn't have an offer. She just wants to talk."

"Bullshit." I sat down on the edge of Jason's desk and looked towards him. "Grace Lansing is alive," I said simply to him. I don't know who was more surprised, Elle or him.

But Jason apparently trusted me enough not to argue, and I continued. "And because she's a control freak, I'm betting that everything we say here is off the record. Can't let Lucien know that someone's been manipulating him all these years."

Elle didn't exactly nod, but I knew I was right even before the slight jerk of her chin. She sank down into one of the chairs across from the desk and put her sunglasses back on.

"You can't open them by yourself. You wouldn't be here otherwise. So Grace realized she screwed up, and now she has to give me back what she stole. Or she's never getting out of there again."

"She didn't 'screw up,'" Elle returned hotly. "If she'd wanted you out of the way, she would have killed you."

"Yeah, yeah, I'm more useful to *everyone* alive, I know. No one will shut up about it."

"Then you'll come," she asked, not entirely convinced that I would.

"Tell me what happened to you," I said, "and I'll think about it."

She sighed, throwing her hands up in the air a little. "What happened to me is a very boring story about a very naive girl. And then I learned better."

"*Girls*," I corrected, because I hadn't forgotten that for all the talk that there were two girls who had come to Belle Dam in search of Grace's secrets, only one had apparently made it back out.

"We came because of the Widow," Elle said as she looked out the windows.

I read between the lines. "You came for *power*," I clarified. "Either you wanted what she had, or you wanted to find out how to get it for yourself." I thought about it for a moment, remembering what Grace had told me about her own origins. About how she'd come to found Belle Dam in the first place. "Did you come for the lighthouse, too?" Elle shuddered. "Oh, gods no. We wanted power, sure, but we didn't want anything to do with the lighthouse. That's eight kinds of stupid right there." Her expression was haunted. "Had I known I was going to spend the next ten years of my life inside of it, I might have made a different choice."

No, she wouldn't have. People who were only after power always made the same choices when it came down to it. The power was more important than anything else. "So the two of you came to town, and you planned to divide and conquer. You went to work for Jason, and your friend went to Catherine."

"Carmen," Elle said quietly. "Her name was Carmen."

"What happened to *her*? As far as everyone knows you both died on the beach that night."

"We found a way to slip between the worlds. Carmen ... didn't make it. I did." Each sentence was like another nail into her guilt. I could see the changes coming over her, the gnawing darkness that was eating her up from the inside.

"And you've been doing Grace's bidding ever since."

Her eyes flashed sudden fire, a contempt washing over her face that was more Grace than girl. "Watch your tone," she snapped. "If it wasn't for me, you'd be a lot worse off. Hannah tried to kill you when you first came to town. A bus, right? I stopped her before she finished the job. I even tried to warn you about what Lucien was planning, and I've been doing everything I can to put out all the fires you started while you've been sitting at home feeling sorry for yourself."

"Then where the hell were you when Trey struck a bargain with Lucien?" I demanded. "Because from where I'm standing, that wipes out *any* good will you might have earned."

She made a face, shifting uncomfortably. "I've been ... recovering."

Right. The witch eyes. Elle couldn't handle the power any better than I could. And if her eyes proved anything, it was that she was even worse off than I was. But Grace still kept pushing her to try. "If I were you," I said softly, "I'd figure out that Grace is not the hero in this story."

"Of course she is," Elle said, back on familiar ground again. "She contained the demon and has guarded the lighthouse ever since. You have her to thank that nothing else has come through to this world."

"She trapped the demon in a town full of innocent victims," I returned. "Everyone he's fed off of for the last one hundred years is her responsibility. She didn't trap him here out of some self-sacrificing need to protect the world. She did it because she was pissed and wanted him to suffer. So she took what was essentially a god and made him human. And she probably hoped to claim his power for herself, but she screwed up and found herself trapped in the lighthouse instead."

"You don't know what you're talking about."

"*She threw me out of the lighthouse and ripped out my magic,*" I returned hotly. "Because she passed judgment on me way back when she was still human herself."

"She still *is* human."

"She's a phantom in a tower," I snapped. "She's a ghost that can't get it up for reality."

"She won't be for long."

I snorted. "With whose help? Because the two of you can't seem to do anything but screw it up. She's no closer to being free than she was ten years ago."

"You're wrong," Elle said, still looking troubled. "When you restored that part of Lucien's power to him, the bindings on my lady were loosened. The stronger he gets, the more freedoms are returned to her. Soon, she'll be able to cross over and restore herself."

"In all things, balance," I quoted back to her. It was as close to a law of the supernatural as anything I'd ever seen. "She bound him, and she got trapped. That was the price." *But what if she'd paid a different price,* I wondered. *Why that one?*

I shook my head, clearing my thoughts. Jason stepped up to my shoulder, put his hand on me. "Is there anything else? You've given my son a lot to think about."

Elle looked nervous. Then again, I would too if I had to go back to Grace and report that things hadn't gone according to plan. "Tomorrow," she said, licking her lips. "She'll meet with you tomorrow. You can figure out where."

"If you were smart, Elle? You'd get as far away from Grace Lansing as you could," I said. "You're her handmaiden or whatever, now, but what happens when she gets free? Because you can be naive and think that this has all been about Grace trapping Lucien, but there's more to it than that. This has always been about something more to her. But as far as I'm concerned? You're just as much to blame for this mess as she is. And that's one hell of a target to have on your back."

I turned away, shaking my head. Grace was a sociopath, so she'd probably want to meet in the church again. That much was easy. "And you might want to invest in some eye drops," I called out as she strode from the room.

Once I was sure she'd left, I turned to Jason, who had a deep frown on his face.

"I need a favor." There was a long pause. "Jason? Are you listening?"

"Hmm?" He looked down at me surprised, like he'd forgotten I was in the room with him.

"You know how Grace had a monument in the cemetery? And how it kind of got blown up?" I waited for his nod before I continued. "Do you think you could pay someone to replace it?"

His forehead broke out into lines of confusion. "Why?"

I gave him a small smile. "Because I want to leave her a little message."

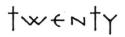

twenty

I spent a day and a half staring at the chessboards.

Sometimes I spun them around. Sometimes I switched from red to white. Sometimes I took pieces off the board or rearranged the ones that were already there. It wasn't enough to play one game, or both games. I had to play all of them. And I couldn't afford a single mistake.

There had to be a way to balance all of the games at once. To keep Jason and Catherine occupied, to manipulate Lucien, and to outsmart Grace. To keep one, or any of them, from teaming up with one another. Riley had said that if I tried, they would overpower me. But they could only overpower me if I gave them the chance.

He showed up about an hour before sunset. I'd changed into jeans and a black turtleneck, thrown something into my hair so it didn't puff up in every direction, and grabbed the most ostentatious pair of sunglasses in my room. They weren't the comfortable, plastic kinds I was used to. They were high-end, black-and-gold monstrosities, and they were perfection.

"I almost feel like a real boy," Matthias crowed as he walked into the library. "Being summoned up to the manor by the little master. It's like a Dickens novel come to life."

I waited a beat and then remembered that Drew wasn't here to jump in and make a crack about Dickens. Matthias glanced down at the boards, his fingers brushing up against one of the white rooks. He looked at me with a raised eyebrow as if to say, *well?*

Rather than answering, I shifted a red pawn diagonally into the space held by the rook and knocked it over. "You'll have better luck with a bishop," I said. I snagged the piece in question and rolled it between my fingers.

"So why am I here, little Thorpeling? I've already told you that I'm not going to be able to help you in this little endeavor." Matthias was an old demon, not quite as powerful as a Rider, but probably close. He was trapped here just like Lucien, only the difference was that his chains were a little easier to unlock. He'd been bound to protect the first church in Belle Dam, and only two bricks remained from that structure. Destroy them, and Matthias would be free.

My attention stayed completely on the board, leaving Matthias to skirt the edges of my attention. He was just a demon like Lucien, and they thought that by entering a room they were immediately the most important part of it. Just like they thought that Belle Dam was only special because of the monsters that it caged.

That was about to change.

"I've got her over a barrel," I said, nodding to the game board. The red pawn was one step away from the opposite side, where it would earn a promotion and become whatever piece I desired. There were no immediate moves for white that could stop it.

"The first rule in dealing with women, is *never* expect that you have them at all," he said. "They always have a way to surprise you."

"Does that go double for demons?"

His lips quirked like he wanted to smile, but he resisted. "I've already asked once. Why am I here?" His foot tapped a restless rhythm against the carpet, like I was keeping him from something far more interesting. Knowing Matthias, that might not be far off track.

"I ... need a lawyer," I admitted.

Matthias stared me down for a good minute. All the sound in the library seemed to dwindle down to nothing— even my heart silenced itself in my chest. "How, exactly," he started, and then just as quickly stopped. Another silence began. Matthias lowered himself down into one of the chairs, and his attention came down on the chess sets.

"Interesting," he murmured to himself.

"I need to understand a few things, too," I added in a sudden rush. "I can't make a plan until I know everything."

"So it would seem," Matthias said. Then, louder, he called out, "Bring her in, if you please."

I shifted in my seat, the chess piece still tucked between my fingers like a lifeline.

Drew strolled into the library, pushing a wheelchair. And sitting in the wheelchair was none other than Riley.

"I just get so lonely. I wanted some friendly faces." Matthias said in explanation. "Now the gang's all here."

¤　¤　¤

Drew didn't seem surprised by the gathering, nor had he been particularly shocked when Matthias arrived and pulled both him and Riley out of her hospital room before heading over to the Thorpe estate.

"Figured you needed my help again," he said. "Not like you can even step out your front door without screwing something up. I'm used to it by now."

"Thanks," I responded dryly. Drew the dick was in fine form this afternoon.

Riley had undergone the most startling transformation. Her wild hospital hair had been brushed back and tied up in a ponytail, and the outfit she wore … well, it was Amish goth. A collarless, black button-up done up all the way to her neck. A long, ankle-length black skirt with black lace at the bottom. And gloves.

"Grace wants to meet with me," I said, pretending that Matthias hadn't just turned my afternoon into a circus. "And I want to be prepared."

"So pack a lunch," Matthias replied. "Or an extra pair of underwear. I don't know how you think I can help you."

"If that was true, you wouldn't have shown," I said. I gestured towards Drew and Riley. "And you certainly wouldn't have brought the two of them unless they were important somehow."

Matthias rolled his eyes.

I continued, "Grace is going to have terms, and I can't afford to let her have the upper hand. So how about you stop being a pretentious twit for half an hour and remember that if things go south, I'll still have my powers back and I can make your life more miserable than it already is."

"Do you even know what you want yet? A day ago, you were all set to run. Now you're suddenly ready to fight?"

So he knew about that, huh? Matthias was paying more attention to my actions than I'd realized. "Isn't it obvious, Matt?" I wagged the chess piece in his direction. "I want to stop all of them. Not just Jason and Catherine. Not just Lucien. *All of them*. At the same time. Because every time you cut a head off this feud, it turns out there's a whole other layer you never saw coming. So you're going to help me tear out the roots ... or you're going to be the first demon I destroy."

Matthias kept his silence for only a span of seconds before the tension in him vanished like vapor. "Then once again, I've come to your rescue. Because without the girl, you'll never figure out what you need."

I got up and held out the red bishop to her. She looked up at me, eyes in wonder, even as she snatched it out of my hands and clutched it to her chest. "Are you going to break him now? Rout his forces, fire flies, calcaneus on vertebrae, checkmate?"

I knelt down in front of her, glancing towards Matthias who gave me an approving nod, and then turned to her again. "Riley, it's not enough to break him." She grew still in front of me. Her lips compressed into a bloodless line. I took a deep breath. "He needs to suffer first. They all do. Can you help?"

"Braden, what the hell are you doing?" Drew demanded. "Riley's not a part of this. Not anymore."

"She's still a part of this, Drew," I said, refusing to break my connection with Riley.

"Didn't you do enough damage the last time? She's here because of you," he snapped.

And like that, the air went out of me. What was I doing? Using Riley? Asking her to help me destroy my enemies? That's something Lucien or Catherine would do.

Riley reached out and tapped my glasses. Her demon-blue eyes never blinked. I hadn't noticed that before, but now it was all I could see. "Blind boy needs violet boy. Violet boy can save them. Violet boy can save us all. Violet boy can destroy us all."

"But can I be one without the other?"

"Like hell," Drew snarled, but just as he leaped up in outrage, Matthias was there at his side, a finger pressed against his temple.

"Sleep," the demon whispered. Drew sagged back down like a puppet with its strings cut. Just before he crumpled down onto the floor, Matthias gave him a healthy shove and he ended up sprawled over the side of the couch.

"There is one more thing you need to know," the demon said gravely. "And I'm afraid that our young mister Armstrong won't be quite so receptive."

¤   ¤   ¤

A half hour later, I still couldn't feel my legs. Riley was happily ensconced with the chess sets, and though she didn't touch a single piece other than the bishop clutched between her fingers, she was captivated. Matthias had stoked a fire in the fireplace, though I was vaguely aware that there was no kindling inside to burn, nor wood of any kind.

Drew started to stir, and I looked away.

It all depends on how much you want this," Matthias had said. *"And how far you're willing to go."*

"What happened?" Drew slurred the words through a yawn until they were nearly one long, stretched out syllable.

"We'll just leave the two of you alone," Matthias demurred, pulling himself to his feet. He sauntered over to where Riley's wheelchair had been parked and smirked over his shoulder. "Make good choices, Mr. Thorpe."

I couldn't tell if he meant it more as a condemnation or a warning. All I knew was that it wasn't an innocent piece of advice. Matthias had just as much to lose in this as anyone.

The grandfather clock struck at the hour, clear bells pealing out a chorus of time. Lucien had kept a low profile since the wake. Were the church bells still doing their job and keeping him out of the way? I couldn't imagine that would keep him down for long, but yet it already had.

"Where's he taking her?" Drew pulled himself up into a sitting position and scrubbed a hand against the drool oozing the side of his cheek. "What's going on?"

"I need you to listen to me very carefully, Drew." The fire was like a swinging pocket watch. Hypnotizing. My head felt strange, like it was filled with sunset clouds, all reds and pinks and purples. I wondered about the fire, about what would happen if I slipped my fingers against the salamander and vermilion and collected it like dewdrops. Would it even hurt? I shook my head and turned away, unable to even feel the flames against my skin.

While Drew had been asleep, Matthias had had much to say. He'd even brought me the elaborate gold pen and heavy card stock notepaper. I used it now to write down two locations. "After you take Riley back," I said, handing him the card, "I need you to pick something up for me. And then tomorrow night I need you to meet me there."

"Are you going to tell me what the hell's going on? You let demon boy put the mojo on me?"

I looked towards the door. Chewed my lower lip. Hesitated. Panicked. Matthias had said not to tell. Matthias said that nothing good would come of it.

Matthias wasn't the one who was going to have to pull all the strings.

"Have you accepted anyone as your personal lord and savior lately?" I asked.

twenty-one

The church doors were unlocked. The moon had appeared from between the clouds only minutes before, a slow and methodical fire that burned at my back. The church itself smelled like funerals and spice, of things celebrated and forgotten.

Elle was alone, knelt down in front of the chapel candles, a fire stick clasped forgotten between her hands. She could have been lost in prayer. She could have been dead. It was hard to say. Or care.

"She's waiting for you upstairs," Elle said, only moving her lips. "Be careful."

"There's not much she can still take from me."

Elle turned her head to look at me, her eyes sad and serious. "Don't let her prove you wrong."

To the right of the chapel was an open door, and behind it, stairs that led up into the darkness. I climbed towards my meeting with Grace, tired of her fascination with heights. I blamed the burn in my legs on nerves, not the climb. Grace had a hundred years to plan for this. I'd had about thirty-six hours.

I came to the crest of the bell tower, which was now apparently just a tower. The axle the bell had hung from was still there, as were the metal links that had helped it sway back and forth, but the bell itself was missing.

"He dares only strike at one a day," Grace said, again from her perch at the window. She looked out at her city, the belle dame of Belle Dam. It was meant to be ironic, I knew now. A "beldam" was a hag, or a witch. She'd named the city after herself twice. "It must gall him, to dirty his own hands. To have a fraction of his old strength restored, and yet the bells cut through his dark power with every passing hour."

"Good job. You've given him a scare," I said dryly. Grace didn't torture Lucien like she wanted to crush him. It was all with an air of grotesque passion. If she was a cat, then he was the prey, and she only toyed with him before the passion to consume him became too much. Until all that was left was to lick the blood from her fingers when she was done.

I just wanted him to suffer, even destroy him if the opportunity presented itself. Somehow, that had become the less creepy alternative. I wanted to become a monster, and somehow that made me the hero.

"Shouldn't you be out there right now, pulling his pigtails?"

A breeze cut through the open walls, and I had the sense it was raveling around her like a shawl. "You grow bold," she whispered. "Stupid boy. What would the world lose if the

Thorpe line withered where you stood—if I took back the life I returned to you?"

"Did you come here to make threats," I said evenly, "or did you come to beg me for my help?"

That drew her up short. Grace pursed her lips, magma-eyes churning. "You don't know any—"

"—I know *exactly* why I'm here. Do you think I couldn't figure out what happened? If so, then I'm not the stupid one, am I?"

I'll give her one thing. The zombie witch with inferno eyes had a great poker face.

I gestured between the two of us. "We're still connected. You might have taken my power, but I can still *feel* it. I know you tried to have Elle do your dirty work for you, and that didn't work. I know it's *killing* her. And as long as the wellsprings are dormant, you're still trapped in the lighthouse."

"Abomination," she hissed.

"Sticks and stones," I sing-songed. "You wanted his power for yourself, but you ended up trapped. And I unlocked the first wellspring. That's it, isn't it? I started releasing that power, and now I'm the one who has to finish it. And you can't touch a drop of it without me. But you lost control and came after me. Screwed yourself over, didn't you?" My lip curled. "In all things, *balance*." It wasn't quite the B word I wanted, but the meaning was clear.

There was a moment, a single second in space and time, where the fire in her eyes kindled and weighed against itself. I could see it in the glow of her power and in the tension that had thickened the room. On one side of the scale was my annihilation. On the other, my survival. The difference between them was less than a feather's sigh.

"You misunderstand your position here. Your *purpose*," she said, the flames devolving down into embers. "You only live because of my mercy. But that doesn't make you my equal. Remember that."

"Cut the crap," I snapped. I was curious how far I could push things. If I was wrong, and Grace *didn't* need me, there was only so much she would tolerate. But if I was right, then maybe it was the time to redefine some of the boundaries between us. Starting with ... "You need me. Actually," I said, pretending to think, "You needed the old me. The broken, cursed kid who got traumatized every time he took a hotel shower."

"Your power," she sneered. "What are you but a pawn in a game you barely understand?"

"What are you but an ancient bitch who can't get over her ex?"

"You dare—"

"I dare! Of course I do. So if you're going to kill me, then do it." There was a moment while the two of us acknowledged the challenge that had been laid down. "You need me. And *he* needs me. But look!" I held up my arm, dangled it out in front of her. "No strings. I'm not your puppet. I won't dance because you tell me to. So shut up and listen, because you might have gotten used to the sound of your own voice over the last hundred years, but I don't *care.*"

"How desperate do you think I am? I don't bargain with mongrels."

It was hard to forget that not only was Grace an aged magical revenant hell-bent on revenge, but she was also something of a pretentious bigot. "If you want my help, we're doing this my way. You're not just giving me my power back. You're going to show me how to use it without killing myself. You're going to help me get the control I need."

Grace sneered. "If you think I'm going to unleash you with the true weight of your power onto this world, you are sorely mistaken. Imagine the destruction you could sow in just a single lifetime. This will never happen. I will not allow it."

"Fine," I said, thinking quickly. I couldn't let Grace decide the terms of our agreement without fighting back, but I also couldn't afford to just let her walk away entirely. "Then give me three days." My heart squeezed in tight, constricted like a snake had wrapped around the muscle and was slowly pressing the life out of it.

Only three days. How could I do everything and say goodbye to my life in three days?

"*What?*"

"Three. Days." I said clearly, like it had been part of my plan all along.

I had caught her off guard. She weighed the words carefully, but if she thought it would be that easy to divine my intentions, she was disappointed. Hell, I didn't even know my intentions at this point. Confusion lined her face, and the fire in her eyes dimmed. "To do what?" She sounded almost curious.

"You give me three days back in the world. And then we can negotiate what happens to me. Tear out my eyes, lock me in the lighthouse, but there's no way I'm walking away from this alive. I know that."

The fire in Grace's eyes dimmed completely, and for the first time I saw something other than fire—a shifting of shades that ran from crimson all the way to daisy yellow. Reds and oranges and yellows, each as striking as the next, no two shades quite the same.

Grace knew about sacrifice, maybe more than anyone, but it seemed that self-sacrifice still eluded her understanding. "You... would give up your life?" She looked almost human. Almost sad. Almost.

"I know what's going to happen to me," I said clearly. I did know. I'd known for a while that some journeys don't end well. They just end. "If I'm going to fall, I'll drag him down with me."

There was a startled pause.

Grace's voice was pebbles against stone, as gentle and as tentative as she could. "And what could you do in three days?"

My smile was slow and sincere. "I'm going to tear Lucien apart. You trapped him in this town, but it's become his playground. He has his toys, and his games, and his plans.

He has his pleasures, and I'm going to sour all of them. I'm going to make this place the hell you should have made it in the first place. For him."

"Every cage has its key," she murmured. Another way of saying *in all things, balance*. If I was going to take something from Lucien, I would have to give up something of myself. That was the true nature of power, I understood it now. For every victory, there is a sacrifice. For every power, there is a price. And there is always a loophole.

"The spell over Belle Dam, the one you used to trap him, that continues because you're still alive, doesn't it?" Grace nodded, but my question was rhetorical. I'd already figured out that much on my own. "If I have to bind myself to the lighthouse, then I will. I'll give you my freedom and take up your place."

"The burden of Atlas," she murmured with a small smile. "Do you know how long a hundred years is in this world?"

"I'll finally have time to watch all the Lord of the Rings movies," I offered. "They're just so long." But there would be so much I could do before that happened. Heal Riley the best that I could. Save Trey. Protect Jade. Ravage the life that Lucien had built until nothing was left but a shredded, bloodless carcass. Dig out the roots of the feud and pry them from the town so that no one else would get tangled in agendas and dark motivations.

If I could accomplish even half of those things, I could walk away from the world and be okay.

As if she could read my thoughts, Grace's expression turned severe again. "It is not as easy a thing as this, you understand. There will be factors you haven't thought of. Prices that will have to be paid. How willing are you to take your revenge? What are you willing to sacrifice? Such things will have the highest of costs."

I've already offered her my life, my powers, my eternity. What else can she possibly take from me? "I won't give up Jade and Gentry," I said, the first thought coming into my mind. "And if we do this, you have to help them put a stop to the feud. You'll have stopped what you needed to stop. Belle Dam deserves to heal after everything it's been through."

She inclined her head as she considered. Another smile. "You will be my hands in the world. If you do everything you agree to, we will be in agreement. I will allow the concessions you've requested."

I released a breath. Okay, okay. This could work. Maybe. I couldn't trust Grace, not fully. But at least I could hope that any family loyalty she still possessed might be enough to shield Trey and Jade from the worst of what she could do.

"I'm not just going to take your word for it," I said. "I don't trust you enough not to turn on me the moment it suits your purposes."

The Widow of Belle Dam, who was probably used to people dancing along the strings she'd crafted, narrowed her eyes on me. "Is that a fact," she said coolly. "And will you stroll up to the demon and ask him for a favor?"

"There's more than one demon in Belle Dam," I pointed out, my tone just as sharp. "And it says a lot that I'd trust him a lot further than I'd trust you. Matthias can orchestrate a contract as well as Lucien can."

"A demon only ever looks out for his own interests," she snapped. "What makes you think that the demon can be trusted?"

Because I can give him what he wants. And I can make sure that no one else ever will if he betrays me. "The Grimm owes me a favor. He knows if I get my powers back, I'm going to have a debt to settle with him. He aided Lucien and his restoration."

She tapped a finger against her lips. "And you'll give him amnesty for his crimes against you?"

"So I can nail Lucien to the wall? Hell, yes."

Grace turned her head away, but not before I saw the start of a smile form. *Had she ever met anyone who wanted to see the demon pay as much as she did?* A moment passed, and then I had to know. "What did he do?" I asked softly. "How did it start? You don't challenge the powers you challenged without one hell of a reason."

"We came to this land in search of the lighthouse, a bastion to travel between the worlds. You could enter in this world, climb a thousand times a thousand stairs, and emerge in a world unlike anything else known in this existence. Or so the legends said. But what we found was not another world at the top of the lighthouse. No, what we found was so much worse."

I remembered the lantern room of the lighthouse, the way one whole side of the room had been smashed in, as though a giant had slammed his fist through the roof and walls in a fit of childish pique.

"Maybe it's a long-buried instinct in those of us with the power to challenge the gods, the ones for whom magic was truly meant. We seek out the seeds of our own destruction. We stare into the abyss, and pray that it stares back into us. The Riders first taught man to use magic, wizards and sorcerers who were like gods themselves. But those powers came with deadly strings attached. For me, the search for the lighthouse was tantamount to my survival. For you see, my powers, though they were great, were slowly killing me."

"So it was the same for you," I nodded. Somehow I knew this, but the idea of Grace as weak and frail didn't seem to compute in my brain. I could not reconcile the two images.

"Ahh," she said, another creeping smile tugging at the corner of her mouth, "you don't believe. But it is true all the same. For you see, our power comes tied to the demons, and only through them can we achieve the true measure of our gift. We are bound to them from our very first breath. The only question is how long they will let us linger with our fantasies."

Once, I thought that by searching out Grace's legacy, I might figure out a way to control the powers that I'd been born with. But if it was all a trick—if my destiny had always been to act as a puppet for Lucien's darkness—then

I'd *never* had a chance. My life had never felt as claustro-phobic as it did right now. Even though I could look out and see the city laid out before me, the stars in the night sky, the lights across the bay signaling another city ... my life was such a small thing. An empty box that never had any hope of being near to full enough.

"Oh," I said quietly, sinking down onto one of the boxes that had been stacked up next to the windows.

Grace didn't seem to notice. "I didn't know him for what he was, not at first. But he promised me the great-est gift I could have wished for. Freedom. Freedom from the pain, from succumbing to the weight of a power greater than me. At the time, if I'd known—" she cut herself off, shaking her head.

"If you'd known?"

Grace took a moment to answer. I got the impression she was trying to decide whether to speak the truth, or con-jure up a lie. "If I'd known the price, I might have chosen differently. But then, I might not. If there was one thing I couldn't control, it was the hunger to be free from my curse."

Truer words. But then, as someone who'd been freed from his curse, it wasn't everything it should have been.

"So the Riders bequeath the greatest of powers, but only so long as their pawns become weapons in their own right. And who better than the shadows that first whispered of murder to the first men? So the devil came to me and offered me sweet release. And when our bargain was struck and our hands touched, this man who I thought loved me, drew out the stars that burned within me. An entire life, an entire person crumbled into ashes and blew away into dust. And what he left in his wake was the very creature that tore him apart."

"He stole your future," I translated. "Fed on you the way he feeds on all of them."

"That is what I said," she replied testily. "But because of the bond that had been created between us, I saw the lives left unlived. I saw what I had lost, and vowed vengeance. So came the groundwork of the city of Belle Dam, a city named for my own hubris and my newly stoked rage."

I chewed on my lower lip and looked out again at the city. I wasn't sure what to say. Her story could have been mine. It probably would have, if Lucien had gotten his way. I'd have set him free, and he'd have used the opening to bind himself to me and drain the world from my fingertips.

In a normal person, Lucien's particular brand of vampirism left them an unremarkable husk of a person, dragged down by lethargy and an inability to gain fortune's favor. But what would happen to someone like me? Would I become a vengeance fanatic like Grace?

Or would I become the vision? Is that how it happened? Is that what really brought it about? Lucien, stealing the future I was meant to have, and leaving a psychotic godling in my place? I still remembered the vision she'd shown me, the way I was both more and less than what I was now. Less human, less *concerned,* but more in every other way. My cruelty had no end. My hunger for chaos was limitless. The version of me with violet eyes walked streets littered with bodies, called demons across the lighthouse, and welcomed them like a newest, youngest sibling.

But my fears about that other Braden were not for Grace's eyes, or ears.

I looked back towards the stairs, and changed the subject. "Elle's hidden from him too, isn't she? That's how she keeps moving around town and why he hasn't bothered her yet. If he knew, he'd want to know where she disappeared to, and why she hasn't aged."

Grace nodded. "My will is her will. She has no secrets from me. And my protection falls upon her like a cloak, keeping her safe."

"I want to know how to do that."

Her responding look was sly. "You wish to have my protection? Such an easy thing to request, so different in practice."

I shuddered. "No," I said firmly, "I don't want *your* protection. I want to protect myself. You know as well as I do that all of this depends on hiding from Lucien's sight. I thought about running, and he cut that off at the pass."

"The *girl* thought about running," Grace clarified. "Whatever he plans requires the both of you, but your future remains an unremarkable mirage."

Lucien didn't see me running. He saw Jade. "Have you been protecting me all this time?"

Grace lifted a shoulder. "A wise woman keeps her strategies secret, and her weaknesses tucked out of sight. The girl was an oversight, though. I should have warded all those you came into contact with."

"What do you mean, 'an oversight'?"

Her smile was twisted. "Don't you already know? The girl is tied tight to the plans the demon still has for you. Together, the two of you would spawn a child also burdened with stolen power. Lucien wants the child to replace the one he broke. But the girl has already ruined his plans and he doesn't even know. And now he won't, until he sees it for himself."

Jade. The pregnancy test. Oh God, if Jade really was pregnant, then not only did that mess with Lucien's plans to use me, but also…I shook my head, warding off the thought. And wait, Lucien wanted us to *what*? Jade? And *me*?

"I don't think that would ever happen," I said stiffly.

"Do you even know the costs of what you seek?" Grace asked. "What you will lose? What you will sacrifice? That would be the least of it." Ever since the tide of the conversation had changed, since she'd seen something in me that had caught her off guard, her tone had warmed. No longer a frozen lake but water streaming languidly from an iceberg. A matter of degrees, but still a notable difference.

"I went ahead and filled the boy in on some of the particulars," Matthias called out from the stairwell. "Hope I stole your thunder."

twenty-two

He climbed the steps slowly, emerging in a black leather jacket paired with dark jeans. Dressing down, at least as far as he was concerned. I'd never seen a demon in less than a three-piece suit. "It's been a long time, Warden."

There was a bite to his words, an insult I didn't quite understand. But Grace did. Her eyes flashed sunflare red in an instant. At the same time, Matthias's eyes darkened until the whites were completely swallowed up. Once they were gone, cornflower blue irises began to emerge, like the sun in the middle of an eclipse finally emerging from behind the moon.

"Don't be like that, Grimm," she chided. "What are a few drops of time compared to the ocean of your existence?"

"Oh, I forgot how utterly pretentious you are," Matthias sighed wearily, sparing me a glance. "I don't know how you deal with it."

"Like you're one to talk," I muttered.

"Are you here to bleat about the travesties that have befallen you, or are we here to bind the boy to my will?"

"Someone needs to explain how a partnership works, don't you think?" I stepped in front of Matthias, just far enough that he would have to move to reach me. "No one's binding me to your *anything*. You're going to give me what I want, and I get three days in Belle Dam before you come to collect."

Grace sneered. "And what if I decide that you are too much of a risk to release into this world?"

"Then I know a Rider who will be more than happy to find out exactly where you've been cowering for a hundred years." The expression in her face grew even more severe. "You seem to forget that we are not equals."

That's because I'm better than you will ever be. Grace had let herself become a monster and let the humanity in her wither out a hundred years before. She thought I would believe in her good will—that containing me had only to do with protecting the town. But the truth was that Grace craved her freedom almost as much as she wanted Lucien to suffer. Luckily, I could provide both of those things in equal measure.

"You know my terms," I said to Matthias, taking a step back. He held out his arm, revealing a roll of parchment he was holding. Trust Matthias to bring props. It wasn't enough for the two of them to negotiate a contract, but he would have to do it on something particularly ridiculous.

The negotiation didn't go exactly how I expected. The

vellum unraveled, floating out of Matthias's hand until it was at an even point between the two of them. Words began to stream across the paper, some in white flame that didn't burn the page, while others appeared in icy blue. Fire and ice waged war across the page as words were added, crossed out, consumed and burned away entirely. During the process neither Grace nor Matthias said a word, but their eyes were locked on one another.

As parts of the contract were finalized, as it were, the color faded until they were a dark ink that was a bit too faded to be called black. Bit by bit, the contract was agreed by the two until the regular letters outnumbered those that glowed. Eventually, the colors faded, and the contract floated to Grace's hand. She pressed her index finger against the contract, and though there was no wound on her finger, blood seeped out of it and onto the page.

Matthias walked forward, plucking the contract out of her hands. "Everything should be in order," he said, offering it to me. Where the bloody fingerprint had been a moment before, now Grace's name was written out in an elegant script. "All you have to do is press your finger against the bottom," he said.

Like I was seriously going to just sign the contract without looking at it first. I trusted Matthias as much as I needed to, but I hadn't become an idiot overnight. As it was a simple agreement—power in exchange for Grace's freedom and giving myself over to her within a specific time frame—there was only so much that had to be covered. I looked towards the bottom of the page. "'Subject to the restrictions of the city where the contract originated?'" I quoted, looking to Matthias.

"You cannot use the powers at your disposal to undo what has already been done," Grace cut in, "such as voiding this contract or trying to flee at the nadir of your time. You cannot shatter the cage that defines my revenge and choose to free the demon."

"You are subject to all the rules of this city, whether they are of supernatural or mundane origin," Matthias added. "The contract is legally binding."

Without another word, I pressed my finger against the bottom of the page. The paper wriggled against my skin, vacuuming tight until my blood was drawn from behind my flesh. *Braden Michael Thorpe* appeared at the bottom in a facsimile of my own signature, not nearly as elaborate or perfect as Grace's.

"I hope you know what you're doing," Matthias murmured.

"*Goodbye,* Matthias," I said, turning away from him. The contract was signed.

"Oh don't go far, Grimmling. I want a word when the boy is finished."

Matthias coughed into his fist.

"You know what you have to do now?" Grace asked me, eyes now alight with hunger and need. "You know what you will be required to do?"

I nodded, my skin flushing. Matthias's instructions

back at the house were still caught on an endless loop in my head. My stomach twisted. "I remember."

"Good," she sniffed. "Then you will meet tomorrow at the aperture from which I first drew you from this world. And once you have satisfied your side, I shall restore to you what was yours."

"And teach me to control it," I reminded her. "My time doesn't start until I can control the witch eyes."

"Fine, fine," she waved away my concerns.

I turned to go, only to find that Matthias had already taken his leave.

Grace stopped me just as I began my descent. "Remember what I told you once, blade-hearted boy. This power brought everything I love to ruin, and dug the graves for all those who called upon me. Be careful how sharp you choose to be, because a blade cuts both ways."

twenty-three

When you know your life is about to change completely, twenty-four hours can go by in a blink.

Drew met me on the road that ran parallel to the Lansing estate. The moon was a shrouded mystery in the sky, wanting no part of me tonight. I didn't blame her. All that kept me going was need and the gnawing threat of failure under my skin. Everything had come down to a precarious house of cards, and the slightest spark would send the whole thing tumbling down into flames.

"You disappeared," he grunted, climbing off his bike. I still didn't know if the motorcycle actually belonged to him or how he'd come across it. I wanted to ask, but now was not the time. It seemed … inappropriate.

I kept breathing in and out, slowly. Everything was going to work out. I wasn't doing anything I didn't absolutely have to. All I had to do was get through the night, and tomorrow I could worry about all the next steps. "Had a lot to do today."

That was a lie. I'd hidden away from everyone, locked myself behind doors of wood and ones of silence. I'd thrown my phone off the pier on my way back home from the church the night before. Taken off all the clothes that Jason had bought me, and dug out the few possessions I still had with me when I'd first gotten off the bus to Belle Dam. Found my favorite pair of sunglasses—neon green and black plastic, obnoxious and yet my favorite things ever.

Nothing seemed to fit the way I remembered it. My shirt was too tight around the shoulders and arms, and my sneakers felt like they'd been broken in by someone else's feet. This wasn't me. Not anymore.

But all I had to do was fake it for one night.

"Did you bring it?" I asked.

"I don't like being cut out of what's going on," Drew said, and there was a vulnerability in his eyes that I'd only seen once before. The night Drew found out about his father. He patted something at his side, something left in shadow. "You send me out to run errands but you don't tell me what they're for? Just because my last name isn't slang for *blond douchebag* doesn't mean I should get blown off. You were the one that wanted me involved." He moved to stand next to me, underneath the streetlights. My eyes gravitated towards the thing on his hip.

"No, you're right," I said. "I'll fill you in later. Just ... just trust me, okay? We need that," I said, nodding to the dark brown satchel resting on his side, "safe and sound."

"Freaking heavy," he grunted. "Wouldn't think they'd be so bad."

All burdens are heavier than you think. Maybe not at first, but eventually they'll break you.

I just had to keep going long enough to outrun mine. "Come on," I started down the path into the woods, a path I could have walked in my sleep now. "We've got a meeting to get to."

It took less time than I remembered to find the gaping chasm in the Lansing backyard. There'd been a chapel here, once, but now the only evidence that it remained were some scraps of foundation, and a section of concrete floor maybe a dozen square feet large. I'd destroyed the rest of it, and every living thing surrounding it.

Trees were toppled behemoths all around us, splintered and shattered like shipwrecks. The ground had been freshly turned over that night, but over the past few weeks had finally started to settle back down. I was surprised there was still a path. Maybe I wasn't the only one who'd made the trek out here.

The chapel hadn't been in Catherine's actual backyard—it had been tucked away in the woods somewhere far from the prying eyes of the city's serfs and vassals. But there was always the worry that tonight would be the night that she'd stumble upon me, sneaking onto her land.

Elle waited for the pair of us at the bottom of the pit. She was still wearing sunglasses, too.

"So you're really going through with this?" Drew asked.

I focused on my footsteps. The hill down into the pit was still soft and it would be easily to slip. That would be all I'd need. Put an intricate plan for revenge into motion, and then break my neck just before it all started to play out.

"I have to," I said quietly. I wished for Drew to stop talking. I didn't want to talk to him.

"How do you know you can trust her?"

"She doesn't have a choice. We have a contract." Everyone was signing contracts. Me. Trey. But Elle had managed a way out of hers. So it was possible. Drew huffed behind me, and I headed him off before he could start arguing. I didn't have it in me to do the back and forth with him. Not tonight. "I can open the way so that Grace can come and go as she pleases. I don't need my magic for that. But Grace won't come back to this side without the wellsprings. So she has to train me first, or she'll never be able to go after Lucien the way she wants."

It looked like Elle had woken up on the same sullen side of the bed that I did. "Whoa, you didn't tell me your girlfriend was *that*," Drew said with a low whistle.

Any other day, I would have had a retort. But I couldn't do it tonight. Drew stared at me in confusion.

What I wanted more than anything was to keel over and vomit until there was nothing left inside of me. What I *did*, though, was to keep walking down to meet with Elle where she waited. Most of the damage to her eyes was hidden by her sunglasses, but now that I knew what they were hiding, I could still see the hints of trauma around the edges.

"You're actually here." She sounded surprised. Almost belligerent.

In my head, I could still see the room that had been here once, with the altar set up against one side. We were just a few feet away from it, right at the spot where the worlds had split apart at the seams and created a passage between the real world and the blizzardy nightmare that existed outside the lighthouse.

My hands were shaking.

"Of course we're here. Someone has to keep the kid out of trouble," Drew said.

His concern was a knife in my gut.

"Do you even know why you're here?" Elle asked, looking between us in astonishment. *So she didn't know. Or she didn't think I could go through with it.*

"Know wh—uck!" The knife slid into Drew's gut like butter. My arms were literally shaking now, and I barely had the strength to pull the knife back out. I was glad he was facing away from me, that I couldn't see the look in his eyes. My hands had been cold, but now they were hot. I couldn't figure out why until I looked down and saw the crimson stain spreading down my skin. *This used to be in Drew,* I thought hysterically. Like all I would have to do was slip it back inside him and it would be okay.

The Armstrong line had been Grace's contingency plan. She was the reason that people said things like "there must always be an Armstrong in Belle Dam" and the families were cautious about tolerating the Armstrongs until the next generation came along, and they were deemed expendable.

Drew fell to his knees. He gurgled, and I knew if I looked in his eyes I'd see the question there, so I couldn't. I looked at Elle. Watched her watch me. Watched her see what I was capable of.

She stepped out of the way as a portal started to form, a bulge in reality that threatened to tear through all things. There were no tears in me, even though one of my best friends was bleeding to death. Bleeding to death because of me.

The portal began sucking up his blood like it was a vortex, and not a path between worlds. Individual droplets fell into the edges, crackling with quicksilver. The mercury light that spread across Drew as he shifted was engulfing him now as he was dragged into the portal by a mystical kind of gravity, arcing out against the portal like it was lightning.

Drew had been sprawled along the couch, and Riley was lost in her own world when Matthias continued our conversation. "Do you even know the price that she's asking of you?"

"Then tell me," I'd demanded impatiently.

"The wellsprings aren't enough to earn her freedom." He glanced at Drew, and if I didn't know better I might have described his sigh as soft or fond. "Something that can pry the doors between worlds open long enough for her freedom to stick. That's why she created the Armstrong line in the beginning. So that they would be waiting for her at the end."

Everything came to a halt. "She wants me to kill him?"

"No," Matthias said gravely. "She doesn't want him dead. Dead won't do her any good. To keep the portals open, he must be alive." He steepled his fingers together and regarded me from across the room. "Now tell me again how much you want your revenge upon them."

I caught one last glimpse of the satchel at his side, and I lowered my eyes. "I'm sorry," I whispered, as he disappeared between the worlds.

It only took Elle a few seconds to recuperate. She blinked a few times, then summoned up the vestiges of her enigmatic smile, though now it looked forced and nervous. "Congratulations," she said, biting down on her lower lip, "your visa has been approved." She stepped to one side, now more a cruise director than a gatekeeper. I stepped through the portal without looking back, without thinking of what I'd sacrificed for make this happen. She followed me inside the room of solid white stone. Behind us, the curtain between the worlds fell, and the portal closed.

¤　　¤　　¤

I was gone for twenty-one days.

twenty-four

There weren't any pleasantries exchanged on the other side of the world. I walked through the portal straight into the lantern room where Grace had attacked me once upon a time. The moment Elle stepped through behind me, I felt the portal close up like a zipper being pulled.

The next second I was on the floor, screaming.

Fire burning churning heated words dance like blackberry bushes and accosted gold accents. Screaming, always screaming, and there's a body that won't stop bleeding. Blood teases candy against ravenous maws that could swallow the world but for her standing guard. Blood flows and she keeps bleeding because it's the worlds blood one world seeping into the other like rotten bandages fragrant and raw as it catches fire and burns me and the looking glass cannot save me now. My body screams and veils fall over my face like arrogance, greed, and melancholy. This place is holy. This place is profane. There are seven devils and I might be one.

"Get up."

My head cleared, and inside of me there was a coiled fire where the gnawing void had been. Just like that, my powers were back. It felt good, like the first moment underneath a hot shower, or a warm blanket. But there was still the emptiness to contend with, the feeling that I still wasn't complete. That there was something missing that had once been there.

I killed Drew. I can't believe I killed Drew.

"If you want to learn, get up."

I hadn't even seen Grace yet, but her voice vibrated against my skin like the lashings of a stun gun. My body already felt like it had run a marathon—I was out of practice in handling the visions. This one had come out of the gate swinging, and I hadn't had time to prepare. Every muscle I had was sore, and all of my limbs trembled. Getting to my feet was like being a fawn standing on four legs for the first time. I made it as far as my knees before my body refused to move any more. I laid my head back on the ground, using it like a fifth limb to keep me at least somewhat upright.

"Very well. The hard way it shall be."

Fire scoured the skin from my bones. Pain tore at my limbs, and I collapsed back on the ground into a sea of amaranthine agony. I could feel the heat melting my face, the way that my hair caught fire and burned right down to the root. I burned until I was ashes.

"We have near on to eternity," the voice continued. "I can do this for decades before it grows tedious. Get up."

It took me a few seconds less this time, to get my feet underneath me. But I still couldn't make it up higher than my knees before the next attack came. Blisters erupted across my skin, and my vocal cords melted beyond the ability to function. My agony couldn't make a sound, but still I tried. I tried to scream more than I'd ever tried for anything in my life.

Again, relief. Again, the voice. "Get. Up."

This time, I made it to my feet. This time, I got a look at the woman who was torturing me, and the hellfire lights swarming around her like fireflies. "Fight back," she said calmly.

By the time I'd even managed to process her words, I was back on the floor. Dying. Being torn apart and charred from existence. But again, the pain relinquished its hold on me. Again I made it to my feet. Again she taunted me.

"What sort of warrior are you? Fight back."

This time I made it to my feet before the pain had even stopped. My body grew stronger, reforged a little more with each deluge of pain. Fighting back. This time, when she challenged me, I could feel the light at my back. The spilling, quenching blue that I'd almost forgotten. The light that had come from inside me before, when my life was threatened. When I was in danger. I'd attributed it to the winter voice inside my mind, the insidious part of Lucien that had remained attached to the wellspring power. Corrupting anyone who would touch it.

Even with the blue light, I fell again. But again I rose up. And this time, the light was stronger still, until I was bathed in healing blue, and the rage in Grace's eyes slid over me and around me. Until she was impotent against me, and I was shielded from her.

It felt like a dormant muscle being stretched. With every passing second, I started to understand it better, deepening the light around me and strengthening the shield. Flexing my power to test myself the same way Grace was testing me.

With this victory, small as it might have been, the pattern stopped. There was a curve to her lips, what would have been a smile in anyone else. Anyone that might have had a sense of humor, or even a soul. But Grace was too serious, and too empty, to possess either of those things.

"The first thing you must master is pain," Grace said.

A moment later, a new attack. A new pain. An assault of *everything,* like the world around me had finally grown weary of me and thrown everything it had forward like a psychic shoe bomb.

Winter vengeance and demands of the dead. Marigold melancholy in the veins and deep rose vigils. The house of lights, the waystone, the guide; bright sky potential keening need and frankincense arias worlds where angels flee and demons tread. My word is balance and the law is mine to wield. Do as I say or burn in sunlight the way to the hidden places at the table. Thousands of entrances invasive brigands but only one exit and the hole in the sky. Dark magic lingers like snapdragons in anarchy striking down ancient compacts. Oh how she seethes, and there will be a reckoning. She is not done paying not yet, not until the balance is restored.

The visions stopped just as quickly as they'd begun.

"You don't even know the first thing about yourself,"

Grace said. By the time my eyes cleared and I could see again, she was circling around me. *Like a predator. Exactly like a predator.* Out of the corner of my eye, I saw Elle standing near the staircase, head bowed down and hands clasped in front of her. Praying for me? Or maybe praying for Drew?

"It isn't your fault," Grace continued, still circling me. "It isn't an accident that the powers we possess are lost to the chafing sands of time. The demons call us sorcerers, laughing all the while. We are the demon's hands in the world, the demon's heart. They tie us with strings and expect their will done. And without fail, each generation destroys any information on their predecessors that they can unearth. Because the less you know, the faster you die, and the faster you die, the fewer pawns the demons have in this world."

"No wonder you nearly died." She laughed. "You were trained by idiots."

John wasn't an idiot. Not by a long shot. I snarled, but it only made her laugh harder. "Say another word about him and I'll kill you." Rage and the remembrance of grief surged in my gut, and it took me everything I had to restrain myself. *This was what I'd asked for. This was more than I deserved.*

Grace turned and struck me down again. The explosive red light carrying waves of visions that shoved fifteen thousand hours of memory into my brain at once. All the muscles in my body spasmed, giving out like I'd been hit with a stun gun, and the process started all over again.

Time lacked meaning in the lighthouse. The sky outside was always winter-storm dark, and I never felt hunger pangs or the need to go to the bathroom. I didn't even get that gross feeling on my teeth when they hadn't been brushed in a while. Every time I lay down and closed my eyes, only a second passed before I bolted back upright, fully refreshed. There were no dreams. There was no peace.

Grace thought that torture and teaching were the same. Every session was war waged only between the two of us. It took a lot of rounds before I could summon up the blue light of my power at will and use it to deflect against her. It took even more repetitions before my power could defend me on instinct alone. Even still, with everything I learned, I held something back. I studied her, thought about the way she attacked, the way she thought.

From session to session, I could feel my power changing shapes inside of me, but it was an agonizing growth filled with pains and failures. It happened day by day, but it was a slow progression. I was metal on the blacksmith's anvil, but I was also the blacksmith controlling how and why I was being shaped. My power became something I could control, rather than the thing that controlled me.

"Who do you hate?" she asked me randomly one day.

I wiped my face off with the bottom of my shirt. I didn't sweat, and there was no dirt, but I still *felt* unclean. In need of a shower. "I don't know. You?"

Her lips hinted at humor. "Hatred is what keeps you in control. You can do anything so long as your hatred can rationalize it. Men become monsters with the easiest of justifications. Control your hatred, sharpen it, and you will have a weapon that will last you all of your days."

All three of them? I was tempted to ask.

"Hatred is a whetstone that can sharpen your mind, but hold your grief tight as well. The losses we suffer teach us the control we need. All strong emotions, the ones that scar the world, are the way we find our power."

I spat blood and stepped away from the wall she'd thrown me into only minutes before. "And have you been grieving ever since you came here? I thought time healed all wounds."

Her lips thinned. I realized she'd stopped scaring me a while ago. Grace was a monster, but she was a monster who needed me more than I needed her. "Time heals only what you allow it to. Master yourself and you can suppress the visions, seeing only what you want to see. Be the victor, not the victim." I squirmed, it was too close to the advice Matthias had given me weeks ago. *Be the villain, not the victim.*

I tried not to stare into the furious storm raging outside of the lighthouse. It was like seven kinds of natural disasters rolled up into one chaotic world of destruction. The clouds roiled as though stirred by tornadoes that were thousands of miles across, and blizzards raged at the corners, blanketing the sky in shawls of white. Streaks of glooming black and red light stood out from time to time, volcanic destruction so far from here that it was little more than a splash of color on the horizon.

But it was the lightning I hated the most, because when the lightning struck—a thousand bolts careening out from a single origin—the clouds lit up so much I could see *things*. Faces and hands and slithering pieces that rolled with purpose, so vast that their movements were the cause of the shrieking winds that howled around the lighthouse precipice.

"Again," Grace said, as her onslaught started anew.

¤　　¤　　¤

"What's out there?" I'd fallen over and collapsed, drained. This time, my eyes didn't close, and the passage of time was slow and steady, measured in heartbeats. Hours passed before I finally let my eyes drift closed, only to bolt upright again a moment later. The aches and pains in my body were washed away as usual. Grace stood near the broken wall at her usual vigil. This time, I went to stand next to her, searching the clouds for what it was she saw. Or didn't see.

"The beginning of all things. The end of all things. The punishment and praise of all things."

"The Riders at the Gate," I said.

She spread her hands expansively. "Welcome to the Gate. Enter the lighthouse from a thousand different worlds, and exit a thousand more. You could visit a new world every day for the rest of your life and never double back on yourself."

I looked around as though I could see them, these

doors into other worlds. "This is what you were looking for, wasn't it? You wanted to travel to other worlds? Why?" Wasn't one world bad enough? A thousand more filled with lies, betrayal and hatred? Who would ever want to see that?

"Because I thought the lighthouse was the answer to my gift. There's a connection. The Riders created the lighthouse, leaving a door in every world they could claw their way into, and sorcerers to draw them into these worlds. The Riders know the trick, you see, to a demon walking in the world of men. Cast off enough of your power, or hide it away, and you can enter the world as easily as any demonic dog. No real demon would ever sacrifice their power this way, but the Riders are beyond simple demons."

"And finding the lighthouse was how Lucien found you."

She inclined her head. "He found me because I started searching. I found the lighthouse only with his help. This was his plan all along. Then he stole my future from me, and had to be taught a lesson."

She might have trapped him, but he wasn't really punished. Not yet.

"Again," I said. "The faster you show me everything, the faster I can return."

Grace inclined her head, a smile on her lips.

¤   ¤   ¤

It wasn't all moments of conversation and violence. There were times where she broke through my defenses without even looking in my direction, and when the hit came, instead of debilitating pain, it sank into my skin and electrified my senses. It was scraps of knowledge at first: understanding how to divide my vision so that I could see many different places all at once, how to single out certain kinds of memories, how to pick out liars without unraveling everything that they were. Grace had uncovered dozens of different ways to utilize her power, some of which I'd figured out on my own.

She also learned things in the exchange. The bits of magic that I'd managed, the way I'd destroyed a hellhound, the overwhelming explosion of power that had first brought me here. But more importantly, she learned things about the world. She saw Belle Dam through my eyes: a world where communication was instantaneous, no matter the distance. The vast power of the Internet and the way it changed how people worked.

"You're too slow, too sloppy," Grace said, days later. I was lethargic all the time now, my body shifting into some altered state of consciousness to cope with the fact that I no longer played by life's rules. I'd become hypervigilant, convinced that attacks were coming at every moment of the day. When they didn't come, not for hours and hours, I convinced myself that it was all part of her plan. It only made the paranoia worse.

Grace started lobbing fireballs at me. I could swat them to the side, transmute the fire into water, disperse the fire into a pulse of heat, or even freeze them where they flew.

Every time I found a way to stop them, every loophole

I exploited, she closed it off and made the next volley even more impenetrable. The longer we went, the more the grim line of her mouth tightened. "The point," she said icily, "is to unravel the magic and claim it for your own. Do not dodge an attack you can swallow whole. It will weaken your enemy, and throw him off guard."

Each time the fireballs struck me, the blue aura that surrounded me constantly now would keep them from doing any real damage, but it was still like sticking my finger into an electrical outlet, just for a second. A jolt, like my heart and body were being restarted. It wasn't pleasant.

She wanted me to unravel the spells using only my visions, which was basically the exact opposite of what John had spent seventeen years trying to get me to do. The only problem was that she made it so *difficult.* The witch eyes could unravel even the most complicated spell, laying out the component pieces and the way it looked and felt. But that sometimes took time. I had, at best, a handful of seconds before I took another fireball to the face.

Throughout it all, I watched the calculating twist in her eyes, saw the way she regarded me. And so I took my time working through concepts I already understood. Fumbled through spells that I could have managed in my sleep. Because I didn't dare let her know everything that I was capable of. We were still enemies under the skin.

I hadn't lied when I said I hated her. I just knew how to prioritize.

twenty-five

Neither of us was prepared the day she tried to teach me how to invade another's mind. I'd done things that like before—it was how Trey and I had managed to stop Lucien the first time—but Grace's way was different. Slipping inside Trey had been like jumping onto a moving train and then jumping off before it reached the station. Grace's way was brute force: a constant barrage of power and pressure until the mind cracked right down the middle.

She treated it like a game. First, she would try to batter her way through my defenses, then I would try the same. The price was that every time she broke her way into my mind, everything she touched, she tainted. I couldn't think of one of the emergency room trips with John without feeling her derision soaking into the scene. And she heaped even more anger onto my memories of Catherine, a cold blade of wrath compared to the inferno of my rage.

"You've been wasted," she huffed, hours into the exercise. "Spending your entire life hiding behind others, hoping they would solve your problems so that you wouldn't have to. Hiding behind John, behind Lucien, Gentry, and even your *father*." She sneered. "You are the very definition of weakness."

She moved in for another strike, but her rebuke had pissed me off, and I struck first. As hard as I could. It was the first time I'd ever broken through her defenses, and the first time I'd ever seen the things she saw.

It should have destroyed me.

¤　　¤　　¤

It was the vision. The one that set everything into motion. But the nature of it has changed. I'm no longer seeing it through my eyes. I'm seeing it through *hers*.

It was a simple thing for him, the survivor of a dark apotheosis, to bring forth the lighthouse from between the faded tapestries of worlds dead and buried. Wherever there is power, there are locks. And somehow, for him, the locks swirl around, eager to open though they've lain fallow for the few who have known to try. Wherever there are locks, there are keys, and this boy, this boy will be a key like no other. The ground beneath me trembles, shatters, rends its limbs and grinds its bones and the lighthouse emerges into the world that had lost it a century past.

*He can unlock all of the doors inside—doors I've spent a hundred years beating against in frustration. But for him, they sing. They cry out in desperation—*look at us, open us. Whole *worlds who have no clue that a beardless monstrosity who is barely full grown has sown the seeds of their dissolution.*

I can feel Them. The Storm Demons, the Many-in-Ones, the Riders at the Gate. Circling the sewers and ascending through the aviaries. I've glimpsed them before, in the darkness behind the ever-raging chaos storms between the worlds. They are massive creatures that are not constrained by one world, or two worlds. Entire planets cannot contain the whole of their glory. Such is the way it has always been.

But all things have their endings.

"He comes," they whisper, in voices that are not words but thoughts that pound the air like a behemoth's wings. The Riders at the Gate, banished from all worlds when the second world was still new. Legends say that men were born of the second world. But the Riders, they are creatures born from the first. The first world, broken and bartered by the Riders, and the source of the waterfall from which all evil plunges into the world.

What was once the city of Belle Dam—my city—is now an ossuary worth nothing more than the bone dust it collects. The spells laid into the bones of this town were so intricate, so careful! But he brings it to ruin with ease, drinking down the marrow of the skeleton that makes it all holy. He saw the truth I hid, the truth hidden by the Rider himself, and so he brings my legacy to ruin. Not simply enough to look into the world and let everything he sees ignite into flames. No, the spells in the town ran deeper than that: trickled down through the generations so that the blood, too, was a spell of its own making.

Magics as strong as this tend to spread, it is the nature of all things.

I will be the first. He comes for me, and I see myself pleading with him. Speaking words that appeal to a human side he no longer has. Calling him by names that no longer describe even a fraction of his power. Who was I, he cried and his voice was the lightning itself, to bray at him with my human tongue?

I was the first. But I was not the last by a far cry. He makes it into a game. Trapped and waiting, he calls me the Watcher. And so he makes me watch. They scream when he finds them, going door to door and uncovering their hiding places with eyes that brook no secrets. He doesn't understand the looks on their faces. Their words. Their tears. He has no humanity left to understand them. They are butterflies, and he is the crushing fist.

His face is confused, until it is presented with the blood. Blood is simple. Blood is easy.

Bloody is necessary.

His plan is obvious to me, though I can do nothing to stop him. To commit the most inhuman act, to take his place among them, and become the most heinous parts of himself, the town must first be shattered.

Storm voices scream out. "Destruction. Herald."

The lighthouse tears through this world, leading to both worlds below and worlds above. It is the tree of life, the tower of Babel, the ladder of Jacob. It is impossibly tall, dwarfing even the clouds that have swept away from it like oil from soap. Its size, and presence, are an affront to the world of man, prov-

ing once and for all how insignificant they are in the grand scheme of things.

This should have been my moment, the thought is savage and hungry in my mind. I, who drew the first blood. The Widow upon whom Belle Dam owed its existence. But when he tears my soul from my body, compressing it down until it is nothing more than a shiny bit of carbon, the only victory I have is that I do not utter a single word. With every sparkle of sunlight upon the gem, my soul screams. Eternal agony is a deserved punishment, he tells me, for a soul so wicked as mine.

"Please," the Rider below him begs. The boy looks down, surprised. He's forgotten that his boot covers the neck of the Rider, that at any moment he could crush the life from him. It isn't quite Lucien, not anymore. The skin is cracked and in places ripped away, and he slithers on his belly like the snake he is. He was formidable once, but now he searches for masters and monsters, one to save him, the other to feed upon.

"There is winter in my bones, now," the boy says, and it has the sound of a riddle he hasn't quite puzzled out yet. "You were called Lucien, weren't you? I almost remember." His eyes alight with new knowledge. "The light that blinds thine eyes, fortune; the thousand eyes and the frozen flames. Look at you," he coos at it like a pet. "How tiny a creature you are now."

There are still vestiges of power left within the demon. It would be an easy thing, to empty him out and drain the last of his power away. Lucien tries to cry, but finds himself unable. It unsettles my stomach, to watch a creature like that striving towards an emotion it has never felt before. But it tries harder than it has ever tried before, struggling for survival.

"I will be better than you ever were," the boy promises him. "Because I am a being filled with graces and holy fires. Had the stars favored you differently, we might have been brothers."

A noxious fume of emotions curled around them both, like some strange perfume of souls. "Look at you," he said, caressing the side of the demon's head. "So human. You taste like endings."

"Bear witness," the voices call from the far sides of both heavens and hell. Scattered as they are, in corners of worlds where the lighthouse is barely legend. But they are coming. They come. He turned to me, even though I am dead and ash in this broken world. "They come, and I will welcome them with flames and anguish."

The end of the world begins with a boy, a demon, and a power that should never have been.

¤　¤　¤

Grace disappeared into the bowels of the lighthouse and left me to linger in the lantern room while she soothed her pride. Or whatever it was that I'd wounded.

I didn't let those days go to waste. I continued trying to become the master of my own power and figure out all the different ways it could be used. Grace claimed the only thing one needed was grief, or some other strong emotion, but deep down that didn't seem right.

And if were so easy to master the witch eyes, then why did the demons get involved at all? There were pieces she wasn't telling me, pieces I could discern on my own. Grace had a fraction of Lucien's power herself—maybe not as much as one of the wellsprings, but a few drops at least. Enough to help her control her powers, and enough to let her manipulate the same strands of fate that Lucien did, giving her access to the same visions of the future.

Knowing that she was holding back was annoying, but I also understood it. Grace wouldn't give away everything, not when she was setting me up to take her place. She still didn't realize that I knew, of course.

It was fine, because I did my best work while being underestimated.

When she did return, finally, I saw the grim line of her mouth and knew that our time here was done. "You have three days," she said coldly. "But first, you will fulfill the rest of the terms of your contract."

"Within twenty-four hours," I said, not meeting her eyes.

"You will do it as soon as you leave!" Grace snarled, losing any sense of composure. "You cannot break the bonds of our contract. You belong to me."

"I belong to *myself*!" I fired back. "And you don't have to remind me about what I owe you. I know what I have to do." I had already done enough for her. Now was the time for *me*. For what I wanted.

I turned towards the stairs, realizing that Elle was already there, waiting to escort me back. "You realize if you haven't done your part," I said over my shoulder, "then all of this will be for nothing. I'll be dead and you'll never escape this lighthouse. I won't be the last one born with our gift. Eventually, Lucien will find the skeleton key he needs, and then he'll come for you."

Grace hurled obscenities at me as I descended the stairs, antiquated words in a language I didn't speak. But "Fuck you" had a particular sound to it that was the same no matter what language it was in.

A portal waited for me at the bottom of the stairs, Elle at its side like an attendant at an amusement park. *You must be this tall to travel between dimensions.*

"Make sure she gets her fiber," I said, jutting my head towards my shoulder, back towards the way I'd come. "There's still time for you to escape, you know."

"I struck my own bargain," she said grudgingly. Interestingly enough, her head was still bowed low. She was going to have one hell of a headache for all the posturing she'd done. "I'll stay where I'm at. At least one of us should be predictable."

I paused at that. "Does she know? About me?"

"She thinks you're under control."

"Are you going to tell her?"

"We should all pay for our mistakes," Elle said slowly. "Even her."

twenty-six

Belle Dam had changed in my absence. I'd left in the midst of a prolonged summer with warm days and warmish nights, and returned to full-fledged winter. Returning to a giant pit in the ground was inconvenient when snow had been coming down for days. The snow came up to my knees, and even as I stood there getting my bearings back, a sharp wind sent a sky full of dust spilling out over top of me.

I had to turn around a few times to figure out where I was, exactly. With snow coating the sides of the hole, it was hard to see where the ground sloped gently upwards in the hill we'd used to climb down.

We.

And now there was only me.

I promised myself I would stop and feel what had happened once my time was done. Either I would be successful, or my three days would pass and I'd spend the rest of them in the lighthouse. The difference between a living hell, or just the actual hell.

I felt different now that the witch eyes were a part of me again. I could look out into the woods and see the story of every tree, every path. The people who'd walked these woods, their stories. Their lives and lies and troubles. It was all there, waiting for me. I didn't need the sunglasses now, to shield me from the visions. I willed them to stay silent, and they listened.

My magic curled around me, warming the air and keeping the snow from seeping cold into my skin. I plodded through the accumulation until I found the hill and climbed back up. There would still be a half mile trek back towards civilization, but I could handle it.

"Braden?"

Jade's voice was tentative and disbelieving. She stood at the top of the hill, wearing a bright white parka and snow boots that had probably cost more than my entire outfit. She looked like she'd been standing around here for a while—her skin was pink with cold, and she was shaking.

"Where were you? How are you okay right now? Everyone's been looking for you!"

"Jade, calm," I said slowly. "How long was I gone?"

She shook her head, still bewildered. I guess I couldn't blame her. I'd basically appeared out of thin air after all. "Three weeks? You missed Christmas."

Three weeks. Time had moved strangely in the lighthouse. I would have thought I was gone more like six months.

"Is Drew with you? We know you both came out here and then you disappeared. We found his motorcycle on the side of the road. It wasn't hard to figure out where you'd gone. Where is he?"

Jade's questions kept coming, too fast and too insistent. Her voice became a low buzzing, and I frowned, trying to concentrate on it. My ears popped, once, twice, a third time. The wind whistled through the trees, the crackle of broken branches, traffic in the distance, water crashing against the rocks, people crying, laughing at jokes, yelling about the milk, "why the hell didn't you get the milk like you said you would I ask you to do one thing you stupid—"

Everything stopped when I closed my eyes.

Inhale. Exhale. Maintain control.

"Drew isn't coming," I said, once the vertigo and overwhelming pressure in my ears had settled down.

"But I have to talk to him," Jade whispered. Her eyes glistened in the faint traces of moonlight. A shudder passed through her, and then she was fine. Strong. "Come on, we should get you home."

I followed Jade out of the woods, but I didn't tell her I wasn't going home.

I never would again.

¤   ¤   ¤

After Grace's lighthouse had disappeared from the world, the city had built a replacement. Not as grand, not as interesting. But it did the trick as well as anything, I supposed.

I'd left Jade at the street, telling her a heavily censored version of my plans for the evening. I knew she might be necessary later, so I told her where to meet me, and when. If it worked, I would need a familiar face. If it didn't work, I might just need the distraction. After she left, and it had been such a struggle to *make* her leave, I'd moved on to my next destination, the lighthouse, and my next appointment. My schedule was packed, considering I'd spent the last three weeks in phantom boot camp.

"It's about time," Matthias grumbled, climbing to his feet. He'd been perched carefully on a rock, clearly waiting. I looked around in alarm.

"Jade was waiting for me."

"You're lucky it was the girl," Matthias said. "Everyone knows you boys were playing with things you shouldn't before you disappeared. She's not the only one whose been lurking around. This town does so enjoy its rumors, especially when they're salacious."

Rumors were the least of my concern. "And Lucien? Is he up and walking around yet?"

Matthias nodded. "For almost a week now. Those church bells were such nasty business. I heard he's trying to have them all melted down into scrap. But he has bigger problems at the moment. It seems your dear old father isn't too thrilled with his son's disappearance. And he's got only one target in mind."

"Catherine and Lucien," I confirmed. "Have they come to blows yet?"

Matthias sighed in regret. "Sadly not. I was hoping there would be a bit of bloodshed to welcome you home, but *someone* has been a most unhealthy influence on poor Jason. He's trying to be *rational.* There is no body, so he assumes his son still draws breath. He doesn't dare strike out at them until he knows what they want."

A better son would have made contingency plans. Made sure his father knew that he was going across worlds and might never come back. I ... hadn't thought that far through.

No, that wasn't true. I was so wrapped up in what I was doing that I hadn't stopped to think about what would happen when I was gone. Or what would happen if I'd never come back.

The demon smiled. It was like looking at a wholly different person, now with my power returned. I could see hints of the demon at his edges, features that were too sharp, too pointed. Even more, I could sense the scope of the power he'd left behind when he incarnated in this world. Unlike Lucien, who'd had his power ripped out of him, Matthias had left his power behind, and was free to collect it at his leisure once he was released from this existence.

"Your secrets are safe ... for now. But if the girl knows you're back, then word will start to spread ... " he trailed off, obviously baiting me.

I studied him. Matthias was always up front to a point. He was smart enough to know that our fates were entwined. If I fell, his part in my plans would be obvious to every one of the factions colluding here in town.

"Anything else I need to know?" I asked, trying to mask my fear.

"Perhaps you don't understand the nature of the feud," Matthias said, brushing sand off of his pants. "The only thing that could possibly be worse than your disappearance off the face of this world? Is your sudden return. It will only take one spark for this town to go up in flames the likes of which none of us, humans or demons alike, have ever seen. You need to show caution now. Or you might find your hand basket to hell a little overcrowded."

"Matthias," I started, but he didn't let me finish.

"There is one thing I desire most in this wretched little world," he said, his posture stiff and unyielding, "and I will not have it if you leave nothing but a ghost town in your wake."

I thought of the way Belle Dam had looked in the vision—broken and burning. What had Grace called it? *An ossuary.* Like the city was nothing more than an empty pit filled with bones of those who had once lived there. That could still happen.

"Don't do this," he pleaded urgently, "let the Rider's power lay fallow. Fulfill our bargain, and I will help you."

"Cross your heart?" I asked, finally feeling three weeks without sleep catching up to me. Bones were never meant to be this heavy.

"No," I said, ending the discussion. "What time is it?"

Matthias looked down at his watch. "A little after nine, why?"

I shook my head. "Come on. We don't have time to play games of 'what if.' I chose my path." And without another word, I walked towards the water. Matthias was a cautious predator behind me. The closer I came to the shore, the farther the water receded. I didn't part the sea or anything major like that, I just... moved it back. Moisture leached from the wet sand where I walked, and the bay waters retreated. The ground dipped downhill, but still we walked, and still the waters were repelled. We didn't walk far, maybe five hundred feet before I stopped us. The sand beneath us was hot, an impossible warmth for something that should have been under fifty feet of water.

I could have done all of this from the shore, of course. Matthias wouldn't have cared either way. But I wanted him to be reminded of the power that was mine. The sound of locks turning exploded in my mind, and the ground beneath us rumbled like a bank safe the size of an aircraft carrier being spun down in the earth below us.

Locks clicked into place, spun open, and in seconds the door into the wellspring started to open in the earth. The power, a kaleidoscope of energy that didn't feel magical *or* demonic, but some blending of the two, sailed up and lapped at my feet.

I reached out, palm facing the ground, and drew the wellspring into me. Winter solace surged into my bones like it had always been meant for me. Icy demon power reacted against the fire of my magic, and the two waged a war inside of me. But neither of them was in control. I was. I pushed them both down, and thought it felt like only seconds, I knew that almost an hour passed as I struggled to maintain my control.

"Okay," I said, rasping. "Okay, we're good."

"*We?*" Matthias asked, his apprehension thick like a cloud around him.

The Grimm is afraid, the winter voice in me murmured. Without even thinking about it, I clamped down on that part of the demon's power, with its whispers and attempts at controlling my mind. I was my own person, and I wouldn't become the broken thing that any of them wanted. I locked the winter voice away and pushed at the fires burning inside of me. *I controlled these powers*, I wanted to shout. *Me!*

"Nothing to worry about yet, Matthias, I'm still just as obnoxious and adorable as always," I said after taking a few deep breaths. We walked back the way we came, maybe moving a bit faster as the returning water nipped at our heels. "Get your phone out," I demanded, once we were back on the real shore.

Matthias had it in his hands before I was even done speaking. He was probably scared of what I would do if he said no. "Text Jason. Tell him Catherine's willing to meet to discuss the ransom demands." The demon's eyebrows lifted. "Then text Catherine, and tell her that Jason's going to take a son for a son if she doesn't meet him."

"When?"

"Tell them to meet at midnight." I squinted up at the beacon shining above us. With my new control, I could choose to repress the visions, but I flitted through the different layers to the world until I found the one I was looking for. There were many, many spells that had been laid over the foundation of Belle Dam. The first one I'd noticed had been the dark eye that hung over the town like a damning albatross. Lucien's eye. Lucien's power.

Grace had weakened him for a while, but he was stronger than ever. Stronger than he had been the last time we'd faced off, in his office.

I had to be stronger, too.

"Where are you going until then?" Matthias asked, unable to repress his curiosity.

"Don't worry, Grimm. I have a plan. But a great magician needs an assistant, you know."

There were, after all, three wellsprings in the city. Lucien possessed one, and now I another. Grace had never been specific about the ownership of the wellsprings—she demanded their power, but she never said she wanted *both* of the ones that remained. I had claimed one for myself, but there was still a third that would level the playing field. If I was right, each of us would be a match for the other.

But first, I would set the rest of the pieces into motion.

Twenty-seven

The hospital lights flickered when I came off the elevator. The whirling storm of magic in me clawed for release, but it only took a fraction of my power to move undetected down the halls. The power trickled out of my fingertips, smoothing away the sounds of my passing, the sight of me walking off the elevator, and the smell of seawater that still clung to me like cologne.

Magic came so much easier now that I could hold the visions back. *Is this what it was always like for you, Grace? How could it not be enough for her? Why had it been so important for her to seek out more and more power? This was ... it was everything.*

Riley's room was at the end of the hall. Everyone else was asleep, but I knew she'd be waiting for me. Something in me had been waiting for this, but it was hard to say where the feelings were coming from. With the wellspring power inside of me, there was a dark potential that could go awry at any moment if I lost control. Was I really looking forward to seeing Riley again? Or was it the winter voice?

What had happened to Riley was an accident, the reaction of my power against Lucien's. But both powers were inside of me now.

I didn't expect to see Riley sitting up when I walked in. But what was more, I didn't expect the change in her eyes. Ever since Lucien had attacked her, Riley had the cornflower blue irises of a demon. But now the blue had faded, and in the light her hazel eyes shined like gold.

"Riley?" I whispered.

"Braden," she whispered, her eyes shimmering with tears. "What did you *do*?"

She knew. What I'd done to Drew, and why I did it. The fact that I hadn't even cried yet. Riley had been broken beyond repair, but somehow she still found her way back to herself, and she knew what I had done. How easy it had been.

I was a monster, and now I wasn't the only one who knew it.

My steps faltered. My brain skipped off the track and I fumbled for something. Anything. But there was no way of making this right. Not yet.

I crumpled down into the chair at her side. I couldn't bear to look at her anymore.

"It was the only thing that made sense," I whispered. "I knew it was wrong, but I had to. It was the only way that Grace could be free. She'd been planning this for years—she needed a sacrifice so she could cross over permanently. The same way Elle used her friend to make the journey before. But Grace is in another league, so she needed someone that had enough juice to make it happen. That's why she made the Armstrongs the way they were."

I put my head in my hands. "You were the one that said that there was only one way to beat them. I tried, I really did, Riley. But I couldn't see any other way. I had to bargain with Grace to get what I wanted, but I can't let her out. Leaving Lucien here would be bad enough. I can't imagine what the two of them would do. They're both monsters." Out in the hall, a phone rang. "But that doesn't make it okay, Ri," I whispered.

"Common comes the advancing knight." My head whipped up, Riley's eyes had returned to their inhuman blue, the awareness in them, gone. "Crawling through spider webs, weaving doom inside traps inside gambits."

This wasn't happening. "Riley?"

"Stop sleeping," Riley chided, tapping me on the temple. She stared at my head like she could see through my skull. At the sound of her, the winter voices began crawling through my body like worms, inching towards the light. Riley cooed, and I stumbled back.

I am in control. Not you. I don't want you here. Stay down. Stay asleep.

Magic might have become easier to manage with my powers under control, but maintaining control was an infinitely more vexing struggle. All it had taken was two little words, and a surge of demonic essence slipped out of my grasp. It was the difference between standing on a window ledge a thousand feet in the air, and then clinging to it by the fingertips a moment later.

I am in control. This is my body. My life. I pushed back, fighting every impulse and icy rationale. I tried to shut out the voices, but I couldn't. *Break her. Free her. Let her be your dark prophet, let her be your lantern guide. Human with the demon mind, she could be useful.*

Riley was more dangerous than I had thought. "Why are you doing this?" I managed to grit out, squeezing my hands into fists. I concentrated on each breath, on the warm air entering my body, the heat against my skin.

"You need him," she laughed, like this were all a joke and I just hadn't caught on yet.

"I can do this without him." Riley insisted on acting like we were two separate entities, me versus the violet-eyed version of myself.

"But why would you want to?" She giggled, manifesting the chess piece I'd given her from between her hands with a magician's flourish. "I like him best."

"Riley," I took another deep breath, "I want to help you. That's why I'm here. Do you remember what you used to be like? I want to take you back there. You shouldn't be stuck in the hospital like this. It's my fault you're here."

"It is," she agreed, but her voice was flat. "I get to watch the pieces move."

"I want to help you," I continued. "But I need your help first."

Her head craned to the side. "You want to punish. I want to help."

"Okay, good." I reached over, and took one of her hands between mine. Her free hand still held the bishop, and she squeezed it tight in her fist. "You told me to come back when I had my power again." I faked a laugh. "I'm here. Bright and shiny as usual."

She pulled her hand out of my grasp and wiped it against the sheets of her bed. "I said I wanted violet-eyed boy. You're not him. I want him."

"He's already here," I said, desperately trying to think of a way out of this. If Riley got too upset, I didn't know what I would do. When she lost control, she was violent and unpredictable and the nurses would have to sedate her. Which meant she wouldn't be able to help me, and if she was unconscious, I didn't think I could help her either.

She lunged at me so suddenly that I couldn't react in time. The blue aura that surrounded me in dangerous moments flared to life and then dwindled down to a dampened smolder around her hands. The moment that her skin touched mine, the power of the wellspring surged up again, and I was consumed.

We have been waiting and we are so patient, loving and kind and helpful. All can be yours just cast off what matters no more. Who needs them, the ones that hurt and betrayed you. We can make them suffer. We can show you how to destroy them. Sometimes they don't have to die to be broken and it's better when they live. This city is yours, here you can test your-

self, become what you are meant to be. We have been waiting for you, only you, it's only ever been you.

Before, there had only been one voice in my head, but now there were dozens. Maybe thousands. Or maybe only one. It was hard to say for sure. I could feel the two different antithetical energies rustling around in my essence, two serpents locked in an inevitable contest for supremacy. The fire of magic, the churning engine behind the witch eyes, and the calculating, slow-moving glaciers of the wellspring. They'd fought before, and broken Riley in the process.

She was screaming next to me, but she was laughing too. The bed rattled, the room shook. Lights exploded. The hospital was going to collapse around us, and still she would not let go of my head.

Let us in, and let us breathe. We are your right hand, we are fate given flesh. Accept us now. Accept what we offer. Together we will show you how to humble them all, how to make the city kneel before you and beg you to end their suffering. There is a vast universe where you can be everything you wish to be, no matter how contrary. Worlds of malice and worlds of compassion. Worlds where you are everything and worlds where you are the void.

All I could hear was screaming wind and laughter. I tried to fight back, but I was just one person against a power that had raged for thousands of years. I was out of my league. *Let us in,* the voices whispered.

Fine, I agreed.

And just like that, she patted me on the cheek. "There

he is," Riley said, sounding so much like the old Riley that I couldn't process it. I was already reeling, and this was too much. She was too much.

New strength surged into my arms and legs, my mind cleared of all the debris of the last few weeks. It wasn't a sudden change like I expected. There wasn't a switch to flip, from human to inhumane. I didn't look out at the world like a stranger. I knew what the thoughts of the other me had been like. I knew how foreign this world had seemed to the other Braden.

But I was still myself. The demon power poured through my veins like a surge of adrenaline, and the power of the witch eyes curled around me and inside of me, a fire that would not go out. Somehow, the two powers had achieved a balance.

"Now we can begin," Riley said, and took my hand in hers, sliding her fingers between mine.

twenty-eight

The contact between us kept the power inside me writhing, electric and angry. Demanding release. I couldn't leave Riley like this much longer if I could help it. Whatever she was becoming, it seemed like it was getting worse. Or maybe it was finally revealing itself, now that I had my powers back. She'd been broken by a combination of Lucien's power and my own, but more and more it seemed like the demon was stronger in her.

Her hand in mine was icy, but her grip was inhumanly strong. She could have broken my bones if she wanted to, I had no doubt.

"Tell Riley where you want it to hurt," she whispered, leaning close to me. I wanted to squirm away, because this wasn't Riley. More and more, she was becoming what I would imagine Lucien and Grace's child would be like.

"Lucien hides behind his abilities," I said, licking my lips. "He relies on them for everything. I've tried using them before, but it's too much chaos in my head. There aren't just a thousand different outcomes to anything, there's a thousand times a thousand. And that's a few hours' worth. I can't keep up with them the way Lucien does."

"I don't hear a request."

Yes, definitely the sooner the better. "I have a plan to take it away from him, but I want to do something else first. Something...worse."

A slow smile started to creep across her face, off-putting in the way that muscles seemed to contract at random, rather than by intent. Like someone trying to mimic smiling when they'd only seen the anatomy of one, muscles tightening, pulling against bone for leverage.

"You want the confluence," she said. Her hand slipped out of mine and then brushed against my temple again. "Open your eyes. See the dark lines. See the futures, the threads."

The demonic power in me reacted, again, to her words. I tried to pull away, tried to throw myself off the bed and away from her, but awareness of my body faded as my vision was clouded with futures.

The world became a creature of fog, sweeping in from the sides and giving contrast to the thousands of colored threads that spilled out in front of me like an explosion of iridescent fishing line. Each thread twisted around others, knotted up, wrapped around, intersected, and cut off other threads. Even just an inch in front of my face was a maze of colors I could barely decipher. And Lucien could sift through thousands of them in an instant. It was his birthright the same way the witch eyes were mine, but I hadn't even mastered my gift. I had to have Grace's help. So how would I ever master Lucien's?

That's what Riley was for.

You want the confluences, her voice pressed into my head from the outside, ringing in my ears. *The places where futures intersect.* Her fingers floated into my vision, filled with sparkling stars and transparent against the wave of potential in front of me. She strummed her fingers along the threads like they were strings on a guitar, tugging on places where five, ten, twenty lines all came together.

Take away one point, but she didn't finish the thought before the confluence went dark, *and everything is dominoes.* All the threads that had spilled out of it, maybe twice what had entered it, vanished. Dark fog appeared through now-empty spaces in the future weave. *Take away many points, and what will he have left?*

One by one, the futures started to vanish, until all paths lead to the same five or six outcomes. And then even those, too, began to fade away until there was only one left.

A future that ended with my boot on Lucien's neck—and the town around me charred from existence.

Only in this version of the future, Riley was there. Her hair was hacked short, her face gaunt and skeletal, and eyes burning like gas flames. She stood behind Trey in placement, but her role was clear. Protégé. Handmaiden. Whatever it was that Elle fulfilled for Grace, Riley would be for me in the dark turn of my future.

It was enough to send me recoiling back. The connection between us split with an awful screech of mental feedback, the psychic equivalent to a microphone going rogue. The visions faded, and Riley sat there watching me with disaffection.

I can't let her stay like this. She can't become ... whatever that was.

I didn't think it through. The power in me swelled, responding to my need. Whatever Lucien and I had done before had attacked Riley's mind: scrambling what was there, twisting it and perverting its shape. She'd come out of it broken and inhuman. But I had both of the same powers inside of me now—the witch eyes and Lucien's wellspring essence—so in theory I should have been able to.

But I'd never seen Riley's mind without my sunglasses on, so even if I could figure it out, I wasn't sure what it should look like before it had been altered. Her mind now was a towering stack of faded blue bricks, aged and dark in some places, faded and bone white in others. There were holes in the wall, entire sections where the bricks were missing. By any rights, the whole thing should have toppled to the ground, but somehow there was an equilibrium formed by the bricks and emptiness.

"All the king's horses and all the king's men couldn't put her back together again," Riley said with a giggle.

"King me," I muttered back as *there—that spot right there*—the wall was different. Squid-spongy instead of stiff and unyielding, bricks the same shade of blue as Riley's eyes.

It's just a stain, the winter voices whispered slyly, *you can strip it away. We can show you how.* I sucked my lower lip down between my teeth and bit down, focusing on the wall. Everything felt...jumbled. Like the colors were wrong and the wall wasn't supposed to even be a wall at all. It had been taken and shaken around like a handful of dice, its purpose completely changed.

The winter voices were right, though. I could feel the way the stain had a sticky side to it and how easy it would be to tear it away. As soon as I started to tear, I realized my mistake, although it was already too late. The spot was cornflower blue for a reason—it was a fraction of Lucien's power just like the wellspring, although this had the added benefit of coming directly from the source.

In contrast to the depths of the wellspring, it was a miniscule bit of demonic power. But size didn't always matter, and taking in a little more demon into me was just like adding a guilty conscience to an already bad day: it just made things worse.

The winter voices surged into a furor of words, in languages I didn't even think had ever been spoken out loud before, just before the English my mind translated it to. *Riders at the Gate. So many sins at our fingertips. Agony first, then the blood. Open doors and throats and don't mind the mess. Thrown from the lighthouse, not messy enough. Decapitation much better. Funnier. So much humor in the moment the light fades. Let them all diminish. It's time. It's time. Waited so long and now there is—*

"No!"

But even as I fought against it, I could feel the part of me that was in control slipping away, and something else rising up underneath it all. Like a combine scything through wheat fields, it roared across the landscape of my mind, blades of diamond dicing away at all the chaff and wasted potential.

This is how it happens. This is how I become the dark thing.

There was too much in me now—too much demon, and not enough human. How Grace ever thought she could control the power of the wellspring was beyond me. I only had a fraction of it inside me, and it was too much. It felt like I was a balloon that had filled far past the point where it should have exploded, only I hadn't yet. But it was only a matter of time.

"Braden?" Jade appeared at the door, an angel dressed in black.

"No!" Riley screamed, a renegade fury in her voice. She lunged off the bed and it was only at the last second that some part of my brain rebooted, and I slammed a wall of magic in between the two girls. Riley had found a knife somewhere, long and sharp and gripped by the blade rather than the pommel, causing blood to spill from between her fingers.

The blue light erupted around me like a security blanket, and instantly the shifting balance in my head reversed, and the demonic energy was no longer in control. As my mind cleared, I realized how close to slipping I was. *Three days? How am I even going to manage three more hours?*

Letting the wellspring power run free, listening to the winter voices, all of it was designed to make me weak, and exploit those moments.

Wisely, Jade didn't say anything at first. She just stared at the scene in front of her with wide, terrified eyes. Riley fought against the barrier, blood splattering against the air and smearing against it, making the invisible slightly... not. Her eyes and face were still screwed up in an animalistic fury.

"Jade, keep talking," I said. Maybe if I had something to latch onto, something I could focus on. Because I had to try again. I couldn't leave Riley like... this. There had to be something I could do.

"What do you want me to say?" she asked.

"I don't care," I whispered, feeling nerves and exhaustion skipping along the edges of my awareness. I might not get another shot at this. I had to do *something*.

Again I tried to fight the wall, to tear it apart piece by piece. I could tear away the weak parts, where there was nothing but stain upon the bricks, but that hadn't worked out so easily last time. Then I realized I was going about it all wrong. Instead of stripping the stain from the bricks, I started moving the bricks themselves.

I couldn't even say for sure what Jade said in the background, but the sound of her voice was a soothing buzz against the harshness in Riley's mind. I could feel the sweat pooling under my arms, down my back, even in the backs of my knees, but the more pieces I started to move, the easier they started to give way. The entire structure of Riley's mind started to fall into a different shape, and even without some sort of blueprint to work off, I could *feel* where pieces were meant to go. Bit by bit the color, and even the texture of the bricks began to change—some became like glass, while others glowed with an inner source of light stronger than any light bulb.

Even as I worked, I could sense something awry. An integral part missing. The more I worked, the more apparent it became. Until finally the wall was torn down, and Riley's mind was the maze it must have been before, and it was ... void. Empty.

I pulled back my vision, slipping through the folds and layers that had returned to Riley's mind until like a nighttime flower, its bloom reversed upon the light's return.

Riley had slumped down on the side of the bed, the knife clattered to the ground sometime while I was gone. Her eyes were wide and empty, and I reached out, terrified that she was dead. That in my need to cure her, I'd somehow killed her instead.

"Braden, she needs help. We have to call the nurses," Jade said, her hands pressed against the barrier that divided the room.

The winter voices had gone sullen and silent when I'd regained control of myself, but when I reached out and touched Riley, I could feel their intrigue. They recognized something in her—something I didn't at first. *Her future. That's what's missing.*

I'd tried to stop Lucien from devouring Riley's mind, but I must not have been fast enough. He'd still managed to drain away the future potential she had, stripping her life down to its bare minimum.

With a tired sigh, I waved the barrier down and climbed to my feet. "Go call the nurses," I said.

Unfortunately, my night was far from over.

¤ ¤ ¤

When it came down to it, the fact that I could bring Belle Dam to its knees with only three text messages was pretty impressive. I'd instructed Matthias to send the first two, and Jade to send the last before I left the hospital.

There were a few cars on the road, and I stayed tucked into the shadows until they passed. As I crossed into the town square, Trey was already waiting for me. It was still ten minutes to midnight, when I'd told him to meet me, but he paced like he'd been here twice that.

He kept passing by the same city bench, turning towards it long enough to glare at it, like it was somehow responsible for his predicament. Just like in the hospital, I used my magic to smooth away any signs of my approach and kept out of his line of sight. I couldn't say why I did it at first, especially since Trey was probably worried. I'd disappeared without a trace for weeks, and then he gets a text from his sister to meet me at midnight? Not traumatic at all.

I cut across the path, making sure I slid into his line of sight as I finished my approach. As I stepped into the streetlight, Trey sucked in a breath. "My god, you're okay," he muttered. He moved for me at once, the tension holding him upright squeezed out of him. He looked like he hadn't been sleeping. For all I knew, he hadn't.

"I had to go away for a while," I said, knowing how that sounded. "I couldn't tell anyone what was happening."

He shook his head, like it was that easy to dispel dark thoughts. "I thought my mother, or Lucien—I thought someone had taken you! My mother was *offended,* like it was so unthinkable, when I accused her of doing something to you. Like she's suddenly Mother of the Year or something." And then a moment later, a soft admission, "I knew you'd come back."

"We don't have a lot of time," I told him. "Still a lot to do, if you're up to it."

"What happened to you?"

I shook my head. "It's not important right now."' I slipped inside his arms, felt his warmth and the beat of his heart against his chest. Trey wrapped his arms around me with a sigh.

"What's going to happen?" he asked, sounding resigned, like our lives would always be like this. Maybe this *was* what my life would always look like.

"Jason and Catherine are meeting me. Or at least they will be in," I grabbed his arm and twisted it so I could read his watch, "eight minutes."

Trey got a weird look on his face, and then carefully reached for my sunglasses. When I didn't resist, he slid them off my face. "Your eyes are blue," he said, but it sounded almost like a question.

"It's probably just a trick of the light," I said. My eyes were never *just* blue.

"No, they *are*," Trey insisted. He walked me over to one of the cars parked on the street. My eyes were glowing, but now they were the same sapphire blue that I'd seen in the lighthouse. Before Grace had stolen my powers, my eyes had always been a kaleidoscope, a constantly changing barrage of colors. Now, though, they'd seemed to settle on just one. I looked at myself in the window, thinking it over. I even tried a few different angles, before I concentrated and the color faded. My eyes were still blue, but not the phosphorescent kind. Just normal blue.

I looked at his reflection in the window. "Did you bring it?"

He patted down the breast pocket of his jacket. "You asked so nicely."

I was pretty sure I hadn't asked him at all. The text Jade had sent was basically HE'S OKAY, MEET IN SQUARE. BRING CONTRACT.

"Are you sure you're okay?"

I looked towards the west, almost as though I could see Grace's lighthouse on the skyline. I could feel it in the back of my head, a throbbing presence just waiting for me to return.

"Come on," I said, ignoring the butterflies in my stomach. "Time for a party."

twenty-nine

Up until this point, all my experiences at Fallon Law Offices had taken place in Lucien's office. But there was a conference room on the far side of the floor that was much more appropriate for tonight's agenda, and it had a fantastic view of the harbor.

Working together, Trey and I cleared the room of all but four chairs, one at each of the cardinal points of the giant rectangular conference table. I could have conjured everything out of the room—depositing it in another room or even another floor if I'd wanted, but I didn't want to use any magic just yet. I didn't want Catherine or Jason to get gun-shy.

Jason arrived first, which was no surprise on both parts. Jason was obsessively early for everything, and Catherine preferred to make an entrance. They both stalked into the conference room like they were the most important people in the town. Again, not a surprise.

Trey and I waited in Lucien's office with the lights out, while Jason and Catherine both headed for the conference room where the lights were blazing. I left Trey to wait, and took a deep breath as I crossed the floor and headed in to start the showdown.

The spotlights at the corners of the harbor gave it a soft glow. All of the boats had been pulled from the water by now, stored for the winter just a few hundred yards from the water. As I approached, my feet barely making any sound, Catherine and Jason circled each other, wearing identical masks of disgust and loathing.

"I hope you don't think this is funny," Catherine said, seething. "It's one thing to fill my son's head with sorts of propaganda, but this is unacceptable."

"She didn't kill me, Jason," I said, strolling into the room like I owned it. "She didn't have anything to do with my disappearance, either. I wasn't kidnapped. I was healing."

Catherine shot him a look of triumph, as if anyone cared that my arrival vindicated her from suspicion. Other than that, though, she kept her surprise at my arrival hidden. Like she'd expected it all along.

Jason was half out of his chair before he caught himself, and his forehead screwed up in confusion. "*Healing?* What does that mean?"

I relaxed the illusion over my eyes, let the color shine forth again. "Healing," I repeated, this time with more meaning.

Catherine started gathering her power, a cascade of diamonds and silver energy that swirled around her to my eyes. But the benefit to having a demon's power tucked away inside of me was that it gave me a portion of his power.

And there was no power greater than Lucien's insight into the future. I might not have been able to sift through the threads of what could be as fast as he could, but I also knew what to look for.

My magic swarmed through hers, tearing spells apart faster than she could try and focus them. I saw every spell before she even had the chance to think it up. Each time, the tearing was a static shock to her system, throwing her a little more off guard. It was a hard balance, keeping one hand on my magic and the other on the demon power coursing through me. Too much power. Too volatile. This was dangerous.

But we want Catherine contained, don't we?

It was getting to be too much. The winter voices were more numerous now, getting stronger in my head. I could feel my control shaking, like muscles that have been asked to do too much.

"Enough," I snapped, severing the latest spell and, taking another page out of Lucien's book, creating a binding circle all around her. Unlike Lucien, though, I didn't need a witch to back me up. I slammed enough energy around her to keep her contained, a complicated pattern of sigils springing to light beneath her, something that was pulled from the deep recesses of my power. But whether it was Grace's memory, or Lucien's design, I didn't know.

The moment the spell went up, I sagged a little. Jason was there in an instant, his arm on the small of my back. Not holding me up, but just … there. Catherine looked furious, but she glided back down into her seat with all the dignity of a queen. She didn't act like someone who was trapped in a three-foot-wide circle.

"What's going on?" Jason asked, lowering his voice so it wouldn't carry much past the two of us.

I shook my head and gestured for him to take his seat again. There was sweat on my forehead, but this had to be done. I didn't have a choice.

"Do either of you even know why there's a feud in Belle Dam?" I looked between the two of them: condescending Catherine who was too above it all to answer, and confused Jason, who had no idea where the conversation was heading. I went ahead and answered for them. "There's a feud because someone told you there was. Just like they told your parents, and their parents. But how many people do you think actually knew *why* there was a feud?"

"Oh, please tell me there's a point to all this," Catherine remarked, her eyes tilted toward the ceiling.

"Part of it's so you'd be manageable. Quiet. You wouldn't ask questions." I circled the table. "Never wondering why Jason was so convinced you killed his wife," and as I circled Jason, adding, "or why Lucien was so eager to take your son away."

"The feud makes both of you stupid. It makes *everyone* stupid. How many people do you think know that witches and demons walk the streets of Belle Dam? How many people may not know *that,* but they know that if you want something that seems impossible, you do Jason Thorpe a favor and hope he'll do one for you. Or that Catherine Lansing has a way of finding out secrets that *no one* knows. Everyone in this town buys into the delusion that it's just a normal town, but it's not. Everyone, including the two of you, buries their heads in the sand."

I dropped a manila folder filled with papers onto the desk. "That changes tonight."

¤   ¤   ¤

I let the silence build, waiting for the moment one of them cracked. I knew it would be Catherine. Jason had a mountain of patience. He'd rather wait there a thousand years than allowing someone else the pleasure of seeing him crumble.

"What is that?" she demanded.

I faked surprise. "That? *That* is the contract that Lucien talked your son into signing. He gets all the magical vitamins he needs to cause trouble, and Lucien gets to dismantle his life in exchange. Sounds fair, right?"

Catherine's face went white. It actually wasn't even fair to call it just white. It was more like she went from living to corpse in a microsecond. Since the folder was too far out of her reach, I did her a solid and slid a copy towards her end of the table. Then I did the same for Jason.

The contract was longer than the one I'd signed with Matthias, and it wasn't just ironclad, it was clad in iron, steel, titanium, lead, and diamonds. Lucien had thrown in contingencies for almost *everything*. Even implausible scenarios like if I somehow scooped Trey's essence out of his body and transplanted it into someone else, the contract was still valid. If I killed Lucien again, Trey suffered. If I banished Lucien, Trey suffered. Even if I did nothing and left Lucien alone, Trey suffered.

He'd had a few weeks in the Lansing chapel to do nothing but stew over how I'd beaten him. He'd probably spent all that time figuring out just what sorts of clauses to throw in to cut me off at the knees. But he hadn't considered the most basic point of all. I still had one avenue I could use.

I nodded towards the doors, where Trey stood in the shadows. He joined us in the room, and closed the doors behind him. "It's true, I did." He gave me a tight smile, and moved to stand opposite me on the other side of the table. "What's this?" Trey asked, indicating the glowing circle of sigils in the carpet below his mother.

"Know how when you're in kindergarten, your report card is all checks and check minuses?" I waved towards Catherine. "Plays well with others. *Big* check minus."

Catherine hadn't even lobbied a verbal protest yet, and the chance to do so had just been snatched out from under her. "This isn't possible," she insisted. "Why would you do something like this, Gentry?" She looked bewildered and devastated. There was even a touch of anger, like Trey had done this just to hurt her personally somehow. Like Trey would hand over his future for something frivolous.

Then again, she might call saving my life frivolous. "I think the more important question is why you still don't believe that your new pet demon has a hard-on for destroying your son." Trusting Lucien wasn't the greatest of Catherine's crimes, but she'd enabled him to continue hurting people all over the city.

"There—there has to be a reason," she said, voice a bit weaker. It didn't take her long to recover. She turned towards me, her cold eyes narrowed. "What is this meant to be, then? Some sort of *intervention*?" She snarled the last word with a rage that surprised me. Catherine was the ice queen. Not the out-of-control hothead.

"Your son just told you that he sold his soul to the devil, and you think this is about me?" I glanced at Jason, who had his fingers steepled in front of him, taking it all in.

"Braden?" Jason said my name like it was a question, but I'd learned enough about him to be able to read the question behind the question. *Is this really worth it? She's a crazy, narcissistic twit who never met an actual color scheme she liked.* I may have embellished on his expression a bit. "The feud?"

"We're getting off track," I agreed.

"I would hate for him to lose his place," she spat.

I looked between the two of them. It wouldn't be enough just to get Catherine in line. That was exactly why the feud was such a problem in the first place. For a minute, just one, I had to forget that Jason was my father. But was it something that he would even be okay with? Could Jason even become something more than the secrets and lies that surrounded Belle Dam?

"Do you really think you of all people have the right to walk in here demanding change?" Catherine interrupted. "Everything horrific that happened in this town only happened once you entered the picture. Your mother's death, your uncle's. Those fall on your head, not mine."

I probably would have set her on fire if Trey hadn't gotten there first. He slammed his fist down on the table in front of her, and shoved the contract towards her face. "Is that Braden's signature on the bottom?" he demanded. "Is it?"

Catherine had to shift her head back, and even though the circle should have stopped Trey from getting too close to her, a golden aura spread around his skin where it pierced the binding, but the spell didn't falter. I didn't know if it was my magic making allowances for Trey, or his own complementing mine, but either way it was the golden light that drew Catherine's eyes. The manifestation of her son's new abilities.

Her eyes flew to Jason's, and for the first time, I saw the fear there. Catherine still didn't grasp what we were all doing here tonight, but she knew the cease-fire she had with Jason was more than broken. Now he had a reason to go after her son, if he wanted. Trey being normal had kept him safe, but Trey tapping into his powers? The powers that Catherine had deliberately kept from him? That made him a target. The same way I was a target.

"I haven't made myself clear," I said. "So let me tell you about what's really going on in Belle Dam, and why the two of you have been played for suckers." Trey pulled out his chair, and then to be a bit of a smart ass he extended his hand and did the same for mine with his golden magic. I ran my fingers through the strands as I sat. They felt like warm syrup and something more that was just *Trey*.

"It started with a girl who saw things that no one else could see, and the demon that stole her future ... "

¤   ¤   ¤

Neither one of them spoke, and it was hard to say how much of the story they believed. Lucien, a demon older than time, and Grace, a woman still alive long after she should have died. The feud between *them* that had trickled down into the city, and the real issues plaguing the city.

"You can't possibly expect me to buy into this," Catherine said, with a pinched expression on her face. It didn't surprise me that she wasn't receptive to what was really going on here. She, like Grace, had a way of only seeing things from her own perspective. It was like once she made up her mind about how the world worked, nothing could change her perspective.

"It's all true," Trey said firmly, staring down at his hands.

"You've seen her, then?" Catherine challenged. "This mysterious ancestor of ours with all the answers?"

Trey looked uncertain for only a moment before his jaw hardened. "Braden saw her. She attacked him. And then she fixed him."

"How convenient," Catherine said, "out of the goodness of her evil heart, no doubt. So he can't decide who the villain is supposed to be in this little story, and we're supposed to go along with it? Who is it this time? Lucien? Her? Me? This is one ridiculous claim after the next."

"D," I said. "All of the above. You're all the villains, in some way." *But me most of all,* I thought uncomfortably.

"So what is it you *want* from this little intervention?" Catherine asked. "Turn away my demon and let your father walk all over me? Do you really think I'm that stupid?"

"You should probably stop using that word," I said carefully. "This isn't an intervention. It's a coup."

Catherine's whole body slowed, and her head moved at a glacial pace as she tilted it towards me. "Excuse me?"

There was a mocking laugh that had been building in me since the first time I'd been met with Catherine's arrogance. She really did think she was the center of the world, and finally I could make her understand. "Did you really think I need anything from you?" I shook my head. "Grace coming back means there's a third side this idiotic feud. The only reason you're here is because you're going to help me clear off the board a little."

"Braden, what are you planning?" Jason asked skeptically.

"That depends on what you want to hear about first. The bad part of the plan, or the even worse part?"

"Braden." Jason's growl made me smile. I knew that tone of exasperation. John had used it often. But thinking of John reminded me of Catherine, and the smile faded.

"I know you want to help, but you can't." I tried to

be as concise and to the point as I could. Jason understood brevity. He opened his mouth to argue, but I ran over his protests. "And I can't let you interfere, either. This is going to be hard enough without the distraction. So we're going to compromise." I looked at Trey, biting my lip. "And this is the part where we lose them." Trey nodded, because I'd already told him what I was planning. *Some* of what I was planning.

"I could strip the magic out of you," I said to Catherine, "but then I'd have to do the same to him. So at least this will still be fair. I'm going to bind your powers together. You'll still have your own power, but you won't be able to access it unless you learn to work together. Maybe that will get you both to start using your magic a little more wisely. You'll be able to make sure Jason can't act against you, and he'll be able to do the same to you."

There was a long silence in the room. A hundred years of hatred seeped in while we were talking, and stole the air. A dozen generations of Lansing and Thorpe ghosts crowding around at the corners, screaming their dissent.

I knew there was no way they'd go for it. And I wasn't surprised when both Jason and Catherine leapt to their feet with angry protests.

I nodded to Trey, who started whispering under his breath. By degrees, both Jason and Catherine's voices dwindled down to nothing, though they were clearly still trying to shout out their disapproval. We just couldn't hear them. The moment they both realized their voices had been stolen, Jason and Catherine paused. I thought for sure that Jason would storm from the room, and I'd have to stop him. He remained standing but he didn't move, surprising me.

"You don't get a choice in the matter, and there's nothing to negotiate," I added, watching Catherine carefully. Unlike Jason, she was fighting Trey's spell. I could see him sweating across the table, and the net-like layers of magic crossing her mouth kept bulging outwards and then retracting, like a balloon being filled and then emptied. The spell finally snapped after almost a minute of this, which was about thirty seconds longer than I'd expected Trey to be able to hold out.

"Do you really think I'll stand idly by and let you take over my town?" she snarled.

"I signed a contract of my own," I said quietly, getting up and standing by the window. "This power I have? It's only mine for a handful of days. But I'm not going to sit on it, and squander it the way Thorpes and Lansings have done for generations. I get three days in Belle Dam to do *whatever* I want. Understand this: I can, and will, make your life *very* difficult in the meantime. I will tear down every obstacle between me and what I want. It doesn't matter if it's people, things … or even places."

I turned my back to the window, the view of Belle Dam and the harbor in the distance. Catherine's snide dismissal hung in the air.

Now.

It almost seemed like the windows started shaking even before the harbor caught fire, before boats and buoys exploded into kindling and ash. In my mind's eye I watched them like a line of matches, each explosion causing the next in line. Ships passed from grandfather to grandson ignited just as easily as the rarely used luxury boats that left the dock only rarely. Catherine and Jason had a front-row view, and I had their expressions at the moment they changed.

The building shook, the windows rattled and threatened to break, the sky became a fireball that bathed Lucien's office in red light. The corona spread around and behind me, draped like a shroud of force and flame.

I waited long enough for their masks to crackle, then collapse. Silence wrapped its hands around their necks, choking their words. They stared, and stared, and I did not blink. I would not be the first to look away.

"I'm not playing around," I said, barely a whisper. "Do we understand each other?"

thirty

I let them take it all in. Even Trey, who knew it was coming, was stunned into silence. In the distance, sirens screamed to life, the pitch of the fire trucks higher and longer than that of the squad cars blazing through the city.

Thirty seconds after the blast, the phones of the two most important people in town started going off in a rapid fire stream. By mutual, silent agreement, both Jason and Catherine pulled them out and shut them off. No one said anything, and the port in Belle Dam continued to burn.

My contract with Grace forbade me from altering the spells that had been laid into the town's foundation. At a glance, that meant I couldn't go around destroying the city building by building, because the lines of the city—the buildings, the streets, the woods—had been part of the binding spells that trapped Lucien. Break down those elements, and the spell would start to falter.

But the harbor wasn't a building. It was an outpost on the water. Fair game.

"Lucien would like nothing more than to tear through this town and cause destruction like you've never seen," I said. It was a testament to how quiet the room was that my voice carried as much as it did. "If you push me, I'll save him the trouble."

I relaxed my fist, and the amber glow in the office vanished as a dozen fires a mile away were instantly snuffed out. "Lucien lied about a lot of things, but he told me what the witch eyes meant. What this *power* meant." I stared at the pair of them, struggling to remember the days when I'd hated one and feared the other. "It's supposed to burn through you. To cripple you. That way, when the demons come, you'll take any bargain they lay before you. You'll become their instrument. I chose to become a different instrument instead."

"Braden," Jason whispered, and I saw in his eyes that he *knew*. That all his searching, all his sacrifice had been in vain. He'd found a way for me to escape and left the choice up to me. But I hadn't chosen him. Again. "What did you promise her?"

"Just the three days," I lied. Because as long as it was only seventy-two hours, it was manageable. I couldn't think about what happened on the other end of the countdown. I cleared my throat. "If you cross me, I'll destroy you, and I won't even break a sweat. The harbor is your only warning."

"I don't have to listen to this," Catherine scoffed.

I extended my hand, *pulling,* and something that was a glowing mesh of crystals, flames, and spirit slipped out of her like taffy. Catherine exhaled, her knuckles dug into the armrests, and her eyes widened as it drained out of her. I let it continue, let her feel the very power she clung to bleed out of her. Let her know how it felt to be helpless and weak.

I could feel the winter voices stirring inside me, feel the malignant part of my power rising in response to the rage Catherine stoked in me. I never knew I could want someone dead so desperately, and yet struggle so hard to keep from killing her. If I lost control now, I knew she'd never survive.

"Like I said, I can take your power if that's what you would prefer." I walked over to her, and leaned against the edge of the table, looking down on her. "Do you think I won't? You'd deserve it. I can *ruin* you."

Catherine gaped at me, and it took everything in me that I didn't just end her life there. To see the light in her eyes die the same way she'd made John's light disappear. "You'll beg, but I won't kill you," I said finally. "Because every day, I'll have something so much worse in store for you."

It was a fine line. I couldn't know with any certainty which actions would lead me down the path of Grace's prophecy. I didn't even know for sure that our bargain could have stopped it. What if I fell faster than expected? Could I still wake up a boy, and be a monster before the setting of the sun?

No. I released the crystal spell and waited until the look of recognition and relief settled across Catherine's face. I wouldn't take her power now. That I could was enough.

"It's after midnight," I said, looking to the wall clock. "Two days left."

Catherine swallowed, but wisely held her tongue.

"This is all the mercy you get. Step out of line and I will tear your life apart, piece by piece." I glanced over my shoulder towards Jason. "Either of you. I mean it."

"Braden," Jason said, stepping forward. "You need—"

"The feud ends here," I said, talking over him. "Belle Dam's out of the demon-dealing business. You brought this war to us. Trey bargained his life for power, just as I did with Grace. When they come to collect, who's going to pay? You? Her?" I shook my head. "Kids always suffer for the sins of their parents," I muttered.

Before I could listen to any more of their defenses, their complaints, or their arguments, I focused on the magic churning a hole inside of me, and concentrated on the magic inside of *them*. Catherine's magic was crystal and yet fluid like blown glass, eschewing function for appearance. It was lavender and rain, chiming and the music of flutes. It smelled of baking bread and tasted like spice.

Jason's was a thing of function, straight, sharp lines and segments. It was bits of black and white woven together in interlocking pieces, built up over time like the bricks in a wall. Every edge was sharp as razors, dull polished steel and hot ashes. It smelled like the incense they burned at church, and the way clean smelled in a hospital. Trumpets blared and drums beat in a perfect steady rhythm.

Their powers were so different, it should have been

impossible to bind them together in the way that I'd wanted, but three weeks of training with Grace had taught me new definitions of what was both possible and what was wise. It was possible that there would be some damage left in my aftermath, and at least this way I was giving Catherine and Jason the opportunity to fix it once I was gone.

Actually binding their powers together was easy when it came down to the practice of it. I braided the power together, drawing it tight down the line like it was rope. There were benefits to what I was doing—collectively, they'd be even stronger than the two of them had been on their own. If something bad *did* happen in Belle Dam, they might be better prepared for it.

If I'd had time, I might have tried to work out a way so that the connection would pass down the family line, so that the two families would always have to work together if they wanted to accomplish anything. But I still had a sinking feeling that the Thorpe line was going to end with me.

It didn't take as long as I feared it would. Their individual strengths bound together until they were not two separate sources of power, but one split right down the middle.

After the cloud of magic had left my eyes and the room started to come back into focus, I realized my hands were on the table, and I wasn't so much standing as I was being held up. Trey was at my side, his arms wrapped around my waist, keeping me vertical. Fatigue washed through my body like it'd been there for years and I'd only just noticed, but I managed to regain my own balance. Trey didn't pull away.

"Is it done, then?" Catherine demanded frostily. Her skin was flushed red, as was Jason's. I'd been so focused on what I was doing that I hadn't stopped to wonder what the binding must have been like for them. Or how they even felt about it. I'd basically just crippled something that had sustained them both for the majority of their lives. It was almost worse than what Grace had done to me, in a way, because even though Grace had taken my power from me, she hadn't left me with the illusion of independence I'd fostered onto them.

But I couldn't worry about that right now. "I need your sister," I said softly to Trey. "And there's still a lot to do tonight." We walked around the table and out of the room before Trey looked back and stopped us. "Hey," he said, nodding back the way we'd come. I turned, still seeing the glowing sigils in the carpet that bound Catherine to her spot.

"Oh, right," I said, waving my hand. The binding circle evaporated, and some of my innate power swept back into my body. It alleviated some of the fatigue I was feeling, even though I was still so tired. If only I had time to sleep for a week, I might actually feel rested. But I only had so many hours left to my life.

Every one counted.

thirty-one

Trey didn't ask any questions when I directed him to get in his truck and start driving. We picked Jade up on the way, and she'd dressed for something more clandestine than I had planned. A black turtleneck, black skinny jeans, and knee-high leather boots. I let the siblings take the seats in the front, and I squeezed myself into the space in the back. I needed to focus on other things anyway.

"Okay, now that Jade's here, will you *please* tell me what we're doing? I've only got half a tank. At least tell me if I need to fill it up," Trey asked, having clamped down on his curiosity for an admirable twenty minutes.

"First, we need to get a big group of people together. Do you think we can throw together some sort of benefit at the Harbor Club by tomorrow night?"

"You're kidding, right?" Jade tapped the clock on the console. "It's almost one in the morning. And you want to throw a dinner party in eighteen hours? It's not possible." Even though the radio was on the lowest volume it could be on and still be considered "on," Jade kept fiddling with the station. "What do you need a big group for, anyway?"

"The next part of the plan. The more people we can get together, the better."

"Well," she said, pursing her lips in the mirror. "There's always the dance. Winter formal's tomorrow night. That work? Or do you need adult-type people?"

The winter formal? Seriously? It was like a sign from the deities behind every high school rom-com I'd watched growing up. "No, that'll work."

"Braden!" Trey's voice was sharp. "Explaining. Now."

I huffed. Of course Trey would run right over talk about the dance. "Riley told me about a weakness of Lucien's that I can exploit," I said, because it was as simple as I could boil it down.

"Aren't you scared that he's going to see what you're planning?" Trey asked, watching me from the rearview mirror.

I shook my head. "And that brings me to what Grace told me. The more people that know about her, the more likely it is that Lucien finds out. So she's been hiding all of us from his abilities." I nodded towards Jade. "That was how Lucien knew about us leaving together. He read it in your future. But she fixed her oversight after that."

Jade turned around in her seat. "What do you mean 'her oversight'?"

I shifted in my seat, and smoothed out the creases in my pants. "That thing you wanted to talk to Drew about," I said evenly, despite the fact that I had no business knowing about it. "Lucien had something else in mind for you." *And that's probably the reason that Drew had to die, because there was going to be an Armstrong to replace him.* The thought made the bile churn in my stomach.

"Oh," Jade said quietly, sitting back in her seat.

The hurt in her voice got Trey's attention, and he wouldn't let it go. "What's he talking about? What thing? You and Drew were talking? You promised me that was over."

"And you promised Mom that you wouldn't see Braden anymore," Jade said, sounding exhausted. "We tell people what they want to hear. It's what we do."

"Wait, you told your mom you wouldn't see me anymore?" I asked, forgetting anything about concentration or focus. I leaned forward in my seat, like proximity to Trey would somehow make this clearer.

"It was a while ago," he said, evading an honest answer. "Before anything seriously started to happen with us. She was just worried that you were going to screw up her timeline of my life."

"You could have always told her no," Jade said. "She got used to controlling you because you let her. It's not her fault you flipped the script once Braden came to town."

"Are you seriously defending her?" he demanded. "Do we really need to go over this again?"

"I'm not defending her," Jade said, raising her voice. "I'm just saying you were the perfect son until one day you weren't. No wonder she went over the top."

"I can't believe you're seriously doing this right now."

The car started to accelerate as Trey took his worsening mood out on the roads. I'd been in a car with him once before when he'd lost his temper. It hadn't ended well. I hoped we could avoid a repeat performance. "Unbelievable." Trey's seething frustration was a tangible thing, it pressed into every inch of space inside the truck, stinking like ashtrays and muddy water.

"Stop here," I said calmly. When Trey didn't stop fast enough, I reached out with my magic and cut the feed of gas to the engine and eased the brake pedal down. Trey spun around in his seat, fixing me with a dark look. I didn't say anything, just pushed him towards the door. Reluctantly, he got out, and I climbed out over his seat and followed.

We were in the middle of town, equidistant from the Lansing and Thorpe homes that marked the western- and easternmost points of Belle Dam. It was a residential street like any other, only this one was important. At least for tonight.

I knew I needed a big gesture, but there were also things I could set into motion tonight that would play out almost immediately. When Jade got out, I held out my hand and she gave me the blank greeting card and a pen. I scrawled a quick message ("She knows about the money"), shoved it in the envelope, and tucked it into the first mailbox on the left side of the street.

The Lansing siblings looked at me with a mixture of annoyance and expectation. Their fight might have ended unceremoniously, but it was clear they'd both turn on me if I didn't start explaining myself.

"Lucien sees futures, which are shaped like tree branches. They all split off from somewhere. If you can get down to the root of something, though, and cut it out completely, it wipes out a whole line of futures."

I nodded towards the darkened house. "He forgot the mail last night. He'll wake up in the morning, remember, and see my note. He'll confess the gambling to his wife, she'll force him to get help, and he'll never end up going to Jason for help paying the mortgage. Because he doesn't get indebted to Jason, he doesn't take the promotion that Jason gets him, which means he doesn't move. And if he doesn't move, his grandson never inherits the house where something integral happens when he's sixteen." I shrugged. "A lot of futures change based on what happens in that house. Now they don't."

Both of them stared at me blankly.

"Come on," I said. "Three more things to do before we can stop for the night. Next I need a St. Christopher medallion, two dollars in quarters, and a pocketknife. Then we can go to the preschool."

Their blank looks got even blanker.

"I'm kidding," I said with an annoyed sigh. "Seriously, you guys are no fun."

thirty-two

Three more stops took the rest of the night and well into the next morning. We stumbled into Jason's house a few hours before noon and down the hallway to my room. Jade walked right into one of the guest rooms, while Trey hesitated outside my door.

I pulled him into my room. Not that it mattered much, because less than a minute later he'd fallen asleep on my side of the bed, his shoes and jacket still on. I huffed out a breath, sat down next to him, and finished what he should have, pulling the shoes off his feet, and his arms out of the jacket. Then I pulled the comforter out from under him and wrapped him up in it.

I left him there and wandered down to the library. Even though my body was exhausted (when was the last time I'd actually *slept*?) my mind still charged ahead like business as usual. I couldn't waste any time with sleep. Not when I didn't know how things would turn out.

Jason had left the chess sets where I'd abandoned them

weeks before, but the pieces had all been shifted. Games that I'd been playing had their fortunes reversed, and now the losers were winning and the winners were in retreat. Was it his way of telling me that things would be okay? Or maybe his hope that life would follow the chess analogy closer than usual?

The dance was ideal for what I wanted to do next. Luring Lucien out into public was integral, and thinning the future pool would help with that. When thousands of threads disappeared, leaving gaps in the mosaic, Lucien would notice. Be curious. And at the dance, I was going to make him have a full-blown panic attack.

Or I'd die trying.

Before I knew it, it was time to get ready for the dance. I wasn't sure where the afternoon went, but I had a sneaking suspicion that my exhaustion was a bandit hiding in the blind spots in my vision, snatching out bites of time for moments of total blackout. More than once, I started working my mind through something only to suddenly realize my thoughts had been disrupted and my neck muscles were unusually stiff.

It was impressive with how little effort Jade put into the formal. She'd brought a dress along at some point, and I meant to ask if she'd just moved into the house entirely, but I figured it was best if I didn't raise the subject. Trey was gone when I went back to my room, the bed made and no sign of him.

"You should talk to your brother," I said, after coming

back from a shower that had seared the skin right off my body.

"About?" Jade lay on my bed, her hair tossed casually above her.

"You know what," I said. Just because we kept skirting the issue didn't mean I wouldn't force it. If Jade really was pregnant, she was going to need *someone* to look out for her.

I headed into the closet, grumbling at the size. It was bigger than the bedroom I'd had growing up. Maybe even bigger than my room and John's combined.

"What are you going to wear?" Jade asked, which was code for *We're not talking about it*. Which was fine. I probably wasn't the best sounding board at the moment anyway.

I slogged my way to the back of the closets where the suits were. Jason really must have assumed I would be the junior version of him, because there were a dozen identical black suits lined up one next to the other. But I didn't want black. Black was Jason's color, the same way that white was Catherine's. I was somewhere in between, and so it was fitting that I pulled the only gray suit off the rack. It wasn't one solid color, but made up of slightly different shades of gray.

Jade sat up in surprise when I walked out of the closet with a suit in one hand, as well as some of the sunglasses she was always pressing me to wear.

"Shirt?" she asked, eyeing me critically.

I handed her the suit, then walked back into the closet, emerging a few seconds later with a button-up that was a slightly brighter shade of gray. Jade frowned until I reached inside the suit and pulled a dark burgundy tie out that matched the suit's material perfectly. Setting the shirt inside, and putting the tie on top showed the ensemble and the way the patterns played off each other.

She raised an eyebrow slowly. "After all this time, you suddenly have a keener fashion sense than me?" She looked annoyed. Jade looked down at her phone, sitting on the edge of the bed, her frown intensifying. "I texted my brother almost an hour ago, and he hasn't responded yet."

Panic start scurrying up my spine until I saw the smirk that she was trying desperately to hide. "What did you text him?" I asked, putting a clamp down on my emotions.

"I just asked him what color his dress was going to be," she said innocently. "You have to get a corsage that matches, right?"

¤   ¤   ¤

Jade raised, and then summarily dismissed, the problem of tickets. "You were supposed to buy them weeks ago. They collect them at the door." Jade tapped her nails against the hood of her car. "But they'll probably let us in anyway," she mused, ducking down to check her makeup. "I can't think of anyone that would want to piss my mom off. Jason either."

But to her credit, riding in the car with Jade wasn't the white-knuckled nightmare it had been in the past. If anything, it was making a case that Jade had been replaced by a body snatcher. She obeyed the speed limit, barely talked, and focused on the road.

I think it was the closest that either one of us had come to acknowledging the baby elephant in the room. Jade herself looked amazing. Her honey-colored hair was pinned back in a way that I still couldn't figure out. It didn't look like hair product, it was too short for a tie or a clip, but all the same it swept up and back, and looked fantastic on her. She wore a sapphire-blue dress, darker than the aura I'd learned to channel recently, but easily just as beautiful. She'd even paired them with real sapphires in her ears and around her neck.

If there was any sort of "Best Dressed" award at this thing and we didn't win, then the city deserved whatever it got in the future.

The hall was on the south side of town, far from the shore and downtown. It wasn't anything special, just a flat, rectangular building with some hedges for landscaping. Colorful dresses abounded as many of the other kids attending straggled in as well. The weather was warmer than it had been, the leftover snow and ice melting overnight while we'd been busy driving all over Belle Dam.

No one stopped us as Jade walked right past the teachers at the door, with me in her wake. If anything, the teachers who saw us started whispering amongst themselves more than any of the students.

The hall itself was a far cry from the mediocrity of the building's exterior. Someone had rigged up tiny spotlights, pastel shades of blue, purple, and green. The spotlights moved every few seconds, just slightly, but it was the effect they created that was so impressive. Someone had hung probably a thousand prism crystals, and the light beaming through them created a shimmering landscape on the ceiling.

I laughed at the sight of it because it was a rare moment of unexpected beauty. That someone had thought this up, and brought their version of a winter wonderland to life was impressive, to say the least. Round tables done up in blues and whites, along with matching centerpieces, lined one side of the hall. Everything had been considered, and it was exactly like walking into the kind of school dance that I'd only ever seen on television before.

"Yeah, it's okay," Jade said on my arm, trying to sound bored but looking impressed all the same.

"Are the dances always like this?" I asked.

She shrugged. "I think so. The school always goes all out. I think the dances were really important to ... " she stumbled over her words, and then forced herself to continue, "to Catherine when she was in high school, and that never seemed to go away."

Just another way Catherine's influenced the high school. But something like this wasn't Catherine's usual brand of awful. Why couldn't they do more things like this, and less with the trying to ritually murder each other?

We walked further into the hall, and I led her towards one of the corners, one with a good vantage point of both the way we'd come in and the hall itself. There were about a hundred students here. I guessed that there were five to six hundred kids enrolled at the high school. I leaned closer, to be heard over the sound of the music. "How many people do you think are going to be here tonight?" I asked her.

Jade's eyes narrowed in thought. "A lot of the seniors, probably. Last winter formal and all. A lot of underclassmen, too, because it's the last dance of the year that's open to all students. Prom's for juniors and seniors only." She did some quick math in her head and said, "Maybe about three hundred all together?"

Three hundred would work. I licked my lips, pulled the sunglasses from my pocket and slid them on. "That's perfect," I said, smiling wide.

"Do you know the only thing worse than a Thorpe and a Lansing going to the dance together?" A voice interjected loudly, over the music. "When two Lansings fight over which one is really his date."

Trey stood there, looking amused. He'd gone the traditional route, wearing a black suit with the jacket unbuttoned, a black vest visible underneath, hiding a gray tie. He looked ...

"Wow," I said, forcing my eyes up to his face. My own suit felt a little tight around the shoulders, but Trey's looked ...

"Hi," he said softly, with a warm smile.

"No, that's fine, I spent hours getting dolled up to be the dateless girl," Jade said with a sigh, stepping away from us. Trey's eyes drifted towards her, and his expression tightened, but she pressed her hand against his arm. "I won't go far," she promised. "I know Braden didn't decide to come to the dance because he didn't have anything better to do on a Saturday night. Something's happening."

"Something's always happening," Trey muttered. He didn't like his sister getting involved in the goings on in Belle Dam, but none of us could pretend like it wasn't happening. Jade wasn't stupid. She was actually more astute then most of us gave her credit for. Mostly because she was smart to stay out of things as much as possible. She knew this wasn't her fight.

Jade seemed to realize that we'd exhausted this particular topic of conversation, at least as far as it could happen in public. "Save me a dance," she said to me, squeezing my arm even as she looked over my shoulder for someone's date to snag. Her neck craned as she scoured above the heads and shoulders of most of the student body, and it took me a moment to realize what she was doing. Looking for Drew.

I blanched and looked away.

"Come on," Trey said a few moments later, nodding towards the dance floor. One of his hands reached up and carefully pulled the sunglasses off of my face. Having them back on had been nice: a barrier against everything that was going on. I could hide behind them, and no one could see what I was thinking. "I want to see who I'm dancing with," he said, tucking them into my pocket.

I pulled up short, shaking my head. "I don't dance. And besides, I'm not here to have a good time. You *know* that."

He had an easy smile on his face. "One dance won't set the world on fire."

"I kind of hate you," I whispered, even as I let him lead me out into the middle of the dance floor. His timing was impeccable, of course, because the moment he stopped and turned around to face me, the music changed and a slow song started. Of course. Trey's smile erupted into a full-blown laugh, and his arms slid easily around my waist, tightening the gap between us. I slid my arms around his neck, and ducked his head so we were eye to eye.

"Coincidence?" I asked, as one of his hands shifted, sliding under the bottom of my jacket.

"Maybe," he agreed, dragging his mouth closer to mine, and I couldn't look away from his lips. I bit the inside of my cheek, and looked up into his eyes. We swayed and moved to the beat of the song, and even though I'd never slow danced before, Trey kept control of both of us, setting a pace that I could just follow.

It wasn't until the song hit the refrain that I really started to laugh and loosen up. "You had this planned," I accused.

"Maybe," he said, noncommittal. I only knew the song because Uncle John had listened to it a lot when I was growing up. "In Your Eyes" by Peter Gabriel.

"You are a nerd," I told him seriously. "Did you scour through every song that had 'eyes' in it somewhere so that there'd be a *moment*?"

The humor dropped off his face, and Trey pulled away enough to look over my shoulder. His mouth had settled into a sharp line. *Oh.* He had. And here I was, being an asshole about it.

"Sorry, I don't do well with romantic gestures," I said, leaning closer into him. "My first kiss was while I was on the run from some hellhounds. Did I ever tell you that story?" Trey finally looked down at me, and though he tried to stay stony and cranky looking, a smile was threatening to break out. "That guy was a good kisser," I sighed. "I wonder whatever happened to him."

"Chased away, I imagine," Trey said seriously. "You *have* heard of breath mints, haven't you?"

I was so caught off guard I lacked any sort of retort at all. And the longer the silence, the wider Trey's smile. "But his loss is my gain," he whispered into my mouth a moment later.

I shouldn't have kissed him. I should have pulled away. This wasn't about having fun or being with a boy. This was supposed to be about Lucien. About finishing what Grace had started.

But this was the only time I was going to be at a high school dance. The only time I'd get to be in a room like this, have a gorgeous guy spinning me around the floor and know for a fact that it was okay. That the moment was perfect.

That I was happy. God, what would John have said, to see me right now? Being a sap and getting run over by *feelings*.

I leaned in to Trey's kiss and tried to surreptitiously pull one hand away to wipe at the corner of my eye. But Trey's hand got there first, and I opened my eyes, startled. His eyes were still closed, but he *knew*. His thumb rubbed soothingly across my cheek, but he never pulled away, and eventually my eyes closed again, and I lost myself to the moment.

No one came to interrupt us or to tell us to stop. No one paid us any attention at all. But eventually the song ended, and Trey and I pulled apart. My brain was in a haze, and I couldn't seem to remember what was wrong with staying here and dancing with Trey all night long.

"You needed a crowd, right," Trey said, his hand still cupped around my face. "You've got one."

Sometime during the song, more people had poured in. Trey pulled me close to him, and even though it was a faster tempo, we danced and laughed, but the reminder that tonight wasn't just about spending time with Trey stuck in my head now.

Five minutes. Then ten. Finally, what had been a small crowd when we first walked in packed around us. I could see why they went with the hall. It was bigger than the Harbor Club, and they were going to need all the space if people kept coming in at this pace. I didn't do an exact head count, but it looked like at *least* the three hundred Jade had predicted were already here.

"I'll be right back," I murmured. I pulled the sunglasses out of my pocket and put them back on, darkening the room significantly but returning me to my comfort level. I walked through the crowd like a zombie, my thoughts not with what I was about to do, but on Lucien. Where was he right now? What was he planning? He hadn't come after Trey yet, but he would.

I vaulted up the steps and onto the stage, staring out over the crowd. I opened my vision, seeing past the normal world and into the secret sight of the witch eyes. *Three hundred and twenty-seven people. Sixteen adults. Thirty are drunk, two of them teachers. There's a kid I've never met, a kid named Stephen, and he's got a flask he keeps refilling out at his car and sharing it with friends. One of the teachers caught him and drained the rest of it himself. The girl with the swimmer boyfriend is about to hook up with her best friend's brother, and a couple of girls are sharing the first of many significant looks.*

I took a deep breath. This was it. The beginning of the end.

I opened my eyes. Time to begin.

thirty-three

It was the crystals that made it so easy. The way they hung and sparkled along the ceiling like a cavalcade of stars. It was easy to focus on them, and easier still to link the lights with my magic. Someone turned a spotlight on me, I couldn't say for sure if it happened because I wanted it to or if someone simply decided that a Thorpe on the stage needed to be lit. Either way, the beam struck me as my head faced the stars, and little by little the room started to follow my gaze. To see what it was that I found so interesting. And that's when I had them.

The lights hypnotized them. One by one, the crowd fell under my sway, lulled into silence by the sparkling metronome of lights. There was a pattern deep in the flash, coached by magic and focused through me. I could *feel* it as each person was added to the collective. Magic rushed through me, a cleansing fire that warmed my bones and gave me the strength to get through this.

Someone turned off the music. All movement in the

room stilled. Even Jade and Trey were caught up in the moment, eyes vacant and jaws slightly parted.

From here, I could have done anything to them. To *any* of them. They were puppets, and I was the master. No one would stop me if I walked the crowd and thinned the herd however I saw fit. I was a god to these tiny creatures, and they would learn to fear me, and rightly so.

No. That wasn't me. I shook my head, and focused on myself. On the reasons that I was doing all of this. This wasn't about controlling anyone. It was about freeing them.

"You may not know me," I whispered, and yet my words carried to every corner of the room. They couldn't hear me but it focused me to use my words. "But I know all of you. All your lives, you've been pieces on the chessboard. Pawns. But even a pawn can fight back if he knows how. So tonight, I'm giving you that option. All you have to do is look me in the eyes, and say yes."

One by one, the crowd turned down their heads and looked towards the stage. It was like staring into the heart of a zombie apocalypse, just waiting for the starting gun to ignite everyone into motion.

This was only half of the process, though. Using a trick I'd learned from Grace, I split my vision until I was seeing two different things at once. My magic coiled around me, and I split my sight again. And again. I split it three hundred different ways until I saw the world the way a fly does, out of a thousand different eyes. I looked every single person in their eyes, all at once, and I didn't collapse under the strain.

Blue light began to fill the room, a beacon of magical energy that could probably be seen from space. Grace would no doubt feel it, as would any witch worth their weight. But just as quickly as it built, I turned the demon's power loose, circling the exterior of the building like a guard dog, building up wards and protections to keep what we were doing in here secret. To hide from prying eyes.

As far as the adults were concerned, it was nothing more than a momentary blip—a pulse of energy far on the other side of town. Certainly nothing to get out of bed for. At least, so long as Catherine and Jason did what they were supposed to, and stayed the hell out of it.

The blue light continued to glow until it drowned out the other colors in the room, and everything was washed in azure and cobalt.

"Do you want to make your own path?" I asked them. "Do you want to hold your own destiny again?"

As they said yes, one at a time and each one a significant moment in its own right, the spell snapped into place. Magic wrapped itself around all of them, no matter if they were sixteen or sixty. Everyone in this building was part of the same moment, but for each of them, it was a new start.

A free start.

It cost a lot of power. A *lot*. I staggered back as the light diminished and the magic started to fade. But even as weak as I was, I smiled as the dance picked up exactly where it had left off a few moments before. No one was any the wiser about what happened, the spotlight clicked off, and I hopped down off the stage.

But I had just given three hundred twenty-seven people the same gift I'd been given. Freedom from Lucien's sight. Freedom from his influence in their direction in life, freedom from the never-ending hunger that meant Lucien was devouring someone's potential. As far as Lucien was concerned, there was a tangle of threads that had suddenly vanished completely, and I was responsible.

If nothing else, I'd done one thing good with my power. I'd saved over three hundred people from his influence.

Trey was on me the moment my feet hit the floor. "Everything okay?"

I nodded, leaning on his arm. "We're good."

"What do we do now?" he asked, eyeing the door.

"Now we wait," I said. "And hope that Lucien was paying attention."

¤   ¤   ¤

An hour passed, and even though I thought it would be impossible to relax, Trey proved me wrong. We moved across the dance floor a couple of times, he threw his sister into my arms until we were dancing and laughing too hard to even move, he pulled me up against him near the drink table and kissed me chastely, slinging his arm around my shoulder. It was the most surreal night of my life, the two worlds I couldn't manage to maintain on my own had been woven together so seamlessly.

It made me wish I'd made different decisions. Maybe I could have found a way to balance school on top of all this. Maybe I should have tried harder.

"Stop brooding," Trey whispered. We were dancing to another slow song, our foreheads pressed together.

I mustered up a smile. "I'm fine. Just . . . thinking."

"Well, stop. Everything's going to work out."

I didn't get it, this *faith* he had. He really did believe that everything was going to be okay. "How do you do that?" I asked honestly. "You know what we're up against, right?"

"I know they're up against *you*," Trey said, his smile never faltering. "And you have this way of always making the unexpected happen." He lifted his head away, and looked around the dance. "Four months ago, who would have put odds on a Thorpe bringing not one, but *two* Lansings to the winter formal as his dates?"

I laughed. "It's just a shame that Jade looks so much better in a dress than you do," I teased.

Trey's expression changed, and he pulled me in tight against him, his entire body suddenly tense. "Look," Trey said into my ear. "It worked. He's here."

Like it was a move we'd practiced a thousand times before, we swayed to the music, but each movement turned us more and more until I spotted him, lurking underneath the curved staircases that led to the upper landing. This time it was Trey who reached into my pocket and put the sunglasses back on. It was all about appearances.

I left the safety of his arms and walked towards the stage. I didn't even have to focus my power, people moved out of my way simply because I wanted them to. A hall full of teenagers, and so many of them were turning to watch me. *Did they know what was going to happen? Or were we still connected?*

I climbed the stairs to the stage slowly, one foot in front of the other. Walked to the edge, then looked out at the crowd. The magic I had inside of me split through my skin, and I felt like a different person from the one who'd been trapped in Trey's arms just a few moments before. I was something new. I could have anything I wanted, all I had to do was want it bad enough.

Heat and cold warred within me, and ice came out the winner. My skin hardened into frosted armor. This was my moment. This was the beginning.

A crook of my finger, and the spotlight clacked loudly on, and my world was a luxury of light. For seventeen years, that much light pouring right into my face might have kicked off a world of trauma. But tonight, it was like a baptism.

He couldn't help but spot me. And like a moth to the flame, he headed towards the spotlight, and towards me. The winter voice whispered murder in my ears, and my power surged like barely constrained waves. But it wasn't the right time to break him. First, he had to suffer.

"What did you do?" Lucien hissed, climbing the stairs and circling me.

"That's enough," I called out, but I wasn't talking to him. He still didn't merit all of my attention just yet. Magic and demon power surged within me, and I could feel the two powers warring against each other even as they complemented so perfectly. It was almost like a drug, the feeling that coursed through my veins. But the demon power was still coming out on top, feeding on all the dark thoughts that Lucien had brought in the door with him. If there was anyone who deserved my darkness, it was him.

The world stopped around us. It wasn't enough to make everything quiet, as I'd done before. He needed to know the power I had at my disposal. So I plucked the two of us out of time and didn't even have to pause to catch a breath. The world froze around us, but it was a moment of iced over motion. Teenagers who'd been dancing a moment ago were in two places at once, in two moments at once. The music hummed in the air, a note dragged out so long it was a weeping cry. Smells were more potent, and the air had a texture. The world was so alive that if I wasn't buffered by my powers, it would have driven me insane.

The room had grown so quiet I could hear dreams being born almost as fast as dreams were broken.

I had his attention.

"You ... what did ... " His eyes scanned futures, as he'd been doing ever since he walked into the hall.

"You've probably forgotten why I terrify you, right?

Why you're so scared of me?" I made a beckoning gesture with my hand, and pulled Carter out of the crowd and into this moment between moments.

Carter had been a friend of Jade's, once upon a time. When he found out I was living at Jason's, Carter thought he could get a little payback. Kick the crap out of me because of something Jason had done. He deserved anything I chose to do to him. He was an ant. He didn't matter.

Carter, who probably thought the rented suit he was wearing looked good on him, who probably thought he was getting laid tonight, even though his date was already making eyes at one of his teammates. Carter, the only person in the hall who I hadn't looked into half an hour before. The lone beacon that had led Lucien right here. Right to me.

Carter hopped up onto the stage, and I lowered my hand. He fell to his knees and looked up at me. *Break him break him break him,* the winter voices chanted in my head. I was tempted.

"Look at me, Carter," I whispered, and to his ears, my voice was a melody. A song he would never hear again, no matter how desperately he searched. "Remember when you thought you were better than me? When you thought you would teach me a lesson?"

His head dropped, but I didn't need to see his face to know the flush that was spreading.

"You are blessed, aren't you? I should eviscerate you for what you did, but instead, I'm granting you asylum." I passed my hands over his head and tugged his head up. I looked into him and spread the tiniest part of my powers. Magic wrapped around him like fishing line, constricting until it was tight against his skin. One moment visible, the next absorbed inside. It was a small magic, but if I wanted to make the effect permanent, a part of me would always reside in him. A part of my power would always be lost.

By the time I'd turned back to Lucien, I knew he'd seen it firsthand already. The way Carter's threads just vanished from the futures that Lucien traveled so extensively, making them duller and more faded than they were a moment before. "I've found a better use for your powers, Lucien. Take a look around. Congratulate them. It's a brand-new day. A graduating class free from you."

"A party trick," Lucien sniffed. "Nothing more. When you die, the magic will be revealed, and everyone goes back to where they belong."

"Except you," I said with a smile. "You'll never find your way home. And you'll never find the rest of your power. Because I'm not going to die, Lucien. I know something you don't know."

"Do you forget who you're talking to?" he demanded, swelling up where he stood. It was funny how impressive he'd looked to me that first day, and how the shine had faded. His suit was expensive, but mine looked better. He was … haggard, in a way. His clothes didn't fit quite right, as if even the natural fabrics of the world knew he was just a pretender to a humanity he eschewed. He was playing dress-up, nothing more. "Do you forget the things that I hold over you? I can take him at any time."

I realized now, in a moment of clarity, why I'd let the winter grow so strong in me. And in a rush of clarity, I saw the path that was opening wide before me, a path I was stepping onto, even now. The vision of the future, the one in which I brought ruin down upon the town, it all came down to this night. And it was as simple as the war inside of me. Grace's ruby, burning eyes, the cerulean glow and warmth of my own. And the pale, cold cornflower blue of the demon eyes. It was all of them together. All the darkness and light inside of me, all of what I was and what I could be.

I released the illusion over my eyes, allowed them to glow, already knowing what Lucien would see. They weren't quite violet yet, but with the powers churning inside of me, they were well on their way. And we both knew it.

Lucien took a step back, and I pressed the advantage. "How many futures do you see?" I asked, though I didn't care about the answer. All I cared about was making *him* care. "Ten thousand? Twenty? Isn't that far less than yesterday and the day before?"

Lucien's eyes twitched, he couldn't help himself. His eyes darted left and right, and I watched him count. Grace was right about one thing—the future controlled Lucien as much as he controlled it. A weakness I would have never thought to exploit.

"I told you I would make you pay," I said softly. No one mattered except the two of us. "I know how much you like to play games, but now it's my turn." I leaned in close, and smiled as he shifted back almost imperceptibly. "I'm going to destroy you, Rider, but first I'm going to make you watch. Make you *helpless*. Take every possible future away from you until the only thing you can see at the end of that long tunnel is the color of my boot just before I crush your neck."

Lucien was stone, unmoving. Unblinking. Frozen, or considering his next move, I couldn't be sure. But I definitely didn't care.

"What good will the future do you then? What games will you play when you don't know the outcome? Do you remember teaching me that exposing someone's weaknesses, and using it against them was fun?" I grabbed him by the tie, and pulled him towards me. He didn't resist. "I'm having the best day ever," I said, whispering into his ear.

"What do you want?" he said, and it was a voice crumbling with frailties. I sneered. How had something that had once been so great become so riddled with flaws?

"You're going to undo what you've done. Take back the power you exposed in Gentry, and restore whatever it is you took out of Riley. And when both of those things are done, you and I are going back to the lighthouse. You think my power will vanish when I die, Lucien? Then I just won't die. All to spite you." I took another step forward and nearly crowed when he took another one back. *How he fears me! It's intoxicating!*

I flicked my wrist, unraveling the bubble I'd trapped us in, and returned us back to the stream of time. The music cued up in a jangled rush at first, as the noise took moments to stabilize.

"Do you think if I keep staring at you," I cocked my head slowly to one side, "that you'd actually lose control of yourself? Wet your pants like a small child?" I took another step forward, and then Lucien was on the edge of the stage, his balance threatened.

There was a hand on my arm, mewling words interrupting my moment. I could still break him, and then watch the weakness wash over him completely. He would deserve it, having become such a lesser, broken thing. I wondered if I could make him drown in it.

The voice kept interrupting, growing more and more insistent. I turned, and the demon in me didn't recognize the human at my side at first. He was fair, and this body reacted to his touch, but names were worthless things, easily cast off and forgotten. And so his name escaped me.

As did my name on his lips. Repeated, over and over again, in his simple human tongue. The magic inside of me, the fire, renewed its efforts, and burned through the frozen fog in my mind. My eyes cleared, and I felt ... *feelings.* A rush of emotion that clogged up my brain with so many different impressions.

And Trey, talking urgently in some kind of babble, his face bathed in indigo. But slowly, the light shining on his face—the light from my eyes—grew darker, and left the shades of madness for familiar blue.

I smiled, once I felt more like myself, and even though

Trey looked like he wanted to punch me in the face he grabbed me and kissed me once. "You looked like you were about to eviscerate him," he whispered in my ear.

Lucien, still on the edge, looked green around the edges.

I was, I thought to myself. *I might have let everything else go just to tear him to shreds.* The demon inside of me wanted it. Wanted to tear Lucien apart and take his place. The same goal that Grace had, once upon a time. It was hard to say if that was still her motive as well.

"Do it," I said to him, trying to sound in control of the situation. Lucien might be cowed into doing what I told him for a time, but the promise of violet-eyed destruction would only get me so far before I had to back it up.

The lawyer was on the edge of the stage one moment, and the next he had supernaturally slithered in between Trey and me, a striking blur of black that had his hand pressed against Trey's chest. Unlike the sparkling black and white that came from Lucien stealing someone's potential just by laying his hand on theirs, this time he drew golden fire out of Trey's skin. For a moment, even Trey's eyes flashed gold, before settling back to their ordinary blue.

"The contract between our parties is officially nullified," Lucien said sourly, pulling his hand away the moment the fire died.

It wasn't that he'd taken Trey's magic—I hadn't forced him into the same situation I'd gone through myself— he just returned it to the way it had been before Trey had made his bargain. Potential, but with little actual knowledge or ability. Every witch had a certain affinity for it, but without training and constant usage of their gifts, it would never grow into the power it could be. Lucien had only fast-tracked him along the process. For a short time only, it now seemed.

Trey didn't have much time to recover or to lob his own protests because almost as soon as his eyes were clear again, I was heading for the exit, his hand clasped in mine.

Riley next. And then Grace. And then this would all be over.

thirty-four

I wasn't stupid. My victory over Lucien was only momentary. It wouldn't last, and his next strike would come sooner rather than later if the sour, speculative flicker of his eyes had anything to say about it. I hadn't beaten him, not really. Not yet.

But it would be so easy, the voices whispered, as I knew they would. It became more and more difficult to ignore them. They were bad thoughts that grew roots instead of fading away. There was a part of me that liked what they suggested, that hungered for new ways to inflict pain on the people that hurt me.

Trey was docile at my side, stumbling along after me. Once again, the crowd parted before me, eyes wide with some mix of fear and wonder. I couldn't say for sure how much they would remember about what I'd done or what had happened to them.

In the back of my mind, I'd been a little afraid that the dance would turn into round three for Lucien and me.

Twice now, I'd squeaked out a victory against him, but each time had cost me too much. The first had almost killed me, the second had almost killed Riley. I didn't want to go three for three.

I waited until we were outside to check on Trey. His pupils were blown wide, his shirt was rumpled, and he looked like he'd just run a marathon, but there didn't appear to be any lasting damage.

"Are you okay?" I asked, leaning a little too close.

Trey pushed me back, pulling away the moment he recovered. Having the bargain broken took a lot out of him. "You didn't have any right to do that. I knew what I was getting into."

There was a buzzing from behind me. I looked over my shoulder to see Lucien standing there on the fringes. Waiting. He pulled the phone out of his breast pocket a moment later, his sneer an angry slash across his face. "Stupid woman, I don't have time for you."

I ignored him, focusing my attention on Trey. "And if you didn't think I was going to fix it, you're an idiot. You're not sacrificing yourself for me, Trey. There's been enough of that to go around."

The scowl hadn't quite left his face, but he still read too much in my words. "What's that supposed to mean?"

I couldn't admit to what I'd done to Drew. None of them would understand why I'd had to do it, or what the cost had really been. All they would see that Drew was dead and that his blood was still on my hands.

"Where are you guys—whoa," Jade pulled up short behind us when she saw Lucien standing to one side, watching us all with contempt. His phone buzzed again, and I thought back to what he'd just said.

"It's Catherine, isn't it?" Lucien's face gave away nothing, but I didn't need the confirmation. "Answer it," I commanded him. "Tell her to meet you at the hospital."

Trey grabbed my arm. "What are you doing?"

"Two birds, one stone." With any luck, I'd still be the stone.

¤   ¤   ¤

For everything that I'd been through and how much of a struggle it had been to try and restore Riley on my own, to have Lucien walk into her hospital room and instantly make everything better was a blow to the ego. What was worse, he knew it.

As easy as it was for the Rider to drain the future from a person, it was just as easy to replace what he'd stolen.

I'd followed him into the room, Trey and Jade somewhere behind me. I didn't trust Lucien, and I unveiled my eyes the moment he reached for my friend. But the stars and sparkles that trickled out from Lucien's hands slipped seamlessly into all the empty spaces that had been left behind in Riley's mind. Everything he poured into her made an immediate difference, like electricity restored to a house that had gone without it for so long.

"Impressive," he tossed over his shoulder. "I would have

preferred it if what you'd stolen from me had been returned, but you nearly managed to undo what you broke in the first place." His eyes glittered, but he kept his rage under control. "You do so enjoy taking my things, don't you?"

"I wasn't the one who broke her. You fed on her. I was just trying to stop you."

"Yes, and you made things so much better by interfering, didn't you?"

Still so arrogant. Throw him from the window, let his body shatter upon the concrete. Soften him. Soil him. Make him regret every silver word.

It was interesting, the way that the winter voices held no loyalty. By all rights, they were manifestations of Lucien's power. They should have been trying to return to him, or at the very least work towards his own agenda. But they never had. They wanted him destroyed as much as anyone.

"You think you have me under control. That a few bells are going to keep me docile? What fairy tales have you been reading, boy? I am still what I am. Just because you've stolen a part of my power does not mean we are equals."

"Doesn't it?" I asked evenly.

"I am the lightning and the thunder that shatters the sky. You are barely a spark, burning bright and then burning . . ." Lucien dropped his hands from Riley, who still hadn't stirred. "Out. Now why don't you tell me how you managed it? Because I'm curious, boy."

It hadn't been enough. If Lucien had returned everything he'd taken from Riley, then why hadn't she woken up? I thought I'd fixed the rest of the damage, restored her mind to as close as I could get it. But there was nothing. Riley was silent and still, which meant that she was almost entirely unrecognizable.

"My name's Braden," I grunted, and without thinking it through I thrust my hand forward and into his chest. Lucien gasped as my hand sank into his vital organs, or their demonic equivalent, and rooted around among all the things inside. A small smile started to form when I found what I was looking for.

I walked calmly towards Riley, the weight of Lucien on my arm negligible. His feet dangled almost a foot off the floor, but I had no trouble carrying him. I rested my free hand on Riley's forehead. Starbursts and coronas, comets and solar winds swept out through Lucien's gut, up through my one arm and down the other, and sank down into Riley's skin.

"Don't think you can screw me over, demon." I didn't recognize my voice. Still split open by my fist, Lucien made gasping noises that sounded like breaths, but as far as witty retorts went, it failed.

Once the last of cosmic essence dripped out of my fingers, I tossed him forward. Lucien's shirt was torn open, but the skin underneath was smooth and unmarked. Not even a scratch. I flexed my hand once, twice, looking for traces of blood. With Drew, there had been so much. With Lucien, nothing.

Lucien's eyes were wide, and his panting had only

grown worse. *Yes, that's the stuff. Fear. Terror. Deep down in the hollows of his bones, carving in the memories that will make him fear me forevermore.*

But for once, those thoughts weren't courtesy of the winter voices.

They were mine.

Before I had time to think about what that meant, or to work through what had just happened, Jade hurried into the doorway, looking back towards the way she'd come. "Catherine just got off the elevator," she reported.

It was time, then.

I extended my hand to Lucien, but when he didn't immediately take it, I kicked him, clocking him right in the spot where my arm had been. "Get up," I snarled, and a second later his hand was in mine. I pulled him to his feet, spent a few moments straightening his jacket, adjusting his tie, using a slip of magic to restore the damage to his shirt. Then I placed my palms on either side of his face, pulled it close towards me.

"Hear her out," I said with a smile. "This ought to be good."

I knew as well as anyone that Lucien was biding his time, waiting for the opportune moment to strike. But he couldn't read my future, and it kept him off his game. I just needed him to stay off it a little while longer. Luckily for me, he'd needed another demonstration of what I was willing to do.

Since she'd been the one keeping lookout, Jade had

missed what had gone down between us, but Trey had been here the whole time. I'd forgotten. His expression was dark, his arms crossed in front of him. Concern rolled off of him in waves, but I pushed him to the side of my awareness, and took a seat at the end of Riley's bed. She still slept, but it was only a matter of time now.

Jade and Trey crossed the room as well, setting up next to the blacked-out windows. About as far from Catherine and the demon as they could get. And even putting Riley's bed between us. *He starts to fear you,* came a whistle in my mind. *Yessss.*

Of course Catherine's ego preceded her into the room. "Have you really forgotten how this arrangement works, Fallon? You come when I call, not the other—" she stopped abruptly once she realized she wasn't alone with Lucien the way she thought. "What are they doing here?"

I offered her a grin and an enthusiastic wave, but I kept my mouth closed. This would be good enough without my two cents.

If looks were weapons, Lucien's glance towards me would have been a poison dart. He cleared his throat, trying and failing to summon up his immaculate aplomb. "What do you want, Catherine?"

She should have noticed that something was wrong with him, but Catherine was always too self-involved to notice the things around her. "I've been trying to reach you all day. Where the hell have you been?"

And for a moment, Lucien forgot the situation he was

in. I could see the irritation sweeping through his body, stiffening his spine and lacing his words with acerbic bite. "I am not your *pet,* to come when you call me because a manicure ran long. I have my own concerns. My own interests."

"Like forcing my son to sign a contract with you?" She didn't even give him a chance to reply. Her arm darted out and slapped him across the face. Then she hauled back and did it a second time.

Lucien wasn't human, and I'd seen him go through enough to say with certainty that he was a durable sonofabitch, but his head snapped back just like any man's would after the second strike.

But it wasn't the change in Lucien that surprised me. It was Catherine, specifically, the tears in her eyes. She stood there, hand pressed over mouth, as tears spilled down over her face. She was shaking, I realized, though she tried to press her hands close to her body to hide it.

"What were the terms?"

Lucien rubbed at his jaw, eyes narrowed down to little slits as he turned back to her. His entire posture shifted. A broken demon and a prisoner in this world, but he still wore the shape of a man and still had height, weight, and strength on her.

"Forget that," Catherine continued, still not realizing the danger that she was in. "I'll do it. I'll take his place. You can negate our deal, or add the terms onto the one I've already signed, or whatever."

"Mom, no," Trey protested. Before he could say anything

else, I placed a wall between us, as easily as breathing. It was as cold as winter silence, bitter to the touch, a construct of demonic ice. Trey continued to shout, but no one could hear him.

Lucien's rage vanished in a moment, replaced by a smile full of contempt. "Do you even know what you're offering up? You haven't even *seen* the terms."

"I can guess." Catherine's bitterness had consumed her. There was a nasty look directed my way before she continued. "You'll take my future, leaving me an empty shell destined for nothing but mediocrity. Maybe even kill me. I don't care." When she looked up at him again, her eyes blazed with her conviction. "But you won't take my son. I don't care what the cost is. I'll pay." She took a shuddering breath, and even I knew it cost her plenty already to add the broken "please" after it.

Lucien looked to me, waiting for my reaction.

"Nah," I said, loudly for Catherine's benefit. "I don't think so."

Lucien turned back to her, spreading his arms as if to ask: *Well, what do you expect me to do?* He was enjoying this little show, even though he wasn't the one pulling the strings. Of course he did. Demons loved causing trouble.

"Stay out of this," Catherine snarled.

"Do you really think you get a free pass, Catherine? Are you really that naive?"

She lunged for me, face contorted with rage until she resembled the monster she really was. Catherine did *ugly* about as well as Catherine did anything: full tilt and holding nothing back. Her rage was a contorted creature. Lucien grabbed her by the arm and held her back from making a dangerous mistake.

"He's my *son*! You won't take this away from me. This is my right!"

"No, not quite. This is your punishment."

I closed my eyes, feeling the darkness welling up within me. *Yes,* the voices hissed, *take this away from her. Break her so exquisitely that she will never be repaired.* When I opened them again, the world spiraled into shades of violet, symbols in patterns made by claws fluttered through the air, remnants of broken worlds that had been cobbled together to form this one. Catherine's heart, beating a rhythm and pumping incendiary fear coursing through her bloodstream.

She yanked herself out of Lucien's grip and stumbled back towards the door.

I turned to Lucien. My equal. My enemy. My eyes raged violet, and I could hear the Riders calling to me, cajoling from across the voids. Our eyes met, and voiceless conversations that were made up of sun flares and tsunamis passed between us before I finally bobbed my head once, sharply. "Do it."

"Lucien, you can't possibly—you told me you needed him!" She still thought Trey was in danger. It was laughable.

The demon still didn't understand. When I said "now" I meant *now.* My fury became an inferno in an instant, and I reacted. I lunged outside of time as the world fell to freezing around me. The others were trapped statues as I rushed forward, barely feeling my feet touch the ground. Even Lucien was caught up in the wake of time, his eyes stuck on the place where I had been, a cruel smirk forming.

I grabbed his arm, dragged him towards Catherine. I pressed his palm flat against her forehead, held it there, and stepped back through the bars of time's cage, and roared, "DO IT!" My rage would brook no argument. There would be no cease-fire here.

I don't know how it looked, if I was just a blur of speed or if I'd simply disappeared and reappeared standing between the two of them. I didn't care. She would pay. She would pay forever if I had my way.

A demon lives to destroy, and in a way, this moment would destroy Catherine Lansing forever. "You are marked as fortune's favored daughter," the demon whispered. Black fire swirled around his skin, seeped into the follicles of her hair and the beads of sweat on her skin. "You will not die young, a victim of accident or chance. Wherever you will go, good fortune will keep you on your way. Your life will be spared for all of your days. Your mind will be as sharp as it ever was, your memory as clear as glass."

In my haste to see it done, the wall trapping Trey had slipped and shattered. He grabbed me now, fingers digging into my skin. "What are you doing?" he demanded, shaking me.

"She doesn't get mercy. She doesn't get to forget and become something less." I looked away from him, to where black fire was still being swallowed up by her skin. "She killed my uncle. And probably a lot more, too. I don't want her to ever forget."

"Why?" he whispered.

"Because I want her to remember. I was her destruction, but I was also her savior. Someone would have toppled her eventually; she's made enough enemies. Now they won't. Now she'll live."

Catherine looked up at me, and the horror I wanted to see in her eyes was truly there, leaking out the sides. *So fragile,* I thought, looking down at her like a pet. *I could shear your soul from your body and scatter it across all the stars in the devil's sky.*

"You wanted a weapon, Catherine," I said, crouching down in front of her, cupping my hand under her chin and pulling her back to her feet. "Wish granted."

"One more thing, Catherine," Lucien said, coming to my side. In this moment, we were almost partners, with an impeccable sense of timing. "Braden and I came to an agreement last night. Your son's contract was already voided."

"What?" Catherine's head whipped around as she looked at each of us in turn. Too much had happened, her mind had gone through so many different scenarios, but this was clearly not one of them. "Then why..."

I looked up at Lucien and nodded. "Show her the rest."

And so Lucien gave her a glimpse of the power he possessed, filled her mind with visions of Belle Dam's former fate. All the lives that Catherine had affected, or altered, or ended. He put faces to names, reminded her of sins long since past. Things even she'd forgotten. Even the ramifications—things she'd done that wouldn't play out for another generation or two. A tangible glossary of her wasted, pathetic life.

Her punishment was knowledge. Walking the streets of Belle Dam and every time she saw a familiar face, she would be reminded of the crimes she'd committed against them.

"Jade, get her out of here," Trey commanded. Jade did as she was told, first helping Catherine to her feet and then leading her out of the room. Trey stood above me as Lucien backed away. His disapproval hung like a chalk cloud in the air, infecting my skin with it.

"What are you doing?" he asked softly.

Who did he think he was, to question me? Did he not see me just bend the Rider to my will, force him to act as my puppet? And who was he? A boy stupid with the gold in his veins, who could not even comprehend the majesty of what was happening now.

"Remember who you are," the boy bleated. It was hard to remember why I should care. Why his voice affected my body. "This is the demon talking. Not you. You have to fight it."

"I am fighting," I said quietly. "And I've only just begun."

"No," he said, and he risked death by laying his hands upon me. Curiously, I did not strike him down, though the desire was there. "This isn't you. You're not the boy with

354

the violet eyes. Your eyes are blue, or green, but never this. Come on, you can remember. For me."

But it wasn't Trey who broke through to me. It was Riley.

"Braden?" she whispered.

Human instinct won out over demon influence. Somewhere inside of me a flame went out, and when I spun around, I was myself again, my thoughts as clear as they'd ever been before.

It was getting worse. Whatever was happening to me, this *degradation,* it wasn't going to get any easier to control. The longer I was out here, the more likely I would do something I would regret. If any part of me remained human long enough to regret it.

Riley's eyes were open, focused and sharp and a far cry from the girl who'd been lost.

"He came after me," she said simply, eyes staring at Lucien though they didn't have any fear, "and then I don't remember anything." Her smile was slow in coming, but when it formed it was just like the memory of her in my head. A knot in my chest unraveled, and if I accomplished nothing else, at least I'd made good on my promise. I'd found a way to bring Riley back.

"Did you save me?" she asked.

I trembled, and Trey's hands slid over my shoulders, squeezed me and pulled me tight against him. "He did."

"Go away," I commanded Lucien, my voice little more than a rasp. He dipped his head, the curl of his lip the only hint of disdain he allowed to surface. He was well into the hallway before I quietly added, "Don't go far. You have one more appointment tonight."

I'd bargained for three days, but I was barely going to make it through one. Grace had made a very bad deal. She thought she'd won a victory, when she bargained my three days down to three midnights, returning me only hours before the first. She thought there wouldn't be enough time for me to go off the rails. Now I knew it was too much.

Trey started to explain to Riley what she'd missed, but it didn't prove necessary. Despite having spent every day since her attack in a psychotic state, Riley had an easy grasp of what had gone down in her absence. "And now Braden swallowed up one of the wellsprings so that he could go toe to toe with Lucien and not get bitch-slapped again," she concluded.

Neither Trey nor I knew what to say. I rubbed my hands on the bottom of my jacket again and again, the feel of something slick on my skin that I couldn't get off.

"Get out," Riley said finally, and my attention snapped back to her.

"What?"

She looked at me like I'd ridden in on the short bus, then gestured down at her outfit. "If I'm going with you, I can't exactly go in a hospital gown and my robe, now can I?"

"You're not going with us," I said, almost in stereo with Trey's protest. But Riley didn't want to hear it. And since allowances had already been made for Jade, because I honestly couldn't tell her no after what I'd done to Drew, the same went for Riley, too.

She stopped me before I reached the door. "I remember what you're going to do," she whispered, lowering her voice so it was just the two of us. "It won't work."

"No, it will. You've said it yourself all along." The jacket wasn't cutting it so I tried wiping my hands down on the bed sheets. Riley wouldn't need them anymore. "Take in the wellspring, become that thing, and I could beat them."

"Beat them, maybe, but you're not just trying to beat them, Braden." She rested her palm against my cheek, and I flinched at her touch. It wasn't that long ago that she'd hijacked my brain with a little skin-to-skin contact. But nothing happened this time, the demonic power inside me still dormant. "It doesn't balance. There's two of them, and only one of you."

In all things, balance. It had been beaten into my head often enough. My heart thudded and then rolled to a stop in my chest. It wasn't going to be enough.

I wasn't going to be enough.

thirty-five

The last time I'd been in a cemetery, I'd been fighting for my life. Well, actually, the last few times I'd been in a cemetery. The night air was a cool breeze off the bay, salty and fresh. There'd been a morbid tint to my thoughts ever since I'd left Riley's hospital room. I knew this was where it had to end. It was poetic.

This was where it had really started, where Lucien had set me onto the path for Grace, and I'd become so enmeshed in Belle Dam's secrets that I jumped through every hoop I could find.

The cloud cover opened, and a sea of stars wished us on our way. Anticipation whispered through the trees like it was Christmas Eve, though that was days past. Belle Dam was hushed, sleeping lightly, ready to wake up in the morning at the moment that everything was different.

Because after tonight, it would be.

Lucien had vanished into the shadows, likely more comfortable traveling on his own than with a bunch of teenagers. Jade and Riley were insistent about coming along, and neither one would hear a word of argument. But since the real showdown was happening in the lighthouse, and not the cemetery, I didn't lobby very hard against their going with us. Trey shot me a disapproving look, but a few minutes more with my friends was a small price to pay.

Trey drove, but when I tried to take the passenger's seat up front to ride next to him, I'd been pushed into the back with Riley on one side and Jade on the other. This new, restored Riley was a quiet creature, prone to long silences and eyes that held too much knowledge. It was hard to say how much she remembered after what had happened to her, Riley deflected questions with the ease of someone who had been asking them for half her life.

Jade, however, was not prone to any such silences. "I *get* that you're pitting the two of them against each other," she said, repeating my own words back about what I expected to happen tonight, "but what's the outcome? Do you really think that they'll take each other out?"

"Of course," I lied. I liked my version of the story better than the reality. My friends didn't need to know what Riley had confided in me, or my own fears. As far as they needed to be concerned, everything was going to happen just the way it was supposed to. Until it didn't. "They're evenly matched. Or at least, they will be. Then all we have to do is wait them out. They'll destroy each other before breakfast. No doubt."

"And you're not worried she's going to turn on you?

She's already done it once before," Trey said from the driver's seat, and the lack of approval in his words halted the conversation for a minute.

"He's lying." There was no emotion to Riley's voice, and it sounded so strange and flat that I thought for a minute that Lucien had fooled us all, and Riley wasn't fixed after all.

"It's a good pl—" I started, but Jade pushed me back, showing a physical strength that I wouldn't have expected out of her. She leaned in front of me, staring over at Riley.

"What do you mean? What's he lying about?"

Riley's auburn hair was limp and pulled back, and the clothes she wore hung off of her like she was hardly bigger than a hanger. She'd lost a lot of weight in the hospital, and probably still needed to be there for a while. Another reason why jailbreaking her hadn't been a good idea.

"They can't kill each other," she said softly, playing with the fringe on the edges of her sleeve. "He knows that. Everything's too bound up into everything else. He's playing at something else."

I gritted my teeth and tried not to let it show too much on my face. I *was* lying, and Riley was exactly right about everything, but why the hell was she telling *Jade*? Why was she trying to ruin everything? I had one chance, maybe, and the last thing I needed was Riley trying to sabotage me from the sidelines. Especially since she knew more than she was saying. Why blow the whistle on me if she wasn't going to reveal everything she knew?

"I'm not *playing* at anything," I said, my voice harsh.

"Lucien doesn't know yet. That'll give Grace a little bit of an advantage. But being in the lighthouse will give Lucien one, too. He won't be bound so tight." One I could handle. But not both. Each of them had worlds of experience on me, and the times I'd gone against them I'd just barely survived. If they decided to set aside their differences and destroy the upstart who'd brought them together, there wouldn't be enough left of me to scrape off the floor.

Jade's expression hardened, and she turned to look out the window. "I want to see her suffer. She attacked you, she *killed* Drew ... I just ... someone should be there to make sure he gets justice."

"Oh." I saw the expression on Riley's face. She *remembered* what had happened to Drew. She knew who was responsible. Dammit!

"Stop here," I told Trey, even though we were still blocks from the cemetery. "I'll go the rest of the way on my own."

Trey met my eyes in the rear view mirror, his expression perturbed. "It's just a couple of blocks. Relax. You've got this."

"Drew's—" But I didn't let Riley finish. I whirled on her, got in her face.

"Not another word. Just shut up. Shut up! You've been in a hospital bed talking like a lunatic for over a month!" I don't know where the rage came from, but it poured out in my words, fed by the guilt sweating out through my skin and the self-loathing that had been eating away at my insides.

I was close to losing it. I had to get out of the car, which was suddenly smaller than it had been moments before. Legs pressed up against mine on both sides, it was a million degrees, and there wasn't any oxygen. I opened my mouth to take a breath, but there was nothing there. Just bodies, shifting at my sides, pressing in on me. Questions lobbed over my head. Panting breaths that weren't doing a bit of good. Too much. Too much too much too much too—

Red and violet sparks burst out of the console, the emergency brake yanked up and the power siphoned into the sky like a strike of reversed lightning. Rotting guilt, suspicion, so guilty oh so guilty put on the cuffs burning against the skin soft melodies and hot spilled hearts weighed against everything that was to come. Crystal eyes like the Library at Alexandria, filled with books worlds memories than any thousand lifetimes before. Eyes that are not eyes, silvered mirrorglass, eyes sharing burden though burden is unspoken.

My hands covered over my face, my head pressed down over my knees, and there was air—cool air—spilling in at my sides. Time had passed, but I couldn't be sure how much. Long enough that my heart had settled and my breaths came slow and even. Too long.

"Braden," Trey said softly at my side. I looked up, felt the tears on my face, and saw his expression. Stricken, but still determined. Over his shoulder, Riley and Jade were wrapped around each other, Jade having turned so that her body was between Riley and me. Like I was a threat.

I *was* a threat.

"It's getting worse," I whispered.

Trey didn't put it into words, but he nodded. "That's the thing that you're afraid of, isn't it? Whatever it is that you've been running from. Ever since your uncle died."

I hadn't told anyone about the vision. About what I could become. At least not the people in my real life. Lucien knew, of course. And Grace. But I thought if I could shield the rest of them, if I could keep this deep, dark secret away from them, they wouldn't look at me the way Jade looked at me now.

I closed my eyes, and felt something burn out inside of me. "She told Jade." It wasn't even a question. It didn't need to be. I knew from the moment that Riley had opened her mouth that they were going to find out. Riley was going to tell everyone what I'd done to Drew, and worse, she was going to tell them *why*. That I'd done it to get my power back, that Drew's friendship had been weighed against my need to be special, and lost.

"Are you okay?"

I opened my eyes again. Trey was still looking at *me* like I was the one who needed comfort. He wasn't surprised by any of it. "How long have you known?" I asked dully.

"Long enough," he said quietly. "You could have told me."

"Ever notice that I don't tell people a lot of things I could?" I asked. Lucien would be here any time, it wouldn't be good for him to find me having a panic attack, or even a heartfelt conversation in the back of Trey's car. "The more

I talk about … anything, the more chance there is that it all gets screwed up." I sighed. "I screw everything up."

"Ever notice that things get that way even without you?" Trey asked. "Not that I'm not saying you do more than your fair share, but really. You don't have a monopoly on being an idiot." He patted me awkwardly on the knee and then turned around to deal with his sister. I don't know what he said to her, and the truth was that I didn't want to know. The last thing I wanted to deal with right now was Jade knowing what I'd done to Drew. Riley bit at one of her fingernails, having tucked her hair up into a brown knit cap sometime after getting out of the car.

There were so many variables, so many different ways that tonight could go off the rails. But there were a few things that absolutely had to happen. The confrontation had to take place in the lighthouse, I had to do it by myself, and … I had to say goodbye before I went.

But runaway emotions interrupted before I could accomplish any of those things. "Is it true?" Jade demanded, the moment I was out of the car.

"Jade—"

I heard the slap before I felt it. Saw the shimmering line of tears before I saw the animosity in her eyes. It was like it happened to someone else, that was how disconnected I was. I pressed a hand against my cheek, feeling the warmth like it didn't belong to me.

"That's not helping," Trey snapped, moving in between us. Jade huffed and opened her mouth to argue before she gave up and spun around on her heel. When she tried to put an arm around Riley and pull her away, Riley resisted.

"I have to go to the grave," I said, numb to what I should be feeling. "Lucien will meet me there." Maybe goodbyes weren't such a good idea after all. "I'm sorry," I told her, even though I wasn't sure I was. "I had to."

"Braden, shut up." Despite everything, Trey still had my back. I didn't get it.

I made sure to look Jade in the eye. If Riley was to be believed, I wasn't going to make it out of here anyway, so why not. Maybe if I made her hate me—maybe that hate would be better than anything else she might feel. She wouldn't have to miss her friend when she could hate the guy who stole her kid's father away. Maybe my death could give her some comfort. It was better if I deserved it. Cleaner.

"I made a deal with Grace," I said, only looking at her. "She'd fix me, and all I had to do was open the door so she could come back through to this world. But it took a lot to do what she did in the first place. And it would cost a lot to bring her back. I knew that, and," I swallowed, "I did it anyway."

She stared at me like she'd never seen me before. Like the last four months had been a lie. And maybe she was right to do that. Maybe they were. "How?"

I knew instinctively that the question was "how could you?" but I chose to answer "how did you do it?" instead. "With a knife," I said simply. "Grace made the Shifter line as a backup. A way out if she couldn't get back on her own.

But no one ever had the juice to make it across before. Until me. So she needed an escape, and I provided it." I held up my hand, palm out, like she could still see the blood that had pooled against my skin, hot like betrayal.

"That's enough," Trey said, pushing me towards the cemetery. "Go home," he snapped at his sister. "The keys are still in the car. Take Riley back to the hospital and then just go home."

"No, wait," Riley said, trying to twist around Jade, who was suddenly blocking her like this was a football game, and not a goodbye.

"Come on, Riley, you need your rest." Jade looked like all the fight had drained out of her.

"But he's got it all wrong," she said, a hint of her old fire stirring to life.

"No, he doesn't," Jade said quietly. They were a strange pair, Riley in street clothes and boots, while Jade still wore her dress and jewelry. "Drew's gone."

"And Braden will be too," Riley insisted, squirming around Jade. Once Riley slipped past her, she charged towards us, her limbs flailing awkwardly as she ran for probably the first time in a month.

Trey caught her easily enough, scooping her up by the waist, under some misguided belief that Riley was going to hit me. But really, if Riley wanted to try punching me in the face, she wouldn't be able to do half the damage that Jade could have done.

But Riley didn't have revenge on her mind. Once Trey

had settled her back on the ground, she looked up at him and announced, "He's not planning on coming back."

That was why Riley hadn't said anything before. She wanted to wait until the last possible minute and rally a defense. I might have talked my way out of it if I had more time. But the demons under my skin were starting to itch, and I couldn't avoid them for long.

Trey wasn't an idiot. And Riley might have been recently crazy, but she was insistent enough that he glanced over at me before looking back at her. "What do you want me to do about it?" Because it was clear that Riley wanted *something.*

"Braden thinks—"

"Enough of that," I whispered harshly, looking around the cemetery. There was no telling what kinds of ears were listening in. I concentrated on a silvery web, drawing the magic into a complex pattern that created a bubble. For a moment I considered only including the three of us, but whether or not she hated me, Jade was still a part of this in her own way, so I extended the bubble to include her. I lined the spell with tiny bits of demon power. Not enough to make me lose control, but enough to ensure that no one would be able to spy through the fringes of the spell.

"Braden thinks he can trap them in the lighthouse with him. Maybe they'll kill each other, maybe not," Riley said, the moment the spell was solid enough to keep us under the radar. Almost like she *knew* the spell was done. *How much of what we did to her left a mark?* I wondered. Lucien had suggested that she wouldn't be *exactly* the way she'd been before the attack, but there'd been no suggestion about how different she'd be.

Trey turned on me. "I thought the plan was to get them to attack each other," he said.

"It is," I nodded, shooting Riley another glare. Why was she trying to make this as difficult as possible?

"And then?" he asked icily.

And then I rot for eternity next to the two of them, unless one of them gets frustrated and kills me first. But either way, the city is saved.

"It won't work," Riley said. "He won't come back out. And then they'll both be free."

"It's fine, Riley," he said consolingly, patting her on the arm. But his eyes stayed on me. He knew she was telling the truth.

Trey might have been willing to stand around and spend the night wringing his hands about what had to happen, but I wasn't. There was a war struggling across Jade's face, competing feelings gaining and losing ground so fast it was hard to tell what she was thinking. She, too, seemed to be taking Riley at face value.

"There has to be a balance!" Riley shouted from behind me as I stalked away. "Why won't anyone listen to me? You can't just topple the scale! You'll be the one that gets stuck, and they'll be free!"

I hurried faster, like if I could just get far enough away, her premonitions of doom wouldn't be able to catch up to me.

Lucien was waiting at Grace's monument when I arrived, Trey hot on my heels. The demon looked up at my approach, his smirk already drawn tight against his face. "Cute," he said, nodding towards the inscription. *Even a Pawn can topple a King.* "Is this supposed to be some kind of message? You're going to hobble me the same way that bitch did?"

I had crossed the worlds twice before, stepped across the veil and entered the lighthouse. But neither time had I opened the portal myself. But I found it wasn't nearly as difficult as I expected. The demon power in me knew how to bend time and space, and the magic made it all happen.

"Funny. I guess everyone's got to be somebody else's bitch." I shrugged and gave Lucien a grin. "Don't worry, it'll be funnier in a moment."

It took even less time to unlock the last wellspring. The first one had been hidden here, underneath Grace's monument. The second had been hidden underneath the bay, just past the lighthouse. And the third was south of the city, in the heart of a forest that I'd never been to. But I didn't need to be there to do this. Now that the power was inside of me, I could open the last wellspring at any time, from anywhere.

Lucien's eyes widened. He could feel the power being stirred up from deep under the earth. He probably thought that I was going to summon it all and devour it right in front of him. He thought wrong.

A cascade of green and gold energy flowed out of

the forest and high into the air, creating an aurora borealis effect over the city. As the power started to fall back to earth, it approached the cemetery with blazing speed.

But it swept past me. Swept past Lucien. It flowed right into the portal and into the lighthouse itself, just like I had planned.

Lucien looked at me in shock, and then he barked out a laugh. "And finally the boy falters. The lighthouse is *my* domain, you idiot. And with that part of my power restored, I'll crush you easily." And then *he* smiled. "But I won't be quick about it. We have some things to settle between us still." And then before he could see a reaction out of me he leapt into the power and vanished through to the other side.

Trey was at my side. "He still doesn't know?"

"He will in about three seconds." I turned to him. "You're not going. You're staying here and making sure your sister and everyone else is safe. I'll close the portal from the other side. Then you'll be safe."

"Not going to happen," Trey said, glaring down at me. "If you wanted them protected, you shouldn't have voided my deal with Lucien. Besides, I'm not letting you go on your own."

"Trey, I can't protect you in there," I insisted. "This isn't part of the plan."

"Yeah, well, Riley says your plan sucks. So we're going with a new plan." He eyed my forehead. "You're sweating. It's taking a lot out of you to open that portal, isn't it? After everything else you've already done tonight, are you really going to waste what you've got left keeping me back?"

"Fine," I said, glaring at him. Riley's words rang in my ears. Balance. How was I going to manage any of it? "But I swear to god if you die in there, I'm going to kill you."

He leaned over and kissed me quickly. "For luck," he whispered.

We entered the lighthouse. Together.

¤   ¤   ¤

Trey and I emerged directly into the lantern room of the lighthouse.

"What in the fallen Hells is this?" Lucien asked from just in front of me. I couldn't see his face, but I could hear the broken shock. What would it be like, to be a demon who had total purview over the future, and to yet be blind-sided by something you'd never seen coming?

"Close your mouth, darling," a cold voice cut in smoothly. Grace stood in front of us, the veil pulled away from her face for once. The wellspring magic had darkened her eyes until they were more black than red, but here and there were hints of fire. "And say hello to an old friend."

"This isn't possible."

"You challenged my ideas about 'possible' a lifetime ago. It pleases me to return the favor." Grace looked past the demon that started all of this and focused on me. "And if it isn't my little Judas, all dressed up with nowhere to go. You should reconsider your scheme, boy."

My contract with her was crumpled in her hands. She nodded behind me, and behind us the portal flared into activity again. Jade and Riley emerged from the other side, though neither of them looked too happy about it. It wasn't until the figure behind them appeared that I realized what had happened. Just how screwed I was. At first I thought it was Elle, and maybe I could sweet-talk something out of her, but the shape emerging into the lantern room was too tall, too broad shouldered.

The man had a gun in his hands, and it was pointed at one of the girls. He smiled, dipped his head, and murmured "My lady" in respectful tones.

The man working for Grace was Matthias.

thirty-six

"Isn't it interesting," Matthias said, "a hundred years in Belle Dam and finally everyone's paying attention to old Matthias. Bargains keep coming in from all sides. The Rider wants a parley, the Widow wants an ally, and the Witchling wants a mentor. But no one wonders about what Matthias wants."

I kept my face schooled in indifference. Lucien took a step forward, and I grabbed the fabric of Trey's shirt as I pulled him to the side. Putting distance between us and the others, and giving me a better shot at defending him.

I just hoped everyone would keep their heads for a few minutes more. The lantern room was crowded, seven bodies packed inside. Beyond the broken wall, the storms beyond in a jagged fury like I'd never seen before. Jade was looking out through the broken glass in curious horror. Riley was staring, too, but in her I saw the look of someone who knew what was out there. Who could see the shapes writhing behind the clouds.

They shouldn't even be here. Were they supposed to be hostages? Trey would have already been enough leverage. With Matthias closest to the portal, there would be no getting back to the other side without going through him.

There was too much power collected in the lighthouse, I thought, biting down on my lip. Too many of us with power. Grace by herself was nothing, Lucien the same, but now each of us held the core of Lucien's power. Matthias was nothing to sneeze at, though, and with the girls and Trey here … there was too much chance someone would get hurt.

The tension in the air only seemed to make the storms rage faster. Somewhere out there the Riders were doing whatever it is they did. Fighting. Killing. But they had to know we were here by now. The power lurching inside me hummed in resonance. Darkness churned in the distance.

"We can't stay in here," I said quietly to Trey.

"Oh, but finally all the players are gathered in a single room. The woman behind the curtain has been revealed, and the most glorious reunion in the history of Belle Dam is taking place," Matthias said, with a showman's swag. He extended an arm, pivoting to encompass both Grace and Lucien, who had not taken their horrific eyes off of one other. His lip curled with distaste as he had a look around the lighthouse. "It's just too bad that such an epic moment had to happen … here."

"I thought you'd like the lighthouse, Matthias. Isn't it

like demon catnip? Go ahead," I nodded, "roll around on the floor a little bit. We won't judge."

Matthias scowled. He shoved the gun underneath Riley's jaw, pointed up. "Has anyone ever told you that sarcasm truly is the lowest form of discourse?"

Having a gun shoved in her face didn't affect Riley the way I thought it would. She blinked twice, then twisted back to look at the demon. "*Everyone* tells him that," she said calmly.

Lucien was still struck dumb by Grace's apparent resurrection. I could see his eyes darting left and right, tracing back lines of the future all the way back to the beginning. Trying to figure out what he'd missed. I smiled. It was easier than I thought it would be to break him down. Maybe Grace had the right idea after all. All her games, all her tricks, those were the appetizers. This was what she'd really been after.

She'd bested one of the Riders at the Gate. Outwitted him from the beginning.

"Got to say, I'm a little disappointed, Matthias," I called. I wanted his attention on me, and not on Jade and Riley. "You know they've got help lines for people in abusive relationships. Just because Grace hurt you once doesn't mean you have to go back. Or did she promise it would never happen again? That last time was an accident?"

"You think you're so funny." He shifted and pointed the gun towards me. "Does your little group of rejects know what you risk unleashing on the world?"

I let some of the violet peek through my eyes, cracked my knuckles and rolled my neck. Stretches were important before a supernatural showdown. "Want to find out first-hand?" I offered, beckoning him forward.

"Silence." A purple lash of energy cut between the two of us, preceding the whip crack that echoed across the room. "Do you really think me stupid, boy? That even with a contract, I could trust in your loyalty?" Though Grace never looked away from Lucien, nor did she let the triumphant smirk waver, her words were addressed to me. "I know exactly why you came here, boy, and what you hope to accomplish. But the thing *you* need to realize is that I will not be the one trapped in this lighthouse for another hundred years."

"You're not locking Braden up," Trey snapped, stepping forward.

Grace casually flicked her wrist like she was swatting a fly. Trey flew backwards and slammed into one of the stone walls. The air rushed out of him in a startled groan, and then he slumped. *John's eyes, right before the spell struck. Seeking me out. His body, falling to the ground.* I couldn't go through that again.

I ran to him, wishing that just for once Trey would learn to keep his mouth shut. He grunted, which was good because it meant he was still conscious. I only had seconds to decide, and I did something I had been trained not to. Magic wasn't supposed to be used for healing on account of it could make things horribly worse, but the normal rules didn't really apply to me anymore. The warring powers inside of me complied with my need, and delved through bone and surface tissue without finding any serious complication.

"You have a choice," Grace went on like there'd never been an interruption. "You can give up this petty resistance and become my surrogate in this world. Or I will kill every last one of them where they stand."

"And what then, Grace?" I challenged. "What happens after you regain your freedom?"

The darkness in her eyes was eclipsed by the red for just a moment, as the wellspring power in her was pushed down. The power was a part of Lucien, so he never had to fight against it, but Grace ... surviving in the lighthouse for as long as she did suggested an iron will I didn't have. She wouldn't lose control the way I would. At least not at first.

"Everything," she whispered with a smile. "Everything happens."

Lucien wanted Trey dead because if Trey was gone, he thought the vision of me killing him would never come to pass. He feared what I would do to him. So did Matthias. But not Grace. With her, it had never been about fear of what I could do.

It was jealousy.

She wanted to be the one with the power of the Rider. *She* wanted to become something more than human.

"What about Gentry and Jade?" I asked. Grace's expression was blank. "Your grandchildren? Or your great to the power of fifteen grandkids, whatever. You'll kill them?"

An absent roll of the shoulder. "What are they to me? Fruit from a rotted branch. What need do I have of any of them?"

"If you destroy the city, he goes free," I motioned to Lucien. "Have you thought about that?"

At this, Grace gave me her first real smile. Full of teeth, and it might have been pretty if not for the insanity in her eyes, and the rictus grin of her facial muscles. Not a woman who wore smiles well. Or ever. "But I have you to thank for that, fledgling. You may have seen into my mind while I taught you, but I also saw into yours. I saw the competing visions, the different perceptions of what would happen. And I know how you unravel the Rider. So simple. I can't believe I never thought of it before myself."

Lucien's finger twitched, and Grace seized on it, the darkening rubies that were her eyes throwing off more light than they had a moment ago. She bathed in it, so it looked as though she wore a gown of crimson. "How was it my broken little bird described it? I 'tore the stuffing' out of you?" Grace's smile was a vicious blade. "Make even one move against me, Rider, and I will show you just how much I remember about that day."

"I have had a hundred years to dream about what I would do to you," Lucien said aloud in wonder. "I thought it would take my release from your curse and a trip through the Dead Worlds to track you down, true, but so what? Delay only makes the destruction sweeter. But here you are, waiting for me. Just as you always have been."

"Do you truly think you are still my master, monster?" Grace delighted at the play on words, a cold twist on her lips. "Have you forgotten the knowledge the lighthouse holds? I've spent a century learning your secrets. All in anticipation of this moment."

It was like all Lucien needed was a provocation, a reason to strike out against her. The darkness swirled around him, a distortion that blurred everything around it.

But the problem with having a battle royale in the lighthouse, as Lucien should have remembered, was that there was no advantage here. Each of us held a portion of the demon's power, and I just prayed to God that the three of us were close to evenly matched.

"You can't win this!" I shouted, lunging to the left as the black fire Lucien threw at Grace was deflected and hurtled my way. Trey had been working his way towards his sister and Riley, but Matthias had turned the gun on him, a cold, expectant look on his face.

"Abominations should be killed and not heard," Grace snarled, whipping scarlet spells in my direction. They were sharp and thin like razor wire, a version of the same spell that Catherine had summoned up against me once. But every time I stared into the heart of the spells, meaning to unspool them the same way all magic came unraveled under my gaze, they split in two, becoming a laser-red Hydra monster hurtling towards me.

It became a three-way brawl after that, and if I'd thought us evenly matched, I was a stupid, stupid kid. The only thing saving me from being instantly incinerated was Grace and Lucien were flinging spells and demonic constructs at *each other* rather than being distracted by me. I leapt out of the way of a wayward blast, dropping into a roll and lunging free of a nearly unavoidable death.

"A hundred years to lick your wounds, and still you pick the wrong fight," Lucien sneered. "At least the boy was a worthwhile challenge. You were simply pathetic."

Grace screeched in fury, and the walls of the lighthouse started to shake. Dust and pebbles rained down from the ceiling. The sounds she made were a physical thing, an expression of magic.

I know this. I've seen this before. The night Lucien killed John, my chest had been boiling over with emotions I couldn't handle. I'd been drowning in something stronger than me, and it had struggled for escape. Only after I had opened my mouth, after I'd *screamed,* had the power flooded out.

It had destroyed the chapel completely, an explosion of magic Grace had needed to first reach out and open the lighthouse to me.

But if Grace unleashed that kind of power here, what would happen to us? In the distance, I could feel the Riders flowing closer, like bubbles of chaos rising to the surface.

"Enough," I shouted. Power lanced out of me, bathing the room in sharp light. It sliced through every spell and trick, ripped Grace's voice from her mouth, and struck down every projectile. For a moment, the room was still, but even as the blue light started to blush and redden, and the winter voices in my head started calling for more, the battle started anew.

Matthias stood calmly in front of the girls, one hand on either shoulder, tugging them up or down, left or right as the situation dictated. He made it into a dance, a smooth pirouette and turn as they avoided everything that came towards them. Once he lifted Jade several feet off the ground as a low flying blast of indigo razor wire spun across the floor.

I did my best to not only shield myself, but to protect Trey, who was still trying to get to his sister. And while Trey usually had moments of almost inhuman movement, where he would unconsciously tap into the magic that burned within him, none of that was evident tonight. More than once he almost walked face first into an incoming blast. I wasn't nearly as graceful as Matthias was with the dodging, but Trey and I still had all our limbs.

Up until now, I'd played more defense than offense, but after a gout of flame almost caught my shirt on fire, I started changing it up. I turned both my palms towards each other, and channeled energy through my fingertips. Lightning began to arc from one hand to the other, compressing down into a basketball-sized coil of lightning.

I waited until Grace was distracted with Lucien's latest attack. Even occupied with the shadowy sand attack the demon threw at her, she still deflected the balled lightning strike.

It careened towards the broken wall. Stone tumbled down into the gap between the lighthouse and the Widow's walk. Though there was nothing there but open air, the moment the stone crossed the barrier from lighthouse to storm, it incinerated itself into a puff of smoke, immediately swept up into the windstorm.

"Stupid boy," the witch snarled.

Lucien must have realized he wasn't the dominant force he expected to be. "You can't let her escape here, Braden. Help me stop her. You know she's the real danger."

Lucien, asking me for help. *Lucien underneath my boot, begging for mercy.* The flash came fast, and ice grew in my veins. *Crush them both. All. Everything. Destruction is glory. The warmest fires burn from bones.*

Blood rushed to my head and I stumbled, and if Trey hadn't grabbed me in that moment Grace's next attack might have severed my head from my body. The two of us tumbled to the ground in a sprawl, only the voices in my head wouldn't shut up. They were so loud it was all I could hear.

Blue light surrounded me, then flashed to purple. The darker it got, the more I slipped. The winter voices surged to the surface, and I fell back, down into a chasm somewhere deep inside myself where I would never find the way out again.

Something struck me across the face, and just like that I was the one looking out my eyes again. My mouth tasted funny, there was blood smeared on Trey's lips, and my face burned. He still had his hand out, and now I could feel the imprint against my skin. He'd slapped me. But something else.

My chest hurt. Burned. It felt like someone had punched me right in the heart. Only then did I see the lightning trickling across Trey's knuckles, remnants of his magic. Magic Trey shouldn't have been able to access on his own.

Or maybe he could—if the need was great enough.

I touched my lips, feeling the blood there. The same blood smeared on Trey.

Grace and Lucien had forgotten me entirely. Matthias stood, patiently waiting for instructions, still manhandling Riley and Jade into safety. There was a clear shot to the portal. I tried to push Trey towards it, telling him to *go, run away,* now while he still could. Before it was too late.

Wind circled the lantern room, a cyclone. It swallowed sound and replaced it with a dark howl, low and roaring in my ears. I didn't know which one of them was responsible for it, but it was only a matter of time before the wind was enough to tear us all from the floor. And sooner or later, all of us would spill out into the storm. A feast for the Riders.

I climbed to my feet. "As soon as you get the signal, you get them out of here," I shouted at Trey.

"What signal?"

"Just do it!"

Once I had my balance, I counted to three. Took a deep breath. Braced myself. "Now!" I screamed.

I threw my hand to the left and tore it down, like splitting a zipper. Only this time, I was tearing open a portal.

Even on a good day, creating a portal took a lot of energy and time. But this wasn't a portal *to* something, it was a portal *between* somethings. I shredded through dimensions in an instant and the incredible stores of power at my disposal were hacked out of me to fuel the spell.

Trey threw himself towards his sister, and managed to get a hold of both her and Riley and pull them to the ground with him. Matthias, who threw his hands up as though in surrender, is back against the broken, crumbled wall of the lighthouse, framed by leviathan storms raging just beyond.

My strength torn out of me in a single moment, I went from being on top of the world to barely keeping my head up. The portal opened like a stage curtain parting, but then it spilled up from the sides, a circle being drawn against the fabric of reality. But it wasn't the portal itself that was important.

It was what came through the portal.

The body stumbled out and onto the stone floor of the lighthouse, collapsing onto hands and knees. Silver mercury dripped from somewhere in its middle, only losing its shine and pooling into blood as it struck the granite beneath it.

And then Drew Armstrong lifted his head and snarled in fury.

thirty-seven

It's called a game-changer. Something that alters the way the game is played, makes the old rules obsolete and causes everything to be called into question.

For a second time, everything in the lighthouse stopped. Time itself needed a moment to catch its breath. Grace's fury once again became a tidal wave of dark power as her sacrifice was stolen from her. Right out from under her. But even she held her breath.

Drew looked up slowly, and to his credit he surveyed the room before speaking. He turned to each of the demons in turn before looking towards me. "This...was your brilliant plan? Letting them bitch each other to death?"

"Hey, anyone that wants to go back to bleeding out in the empty spaces between dimensions is more than welcome to jump back inside," I snapped back, without any heat. God, I'd missed Drew's mouth.

"That fucking hurt, y'know."

"In a minute," I said frantically, my eyes wide with

nerves. "Drew!" That panicked, high-pitched plea wasn't really mine, was it?

Drew didn't waste another second. His hands slipped into the satchel and he pulled out a pair of black stones. Bricks. In a fluid motion, he slammed them into the ground and they splattered into dust.

"She wants me to kill him?"

"No," Matthias said gravely. "She doesn't want him dead. Dead won't do her any good. To keep the portals open, he must be alive." He steepled his fingers together and regarded me from across the room. "Now tell me again how much you want your revenge upon them."

"She won't like you helping me," I added. "She likes to know that she controls everything."

"There's a way you can fix that," Matthias offered with a sly wink.

As the stones exploded into gravel, brittle beyond their years, they released a pulse of white light. The light traveled upwards, taking the form of a complex geometric design, filled with inscriptions in languages I couldn't even identify. All of it wrapped inside a circle inscribed with pointed stars.

Grace's head whipped towards Matthias, her accomplice, just in time to catch his fingers wagging a goodbye as he evaporated into thin air. Next she whirled around to find Drew, but the bleeding boy wasn't where she'd left him. I caught the rat scurrying along across the floor just as it disappeared into a flash of silver and was replaced by a garden snake. Then a raccoon. Then, just as he reached Jade and

Riley, returning to his human, Drew-sized shape. Through the tear in his shirt, I could see the still-reddened memory of the knife wound, the way it cut across the scar he already had, shaping an X across his skin.

"You think you can betray me?" Grace's fury continued to grow. "I will violate everything you've ever touched. You will leave the world the plague you always were, wiping out everything in your wake."

"Oops," I asked, full of a sudden, maddening calm. "Did I forget the part where I yelled out 'surprise'?" I summoned up every scrap of magic I could think of—everything John had taught me. Everything Jason and Catherine and Grace had ever used against me. Even the darkness I'd seen come from Lucien and Matthias. I used everything at my disposal, fire or ice, good or evil, me or the monster. Spells like steel, spells of thorn and bones, constructs shaped like walls and fortresses and magic like I'd never known.

Lucien and Grace could spot a coup when they saw one. The identical looks of fury and calculation vanished from both of their faces, replaced by determination and understanding.

"I will bury you here," Grace snarled. Her voice ripped through my body like an electric shock.

"Nice girlfriend you've got there, Thorpe." Drew had one hand around Jade, bracing her weight. His return seemed to have struck her a bit harder than everything else she'd just witnessed.

"Time to go," I shouted. I threw as many spells up for cover as I could think of.

And now came the difficult part.

Grace and Lucien on their own were intimidating. Grace and Lucien with a common enemy? Near on apocalyptic.

Within seconds, I was battered by so much magic and demonic fury that I could barely see past the haze of darkness obscuring my vision. I felt the others moving behind me, felt them hustling for the portal that would get them out of here. I just had to keep Grace and Lucien distracted long enough for them to get through.

"Your fate belongs to me!" Grace shouted, and the shiver up my spine reminded me of the contract I'd signed with her. I'd fulfilled my terms. I gave her a sacrifice, a wellspring, and she'd given me power.

"I'm a minor," I shouted back, shrugging off the pit in my stomach. "Sue me."

Slammed down to my knees before I knew it, the warring forces inside of me were nearly washed away. Still, Grace and Lucien battered at the defenses I'd thrown up, and hammered through every obstacle I'd put in their way. *Stop fighting us,* the voices whispered. *It's time. You know it is at hand. Your reckoning. Their destruction.*

Come with us. Become what you have always meant to be.

When they crossed through—one, then two, then a third—I felt it. But there was a dissonance where the fourth should have been.

The demon and the Widow were almost through. Lucien needed escape, and Grace couldn't let me leave. With Drew restored, her pass through the lighthouse had been revoked. I was her only escape. If the portal shut, Grace would do as much to keep Lucien from leaving as she would try to escape herself.

Someone dragged me backwards. *No,* I wanted to yell. I had to stay. Had to make sure they couldn't escape again. I just needed a minute to catch my breath!

But the portal swallowed me up before I could even find my voice.

¤   ¤   ¤

It took precious seconds for my head to clear, for the smell of freezing air and headstones to assail my nose. To remind me of the real world.

"Braden!" Shouting in my ears, shrill and panicked. It worked better than smelling salts, catapulting me back into consciousness. I leapt to my feet. I had to go back before one of them escaped. I had to close the portal from the other side. It was the only way.

Trey grabbed me around the waist. Riley was there, standing at my side, the one who'd screamed my name. She was still screaming.

"Listen to me!" She grabbed me by the arm, her hands wiry but hard like steel. I could feel the magic raging on the other side of the portal, growing closer by the moment. "You can lock the door," Riley insisted. "Just like Grace. From *this* side. But it has to be balanced."

The battle had changed, again, and they were once again at each other's throats. As needs changed, the nature of the fight kept shifting. Now what would it be? Lucien, trying to escape, and Grace, trying to prevent it?

"There are two of them," I said to myself. "I can't make up for both of them. It won't balance."

Behind Trey, Riley and Jade whispered to each other.

Grace had bound herself to the lighthouse in order to bind Lucien to the town. But could it work in reverse? Could I bind myself to the town, in order to keep them in the lighthouse?

"He can't." And now it was Jade who was interjecting herself into the debate, wearing the same stubborn look on her face. "Grace is a woman. If you want balance, you need one, too."

"No," I said, sharper than I'd ever spoken to her before, "If they're bound in the lighthouse, we're bound in the town. I won't do that to you." I took a deep breath. "I'll go back through. I'll stop them."

"And what if you don't? What if Lucien escapes? Or Grace? You think she won't tear this town apart?" Drew jumped in front of me, blocking the path to the portal. "Trap them together for the rest of time and call it a day. That bitch doesn't get a happy ending. Neither of them do."

"My life's not over if I have to grow old in Belle Dam," she said, glancing over at Drew and Riley.

"Ever since I've known you, all you've talked about is how much you want to leave," I growled. "New York, Paris, wherever. You don't care as long as it's as far from Belle Dam as it can possibly get."

"Plans change," she said. And it wasn't like she touched her stomach, or did anything at all to indicate it, but I knew what Jade was thinking. I knew having a kid would change things for her.

"I can't ask you do to this," I said, my resolve crumbling.

"Come on," she said, linking her hand in mine and pulling me towards the portal. "I'll let you buy me one of those BFF necklaces afterwards."

I'd used a lot of magic tonight. Mere remnants of my own remained. The demonic power swelled inside of me. My chest grew cold. I stepped out of myself and turned around, looking at my physical shell in earnest. I was never really impressed with the way I looked. From the outside in, though, I could see a little of that strength that I'd always seen in Jason and John, the Thorpe tenacity that had gotten me this far. I reached into my chest, my real chest, and pulled out the nest of vipers that had made its home in there. Brilliantly hued and pleasing to the eye, they were gorgeous things, but still full of venom and death.

I shoved the demonic power, the wellspring power, into the portal, holding it in the space where the two worlds met. Maybe I'd snatched it from Grace's mind, or maybe it was instinct the way Trey had drawn on magic to protect me.

My eyes burned, leaking. A final demon slithered from

its hiding spot under my ribs, drawn out of me. Sucked into the portal and swallowed whole.

My essence combined with a fluttering of crystal petals that drifted out of Jade's body, forming the center of the portal. A keyhole took shape. And as Jade and I bound ourselves into the ball of energy that had once been a demon's majesty, a lock snapped shut in my head. The portal vanished, my vision blurred, and the next thing I knew, my heart was an alien thing thudding my chest.

The path to the lighthouse closed. Grace and Lucien were trapped together, just as Jade and I would be trapped together.

The sun rose over Belle Dam.

thirty-eight

"So what happens to them now?"

Drew stood at the spot where the portal had been. Dawn had come during our absence, and it peeked through the forest to scatter sunlight around like an offering.

"They're trapped together," I said, dusting off my pants. The jacket was ruined, probably the shirt, too. Definitely the pants. Not that I cared about any of that. "Hopefully they spend it torturing each other every day."

Riley nodded, her expression pensive. "Let's hope."

I ended up in the grass near the path, sitting cross-legged with my head in my hands. For whatever reason, none of us were in a hurry to leave. We loitered in the cemetery. For my part, I couldn't quite believe that it was over. Maybe the others stayed because I did. Or maybe they had their own reasons.

Trey sat down in front of me, mimicking my pose. "Your eyes are green again, you know."

That was news to me. I could still feel a coil of energy

in my belly. My magic was drained, but it was still there. Maybe not as strong as before, I wouldn't know that until I'd gotten some rest and tested myself further.

"No, that's not right." The next thing I knew, Jade was crouched right next to me, almost spilling over into my lap. "Look at me," she commanded, lifting my head by the chin. "They're more … aquamarine. Riley?"

"More like blue. Like those flowers?" She struggled with the word before her face lit up. "Forget-me-nots."

"No way, you're all wrong," Drew said, crowding in between both of the girls, slinging an arm around each of them. "They're definitely green. Like limestone."

"So that's two votes for green, and two votes for blue," I said, climbing to my feet. "I think that means I need a tie-breaker."

Trey linked his hand with mine. "What are you thinking?"

"I think it's time I go home. I want to make sure my dad's okay."

He gave me a funny look as the others started walking away.

"What?"

Trey shook his head. "I've just never heard you call him your dad before."

My feelings on Jason were complicated, but not that hard to understand. Especially now that I knew I'd have time to see how things went. "I think it's about time."

¤   ¤   ¤

Jason hemmed and hawed longer than he had any right to before finally deciding to go with blue-green. A chorus of groans met his selection.

Drew left to take Riley back to the hospital. She'd never been properly discharged, and someone with an actual medical degree was better qualified to make that decision than I was. She hugged me before she left. Drew gave me a flinty look, but he slugged me on the shoulder before he left. We might not be okay yet, but there was hope.

Jade hesitated by the door. I knew what they were doing. Trying to give me some privacy so I could deal with Jason one on one. I appreciated it, but I was still nervous.

"So are you going to mind if we stay neighbors for a while?" she asked, biting down on her lower lip. The first thing she'd done upon coming back to the house was to disappear, only to return a few minutes later with her face clean of makeup and changed out of her prom dress and into yoga pants and a tee shirt.

"Neighbors?"

"I ... kind of never went home—after that night, I stayed here. And then you were gone, and I think Jason was lonely, and so he never kicked me out and I'm getting used to it except your maid hates me—"

"—she hates everyone," I said, interrupting her. "And I mean ... I don't care. As long as Jason doesn't."

"It's fine for now, Jade," Jason said kindly. "Until you decide what you want to do, at least."

If you decide to go home, was what he meant. Both of

us knew it. Jade made a face, but she didn't say anything. I didn't know how she was going to deal with her mother from here on out. Catherine had her monstrous moments, but she also loved her kids. Even I knew that. But I couldn't make Jade's decisions for her any more than she could make mine.

"Maybe just for a couple of months," Jade agreed. "Just ... until I figure some things out."

"And Gentry, you're welcome, too, of course," Jason added. "Although we're going to have a very long and serious talk about appropriate behavior under this roof."

Oh my god, kill me now. I could feel the flush rising in my cheeks, and I had to turn away.

"I'm okay," Trey chuckled. "I've been staying at the cabin. I'll probably stay there for a while. But thanks."

My father nodded. After that, Trey and Jade headed for the door, and Trey shot me a pointed look before he closed the door behind him.

"So I run a boarding house now, I suppose." Jason was being far too easygoing about everything. I kept silent, trying to wait him out. To see how he really felt. The last time we'd talked, I'd taken a lot of his autonomy away.

"I don't have to stay here, if you don't want ... " my voice faltered, and I couldn't finish the thought. The idea that Jason might push me out the door had me paralyzed, my throat locked up like a bank vault.

"You're my son," Jason said quickly, his face screwed up in worry. "You don't have to go anywhere if you don't want to."

I let that go before I started talking about feelings, or something equally as embarrassing. "Have you talked to Catherine?"

Jason grimaced and shook his head. "Not since that night. But ... she'll come around. I think. Eventually. Though I don't know how we'll ever work together."

I patted him on the shoulder. "You'll figure out a way."

He cleared his throat. "And you're sure you're alright?"

"I think so." I took a deep breath. "I think I'm less than I was when I first got here, but still more than I was after the funeral. My eyes are weaker." My fingers tangled with the bottom hem of my shirt, all to keep them occupied. And then. "I can't undo what I did to you. Just in case you were wondering."

Jason put his hands on my shoulders. "I asked if *you* were alright, Braden."

"Yeah," I said, braving a smile. "Yeah, I'm good." I could say it and mean it. That was something new.

¤   ¤   ¤

"I'm not saying we have to do a picnic lunch for everyone in town, but we should do *something*. There's room for another festival in Belle Dam. We should commemorate the end of the feud." Riley's idealism had returned with a vengeance, and now she was on a quest for proper holiday recognition.

"I don't know if the feud's over yet. Might still be a

while," Drew offered. "We still don't know how the town's going to react."

Only time would tell if we'd made enough of a difference, but I knew one thing for sure. The feud wasn't something to celebrate, nor was the ending of it. I certainly didn't want to be a hero. Let Belle Dam have its Widow and her legends about treasures and keys. Let me just have my life, on my own terms.

"Maybe we should start small," Trey suggested. "Maybe something with charity work. Get people to sign up to help beautify the city."

"Or help rebuild the harbor docks," Jade added, with pointed fingers. I sighed. Jason and I had a long talk about how expensive boats were and how many people I'd harmed by destroying all the boats in the harbor. I was pretty sure I was grounded. Or at least I would be, once Jason figured out that he was allowed to do that.

The sensation of feathers tickling against my gut started, the first time in days. It was brief, only a moment or two, but it was enough to get my attention. I left Jade and the others behind, and hurried up the street that had first led me into Belle Dam months ago.

Back then, I'd gotten off a bus and walked all the way to Helen's Diner before I figured out what I was doing. But now I was looking for something more than answers.

I wanted to see the boundary line for myself, the line I could no longer cross. But now that I was there, and I saw the girl standing on the other side of it, I changed my mind.

"Long time no see," I said.

Elle inclined her head. Her hair was tied back in a ponytail, and she wore a leather jacket and jeans. There was a large duffel bag at her feet.

"So you got out. And now ... this is goodbye?" My magic still hadn't returned, but if Elle had come looking for a fight she wouldn't be hiding beyond the town line. I wasn't sure how I felt about Elle escaping. A little piece of me hoped she'd been trapped in the lighthouse with the others.

"I made a bad call," she said simply. "You can't blame a girl for trying to make it in this world."

"'Trying to make it?' Your boss wanted to become a monster, and you helped."

"And you showed me the light, darling."

I could hear the others approaching in the distance. "Don't ever come back here," I said. "I mean it."

"Don't worry, doll face. I'm not equipped to deal in your leagues." Then the smile, the brilliant megawatt smile that had probably gotten her everything she'd ever wanted in life. "Yet."

She picked up the bag and flashed me a wink. "Was it worth it?" I asked. "What you did to Carmen?"

"Take care of yourself, superstar," Elle said before she vanished. Just ... there one moment, gone the next.

I took a deep breath, pushed her from my mind, and reached out. I wanted to feel the boundary with my hands. To know what it was like. Though the air was clear, and there was nothing to deter me, I reached out and pressed against a wall I couldn't cross. It warmed and cooled in alternating currents.

I could feel a vision building, and I opened myself up to it. It was like the very first vision, the one that had set me on the path to Belle Dam, just a slide show of images one after another. *Birds flying free of the city. A rare smile from Jason. Shovels turning over dirt, not for a grave, but for a ceremony. The lighthouse—the real one, not the one from my nightmares. Gentry and Jade, Riley and Drew, and faces I didn't know yet. Words exchanged on the dock, and a hand-shake. A child, a murder, and a ring; but only one of them was mine. A sign growing closer.* Now Leaving Belle Dam, *and underneath it, an addendum.* A City of Vision.

The images faded, and I pulled my hand away from the boundary. Trey came up behind me, and wrapped his arms around my waist. He smelled like sandalwood and coffee.

"You owe me a real first date," I said, leaning up to kiss the side of his cheek.

Trey fought a smile. "I've had some thoughts."

I looked out into the distance of a world I'd never get to see, and the world I had wrapped all around me. Belle Dam could have broken me until there was nothing left, but somehow I'd survived.

"Your uncle would be proud of you," Trey whispered in my ear.

Yeah, he would, I realized.

I was going to be alright. Definitely not today, and probably not tomorrow. But eventually. I'd find a way to make this life work. My world might have shrunk overnight, but it would be okay. This was a destiny I'd chosen for myself.

I savored the view of life beyond the city for just a minute before I turned away. There was enough of a world for me inside the lines of Belle Dam. I could be happy here.

Trey kissed my neck and then pulled away. "Come on, I'll let you take me to Helen's. You can buy me pancakes."

I turned back to the city, shedding my melancholy. I smiled. "After you."

THE END

About the Author

Scott Tracey aspired to be an author from a young age. His debut novel, *Witch Eyes*, was named to the 2012 Popular Paperbacks for Young Readers list in the forbidden romance category and ranked among the top ten gay and lesbian Kindle books of 2011 at Amazon.com. Tracey lives near Cleveland, Ohio, and can be found on Twitter @Scott_Tracey or at his website, www.Scott-Tracey.com.